Wishing for a Highlander

ALSO BY JESSI GAGE

Highland Wishes Series

The Wolf and the Highlander

Blue Collar Boyfriends

Reckless

Jade's Spirit

Cole in My Stocking

Wishing for a Highlander

A HIGHLAND WISHES NOVEL

Jessi Gage

Cover by Damonza
Edited by Piper Denna
ISBN: 978-1-941239-01-8

Printed in the United States of America
2nd edition, April 2014

To Shane, who reads everything I write and doesn't squirm too much. Thanks for being my best friend and for supporting my dream.

Acknowledgements

Thank you to my dear friend, Laura Lee Nutt, who cheered for this book from day one. I wouldn't be here without her honest critique, support, and friendship. Thanks also to the ladies of the Cupcake Crew, Amy Raby and Julie Brannagh. I would have lost my sanity long ago without my weekly infusions of espresso, frosting, and snark. Thanks to my mom for hours upon hours of babysitting so I could seek said infusions—and for occasionally letting me borrow her car. Thanks to my husband, Shane, for humoring me and loving me. Lastly, thanks to Piper Denna, who gave this book a shot and taught me so much with her editing prowess.

Chapter 1

THE FIRST BITE of her sandwich transported Melanie to another dimension—she could swear food tasted better in pregnancy, at least now that the first-trimester nausea had passed. Her lunch break at the cramped but tidy Old Charleston Tea House got even better as she reached the first spicy part in her paperback. The combined pleasures of Golden Monkey tea, perfectly seasoned egg salad, and a succulent make-out scene between a librarian and a rugged Scot had her moaning in rapture before she could stop herself.

"No wonder she's pregnant without a ring on her finger," one of the elderly women at a nearby table said behind her hand. "Look at the trash she reads."

The woman's blue-haired companion snuck a glance at her from behind oversized glasses. "Little slut. Probably counts on her big chest to rope 'em in and then doesn't have the brains to keep 'em."

Melanie plunked her tea down so hard it sloshed and stained the lacy tablecloth. Every Friday, she tuned out the constant complaining generated by these two women, but she'd never been the subject of their biting criticisms before. She glared at the pair over the top of her book.

Both of them suddenly found the view of Meeting Street out the large plate glass window exceedingly fascinating.

"I'm sorry," she said with mock sweetness, "did you have something to say to me?"

Two pairs of watery eyes blinked innocently at her. “What was that, dear?” One of the biddies cupped a hand around her ear. The other adjusted her hearing aid.

Gretchen, her favorite server, wedged herself between the tables, interrupting her view of the biddies. “She said, ‘How did you like the tea?’ Will that be all for you ladies?” Gretchen scooped up the leather check holder with a placating look over her shoulder.

Melanie huffed and folded her arms, but she couldn’t bring herself to hold a grudge, since Gretchen was the one whose tips would suffer if she chased away some of her best customers.

The jingling bell over the door heralded the biddies’ exit, but she still couldn’t get back into her novel. Giving it up as a lost cause, she stuffed the paperback into her messenger bag and scarfed down her lunch without tasting it. Leaving her twelve dollars on the table, she waved goodbye to Gretchen and slipped out into the January chill.

Normally she tried to be a words-can-never-hurt-me kind of girl, but those words had cut right through her tissue-thin, pregnancy-enhanced emotions. It wasn’t the remark about her chest that hurt—she was used to being judged by her blond-haired, D-cup cover. It was the assumption that she couldn’t hang on to a man. That had hit a little too close to home.

Kyle’s last words to her circled in her mind as she reached the bike rack and strapped on her helmet. *“What do you want from me, Mel? I’m not going to change my life because you forgot your pill one day. Don’t all you independent career women want to be single moms, anyway?”*

“Bastard,” she seethed as she hiked up her knee-length skirt to hop on her trusty antique Schwinn. It wasn’t like she’d expected Kyle to propose or anything. Just a little responsibility. A little support. That’s all she’d asked for, and she thought she’d earned it, since they’d been together for almost a year.

But no, all Kyle had for her was blame and a view of his cowardly behind as he ran away from what they had created together. A new life, vulnerable and precious, even more so because she hadn't missed a pill like Kyle insisted. The life inside her was a beautiful miracle who existed despite the minor obstacle of a little manufactured hormone.

All she'd wanted from Kyle was for him to be a father to his child. But all Kyle had wanted was to marry a girl named Becky, whom he'd apparently been cheating with for some time. Now, Kyle was a happily married sperm-donor, and she was left to face a monumental and wonderful challenge all by her lonesome.

As she pedaled up Meeting Street, back to the Charleston Museum, she gave thoughts of Kyle and bitter old ladies the heave-ho, choosing instead to think about what made her happy: her loving and supportive parents, her friends, chocolate cream pie, the escape of a good romance novel, and her work organizing the Scottish immigrants exhibit opening next Friday.

Eeek! Friday!

That was only seven days away! And there was still so much to do, including finding a new keynote speaker for the grand opening, since Professor Calderwood, a distant relative of famous Scottish immigrant Andrew Carnegie, had cancelled. Her brain whirring away with her to-do list, she shoved her bike into the rack behind the museum and got to work.

Hours later, with several disappointing phone calls and much eye-straining proof-reading under her belt, she finally laid her eager hands on the package Dr. Calderwood had Fed-Exed. A phone message indicated he'd sent several artifacts from his personal collection for her to include in the exhibit, and she'd looked forward to opening the package as her reward for an afternoon of hard work.

Inside were five carefully wrapped items: a journal kept by a Scottish relative who had settled in Charleston in the 1890's, a flintlock pistol, an antique rosewood box whose rich, dark finish reminded her of her grandmother's prized hope chest, which had been in their family since the old days, and two gleaming *sgian dubhs.*

She appreciated one of the *sgian dubhs* first, running her gloved fingers over the flat of the blade and the intricately woven leather-wrapped hilt. To think, some nineteenth-century warrior had carried this knife in his jacket or tucked in the top of his hose. A thrill of connection went through her until Alan's voice at her office door made her jump.

"It's nearly seven, Mel. Go home for God's sake."

She lifted her magnifying glasses to her head and smiled at her boss. "This is better than home. You need to see this stuff Dr. Calderwood sent."

He shook his head. "I'll take a look on Monday. Promise. Sam's got a recital at school and I'm running late. I mean it. Go home. You need your rest." He nodded at the barely noticeable swell of her belly.

"I'm pregnant, not an invalid, Al." She gave him a wink to soften the rebuke as she lovingly set the first *sgian dubh* aside and began fondling the other. "I'll go home in a few. I just want to put these artifacts in the safe."

"Uh-huh. Just make sure you wipe all the drool off before you do." He gave a wink of his own before leaving.

"Mmm, finally, it's just the two of us," she said to the knife. "Well," she amended as a stray finger caressed the other *sgian dubh,* "just the three of us." The journal, pistol, and box suddenly looked sullen on her workbench. "Oh. Sorry. Just the six of us, then."

She wished she could spend her evening giving each artifact the attention it deserved, but Alan was right. She could use some rest. And she had a frozen pizza and half a chocolate cream pie beckoning her to her apartment. "Monday," she promised the artifacts as she placed them on a felt-lined tray for the safe.

As she gathered up the packaging materials to toss in the trash, she caught sight of a sheet of paper tucked in the bottom of the box. She pulled it out and gave it a quick scan. It was a letter from Dr. Calderwood in which he repeated his regret that he would miss the exhibit's grand opening and offered a brief description of each item.

She couldn't resist reading the letter in full. The couple of paragraphs about the box were especially interesting.

Rosewood box: Owned by Mr. Andrew Carnegie and bought at auction by yours truly October 1985.

Originating in the Scottish Highlands, as the inscription indicates, the box has an intricate opening mechanism that few have reportedly mastered. With no obvious latch on the outside, it is assumed that a series of pressure points when touched the right way releases an inner spring, which opens the lid. I personally have never been able to open it, and three separate antique dealers have inspected the box and concluded that whatever mechanism opens it is likely frozen with age.

In my research on Mr. Carnegie, I have uncovered an interesting story. In private, he would sometimes joke that his immense fortune was "due to nine-tenths hard work and one-tenth the luck of the Scotia rosewoods."—Personal letter penned by Ryan Helmsford, close friend to Mr. Carnegie in his later years, 1901.—This may have been a reference to the rosewood box.

Perhaps Mr. Carnegie had figured out how to open the beguilingly beautiful contraption and was granted his wish for prosperity.

Smiling at Dr. Calderwood's tongue-in-cheek supposition, she put down the letter and lifted the artifact from the tray. About the size of a small jewelry box and with gracefully rounded edges and inlaid patterns of Celtic knotwork in white gold, it had more heft to it than expected. As the letter indicated, there was no visible latch anywhere along its seam.

Trusting the assessment of Dr. Calderwood's antique dealers, she didn't bother trying to open it, but carefully turned it over to inspect the bottom. The inscription of the maker was still visible, though barely, after several centuries. The cursive writing, aged to a deep brown in the lighter reddish-brown finish read *MacLeod, 1542.* Beneath was the place of manufacture, *Inverness.* The name *MacLeod* didn't ring any bells, but then she specialized in Colonial artifacts of the eighteenth and nineteenth centuries, so she wasn't surprised.

She turned the box upright to set it on the tray again, but a sudden playful urge gripped her. Lifting the box to eye level, she said, "If you're in the mood to grant a wish, here's mine: I'd like a sexy Highlander to sweep me off my feet like in the romance novels. Please," she added as an afterthought.

Scoffing at herself, she rolled her eyes. "As if," she muttered, swiveling on her stool to set the box on the tray. As she turned, the balance of the piece shifted. It felt like something inside rotated and slipped from one end of the box to the other. The box made a series of soft clinks and groans like an old cuckoo clock about to engage. The lid sprang open.

She gasped in surprise. Eager wonder coursed through her. No one had been able to open this box in who knew how long, and she'd done it accidentally. How lucky for her! She'd be the first to see inside since perhaps Andrew Carnegie himself.

She felt proud. She felt giddy.

She felt dizzy.

Really dizzy. As if the seat of her stool were spinning increasingly faster, like the Tilt-a-Whirl ride at Six Flags. Only at the amusement park, her vision had never clouded to black and she'd never tumbled backward off a ride.

The sensations of spinning and falling fed off each other, disorienting her and dousing her with nausea. She released the box to cushion her womb

I'm not supposed to fall. It could hurt the baby.

She landed on her back. The hardwood floor of her office didn't knock the wind out of her like she'd expected it to. It felt like...springy grass?

When the black spots cleared, she stared up at a drab-gray sky. Distantly, the sounds of clanging swords and hollering men pierced the damp air. Rolling her head gingerly to the right, she saw a large, flat stone looming like an oversized domino on the verge of falling. Beyond it rose a grassy hill dotted with smaller rocks and scrubby brush. To her left, a path wound around the hill, and in the distance the edge of a sparse, mist-shrouded forest looked like a nice place to meet a ghost or get murdered. She'd narrowly missed landing in a muddy puddle.

Which was strange since she didn't remember her cramped little office having grass, boulders, or puddles. Definitely no gray sky.

She blinked a few times to bring her office back into focus, but her brain wouldn't cooperate. The scenery stayed put.

A blur of black motion out of the corner of her eye made her think Alan might have heard her fall and hurried back to see if she was okay. But it wasn't Alan with his calf-length wool coat. It was a bulky, shirtless man in a...was that a kilt?—running past her little nook of insanity.

He did a double take and altered his trajectory when he saw her sprawled on the ground. In two heartbeats he was crouching at her side.

The man had wild black hair and a matted beard. Up close, she could see the dark-gray wool of his shoulder-wrapped great kilt was coarsely mottled with lighter gray to give an effect much closer to camouflage than plaid. In one hand he gripped a utilitarian sixteenth-century dirk with fresh bloodstains on the blade.

Great. She'd had a doozy of a pregnancy-related dizzy spell and hit her head. Hard.

While her body lay unconscious on the floor of her office in Charleston, her brain thought it might be fun to dump her into an illusion based on her romance novel.

Could this be the hero who would rock her sexually deprived world and tempt her to forsake her friends, family, job, and all she held dear, in favor of steamy nights in his hay-stuffed bed and a significantly shortened life span due to lack of modern medicine and a diet heavy in salt and low in vegetation?

She narrowed her eyes in appraisal. He certainly had the biceps for it. The boulder beside her had nothing on the man's massive chest. And his eyes were an intense shade of blue that might be appealing if he weren't sneering at her. But he was a little on the hairy side for a romantic hero. Weren't they usually waxed to show off their washboard abs? And she could do without the smears of dirt covering every inch of his exposed skin. And in the books she loved so much, the hero was always taller. But she was short, so why not conjure up a five-foot-eight hero for her five-foot-two self?

The dirk went to her throat and pressed lightly, not breaking the skin but threatening to if she made a wrong move.

She rolled her eyes. "Hello, melodrama, anyone? Like little old me could possibly be a threat to a big, strong warrior like you. Puh-lease. Can we get to the romance, already? I'd hate to waste a perfectly good concussion on the whole build-up of sexual tension thing. What if I wake up before the good part? Although, maybe we could go to your place and have ourselves a little bath first. And maybe comb out that hair. How would you feel about shaving?"

The man bared his teeth. "An addled Sassenach spy," he said in a rocky Highland burr.

"And oddly dressed." He grunted. "Only one thing English lasses are good for, and since skirmishes always give me a wicked cockstand—" With the hand not holding the dirk, he pushed up the hem of her skirt, clumsily, as though he weren't used to dealing with such a snug-fitting garment.

"Really?" she said with another roll of her eyes. "You're going to 'take me' right here?"

She made little quotes in the air. "Come on. Just because I want to get to the good part doesn't mean I don't need a little warming up. Ever hear of preheating the oven? Sheesh, Kyle had more romance in his little finger than you've got in your whole body, and that's not saying much. That bastard."

The man gave up on lifting her skirt and simply ripped his dirk through the thick material, tearing a line up one thigh.

"Hey! That was a nice skirt!"

A surge of fear sped her pulse. This was feeling less and less like something her imagination might have conjured. And yet it couldn't possibly be real. Not unless she'd somehow stumbled into a reenactment, and since the damp, almost balmy landscape looked nothing like anyplace within stumbling distance of the Charleston Museum in mid-January, that was highly unlikely. No, it had to be a hallucination. A frighteningly realistic hallucination.

When the man shoved a knee between her legs and rubbed his non-dirk hand up to grab her breast through her top, indignation filled her lungs. Hallucination or not, she wouldn't stand for being felt up against her will.

"Get your hands off me!"

The man didn't relent, kneading her breast through the lightweight cashmere. Sour breath seared her cheek as he moved over her, pinning her to the ground. "Don't make a fuss, lass. I need but a few minutes and then ye can return to your English bastard and his romantic ways."

The man stabbed his dirk into the grass an inch from her ear in an obvious warning. Her heart jumped into her throat and beat frantically until all she could hear was the thunder of her pulse.

The man held her down with one hand while he reached between her legs with the other.

Seemingly confounded, he leaned back to study her clothing. She sent a heartfelt thank you heavenward for the thick cotton tights that made biking to work in January possible. She took advantage of the moment and blindly reached for the dirk beside her head. When the hilt met her palm, she curled her fingers around it and yanked the blade free.

She'd planned to merely wave it at the man and tell him to back off, but when he cocked his fist back, aiming a punch toward her face, something in her snapped. It wasn't so much rational thought as instinct that drove her to squeeze her eyes shut and thrust the dirk forward.

It sank into flesh. The blow she'd braced for never came.

She opened one eye.

The man's face was a mask of disbelief. Both his hands were wrapped around her hand, around the dirk's hilt. A good two thirds of the twelve-inch blade was buried in his stomach through the diagonal swath of wool wrapped around his torso.

She yanked her hand away. The man slid the blade out of his stomach and a spurt of blood came with it, splattering her bunched-up skirt and marring the peach cashmere of her sweater. The man toppled to his side, groaning and clutching the wound.

Horror washed over her in an icy wave. What had she done?

Defended yourself, her practical mind supplied. But what had felt necessary a few moments ago now seemed like overkill. Torn between running away and offering to help the man, she scrambled backward until her back hit the leaning boulder. Her breath came too fast.

"It's only a hallucination," she chanted to herself over and over.

But her senses conspired against her, insisting this place was real. The blood on her hands quickly cooled, and the moist ground chilled her bottom. Heather and field grass scented the air.

Shouts, groans, and the clang of swords persisted behind the boulder. The man on the ground breathed in and out with harsh whooshes of breath.

No hallucination could do all that. Her imagination simply wasn't that good.

She was inexplicably and undeniably present at what appeared to be a clan skirmish in Scotland, and judging by her attacker's wardrobe and weaponry, it was a far cry from modern-day Scotland. While she tried to process this new reality past several layers of shock, the man on the ground pushed to his hands and knees.

Relief that he wasn't dead made her shoulders sag.

"I'm sorry," she said. "I didn't mean to, um, stab you. But you were going to rape me. I had to defend myself. Is there anything I can do to help?" As she pushed up on shaky legs, she thought about her cellphone, lying on her workbench in Charleston. Even if she'd had it in her pocket, 9-1-1 wouldn't do any good here.

The man struggled to his feet. A glint of bloodied steel drew her eyes to his right hand.

Oh God, the dirk! Why had she let it go?

"There's somat ye can do, all right," he ground out through clenched teeth. "Come 'ere, so I can show ye how a stabbing's done." He launched in her direction.

She screamed and ran. Straight into a hard chest swathed in muted brown wool.

Chapter 2

MELANIE JERKED HER head up, way up, to find deep brown eyes glaring past her out of a chiseled face surrounded by wild, dark-blond hair. One of the man's hands gripped her shoulder.

The other held an enormous Highland broadsword. The look on his face spelled death for her would-be rapist.

Relief washed through her. She was hallucinating after all.

Men this tall, rugged, and handsome didn't actually exist, not on any continent in any time. Air-brushed masculinity like this only lived on the covers of romance novels.

He was definitely something she would have imagined. There. Dilemma solved. She'd hit her head and was having an Emmy-winner of a hallucination.

Drunk with elation that she hadn't really almost been raped and hadn't really stabbed a man, she slapped the muscled arm of her very own imaginary Highlander and quipped, "What took you so long? That was cutting it kind of close, don't you think?"

The man flicked her a distracted glance, then shoved her away so hard she stumbled into a prickly bush. Thorny barbs bit her hands and face and snagged her clothes.

Okay, that wasn't very heroic. Even if it appeared he'd done it to save her from her charging attacker. In the romance novels, the hero always managed a graceful, chivalrous rescue.

While she detangled herself from the bush, the new man dodged the bloody dirk and struck the bearded man with his sword. The warrior had to be at least six and a half feet tall.

Between the bearded man's shorter reach and smaller weapon, he stood no chance. He fell under two ruthless skewerings.

Her gut clenched with horror and sympathy before she managed to remember that none of this was really happening.

But if none of this was real, then she'd bonked her head on her office floor hard enough to endanger herself and her baby. She clutched her belly. *Please be okay, little one. Hang in there. We'll figure a way out of this.*

Looking at her belly, she saw blood still on her hands and soaked into the fabrics of her skirt and sweater. She willed it to go away. She willed the tear in her skirt to close. She willed herself back to her office, back to consciousness.

Nothing changed.

If this was all happening in her head, shouldn't she be able to control it or at least nudge it in a certain direction, like in a dream? Unfortunately, she had no time to ponder why her delusion ignored her whims, because the honey-blond warrior came at her, pushing her against the boulder with the mere force of his presence. His eyes blazed. She gulped, fearing she might be worse off with this man than she'd been with the one on the ground.

"And just who might you be?" he asked in a deadly, deep burr. Every inch of his tall, muscled frame was tensed for battle. His sword, so long she'd be hard pressed to lift it one-handed, remained poised for attack and perfectly stationary at his side. The tight muscles in his forearm didn't even twitch with its weight.

She shook her head, too terrified to answer. Would he accuse her of being an English spy, too? Would he try to rape her?

Was he real? Her stampeding heart thought so.

The new man's eyes scanned down her body, fixing on her belly.

She gripped her slight swell protectively.

"You're wounded," he stated with a modicum of concern, seemingly too distracted by the blood all over her to notice her knocked-up state. He sheathed his sword. Rough hands yanked at the blood-soaked hem of her sweater, undeterred by her swatting.

"I'm not," she blurted, tangling her hands with his. "It's not my blood. Please stop touching me."

Proving he had at least an ounce of chivalry, he stopped before exposing her gently rounded belly. Was that a flicker of hurt she caught in his eyes? For a second he'd almost looked vulnerable. The expression took years off his face. He looked no older than her twenty-six years, maybe even younger.

He took a step back and narrowed his eyes, becoming the hardened warrior once again. "Are ye English? A spy?"

Oh cripes. Here we go.

"I'm not English. I promise you. Not a single drop of English blood in these veins." That was the truth. She was Scottish, Irish, Swedish, and German by heritage and had never been more grateful.

The man harrumphed. "Mayhap. Ye dinna sound English. But ye dinna sound Scots, either. I havena heard speech like yours before." His brow pinched with curiosity, and his lips puckered ever so slightly in concentration.

She sagged with relief. His was not the face of a man who would harm her intentionally.

It was the face of a man who might keep her safe in this hallucination or whatever it was.

Without warning, the warrior grabbed her and threw himself down into the mud, bringing her with him. His body molded along her back, pinning her face down in the puddle she'd nearly landed in when she'd fallen off her stool. A mild pressure in her abdomen made her whimper as their combined weight tried to compress her incompressible womb.

Worry for her baby made her buck against the man. "Get off me!"

He clamped a hand over her mouth.

Pounding footsteps came close. Tension in the man's body made her freeze with fear.

Men's voices came from the other side of the boulder.

"Gunn," the man cursed quietly, hot breath scalding her ear. "The fools willna give up even though they're more than matched by Keith steel. Stay here. Stay down and dinna move."

His weight lifted from her. His footsteps squished away stealthily. A surprised groan met her ears. She looked up to see the honey-blond warrior standing to one side of the boulder with his fist pulled back, apparently ready and willing to deal a second blow to a doubled over gray-haired man wearing the same dark wool as her attacker.

"Go home with you, Harry," the warrior growled. "Ye canna win this, and too much blood has already been spilt."

A younger, squat man in dark-gray wool tiptoed around the other side of the boulder. She opened her mouth to warn the warrior, but he cocked his head toward the sound and quickly positioned himself so he could keep both opponents in view.

"Back with you, Robbie," he said, holding his sword ready. "I didna rise this morning with a particular desire to slay Gunn. But I will if ye dinna go. Now."

Robbie's lip curled as he spotted the dead man on the ground and then took in her prone, mud-covered form. "Ye killed Mack," he accused. "And over a filthy trollop, no less. You'll die for that, Big Darcy." He lunged at the honey-blond warrior—Darcy—and they clashed swords.

The older man pulled his dirk and advanced toward Darcy's back.

"Look out!" she yelled.

Darcy easily dodged Robbie's attack and stabbed him through

the belly with his sword.

At the same time, he pulled a dirk from the sheath on his left hip and jabbed it backward, only sparing a wide-eyed glance over his shoulder for aim. The dirk sliced the gray-haired man in the arm. The man danced back with a grimace.

"Damn you, Robbie," Darcy said to the younger man, who crumpled to the ground clutching his wound. "Why did you attack me?" When the wounded man tried to stand, Darcy said, "Dinna make me finish this. I dinna want your blood on my hands."

"'Tis already finished," the gray-haired man said, advancing again. "Ye've killed my only son, ye bloody Keith. Ye've killed him!"

"I didna ask the Gunn to trespass this day!" Darcy said. "Take Robbie home now and mayhap he'll live. Stay here and fight me and you'll both die. 'Tis not worth it, Harry."

Harry didn't listen. He lunged at Darcy, a suicide move, judging by the watery sheen in the older man's eyes. Her stomach lurched at the needless violence, the wasted lives. She tried telling herself the barbaric fantasy wasn't real, but the desperate wish was wearing thin.

Both gray-kilted men lay dead within seconds. Darcy turned back to her with wild eyes and a hard frown. "'Tis no place for a lass. Come with me. I'll see ye to safety." He took off around the hill with a long stride.

Was he serious? He expected her to follow him? After what she'd just witnessed?

Knowing what he was capable of?

Decisive violence. Swift decimation.

Mercy. Honor. Compassion.

She was done with this hallucination. It was too real. Too upsetting.

She tried clicking her heels together three times as she lay face down in the mud.

"There's no place like home, there's no place like home, there's no place like home."

Cold wetness still seeped past the fabric of her bra. Sharp pebbles at the bottom of the puddle dented her knees. Damn her observant senses and their insistence that she wasn't hallucinating.

The shouts of more men drew closer as Darcy jogged away from her. Hallucination or not, if it was between men in gray kilts who thought "the English" were "only good for one thing" and a man in muted brown who seemed to value her safety and to be morally opposed to killing even if he happened to be very efficient at it, she'd take her chances with the brown.

She scrambled out of the mud. Her loafers squished through the marshy grass as she trudged after her warrior.

§

DARCY LET OUT a relieved sigh when he heard the wee bonny lass following him. He'd have carried the bedraggled, half-dressed thing, but she'd asked that he not touch her, not even to inspect the wounds he'd thought the Gunn had cut into her creamy flesh. Her fearful request reminded him why he'd stopped bothering with dalliances long ago. So long as he didn't try, he need not fear the stomach-curdling flush of rejection.

His memory dredged up the echo of Anya's laughter. 'Twas the first and last time he'd attempted to cozy up with a member of the fairer sex. He'd been eighteen. Against his better judgment, he'd finally given in to Anya's persistent advances. He'd permitted her to lead him to the stables one evening, his cock thrilling at the forbidden mysteries that awaited him while his mind insisted 'twas folly to lie with someone he didn't intend to wed. But Anya's searching lips and roving hands had silenced the thinking part of him.

He'd shed his plaid with eager, shaking hands.

She'd gasped. "I canna take that! No lass could." Seeing his confusion, she'd laughed loud as a braying ass. "Oh, poor Darcy." She pushed out her lower lip. "Ye didna ken, did you? Ye're made all wrong for a woman. A mare, mayhap, but no' a woman."

The next day, his kinsmen had begun calling him Big Darcy, and 'twas how he was distinguished to this day, six years later. He'd thought 'twas merely Anya's gossip that had made all the other lasses cast him sidelong glances and whisper behind their hands, leaving him no single soul within his clan he might offer marriage to. But this stranger had taken one look at him and had seemed to ken. That one fearful request that he not touch her had ripped open the scars of wounds he'd thought long healed.

Och, what was he doing letting memory distract him? He had a woman to get to safety and Gunn to chase off Keith land before any more blood was spilt. Content to hear her light steps not far behind, he dashed into the wood to find the cart where Archie always tended the wounded. She would be safe there. Then he could forget about her odd yet stimulating speech and her frightened, lovely face.

The sound of stumbling made him spin around. She had tripped on a root and was on her hands and knees in the leaves. A muffled cry came from behind her curtain of silvery blond hair.

He ran to her. Rejection be damned, he wasn't about to let a lass weep on the ground if he had strength to carry her. And what man worth his salt wouldn't have the strength to carry such a delicate thing? He sheathed his sword and lifted her slight weight.

Och, did she have to feel so warm and soft against his chest? Did the sight of Gunn blood on her woolen have to tug at him so? Damn his contrary cock for stirring at the feel of her petite, lushly curved body so close to his. Gritting his teeth, he practically ran for Archie's cart.

He made the mistake of glancing down at her face. Smooth

and fair as a polished opal, it would have been glorious as the sun itself if it hadn't been so troubled and smudged with mud.

Mud he'd pushed her into in his haste to protect her from the Gunn. No tears marred her cheeks, but her trembling lower lip, full as a rose bursting to bloom, hinted that she was trying not to weep.

Was it so awful for her to be this near to him? He quickened his pace so he could relieve her of his unwelcome touch as soon as possible.

"Thank you," she said, her voice soft and uniquely accented with a delicate drawl.

He nodded tightly. "Dinna fash. Soon, now, and I shall leave ye be."

Her brow wrinkled. "Where are you taking me?"

"To Archie. He tends the wounded well away from the fighting."

"I told you, I'm not wounded."

Though he was desperate to believe somat other than his proximity was fashing her so, he'd much rather she be disgusted with his oafish size than wounded. Relief at her insistence softened him. "Aye, well, be that as it may, 'tis still the safest place for a lass during a skirmish. Archie'll look after you and see ye to the laird upon our return to Ackergill."

The lass took a mighty fortifying sniff. "You mean the laird of your clan? What clan are you with? Is Ackergill the laird's home? Is it a castle? Oh, God, I'm really in Scotland, aren't I? What year is it?"

"Are ye certain ye arena wounded?" he asked. "Did the Gunn knock you in the head? Those are peculiar questions."

"I suppose they are," she said. "Would you answer them anyway? Please?"

He couldn't refuse her, daft as it was not to ken the year or whose land she was on. "'Tis the year of our Lord 1517.

Springtime, if ye lust to ken. I am Darcy Marek MacFirthen Keith. And aye, ye're in the Highlands."

Her eyes closed. Thick black lashes that defied her pale hair and brows fanned over her cheeks. A single sob escaped her soft lips. She whispered, "I just want to go home. Please, I just want to wake up."

"Ye're awake as they come," He told her. She must have bumped her head even if she didn't admit it. "But if there's aught I can do to wake ye more, I shall. Is it mayhap a strong tea ye need?"

The lass met his gaze with the sad emerald pools of her eyes. He nearly stumbled, forgetting to pick up his feet.

"I can't have caffeine," she said with a sniff. "I've already had a coffee today, and more than one a day isn't good for the baby."

More of her gibberish. *Caffeine? Coffee? Baby?* Did she mean a bairn? She didn't have a bairn with her, unless—a horrible thought struck him.

"Did the Gunn take your bairn?"

The lass opened her mouth, then closed it as if she didn't ken how to respond. At last, she said, "If you mean the man with the beard, 'the Gunn' didn't take anything from me, thank you very much. I meant caffeine isn't good for the baby—the child I'm carrying." She shifted in his arms to lay a shell-white hand on her belly.

Oh, *carrying.* She was with child. Christ, he could see the bulge now that he looked properly. He'd been so focused on the fighting that he'd missed what was right in front of him, an unprotected, pregnant lass—woman, he corrected. And married she must be, if with child.

Och, and he'd pushed her in the mud and lain atop her to hide her lightly colored woolen from the approaching Gunn. What if he'd hurt her or the bairn? He'd owe her husband compensation if so. And he'd never forgive himself.

Size might have its advantages when it came to fighting, but those few boons didn't compensate for the problems it caused. Being the biggest and the strongest had gotten him into far more trouble than it had gotten him out of. Swallowing his regret for how careless he'd been with her, he sought to determine whom she belonged to, whom, saints forbid, he might owe.

"Whose wife are ye, then? Not a Gunn's or I wouldna have had to rescue you from one."

"I'm not married," the lass said. "And thank you for the rescuing, by the way. I can't believe I dropped the dirk. Stupid." She shook her head.

His heart warmed at her thanks. He didn't hear many kind words from the lasses and would take what he could get, even from a dishonored woman who had caught a bairn out wedlock. Oddly, he didn't think poorly of her. Whether it was her vexed brow, her guileless, soft mouth, or her vulnerable size, he had not the heart to condemn her.

He didn't even mind so much that she found him distasteful for being overlarge, although talking with her now, she didn't seem overly upset to be in his arms. He endeavored to keep her talking, keep her distracted from her disgust.

"You never answered my first question," he said. "Who are you? And where are you from if ye're no' English?"

"Ugh. I don't know. Is there an answer that won't get me burned at the stake or locked up in a ward for the hopelessly insane?"

Like most things out of her mouth, that had been a peculiar answer. "You could try the truth," he offered, slowing his pace since he heard Archie's voice not far off.

"No," she said flatly. "I couldn't. At least not the whole truth. How about we just go with my name, Melanie, and with the honest fact that I'm a long way from home and have no idea how to get back." Her green eyes pierced his. "I'm afraid you might be stuck with me, Darcy Keith."

Chapter 3

HE'D PUSHED HER into a bush, shoved her in the mud, squished her with his excessively muscled body and trudged off into the woods with those tree-trunk legs of his, leaving her to jog after him in bloody, mud-caked, nettle-riddled clothes, and all it took for her to forgive him was that vulnerable look in his warm brown eyes. That and the fact she could feel tiny flutters of movement deep in her womb, proof that her baby was coping admirably with the abuse her body had taken in the last half hour.

It was almost tempting to feel relief.

But true relief would only come once she figured out how to get home. She didn't have much in Charleston, but what she had she'd worked hard for and was darned proud of: a few close friends, a small but neat apartment, a job that made up in intellectual stimulation what it lacked in pay, a routine. Her mom and dad were just a five-hour drive away in Atlanta.

What was happening back there while she was here? Was her time going on without her, or had none of her life even happened yet? Was she certifiable for even considering such a question?

As much as she wanted to wrap herself in the cozy blanket of denial, her gut told her that option was long gone. This place was real, and she was really in it. She had disappeared from her workbench at the museum when that box had opened.

The box!

Of course. She'd made a wish and the box had granted it. It was the only possible explanation for what had happened. And if it had dumped her five hundred years in the past because of a bone-headed wish she'd made partly in jest, surely it would return her if she asked it nicely.

She needed that box.

She hadn't seen it back at the boulder, but she hadn't exactly been looking for it either.

She had to go look. It had to be there. It just had to.

She opened her mouth to tell Darcy to take her back, but got a mouthful of evergreen needles.

He shouldered his way through a wall of trees, apparently oblivious to the reaching branches catching at her clothes and hair. Stupid box. This wasn't even what she'd wished for.

Sure, Darcy was gorgeous, but he was no romantic hero. He might look the part, but to play the role respectably, he'd need serious lessons in chivalry. Lesson number one: no pushing the heroine in mud puddles. And who'd ever heard of a pregnant heroine, anyway?

C'mon, box. It wasn't a serious wish. Send me home, for the love of all things Scottish.

Before she could ask Darcy to take her back to the boulder, he set her on her feet in front of a circle of six men in various states of undress and injury. A rickety wagon with no horse occupied the far side of the small clearing. The most able-bodied of the group, a wiry red-haired man, dashed around, wrapping wounds and refilling flasks from a barrel in the wagon. That must be Archie. Grinning over a huge abdominal abrasion, he declared the wounded man needed naught but a daily vinegar rinse and a healing tup with his wife. Looking up, he noticed them.

"Hail, Big Darcy," he greeted with a booming, cheerful burr. "What have ye brought me?"

"Looks like a lass," one of the wounded men said with a grin as he looked her up and down. "A bonny one at that."

"Where'd ye find her, Big Darcy?" another man asked.

"In a mud puddle," another answered. "'Tis clear to see."

"Where's the rest of her dress?" another asked.

"Is that blood beneath the mud?" Archie asked, wading through the wounded until he stood directly before her.

Nervous, she shifted to hide behind Darcy, but he didn't cooperate, turning to go back the way they'd come. Just before disappearing back through the wall of trees, he said over his shoulder, "Though she looks to have taken a bath in blood, none of it seems to be hers. Take care of her, Archie."

He slipped through the trees, leaving her staring disbelievingly after him. The brute hadn't even said goodbye.

Ignoring Archie's hand on her arm and the exhaustion demanding she sit and rest her weary pregnant bones, she marched toward the trees.

Darcy's head poked through, so close that if she'd been a foot taller, he would have headbutted her. "I almost forgot," he said to Archie. "She's no' English."

He disappeared again without even glancing at her.

"Wait!" She shook off Archie's hand and pushing through the densely packed branches.

"Darcy, wait!"

He stopped and turned, though his impressive body clearly strained to get back to the fighting.

"I need to go with you," she said.

"No. Ye will stay here with Archie and help tend the wounded." He strode away.

She trotted after him. "I can't. There's something back there I need. At least, I hope there is. I have to look for it." She caught up and ventured to grab his arm to slow his gait. His skin was hot velvet stretched over granite-hard muscle. She couldn't resist relaxing her grip to smooth her fingers over the enticing flesh. He really was cover model material. But she only appreciated the feel of his tawny skin for a second. She had to get that box. Had to get home.

Alan and the others helping with the Scottish immigrants exhibit were depending on her. Her friends and family would be beside themselves with worry. The dining-room-turned-nursery-nook in her apartment was only half decorated. She had to water her plants.

Darcy stopped walking and stared at her hand until she removed it. "What is it ye lost? I'll look for you. You are to stay here, understand?"

She remembered the sight of Darcy pulling his sword from the bodies of the men he'd killed and how the "Gunn" had pinned her down and threatened her. Maybe she didn't want to go back there. On the other hand, she'd be a fool to trust this warrior to look as hard as she would for her ticket home.

"I have to go with you," she insisted.

Darcy picked her up again, this time not as gently as he had when she'd tripped on the root. He carried her under one arm like a sack of grain, though to his credit, he avoided putting pressure on her lower abdomen.

"I said no, ye contrary thing, and I'm big enough to make you obey whether ye want to or no'." He crashed through the line of trees, stomped past the wounded men, and set her firmly in the wagon. "A skirmish is no place for a woman. I willna be responsible for you getting raped or killed." That vulnerable look softened his hard features for a second. "I could tie you down, but then ye'd be no help to Archie. So what'll it be, lass? Will you obey me or no?"

He tried to intimidate her with his posture and size, bracketing her with his bare arms. It didn't work. Rather, the sight of the succulent, hard mound of his exposed shoulder so close to her face made her wet her lips. His strong collarbones and sinewy neck glistened with sweat, and he smelled of pine and male exertion. Her libido jumped like a feisty poodle.

Jeez Louise, Mel, get a grip. This is not a romance novel. He's not your hero. The box got it wrong. The box was way out of line.

"I need it," she said, pleased her steady voice didn't betray her attraction. "I have to go with you."

"I told you I'd look for whatever ye lust."

Lust. The antiquated word spoken in his deep voice did strange things to her tummy. It took a solid effort not to lick her lips in invitation as the word called to mind activities that most definitely related to wanting.

Home, she reminded herself. She had to get home. "I don't trust you to look as hard as I would. I'm coming with you."

"Where are your ropes, Archie?" he asked. "The woman refuses to stay put. I have no choice but to tie her to the wagon."

Several of the wounded men snickered.

Archie said, "In the foot case there. And bring me some of yon dried moss before ye tie down your woman."

Your woman. The casual declaration made her stomach leap, and the sensation wasn't entirely unpleasant.

"She's not mine," Darcy growled as he opened the lid of a wooden chest in the wagon.

To her horror, he removed a coil of rope. After tossing a yellowish clump in Archie's direction, he came at her.

Her libido disappeared with a poof. She hopped off the wagon, dodging hands that had no business being so quick, considering how large they were.

"Don't you dare tie me down! I've got to get that box. It's my only hope to return home."

He lunged for her, catching her easily around the waist with his long arm, and plunking her back in the wagon. Libido was back. Her body thrilled at Darcy's manhandling, though her muscles struggled against it.

The thought of him tying her up in private might have some

merit, but not in the middle of the forest with several strange men as witnesses. “Okay, okay,” she blurted as he looped the rope around one wrist. “I won’t follow you. Please don’t tie me. I’ll stay. I’ll help.”

He paused to eye her suspiciously.

“I promise,” she said. “I’ll stay here and make myself useful. As long as you promise to look for a rosewood box inlaid with white gold and about yea big.” She gestured with her hands, rope trailing from one wrist. “As long as you swear to look as though your life depends on it.”

She held his gaze, hoping he was getting how important this was to her, hoping she could trust him.

The circle of wounded men went quiet, waiting for his answer.

He bounced on the balls of his feet, clearly impatient to return to the skirmish, but he gave her his full attention and said, “I vow that if your cherished box is on that field, I will find it.”

She relaxed at the sincerity in the promise. “It would be near where you found me,” she said. “If it’s not there, then—” She forced herself to say the rest past her tight throat. “Then I don’t think you’ll find it anywhere.” *And I might be stuck here forever.*

He nodded his understanding, then wheeled around and strode from the clearing.

“Damn,” one of the wounded men said. “I’d hoped to watch Big Darcy bind the feisty lass.”

The other men chuckled. Some of the chuckles ended in pained groans.

She scowled at one and all as she shook the rope from her wrist, but her scowl quickly slipped away. Some of the men were horribly injured. One had a bandage wrapped around his thigh and soaked through with blood. The bandage was obviously not tight enough to slow the flow from what must be a serious gash. Another had a chest wound. He didn’t grin at her like the others, but lay still except for his jumping chest. Pink blood frothed from a wound under his armpit. Another man held a bloody rag to his neck, and an ugly bump under his skin looked like a broken collarbone. Another had a head wound that needed stitches.

She slid off the cart and found Archie. "How can I help?"

§

"I'M AFRAID YOU might be stuck with me, Darcy Keith."

Making his way back to Berringer's field, he tried to forget those sweetly drawled words, but found himself thinking instead that being stuck with a bonny woman with lush curves and a streak of bravery belying her slight stature wouldn't be such a terrible fate. But thoughts like that were neither useful nor prudent. 'Twas impossible for him to do full honor to a woman by giving her a proper marriage bed and children. Thus he had no business thinking of any woman with longing, especially one so small.

He had to help his clan first, but once the Gunn were off their land, he'd find the woman's—Melanie's—cherished box. She said it was her only way home, and home was precisely where he wanted her. Safe with her own people. Far from his futile desires.

Mayhap the box was the only possession she had and she meant to sell it to buy her way back to her people. He still didn't ken what people those might be, but they certainly weren't Scottish and he believed her when she said she wasn't English; her odd speech alone proved as much. Whoever her people were, it was plain she desperately wanted to return to them. Well, he'd help her do just that, and good riddance to her.

By the time he ran back onto the field where his clan had clashed with the Gunn for the third time since Hogmany, and it only April, his kinsmen had driven most of them back over the border. All that was left was to help a few of the battered back to

Archie's wagon where they'd all gather before journeying home to Ackergill.

He carried wee John, who had a gash to his arse that made walking awkward, while Gabe limped along with a little help from his free arm. After depositing the men in Archie's clearing and contenting himself with the sight of the woman dutifully washing Symond's sliced shoulder, he returned to where he'd found her to look for her box.

It took naught but two open eyes to find it. The thing lay half buried in the same mud puddle he'd pushed her into. He lifted it out of the muck and used a corner of his plaid to clean it. A bonny thing it was. Shiny and smooth with rounded edges and inlaid knotwork of white metal on the lid, just like she'd said. 'Twould certainly bring her enough coin to buy passage on a vessel if 'twas over water she needed to go.

He turned the box over to scrub mud from the bottom. An inscription emerged: *MacLeod, 1542. Inverness.*

He nearly dropped the thing.

Trusting he'd read the script wrong, he shifted the box so its base better caught the late-afternoon light. He read it again. It still said 1542.

The little box claimed to be from twenty-five years in the future. Surely someone had forged a few lines to alter the year. Changing a one to a four would be only too easy. But the inscription was written in glossy brown ink *beneath* the stain. If a forgery, 'twould have had to be done before the piece was finished.

Might the box actually be from the future? A frivolous and dangerous thought.

He weighed the object in his hands. Legends were told in pubs about women claiming to have come through the stones like the ones at Loch Stemster from exotic places and future times.

He had found the woman near a great stone.

He snorted and shook his head. He had never put any stock in such tales, and he wouldn't start now. The box was a simple forgery. 'Twas the only solution. But there were some who were more inclined to believe the worst about a person than to trust in reason.

And the king of those paranoid fools was Laird Steafan. Ever since losing his son, Darcy's cousin, at the battle at Creag Kirk four years ago, Steafan hadn't been the same. He would hardly leave the keep for fear of being cut down and leaving Ackergill without a proper leader. He had little tolerance for visitors, more often than not sticking them in the dungeons for the night, rather than allowing them a warm room with a clean bed for fear of what havoc they might cause. Most of all, he mistrusted anything to which a hint of magic could be credited, and if Steafan mistrusted someone, he dealt with them harshly.

All for the sake of Ackergill, his uncle claimed.

For the sake of mild insanity, more like.

But completely sane or no, Steafan was still laird, and the woman would have a hard enough time convincing him she was no threat nor burden to their clan with her odd speech and manner of dress, not to mention her unborn bairn. She didn't need to be associated with a mysterious box on top of it all. Best for all involved if he kept it to himself for the time being.

§

MELANIE'S PROBLEMS SETTLED into the background as she followed Archie's instructions in cleaning and binding wounds until he could get to them with his thread and needle. Broken bones were left for the physician at Ackergill, who she guessed was too valuable to be risked in skirmishes. The man with the lung injury was transferred to a pallet in the back of the wagon, where Archie informed her in a subdued voice he would likely die on the way back to the village.

If anything could keep her mind off her predicament, it was the weight of injury and death casting a pall over Archie's rudimentary field hospital. But even with the heavy atmosphere, the men bantered good-naturedly with her and availed themselves of any and every opportunity to pinch her bottom. The first time, it had been the man with the profusely bleeding thigh. She'd changed his soaked bandage and tied another around the wound so tight he'd winced and asked her if she were trying to sever his leg in twain. When she'd turned to separate another length of linen from Archie's stash, he'd grabbed a handful of her rear end through her skirt and given it a sharp jiggle. She'd spun around and slapped him. Then she'd hastily apologized when he reminded her with a wince how badly his leg hurt. The other men had caught on and, well, her butt was starting to throb—and her left eye was starting to twitch—from all the attention.

More men came into the clearing, both wounded and "hale," as Archie referred to the able-bodied. Fortunately, the wounds sported by the newcomers were mostly minor. Not twenty-first century minor, but minor in the sense that nothing major had been cut off and the men were functionally ambulatory. Several men helped themselves to Archie's stash of bandages and pitched in with the more grievously wounded. From their boisterous banter, she gathered the skirmish was over and the Keiths had come out victorious.

Good. If the men she'd met were a representative sample, she wasn't a fan of "the Gunn."

She searched the milling two-dozen or so warriors for a tall head of honey-blond hair, but didn't see Darcy. Worry tightened her chest. Had he been hurt too badly to make it back? Why did that thought disturb her so deeply? She'd just met the man. And he'd spent half the time she'd known him annoying her.

A tall man strode into the clearing, tall being relative to those in the clearing, and since Darcy wasn't there, the man qualified as tall. He had short brown hair and a closely trimmed beard and said in a booming voice, "Well fought, kinsmen. The Gunn will think twice about trespassing on Keith land again." A round of victorious shouts rent the damp air. "Gloaming comes. 'Tis time to return to our ale and our women." This elicited raucous cheers, punctuated by hoots and whistles. The man smiled briefly, then squinted around as if doing a mental headcount. "Where's Big Darcy?"

"Here I am," came a smooth, deep voice from the trees. When a honey-blond head poked through, followed by a blessedly hale, broad-shouldered body, her chest relaxed.

His eyes found hers, then darted away. He trudged through the men to the wagon where she lost sight of all but the top of his head in the small crowd. She jostled her way through the milling Keith to find him and ask whether he'd found the box, but the bearded man stopped her.

"And just who might you be?" he asked with a firm hand on her shoulder. His ice-blue eyes flashed with suspicion and promises of punishment if he didn't like her answer. Her neck prickled with warning. This was a dangerous man.

They're all dangerous men. Tread carefully, Mel.

Darcy appeared behind the man, and some of the tension left her shoulders. "I found her near the northern hill by Berringer's marker," he said in a light tone that thawed the coldest layer of frost from the bearded man's eyes. He'd also made himself seem shorter by slouching. "Since she'd stuck a Gunn with his own dirk, I assumed she was on our side. Seems she's lost and could use an audience with the laird. What say you, Aodhan, shall we escort the poor thing to Steafan and beg the laird's hospitality?"

"She English?" Aodhan asked, as if she weren't there.

"No," Darcy said with surety.

"Who does she belong to?" Those cold eyes snapped to Darcy

with greater attention than the question seemed to warrant. She had the impulse to say she didn't "belong" to anybody, but she held her tongue, remembering where, and when, she was.

"No Keith or Gunn. That much I've determined," Darcy answered cautiously. "Beyond that, I dinna ken."

Aodhan appraised her like he might a horse for sale. His shrewd eyes softened with appreciation, and his lips twitched with the kind of smile a turkey might see before ending up Thanksgiving dinner. He opened his mouth to say something, but Darcy blurted, "I'll take responsibility for her."

Aodhan gave him a measuring look that bordered on annoyance. Finally, he grunted and moved away to shout orders at the other men.

Darcy huffed a put-out sigh, then turned to her with his mouth pressed in a hard line. "I suppose ye'd better stick close to me."

That was fine with her, though she could have done without the attitude. "Did you find it?" she asked as she followed him to the wagon, already forgetting about the strange little confrontation with Aodhan.

He shook his head and picked up the wagon's jutting handles, lifting its front feet off the ground so the entire rickety thing groaned back on its two wheels.

"Did you find it?" she asked again, her voice sharp with desperation. She needed to hear him say it. She wouldn't let her hope come crashing down around her for anything less than verbal confirmation that the box hadn't come with her into the past.

He walked forward, pulling the wagon and falling in with the departing men. "No," he said, the muscles in his jaw tense.

She stared after him, her legs locked in shock. Men wafting the pungent scents of blood, whisky, and body odor closed around her to follow Darcy out of the clearing. Another hand found her butt and gave two solid tweaks. It jolted her into a jog. She caught up to Darcy, ignoring the snickering behind her.

"What do you mean, 'no'? You looked where you found me and you didn't find it? Are you sure? Did you poke around in the mud?"

"I looked where I found you," he said tightly. "I looked as well as a man can, and yet I am empty handed. I regret that I have no box to give you." With a pained expression, he met her desperate gaze. "I am sorry."

She closed her eyes against a crush of disappointment. If the box hadn't come through with her, then she had nothing tangible with which to buoy her hope.

"I have to go back and look for it," she said, turning to trek back to the field.

"'Tis no' there," he said firmly, putting down the cart to snatch her arm before she'd taken two strides. She met his eyes and the sympathy in them knocked the wind out of her. He was telling the truth. She knew from his sincere expression that no amount of searching back at the boulder would reveal the rosewood box. "You must come with me, Melanie. I need to bring ye to the laird as I would any stranger on Keith land, but then I'll see you fed and rested. I vow I will do all in my power to return you to your people on the morrow."

In the wake of Kyle's betrayal, her first instinct was to bristle at the promise, but with a stab to her heart, she remembered Kyle had never made her any promises. In fact, no man had ever made her a promise before.

She eyed him, unsure how to react. Whether it was the comforting sound of her name marching from his lips in that hearty burr or the earnest gleam in his eyes, somehow she knew that a promise made by Darcy Marek MacFirthen Keith was a promise a girl could trust.

Something in her gut relaxed.

She might not have the box, but she at least had an ally.

She was reluctant to leave the spot where time had broken apart and abandoned her to the past, but when Darcy picked up the cart handles and walked on, she went with him.

§

DARCY SHOOK HIS head at himself as he pulled the cart back to Ackergill. Melanie—Malina he kept wanting to call her in the Scots way—plodded beside him, despondent but no less beautiful for the small crease between her slanted brows.

He'd put that crease there when he'd made her believe he hadn't found her cherished box.

He could wipe it away just as easily by reaching into Archie's healer's supplies, lifting out her hidden possession, and placing it in her tiny, graceful hands.

But her relief would be short-lived. If any of the men saw the thing and word got to Steafan, 'twould go badly for her. And he wasn't sure how much of her suffering he'd be able to bear. He'd met her less than two hours ago, but he already felt protective of her. And it wasn't just that he'd claimed responsibility for her before Aodhan.

His need to protect her had gripped him from the moment he'd seen her, her emerald eyes wide and frightened, her hands shaking and covered in blood. His heart had cried, *Mine*, even though he kent better than to believe he could have a woman for his own. His foolish mouth had verified it soon after, when he'd thought Aodhan had been about to lay claim to her. And Aodhan, the cur, had accepted it without batting an eye. In fact, a twinkle in the war chieftain's usually hard eyes suggested the man found Darcy's claim amusing.

As if to confirm his suspicion, Aodhan hung back to walk alongside him, opposite from Malina. "She doesna look pleased to have been claimed," the war chieftain said in the auld tongue.

Darcy glanced at Malina. She paid them no heed. "I dinna suspect she kens what it means." She spoke English, but a strange version of it. And she seemed too upset about her box to care that he had declared his intention to wed her.

"Ye do realize Steafan will likely wed you tonight when ye present her to him. She'll be sure to understand then."

He jerked his head to stare at Aodhan. "He wouldna."

Aodhan's smirk confirmed what his suddenly thumping heart already kent. Steafan would.

Of course, Aodhan had been there a fortnight past when Steafan had summoned him to his office and threatened to find a wife for him if he didn't find one for himself by Harvest.

"Your brother shames ye, lad," his uncle had said. "Wed and already with a bairn and he two years your younger. Ye're far too auld to nay have a wife, and Ackergill willna suffer a laird with no prospects for children."

"Make Edmund your heir, then," he'd said.

He didn't mind yielding the honor to his brother. Edmund was a fine man, and Steafan made a good point; their family line would carry on with Edmund where it had no chance with him. But the whole argument was pointless. At a whole and hearty forty-five, Steafan wasn't old enough to fash about who would be laird after him, and after losing his son and then his wife to grief soon after, he'd married a young lass. Ginneleah, Aodhan's daughter.

At a fresh seventeen years, Ginneleah had many seasons of childbearing ahead of her. Just because she hadn't conceived in the two years they'd been wed didn't mean she never would. Steafan was bound to have an heir of his own blood. He wouldn't have to settle for one of his brother's blood. But Steafan wasn't one to put hopeful stock in what might happen.

Steafan was a pessimistic, paranoid bugger. And a bully.

"Dinna be so quick to throw away your birthright, lad," he had said. "Remember Jacob and Esau?"

He and Edmund had little in common with Isaac's sons, but arguing with Steafan was as useful an expenditure of time as trying to force a gelding to breed. There was one thing he hadn't ever admitted to his uncle, though, one thing he hoped might sway the laird.

"I canna wed, uncle," he admitted while Aodhan had looked on. "'Tis impossible for me to lie with a woman."

To his dismay, his uncle burst out in laughter, and a grin broke the war chieftain's icy demeanor. His face had burned hot. He'd long grown used to being a laughing stock because of his size, but to bear whisky-slurred laughter in the pub was one thing. To bear the sober mirth of his uncle and the laird's second-in-command in a private meeting felt leagues worse.

"Ye dinna actually believe that, do you, lad?" his uncle had forced through his guffawing.

Seeing the look on his face, Steafan's smile died on his lips. "Christ, Darcy. 'Tis nothing to be shamed by to be large under one's plaid."

Tell that to Anya, he'd thought. Even years later, her horrified expression stuck in his memory like a fly in a spider's web. He couldn't shake the image free, and he was determined never to see such a look on a woman's face again.

"I willna marry, Steafan," he had insisted.

"You will. I willna release you as my heir and I willna settle for an heir with no wife."

He'd trudged from his uncle's office kenning full well he'd be wed within the year and pitying the poor lass Steafan would force into it. But now, with Aodhan whispering in his ear and Malina by his side, lovely as a lily in the gloaming and smelling of exotic fruit despite the mud and blood caking her clothing, he wondered if the saints had presented him a solution that would suit both him and Steafan.

What if Steafan did wed them tonight? What if he kept the lass rather than help her return home? She was already with child. They could be a family and he would never have to trouble her with his bed.

Aodhan's eyes scrunched with uncharacteristic warmth as the possibility unfurled in Darcy's imagination, puffing his chest with pride and filling his belly with nervous flutters. But 'twas a dream and no more.

He shook his head. "I canna wed her, Aodhan. She is lost and wishes to return to her home, her people. I have vowed to help her do so and I willna go back on it."

"So wed her and then send her home to her people. You can tell Steafan she glimpsed under your plaid and ran away." Aodhan's lips twitched, and Darcy felt his cheeks burn. "Steafan willna be able to null the marriage without your consent. You'll be wed as he wishes. You'll have fulfilled the letter of his law, so he willna be able to hound you or force ye into another marriage."

He stared in shock at the plotting war chieftain. He'd never before thought Aodhan less than utterly loyal to Steafan. Yet what he suggested was dishonest. He was ashamed to consider it.

Aodhan's eyes sharpened to their characteristic ice. "Steafan is besotted with your size, lad. It keeps him from seeing Edmund would be the better leader if it comes to that. There are few Keith who can match you as a fighter, and ye're a fine miller and businessman. Ackergill owes a grand share of her prosperity to you. But ye dinna have the ruthless streak a man needs to keep a clan in line. I tell you nothing ye dinna already ken."

He nodded in agreement. He didn't particularly want to lead, and he didn't like the attention of being Steafan's heir. Aodhan's plan was tempting, but there was a flaw in it.

"Steafan is no fool. He wants me wed, but only because he wants me to have bairns. If I wed the woman and she leaves, he'll likely put me in the stocks if I dinna agree to a null."

“I’ll talk to him,” Aodhan said. “I could even make excuses for you. Wed the lass tonight and take her away. Escort her to her home. I’ll tell Steafan you’ve gone searching for your run-away bride. When you return alone, Steafan will have to admit ye’d make a terrible laird if you couldna even keep a wee wife in line. He’ll accept Edmund.” He scoffed, “It doesna matter anyway, since Ginnie is sure to have a bairn sooner or later. Steafan fashes over naught.”

Aodhan made it all seem so easy. He could be wed tonight. To Malina. But then he’d have to help his wife leave him. ’Twas too terrible to consider. “I canna leave my mill,” he protested.

“Edmund can handle it for a time, and I’ll look in on him. The place willna fall apart without you.”

Darcy studied the war chieftain. He’d rarely conversed with the man outside of trading tawdry jests or discussing swordplay tactics on the practice field. “What are you up to, man?” he wondered out loud.

The ice melted from Aodhan’s eyes. “I dinna like to see ye suffer needlessly, lad,” he said and stalked away.

Chapter 4

MELANIE'S FEET WERE killing her. She was used to being on them since she often performed docent duties at the museum, but she wasn't used to marching for upward of an hour over rock-strewn trails cut through darkened forests. On top of burning soles and aching muscles, it also felt like her stomach was trying to eat itself. According to her internal clock, dinner time had come and gone with nary a glimpse of anything edible. If she'd been back in Charleston, she'd have probably eaten two meals that would qualify as dinner by now.

Just when she thought about asking, "Are we there yet?" the forest gave way to an immense, wide open clearing that could have been anything from a swath of farmland to a peat field. Beyond the clearing was a gentle rise dotted with crofter cottages and capped by a utilitarian, three-story rectangle of a castle with glowing windows.

"Ackergill?" she asked, her spirit lifting with the prospect of food and rest. It was the first she'd spoken to Darcy since he'd promised to help her return home. Ever since the hushed talk in Gaelic he'd had with Aodhan, he'd seemed tense, and she hadn't needed any more tension in her life just then, so she'd chosen to ignore him as they walked.

He nodded without meeting her eyes.

Scanning the village, her eyes were drawn far to the right of the castle where three tower-shaped silhouettes with sails stood against the night like pieces on a chessboard. "Ooh, are those windmills?" She'd had a thing for windmills ever since reading *Don Quixote* in her 4th-year Spanish class in high school.

"Aye." Darcy's voice brightened with pride as he followed her gaze. "'Tis my mill. My home overlooks the sea. There." He paused in pulling the wagon to point to the left of the windmills where a two-story house stood dark and alone at the crest of the rise. Now that he mentioned the sea, she detected a trace of salt in the air past the musk of two dozen male bodies in dire need of bathing.

She sighed with longing as the briny scent reminded her of childhood trips to the Georgia coast with her parents. She would see them again, she promised herself. Box or no box, she would find a way.

"It's lovely," she said, cheered with hope and determination.

Darcy fixed her with an intense gaze, picked up the handles and continued on.

"Do you have a large family?" she asked to cover how his gaze unsettled her. The history loving part of her also craved connection with this warrior from the past. She wanted to learn from him while she had the chance. Her grandmother had been from the northern Highlands.

And now, here she was, face to face with the very land to which she attributed a quarter of her blood. What an amazing opportunity!

Darcy shook his head. "My mother died long ago, and my da died four years back. My brother has his own cottage in the village where he lives with his wife. Now 'tis only me at Fraineach."

"I live alone, too," she said without thinking. She regretted it immediately. Women didn't live alone in this time. They lived with their families until they got married. They obeyed their fathers until it was time to obey their husbands. Women's lib wasn't even an embryonic thought.

"Are you a doxie?" he asked quietly. "I wouldna hold it against you if so."

She didn't know whether to sock his arm in offense or to laugh. She settled for a wry smile. "No. I'm not a prostitute. But I do work for a living. Many women do where I come from." How should she put what she did for a living? "I work in a museum, a place for taking care of historical artifacts and making them available to the masses."

"Ye're Catholic, then?" he asked, confusion plain in his voice.

Oh, masses. "No, I'm not really anything religious. By masses, I meant the people, you know, the general population. I take care of old things and tell stories to the people so they can understand history."

"Ah. Ye're a teacher," he concluded. "'Tis a fine occupation if a woman must work."

She didn't argue. Instead, she gazed up at Ackergill Castle as their party wended through what turned out to be an impressive agricultural valley. Up ahead, the keep glowed like a beacon above the cottages, some of which emitted their own welcoming lights.

A glance around at the men showed dirt-smudged faces lifting and brightening. Even the walking wounded kept up as the joy of homecoming quickened the party's pace. To her astonishment, the man with the wounded thigh limped past in an awkward jog, having made it the whole five miles or so with nothing but the help of a crutch pulled from Archie's wagon.

"I need to see the cart back to Archie's," Darcy said, "but my brother's cottage is just here." He paused near a path branching off from the dirt road and tipped up his chin to scan the returning men.

"Edmund!" he called.

A reddish-blond mane came into view as the party of warriors disbanded into the village.

She hadn't noticed him before, but now he stood out to her for his resemblance to Darcy. Around six-feet, Edmund was tall compared to everyone except Darcy and Aodhan, and every bit as muscled as his brother, though his lesser height made him appear bulky where Darcy looked as sleek as he did strong. The two men shared the same square chin, sharp cheekbones, and brown eyes, but Edmund's nose was broader and crooked with a scab of blood over the bridge.

Darcy either didn't notice the newly broken nose or deemed it unworthy of mention.

Without preamble, he said, "Watch the woman, will you?"

Edmund turned wary eyes on her. "This the one the men are talkin' about?"

"Aye. Found her at Berringer's field. She isna clan, and she is my responsibility."

Edmund raised his eyebrows at his brother, then looked long and hard at her.

She offered a tentative smile. "My name is Melanie," she said, curbing the impulse to hold out her right hand for a modern shake. "I'm not an English spy," she added for good measure.

Edmund gave her a wry half-smile. "Well, then, I suppose I can bring you into my home and no' fear for the safety of my wife and bairn." Turning to Darcy, he said, "Will you be along for sup after tending to Richie?"

Richie. The man in the cart with the lung wound. The man whose rattling breaths had ceased about half an hour into the walk. She'd tried to not think about what the sudden silence meant. Tried and failed.

"Aye," Darcy answered with a grim nod. Without another word, he hauled the cart away, leaving her with Edmund.

"This way," Edmund said as he led her to a stone cottage with shutters thrown open to the crisp night air. Golden lantern light flooded out, along with the cries of a young infant. Gesturing for her to enter before him, he said, "So if ye're no' a Sassenach spy, are ye any other kind of spy, or did ye mean ye're no spy at all?"

"I'm not a spy for England or any other country," she said, taking in the warm and tidy main room with its peat fire and sturdy table set for a cottar's dinner. The fragrance of cooked meat and onions instantly made her mouth water. The infant cries, coming from a room with an open door at the back of the cottage, quieted, and the gentle cooing of a nursing mother drifted out to cinch the cozy atmosphere.

"Well, that's a relief," Edmund replied. "The laird would likely skin my arse for offering you hospitality if ye turned out to be any kind of spy."

The comment was good-natured enough, but she caught an undercurrent of something darker. A sentiment for the laird, perhaps, that dipped past healthy respect and into fear? She recalled from what little she knew about feudal Scotland that clan justice ran the gamut from fair to brutally oppressive, depending on the temperament of the laird.

"What kind of man is your laird?" she asked, suddenly nervous about meeting this man who insisted on interviewing strangers before they could be offered hospitality.

Edmund ran a hand over the back of his neck as he made his way to a basin of water set on the floor by the fire. Shucking his cork-soled shoes and knee-high hose, he stepped into the basin otherwise fully clothed, and unabashedly splashed water up between his legs. Though his kilt hid his hands, she could tell he was washing himself, and she blushed at the realization that there were no Calvin Klein boxer briefs under the brown wool. Edmund wore a blocky linen shirt under his kilt, rather than go bare-chested like Darcy. As he answered her, he let down the wool wrapped over his shoulder and pulled his dirty shirt over his head to throw it on a stool by the hearth.

Yup, every bit as muscled as his brother. She averted her eyes from the attractive and very married Highland warrior, looking instead toward the door across the room where the cooing had changed to a soft Gaelic lullaby.

The tinkling sounds of hurried bathing accompanied Edmund's voice. "Steafan is a fair but suspicious man. He isna apt to be as welcoming to strangers as his sire was before him, especially since the ambush at Creag Kirk four years ago. And he doesna need to be, so far north."

The rush of agitated water meant Edmund was stepping out of the basin. The faint rustling of fabric told her he was pulling his shirt back on. She faced him again.

"Ackergill is about as likely to see travelers passing through as the Orkneys. 'Tis not like Inverness, where there are inns and taverns. In the rare event Ackergill sees a traveler come through, he'll be more likely to find himself in the keep dungeon than be offered a room for the night. That way Steafan can ensure the trespasser will do no treachery to the clan."

A chill snaked up her spine at the warning in Edmund's tone. "Is that what I am? A trespasser?"

"Mayhap 'tis how Steafan would view you had Darcy not claimed responsibility for ye. And bonny as you are, if he hadna done it, another surely would have. No. Ye'll nay be treated as a trespasser. But if ye do harm to the clan, 'twill be Darcy who pays for it, and Steafan willna hold back simply because he's our uncle."

Her mouth went dry at the thought of Darcy meeting with any kind of medieval punishment. "Well then, it's a good thing I don't mean your clan any harm. What happened at Creag Kirk to make your laird so suspicious?"

Edmund eyed her for a long second and then nodded. "Ackergill lost twenty able-bodied men to the Gunn and the MacBane," he answered as he stalked to the room where his wife and baby were. "All because a Sassenach spy pitted the northern clans against each other to keep us from joining the fighting at Flodden." He went into the room and shut the door.

She gasped. Flodden. Four years ago would be 1513. The famous Battle at Flodden Field.

The country had lost 5,000 men, referred to as the Flower of Scotland, to the English, along with one of the Jameses—was it James the III or the IV?—she couldn't remember. But she did recall that nearly every clan in the country lost men in that battle. It made sense that England would send spies to try and distract some clans from James's call to fight down at the border.

Well, that explained the general attitude toward English spies she'd encountered.

She'd volunteered to head the Scottish Immigrants' exhibit at the museum to get in touch with her Scottish roots. Looks like she got more than a touch. Run over by a steamroller was more like it. A laugh bordering on hysterical bubbled out of her throat.

Muffled voices filtered through the closed door as Edmund greeted his wife. When less than a minute later, a very male groan accompanied the rhythmic creaking of a piece of furniture, she gaped. Not much for preliminaries, sixteenth century Scotsmen.

Ignoring the sharp grunts of a male engaged in intercourse and the unsurprising lack of happy female noises, she retreated to the farthest place in the cottage from that door, which happened to be the workbench and raised stone hearth that formed the kitchen. She wasn't about to waste an opportunity to study a late-medieval Scottish cottage.

Just as she held up to the lantern light a sharp cleaver with a wooden handle polished from years of regular use, Darcy ducked in the front door. At the same time, Edmund shouted,

"Aye! Christ, Fran, take my seed, lass. Take it. Aaarrghhhhh!" Then barely audible, "Glorious, woman. Ye're glorious."

Darcy paled as his wide eyes jumped from the closed bedroom door to her.

"If I had to listen to them go at it for another second, I was going to put myself out of my misery," she quipped, wagging the cleaver. When his eyes went even wider, she said, "Joking, Darcy. I was joking." She put down the cleaver and raised her hands.

His eyes relaxed and the corner of his mouth lifted. He came to the workbench and picked up the enormous blade. "Well, so long as ye arena using it, mayhap I'll carve the roast."

§

OKAY, SO MAYBE she'd been a bit hasty in her dismissal of medieval Scottish fare.

Edmund's wife, an auburn-haired, generously endowed, rosy cheeked tornado of a woman, had prepared for "her lads" a decadent meal of roasted mutton, a buttery round of bread she called bannock, and a stew of onions and seaweed boiled in spiced milk. The seasoning was perfect, and the meal was both satisfying and nutritious.

"Now, what shall we do about a dress for you?" Fran asked as she busily cleared the table and set the dirty wooden trenchers near the still-full bath basin. "Ye canna meet the laird in these rags." She pinched Melanie's cashmere-encased arm and stopped dead in her tracks. Fingering the material, she commented, "Hmm, mayhap they werena rags to start with. This is a fine woolen, if an odd color, but 'tis no good now, what with all this Gunn blood on it. I'd lend ye one of mine," she said as she guided Melanie to the basin and whipped her sweater over her head before Melanie realized what she was doing. "But ye're inches shorter and I havena time to tack up a hem if ye wish to see the laird before midnight. I'm terribly slow at sewing. I wonder…"

Melanie seized on her distraction and snatched her sweater back to hold in front of her chest. "Um, the men are still here—"

Melanie's protest died on her lips as she met Darcy's eyes. He'd had his head bent in whispers with Edmund until her sweater had been removed. Now he stared at her and nodded absently at whatever Edmund was saying. His gaze caressed her bare shoulders, pausing at her satiny bra straps with their little plastic clips that must be completely foreign to him. A flush warmed her skin, and it wasn't all from embarrassment.

Fran turned her energetic gaze on Darcy. "Do you suppose your mother's dresses might fit?" she asked, oblivious to the heat in his gaze and the unsettling effect it was having on Melanie. "Fetch ye one or two when ye run up to Fraineach. Well, what are you waiting for?" she demanded. "Go on with you. Ye canna go to the laird in bloodied plaid." Fran snapped her fingers in front of Darcy's face until he stopped staring. He towered over the woman, yet he let her herd him out the door like a bashful boy being kicked out of the kitchen for sneaking sweets before dinner.

Without missing a beat, Fran pinned her husband with her glare. "And shame on you, Edmund Alexander MacFirthen Keith, for bathing before offering the clean water to our guest. Since ye're fed and cleaned, make yourself useful. Go fetch some slippers from Hannah. She's got wee feet like Melanie. Then go up to Fraineach and help Darcy."

In the next heartbeat, Fran was bent at Melanie's feet, slipping off her loafers. "Come, now. Let's get you out of these clothes and washed up. The laird won't wait on you all night."

Melanie submitted to the woman's efficient ministrations, because she didn't have a death wish, and clearly to defy Fran was to court a painful death. Beyond raising her eyebrows at Melanie's rounded belly when she'd peeled off the maternity-paneled skirt, she made no comment, much to Melanie's relief. It was awkward enough standing nude in a basin of used, room-temperature bathwater with a stranger rinsing blood and mud off of her, without having to explain being single and pregnant to a sixteenth-century Scottish woman. Fran did not let her get away with being clean-shaven, however.

"Bare as a newborn babe ye are," she said, crouching and frowning at Melanie's shins.

"Under your arms, too. Where did ye say ye were from?"

"Uh, I'm from across the sea," she said.

"Ah, Hasburg, aye? The Netherlands?" she added at Melanie's blank look. "Must be the Spanish influence. Odd, them Spaniards. I've always said so."

"Sure, the Netherlands." Why not? It was a lie, but it would be a lot easier to explain than the truth. Besides, she was shivering too much to expound, and Fran seemed content to make clucking noises and general disapproving remarks about impractical Spanish fashion. To distract herself from the chill, Melanie interrupted Fran. "So, it sounds like the laird is expecting me?"

She made it a question.

Fran made a throaty sound that might have been the equivalent of a modern-day *Mm-hm*.

"The laird will have heard all about the skirmish, and it seems plenty of men laid eyes on you. He'll be expecting you, all right." A wary note crept into her brisk burr, reminding Melanie about her earlier conversation with Edmund.

"Is there anything I should be aware of before meeting the laird?" she asked. "I mean, besides the fact that he's suspicious of outsiders and might punish Darcy if I do anything to harm the clan?"

Fran froze as she searched a drawer. "Punish Darcy?" She stood up straight, a startled look on her face. "He didna claim responsibility for ye before an elder, did he?"

"Is Aodhan an elder?"

"He is," Fran said with a twinkle in her eye that Melanie

didn't understand. She draped a linen blanket around Melanie's shoulders and flitted around the cabin, humming to herself.

Frowning at Fran, Melanie stepped out of the basin to dry herself before the fire. "Am I missing something?"

Fran jumped, as if Melanie's question had pulled her from a private thought. "Dinna fash yourself." She looked down at Melanie's abdomen, which peeked through the folds of the blanket, and her face split into a broad smile. "All ye need ken is that Darcy willna abide your harm. Come, now." With a spring in her step, she led Melanie into the bedroom where her baby dozed with his little fists up by his ears on the rumpled bed. "I've got a shift ye can use that I can trim the hem from, but we'll have to wait on the men for a proper dress. Now, how shall we do your hair? Up, I think. With a crown of heather. Aye. Darcy likes heather."

With Fran on a mission, Melanie had no choice but to follow her and weather the bustling wind of her energy. She dressed Melanie in a long cotton slip and began twisting and piling her hair into a graceful up-do. Laird Steafan might not be known for his hospitality, but Melanie could find nothing to complain about when it came to the generosity of his cottars. In fact, Fran seemed positively delighted to have Melanie disturbing what would likely otherwise be a peaceful night with her husband and baby.

"Thank you for your hospitality," she said to Fran, meeting her eyes in the small bronze mirror on the chest of drawers. "I really appreciate everything you're doing for me."

"Nonsense," Fran said, her smile dimpling her cheeks. "It's not hospitality. We're practically family."

Chapter 5

DARCY HAD BEEN punched in the gut plenty, but never had he been nearly doubled over by the sight of a woman. Malina came out of Edmund and Fran's bedroom dressed in his mother's finest gown, which he'd plucked from the wardrobe up at Fraineach after deciding with no small amount of self-flagellation that he'd go through with Aodhan's plan. The gown draped her from shoulder to floor in forest-green velvet. Gold ribbon wrapped her just below her bosom in a high waistline that hid the gentle swell of her belly. Ivory silk covered her arms and graced her neckline, which was low and so tight her creamy bosom pressed at the silk as if impatient to burst free.

She cleared her throat and he realized he'd been staring at that low neckline and the bounty it tried in vain to conceal. He snapped his eyes up to hers. They blazed with emerald humor.

"I see I'm about the same height as your mother," she said, poking the toe of her borrowed slipper from under the hem.

Fran bustled around her, frowning at the poor gown's straining neckline. "Aye, though ye're a bit more—" She pressed her lips and made a motion with her hands in the general vicinity of her own bosom. "As am I, dear, as am I. 'Tis tight, but 'twill have to do. By the look on poor Darcy's face, I dinna think he minds."

He scowled at his sister-in-law before giving Malina his full attention. "You are lovely," he told her, his eyes catching on the heather crown perched amidst her silvery hair. "So lovely."

Fran giggled.

Malina's cheeks flushed. She said, "You clean up well, yourself. This uncle of yours must be quite the particular man for everyone to have to dress to the nines just to go say 'hi' to him."

He understood only every fourth word that came out of her mouth, but he caught her meaning just the same, since she was eyeing his best shirt and the deep green, finely woven plaid his uncle had ordered from Edinburgh. Steafan had given it to him last year in a ceremony to honor him as heir. "Ye'll wear it the day ye wed and the day ye become laird if the Lord doesna see fit to give me more bairns," his uncle had said.

His gut curdled with guilt. Malina still didn't suspect she was about to be wed. He was surprised Fran hadn't told her. He looked at the woman questioningly, but she turned to a pile of dirty pots by the hearth, leaving him to his own mess.

"Best be off with you," Fran said, her back to them. "Steafan willna like to be kept waiting."

Unable to meet his unwittingly betrothed's eyes, he turned to the door. "Come along, Malina. 'Twill be over soon."

He heard her steps behind him and wished he had the courage to take her hand and have her walk at his side. They went up to the keep that way, her trailing behind him, and stopped before the broad oak door. A prickle on the back of his neck meant the hidden guards were watching their every move. But Steafan would be expecting them, so the guards wouldn't stop them from going in. Likely they wouldn't even bother to show themselves.

But they couldn't go in without first meeting Edmund. Darcy had sent him to fetch a gift for Malina, one that he hoped would make up for his deception.

"The castle looks bigger when you're standing right next to it," she said.

He glanced at her upturned face, innocent and inquisitive as she took in the stark gray wall of Ackergill Keep. The torchlight made her eyes shine like polished gems. Her cheeks glowed with vitality. Almost too bonny she was with her straight teeth gleaming like pearls between her parted lips and her long, black eyelashes, like a woman double blessed by Cliodna.

His heart squeezed with mingled pride and guilt.

"'Tis a fine manor," he said as he returned to scanning the dark lane for Edmund's form. "Not much to look at, but easy to defend. She's served the Keith well for nigh on three centuries."

"Wow, a genuine medieval castle. Why aren't we going in?"

"Christ, Darcy, she looks like a faery princess," Edmund said out of the darkness. He'd come around the side of the keep, giving him a start.

"Dinna be blaming me. 'Twas Fran's doing. Did you get it?"

"Aye." Edmund transferred a heavy velvet sack into Darcy's hand. When their da had been little more than a lad, he'd mined some gold with their grandsire. Most of his take had gone to building Fraineach and the mills, but he'd given some of the raw, precious mineral to each of his sons, making them promise to keep it in Ackergill's treasury in case of dire circumstances.

The sack that settled like a lump of lead in his sporran would be worth a small fortune to Malina, and because it wasn't currency, she wouldn't be hindered in exchanging it for whatever she needed, no matter where she went.

The prospect of parting with the gift from his da compressed his heart with sadness, but he kent his da would have approved the reason. If he couldn't be there to take care of his wife himself, he could at least ensure she and her bairn were provided for. If she was wise with the gold, and he suspected she would be, it could meet whatever needs she had for her whole life.

Surely she would forgive him once he gave it to her. That and her wee box, which sat in his desk up at Fraineach. Then he would take Aodhan's advice and safely escort her all the way to her home. He would do all he could for her, and they would part on good terms.

Once he returned to Ackergill, he could begin to forget her. He'd forget about her brave green eyes, her silvery blond hair that must feel like silk in a man's hands, her lush curves that had so unexpectedly and trustingly molded to his hard planes as he'd carried her, the delicate way her fingers cupped her precious womb, the bonny vision she made in his mother's dress.

Aye. He'd forget about Malina, all right. When the oceans swallowed Scotia and sent her, hills, vales, lochs, and all to the bottom of the sea.

"Best be off," Edmund said. He took her hand and placed it in Darcy's as the woman's da would have done were he here.

Regret sliced his heart. He didn't want to let this woman go. In his bones he felt she belonged to him, now and for all time.

But the feel of her hand, like a chip of smooth ivory that might shatter if a man gripped it too tightly, reminded him just how foolish he was for contemplating keeping her. He could never be a proper husband to any woman, especially one so small. Placing her hand carefully in the crook of his elbow, he met her trusting eyes.

"Best not keep Steafan waiting."

§

MELANIE LET DARCY lead her under the grim portcullis and through a heavily reinforced oak door into Ackergill Castle. Based on the squat building's utilitarian, no-frills exterior, she'd expected the inside to be just as cold and functional. What met her instead was a warm, bustling home, every bit as welcoming as Edmund and Fran's cottage. Hanging tapestries, plentiful rugs and rushes covering the wooden floors, and golden light flickering over every room and corridor made the keep seem much smaller and cozier than it looked from the outside. They also gave her history-loving eyes plenty to look at instead of the mouthwatering Highlander at her side.

He's not for you, Mel. He belongs here, and you belong five hundred years in the future. It's like window-shopping. Just because something looks sexy on the rack doesn't mean you've got to take it home with you.

But surely it wouldn't hurt to try him on…

She shook her head and tried to wiggle her hand out from the crook of his arm; with her fingers in such close proximity to his bulging bicep, she found it challenging to focus on her goal of getting home. But Darcy brought his other hand up to pin hers at the bend of his elbow. Her hand thus imprisoned, he led her past a large room of stone-flag floors and wooden beams where revelers lifted tankards and danced to fiddle-music. That must be the great hall. She craned her neck, trying to memorize every detail of the scene as he hurried her along.

She didn't blame him for being in a hurry. Judging by the look on his face when he'd told Aodhan he'd be responsible for her, he found her presence here about as inconvenient as she did.

Though she occasionally glimpsed in his eyes something much warmer than annoyance, she told herself he just appreciated her the way she appreciated him, as a member of the opposite sex who was easy on the eyes but off limits for innumerable reasons.

Which was why she was in a hurry, too. The sooner she got home, and away from Darcy, the sooner her hormones would cool and everything would go back to normal.

Although, her hormones hadn't exactly been cool back in Charleston. Those fickle, pregnancy-frenzied little chemicals had tempted her into making that stupid wish, and look where giving in to temptation had gotten her. She vowed not to make any more impulsive decisions. She'd keep calm, keep herself out of trouble in this foreign place and time, and find her way home.

If she felt a small pit of discomfort at the thought of leaving, she chose to ignore it. She refused to remember the brief moment of insanity when she'd watched Fran move with such purpose and ease around her cottage, and longed to remain in the sixteenth century for a while where she could roll around in history like a puppy in a pile of clean laundry. She refused to acknowledge her desire to get to know Fran better. Her desire to get to know Darcy better, much better.

This is not a vacation.

More like a nightmare. And she was ready to wake up. She clung to Darcy's words as they'd left Edmund and Fran's cottage: *" 'Twill be over soon."*

The shouts and fiddles from the great hall died away as he led her up a carpeted stairway to the third and top floor of the keep. At the end of a short hall, he stopped before a closed door and knocked. No one answered.

"Go on inside," said someone behind them.

She whirled around to see a man nearly as broad as he was tall, which meant he was about five feet tall and four feet wide at the shoulder, ambling toward them. He had a long black beard and a balding pate too freckled to reflect the torchlight. His eyes crinkled in friendly acknowledgement, but she'd seen enough mob movies to recognize an enforcer when she saw one. The man had a hard mouth and enormous fists that looked as though their sole purpose was to inflict pain.

"Hamish," Darcy greeted. "Is Steafan in the great hall?"

"Aye. But he's expecting you. Word gets 'round." Beetle-black eyes appraised her before his lower lip pushed out in approval. "Help yourself to the good whisky."

Darcy pushed open the door. "Best not offend Hamish," he said quietly after closing it on the short man. He began pacing back and forth over the woven rug before the laird's desk, a walnut masterpiece she immediately went to and began caressing. Carved leaves and vines along the legs and sides teased her fingers with polished elegance.

"Or Steafan for that matter," Darcy went on, oblivious to her fascination with the furniture. "In fact, 'tis probably best if ye leave the talking to me. I dinna wish for your speech to draw my uncle's suspicion."

She nodded distractedly, letting the silky black feathers of a quill in a silver stand tickle the backs of her knuckles. She reached for a silver inkwell with a crystal stopper. When Darcy went still and silent, she glanced up to find him giving her a deadly serious look.

She stopped fondling the laird's possessions. "All right," she agreed. "I won't talk. So, what's the plan here? You say, 'Hi, uncle. This is Melanie. She's not an English spy, and she's just passing through. Just thought I'd introduce her to you, so you know what's going on in your little kingdom.' He'll say, 'Welcome, Melanie-who's-not-an-English-spy. Have a lovely stay.' And then we'll be on our way, right? You'll put me up somewhere until I can figure out how to get home?" Even to her ears it sounded overly optimistic.

He shook his head as if processing her best-case scenario gave him a headache. Finally, his face opened with understanding. His mouth twitched with humor before a shadow darkened his eyes. "'Twould certainly be nice if it could be so simple. But whatever happens tonight, ye need no' fash that I'll keep my word to you."

"I know. I can tell you're a man of your word. Thank you. I think I'll need your help. Without that box, I'm—" Would he know what *screwed* meant? "Knee deep in manure with ankle-high boots," she settled on, channeling her grandmother.

A chuckle rolled from his chest, melting some of the tension from his shoulders. He sobered. "Dinna fash yourself. All will be well."

The door opened. She recognized Laird Steafan from his impeccable dress and regal carriage. He wore a forest-green great kilt shot through with gold and gray in the true clan-tartan style, which would have been rare and highly fashionable at this time in history. It looked just like the one Darcy had put on after dinner, only rather than pleating and wrapping the upper portion around one shoulder, Steafan wore his in a cloak-style so the fabric surrounded him in complicated sheets and folds. A yellowish-orange shirt of heavy, pleated linen peeked around the kilt at the man's neck and wrists. Steafan had brown eyes the same rich shade as Darcy's, but with none of the warmth or vulnerability. His hair was red. Not orange or auburn or reddish.

Red. A shade so deep you could drown in it. His beard and moustache were just as red, as if he'd been snorkeling in a bowl of cranberry juice.

Hamish entered behind Steafan and closed the door, where he assumed a standard bodyguard stance. Steafan strode to the fireplace and faced the room with his doeskin shoes spread confidently and his hands on his hips as if posing for a portrait.

She concentrated on not rolling her eyes.

"Aodhan tells me ye found yourself a wee lass beneath a Gunn," he said in a self-important brogue, bypassing any kind of greeting.

She frowned, not caring for his interpretation of where she had been found. She had, in fact, gotten out from under the Gunn well before Darcy rounded that boulder.

"Uncle." Darcy inclined his head respectfully. "I present to you Melanie. She isna from Scotia, but Aodhan and the others agree she isna English. She seeks our hospitality."

Steafan's shrewd gaze snapped to hers, and she averted her eyes to the plush rug, as she imagined a harmless, obedient woman of this time might do. After everything she'd heard, she didn't want to give him any reason to mistrust her, and acting like an empowered, independent, twenty-first century woman would most definitely rouse his suspicions.

"Aodhan also tells me ye've claimed responsibility for her."

"I have," Darcy said.

"Why?" Steafan asked.

"Because I thought Aodhan was about to, and I didna want him to have her," he answered without skipping a beat.

She dropped the act and turned a sharp look on Darcy. *Have her?* Had she been in danger of being had by Aodhan? If Aodhan didn't "have her" did that mean Darcy did "have her?" She opened her mouth to ask what the heck she had missed, but Darcy silenced her with a warning look as if he'd anticipated her confusion.

Steafan burst out in good-natured laughter. His hands came off his hips and he transformed from a terrifying laird to just a man. "Your honesty is always refreshing, lad." As his laughter died off, he went to a table by the hearth and poured two glasses of amber liquid.

Offering one to Darcy, he raked his gaze over her in a blatant appraisal that made her feel more vulnerable than any twenty-first century man ever had. She resisted the urge to place her hands protectively over her belly. Drawing attention to what the dress's empire waist hid probably wouldn't be smart.

"A bonny wee thing you are," Steafan said more to himself than to her. He threw back his drink and set the glass on the mantle, then moved so close the smoky notes of scotch on his breath seared her nostrils.

Beside her, Darcy sipped from his glass. Though he appeared at ease, his arm brushed her shoulder in a tight, jerky movement betraying his tension. Steafan might be relaxed for the moment, but Darcy's body language communicated how very transient Steafan's good moods were apt to be.

Though uneasiness churned in her, she held her tongue as Darcy had instructed, reminding herself that she was in a potentially dangerous situation. *Do not offend the temperamental laird,* she repeated to herself.

Steafan turned his attention to Darcy. "You have come in your finest plaid, and that is one of Janine's gowns." He nodded in her direction. "One of her finer ones. Your da would be proud to see your betrothed looking so bonny in your mother's dress."

Betrothed?

Before she could react to what Steafan had just said, he clapped his hands and turned to Hamish. "Fetch Aodhan. He's in the great hall. You and he shall serve as witnesses."

Hamish left obediently.

Ignoring Darcy's warning grip on her elbow, she faced Steafan and said, "Excuse me, did you say betrothed?" She wheeled on Darcy. "Did he say betrothed? Why would he say that? What does he need witnesses for?"

Darcy's shoulders rounded.

Steafan chuckled. It was a self-satisfied sound. A mean sound.

"Aye," Darcy admitted, meeting her eyes with seeming difficulty. "He said betrothed. We are to be wed this night, Malina."

"What?"

Steafan's chuckling increased in volume and irritation quotient. She glared at him, and he showed his teeth in response. "Be careful, lass. I am not one to cross. You arena in a position to demand explanations. If ye want them, ye'll have to ask nicely."

Her jaw fell open. "Who do you think you are?" she asked as Darcy pulled her behind him.

"Dinna listen to her, uncle. She is from afar and she doesna ken our ways."

She strained to look around Darcy and saw Steafan's eyes darken with fury. "She asks who I think I am, lad. Mayhap a night in the stocks will enlighten her. Your wedding can wait until she understands who her host and future laird is, and has learned not to cross him."

Uh-oh. So much for remaining inconspicuous and keeping herself out of trouble. But how was she supposed to remain contrite and silent when she'd just learned her only ally had manipulated her into this...this...she didn't even know what to call this. The Scottish version of a shotgun wedding?

"No," Darcy said, his voice near a growl. "Not the stocks. She willna speak out of line again." As he said it, he cut her a warning glare over his shoulder.

She gave Darcy The Look, the one that let a person know he was one step away from meeting with serious harm. She'd been wrong; this wasn't a nightmare. This was hell. Fear and betrayal iced down her spine. Darcy's hands, which had infused her with comfort earlier, now made her feel trapped. She wrenched her arm out of his grasp and backed away, scooting behind Steafan's desk to put the enormous thing between her and the two treacherous Highlanders.

Make that four treacherous Highlanders. Hamish and Aodhan strode in, Aodhan's eyebrows climbing his forehead.

"I see ye've told her what it means for a Keith to claim a woman," he said to Darcy. Looking at her across the desk, he said, "Dinna be hard on the lad. If he hadna done it, I would have, and me with three daughters for you to become second mother to. I would ha' been good to ye, lass, but Darcy, he will worship you." He winked at Darcy, then spread some papers on the desk and reached for the black-feathered quill. "I have the contract ready, Steafan. Begin when ye wish."

Steafan smirked at her. "What'll it be, lass, the stocks tonight, or a wedding?"

"The stocks," she said without hesitation, relieved she seemed to have some choice in the matter. What was a night of discomfort compared to the stripping away of one's choice?

Darcy surged around the desk and shook her by the shoulders.

His eyes blazed with desperation. "Dinna do this," he said close by her ear, his voice urgent and low, private from all but perhaps Aodhan, who stood near the desk. "A person in the stocks must be stripped to their skin and placed in the courtyard for the entire clan to laugh at and spit on. I'd sooner defy my uncle and be banished from Ackergill than see you dishonored so. Dinna make me do that, I beg you."

Fear kicked her heart into her throat at Darcy's manhandling. But as his words penetrated, she stopped fighting his hold. He was serious. He'd abandon his home, his mill, Edmund and Fran, everything he had, all to keep her from a night's humiliation.

He might be a manipulative, lying brute, but he seemed to care for her on some level. She looked hard in his eyes and saw vulnerability glowing behind a glaze of very real fear. Fear for her and for what her actions might cause him to suffer.

She shoved away the sympathy he didn't deserve. He projected an air of absolute honor, but honorable men didn't trick women into marrying them. "You lied to me," she seethed. "You told me you'd help me get home."

"And I will," he said. "Do ye nay remember what I told you before Steafan came in?"

She remembered the words verbatim. *"Whatever happens tonight, Malina, ye need no' fash that I'll keep my word to you."*

Malina. The mere memory of her name spoken that way softened her, damn her romantic heart.

"Trust me," he urged.

She glanced around the office to see Aodhan nodding his encouragement. Steafan watched them with an amused tilt to his mouth and a triumphant lift of one eyebrow. Hamish stood at the ready, his hands curled into cruel claws that she had no doubt would make quick work of stripping her naked and binding her in stocks. Stocks, for heaven's sake! She was being threatened with a humiliating and painful medieval punishment. Did she really want to be subjected to that when the alternative was marrying a gorgeous Highlander who would keep her safe until she could figure out how to get home?

Of course, that was completely contingent on Darcy keeping his word to her, something she no longer had any faith in. A man who could manipulate a woman into this position was not a man she'd trust to keep his word, no matter how sincere his face. He probably used those vulnerable-seeming eyes to get women to swoon over him left and right. He was probably a master manipulator who was laughing at her behind his concerned exterior. And she'd fallen for his tricks.

"Trust me," he said again.

She no longer believed anything Darcy pretended. He wasn't her ally, after all. Part of her crumbled at the loss. But in a room full of dangerous men, she suspected he was the least dangerous, at least to her. Determined that if he broke his word, she'd find a way to make him suffer, she said for the whole room to hear, "Fine. I'll marry you tonight. Congratulations on being slightly more attractive to a woman than the stocks."

Darcy flinched. His lips pressed together as he released her shoulders. Before he turned his back on her, she felt a fleeting regret that she'd caused his eyes to swim with hurt. Boy, was he good, getting her to feel for him. She tamped down the useless sympathy and faced a beaming Aodhan and a disappointed-looking Hamish.

"A feisty wife ye've found yourself, lad," Steafan said. "A fine Keith she'll make. Come, lass." He held out his hand to her as he positioned a wilted Darcy in front of him. "Stand with your groom."

Fury robbed her of grace as she stepped up beside the traitor. Steafan spread his arms like a clergyman addressing his congregation.

"Tonight we secure the handfasting of my nephew and heir,

Darcy Marek MacFirthen Keith, and his bride, Melanie."

He grabbed her right hand, and before she realized what he was doing, used a silver-handled *sgian dubh* to cut a stinging line into the heel of her palm at the base of her thumb. He did the same to Darcy and pressed their palms together. She tried to yank her hand away, but Darcy linked his fingers with hers. Despite everything, the strength of his fingers closing around hers caused a little flutter of excitement in her belly. She hated him for being so irresistible. She hated her body for desiring him even as she reeled with the force of his betrayal.

"Say the vows," Steafan commanded Darcy.

Darcy hesitated.

She refused to look any higher than his shirt laces.

"Say them or I'll finish the ceremony without them."

He huffed a sigh that made her chance a look at his face. His eyes were apologetic and still wounded as he gazed down at her. "I take responsibility for this woman before my laird and clan," he said softly. "With my body I will guard her body. With my life I will guard her life. What I have is hers and all that I am."

The sincerity of the words stunned her. She forgot to be angry for a few heartbeats.

Steafan said, "You are now handfasted by word and blood. Only death shall break this bond. The blessing of the laird be upon you." He released their hands.

She gaped at the finality of his proclamation. "That's it?" she asked. "You're not going to coerce me into saying anything?"

Steafan smiled wickedly. "'Tis done. Ye're a Keith now."

She was married. Good heavens.

Indignation and giddy joy collided in a turbulence that pushed her already fragile emotions to a cliff's edge. If she opened her mouth, she'd either scream or sob, so she pressed her lips closed and glared at the man whose fault this was.

Darcy shrugged one shoulder and said, "I may be only slightly better than a night in the stocks, but at least the whole clan willna see you undressed and bent over for their amusement."

"Aye," Hamish said behind her. "Only Darcy will have the privilege of seeing her that way."

She gasped and spun around to face Steafan's henchman.

Darcy moved in front of her, his hands curled into fists. The back of his neck flushed red.

She tried to peek around him to see Hamish's reaction, but Darcy kept her behind him with one strong hand on her hip.

Steafan's sharp voice peeled through the office like cracking thunder. "Enough, Hamish. I dinna want fists in my office. And show some respect. My nephew is wed. I have lusted so for many years and can now rest assured that should Ginneleah give me no sons, Ackergill shall be led by a true man."

Darcy's grip relaxed just enough that she could peer around him. Hamish didn't look contrite in the least, but his fists had uncurled. That was something.

Under Darcy's watchful eye, Aodhan came forward with a handkerchief and dabbed her palm where her blood and Darcy's mixed in a grisly smear. He kissed her cheek as he held her hand. "You are welcome among the Keith, lass. Dinna let Hamish offend you. He is merely jealous." He cleaned Darcy's hand as well then clapped his arm. "Good lad. I kent ye'd wed one day, despite all your havering, and a fine wife ye've taken. Your da would be fair proud."

Darcy stared at the Keith war chieftain as though he'd sprouted medusa snakes. "Thank you, Aodhan."

"That he would," Steafan agreed. "Now kiss your bride, man."

"If I kiss her now, she's likely to bite my lip off."

Aodhan and Hammish chuckled. Steafan said, "If she tries, then ye'll give her a taste of a husband's discipline." The laird pinned her with a look of challenge.

She glared right back.

"Kiss her," he commanded.

"I'm sorry, Malina," Darcy whispered, as he dipped his face to hers. To his credit, he did, in fact, look sorry.

But neither his apologetic look nor his special version of her name softened her this time.

She tucked her chin and growled, "Don't you dare."

He paused with his lips an inch from hers. He sighed, his breath sweet and smoky from scotch. Then he closed the distance and pressed a quick kiss to her mouth.

When he lifted his face, she wound up and let her hand fly for a good slap. He caught her wrist. Damn his quick reflexes.

Steafan chortled while Darcy's fingers encircled her like a living handcuff. "You willna raise a hand to me ever again, Malina mine," he said in a quiet voice laced with steel.

That voice alone might have cowed her if she weren't spitting mad. But something was off about his expression. He didn't look angry that she had tried to slap him. He looked apologetic, sympathetic. She didn't trust the expression for one instant. But when he increased the pressure of his grip and his eyes intensified with an imploring look, she wondered if he was trying to pass along some hidden message to her. She stopped trying to pull out of his grasp and tried to read him, tried to see past what he wanted her to see, to the heart of the man.

Beneath everything else, the liquid depths of his eyes shone with earnest vulnerability.

Surely no man, no matter how good at manipulating, could pretend so many different things with a single look. What if he was sincere? What if he was as much a victim of Steafan's bullying as she? What if he was doing the best he could to salvage a hopeless situation? He certainly hadn't seemed happy about saying those vows. Oh, God, what if he was as upset about their marriage as she was?

Why did the idea cause a splinter of hurt to snag her heart?

Darcy's eyes were trying to communicate with her. In the frozen moment, she realized what the message was. *"I'm pretending to be what my uncle expects me to be. Please understand."*

"No self-respecting Keith will suffer his wife to abuse his person," his mouth said. "Do you understand?" He tilted his head, pleading with her to go with the act.

"I apologize," she gritted out, giving him The Look again. "I won't try to hit you again, husband of mine. As long as you don't try to kiss me again."

Steafan coughed with surprise. "She'll be a wife worthy of you, Darcy lad," he said. "A wife worthy of dwelling in Ackergill Keep one day."

Darcy released her wrist and in the next second, she was surrounded by Steafan's suffocating arms. The man planted a wet kiss on her cheek. If she hadn't been frozen with shock, she might have tried to shove him away. It was probably good that she didn't, since Darcy's stunned gaze proved Steafan in an affectionate mood was an exceedingly rare thing.

"Welcome to the Keith, lass," Steafan said. "I'm glad I didna have to put you in stocks tonight."

Chapter 6

DARCY'S UNWILLING WIFE stormed out of Ackergill Keep with him trotting like a scolded puppy at her heels.

"It doesna mean anything, Malina," he said, following her into the thick darkness that cloaked the road between the torch-lit lawn of the keep and the meager glow of the village below as the cottars prepared for bed. "'Tis just a piece of paper. This way Steafan will stop harassing me to wed."

She made a noise like a stifled scream, and her stride quickened.

"I will still help ye, lass," he said and winced at the desperate note in his voice. Firmer, he said, "Did ye hear me, Malina? I said I will keep my word to you." Determined to face her wrath like the warrior he was, he caught her arm.

She spun around, and to his dismay, tears stained her cheeks. She swatted at them and wouldn't look him in the eye.

His stomach contracted with regret. Och, he'd never meant to make her weep. He shouldna have pretended ire with her, even if it meant angering Steafan. "Malina—"

Her shiny eyes flashed. "Don't you call me that ever again! You bastard!"

He nearly recoiled from the whip of her anger, but he'd faced enough Gunn and MacKay to stand his ground against a wee, fiery woman. "Haud your wheesht, wife," he growled as he pulled her to him. She'd draw the attention of the whole village, and the last thing he wanted were more witnesses to the debacle he'd landed himself in. Come to think of it, he was not some repentant mutt who ought to be whimpering for his sins. He didn't regret keeping her and her unborn bairn safe from Steafan's stocks tonight. He didn't regret taking full and permanent responsibility for a woman with child lost in a strange land. He didn't exactly expect her thanks, but he didn't appreciate his bride calling him a bastard on their wedding night, either. "I willna have ye maligning me for the whole of Ackergill to hear."

"Oh, you *willna*, will you? And just how do you plan to stop me? Will you dole out your husbandly discipline and make your uncle proud?"

"Och, woman. I am not your enemy." He darted a glance around the road to make sure no one was gawking at them.

"You're not my friend, either, Darcy Keith," she said in a respectable volume, though the sparks in her eyes suggested she'd prefer yelling at him some more. "You betrayed me. You told me I had to meet the laird in order to spend the night here. You made it sound like a formality. You didn't say anything about ending up married. Married! Damn it, Darcy." She shook her head, seeming at a loss for words, and turned her back on him.

Her legs—he remembered how shapely they were from seeing her in her half-dress—carried her down the hill at a remarkably swift walk considering how short they were. His legs were longer, and he used them to his advantage, outpacing her and planting himself in her path.

"You're going the wrong way, Melanie." He deliberately used her name the way she had told it to him rather than the gentler version of it that caressed his tongue like poetry. "Our home is that way." He pointed off the road where a wagon-rutted trail cut across the slope until it bent up to the cliffs, where Fraineach stood proud and strong overlooking the sea.

"I'm going to Fran and Edmund's," she said, weaving around him without slowing.

He was tempted to let her go. Mayhap a night away from him would do her good. Mayhap by morning, she'd be willing to speak to him with a civil tongue. But he couldn't leave her so angry. 'Twas bad for one's slumber to lie down with an angry heart, and he suspected with the day she'd had that the poor lass needed her rest.

"Melanie, wait."

"I don't want your help. I don't want you." Her rejection slit open his heart.

Having nothing else to lose, he blurted, "I have your box."

She stopped in her tracks but kept her back to him.

"It was right where ye said it would be. In the mud by Berringer's marker."

She turned slowly to face him. Even in the moonless darkness he could tell her face was ashen. "Are you lying to me right now, or were you lying when you told me you didn't find it? Is anything that comes out of your mouth the truth?"

Anger heated his neck at how blatantly she questioned his honor, but shame kept him from unleashing it on her. "I admit I lied to you," he said. "'Twas only to keep you from revealing aught to Steafan that might have seen ye lashed to a stake and burned before the dawn."

She cocked her head. "What makes you think I might have said something to earn myself a burning at the stake?"

"I saw the date on the box," he said quietly.

She blinked. Her eyes went unfocused. "The date," she said, lost in her own thoughts. Suddenly, she turned her wide eyes on him, and he recognized fear in their emerald depths. "A forgery," she said. "That's all." She waved her hand, dismissing the issue of the date, but the choppiness of her breath when she inhaled betrayed the fact she was terribly afraid, and something else. Desperate? "Where is it? Do you really have it?"

He nodded. Uncertain what possessed him to give voice to the irrational suspicion, he blurted, "Ye didna simply wander here from your homeland, did you?"

She opened her mouth, but no sound came out. Her lack of denial was as good as a confession. She had come here by magic.

But she didn't seem like a witch. Granted, he'd never met one, but he imagined the wicked beasties weren't afraid of their own magic. Malina was cross with him, but she wasn't evil. No, he sensed a sweetness in her that he longed to explore. But there would be no exploration of this intriguing creature.

"We shouldna speak of such things where unseen ears may hear. Come. You shall rest tonight at Fraineach and in the morn I'll keep my word to you."

§

THE BRINY SCENT of the ocean grew thicker in Melanie's nostrils as Darcy led her up the path to his home. Faintly, as if from far below, the crash of surf against rock slithered up and over the cliff-edge on which the stone manor house he called Fraineach perched like a shale-cloaked sentinel. Despite her frayed emotions, her sense of sight longed to join her other senses in celebrating what must be a breathtaking ocean-side view in the daylight.

She tamped down her wonder, refusing to enjoy any more of this place. However lovely her surroundings, they were her prison, and however fascinating the man she'd thought to be her friend, he was her jailer. Until she got her hands on that box. Then she alone would be master of her fate.

She was such an idiot for trusting anyone else. She should have found a way to go back to that field and look for the box herself. From here on out, she'd do things her way. No more waiting around for a man to keep promises.

Hands clenched with purpose, she followed him onto the

quaint stone porch and through the front door. "Where's the box?" she asked, not willing to waste another moment of her life in the past.

He lit a lantern, and as it flared to life his handsome face looked drawn and stark. "Dinna ye wish to rest? Ye were nearly falling over with weariness when we came into Ackergill. That was hours ago."

"I'll rest when I get home."

He nodded. "'Tis as I suspected, then. 'Tis magic that brought ye here." It wasn't a question, so she didn't answer. He ran a hand over the back of his neck in the same gesture of discomfort she had seen Edmund use. "I thought at first mayhap ye would sell your wee box for passage on a ship. But 'tis no' over water ye need to go, is it?"

"No," she said simply.

He closed his eyes and released a breath. After lighting a candle, he took it with him as he left the comfortable parlor the front door had spilled them into. His footsteps sounded in an adjacent room.

Seeing him so dejected made guilt settle in her chest. She ignored it. Darcy had no right to her sympathy. He'd come right out and told her their marriage meant nothing to him. It was nothing but a convenient way to escape Steafan's demands. How insulting. And hurtful.

He came back to the parlor, and when he moved into the lantern light, he looked even more resigned than when he'd said those vows at Steafan's behest. She wanted to tell him to stop his acting, but he held out the box, and all thoughts of Darcy evaporated as her gaze zeroed in on her ticket home. She grabbed it, and the sleek wood with its cool knotwork felt like long lost treasure in her hands.

"I wish to go home," she told it, turning the piece upside-down as she had at her workbench. Righting it again, she waited for the tiny clinks and groans that would precede the opening of the lid.

Nothing happened.

She tried it again, mimicking the way she'd handled the box several hours ago in Charleston. Nothing.

She gently shook it, repeating her wish and adding a shaky "please" at the end. She tilted it from side to side. With every attempt her movements grew jerkier, more desperate.

"It's not working," she said with an edge of panic. She kept trying to no avail while Darcy stood by and watched. "It's not working! Why isn't it working? I'm doing everything the same." Her eyes swam with the heat of tears she refused to let fall.

"Mayhap ye need to be by the marker."

She looked sharply at him. "Right. The stone. Maybe it's some kind of portal. Maybe it's in cahoots with the box."

"Come along, then," he sighed. "Best get it over and done with."

§

DOWN AT ACKERGILL'S stables, Darcy saddled Rand, the horse his da had bought for him on a trip to Inverness the year before his death. The dun gelding was a full seventeen hands at the withers and strong as a draft horse. He could carry Darcy farther and faster than any other horse he'd tried, and didn't shy from a skirmish when horses were called for. Usually a pleasure, saddling Rand tonight was a terrible duty.

He'd thought he would have weeks to ride alongside Malina as he returned her to her home. If 'twas a sea voyage required to bring her home, he might have had months with her, and a unique adventure as well. But 'twould nay be weeks or months he'd have the pleasure of keeping his vow to protect her.

'Twould be an hour at most.

He couldn't abide the thought of saying goodbye to her so soon. Even though she clearly didn't want him, his heart lusted for her as his lungs lusted for air. When her box took her away, 'twould be a blow worse than any he'd yet received in battle.

While he worked on Rand, his wife turned her box every which way. Her eyes blazed with concentration as she whispered her wishes to it. She looked so lovely in the orange glow of the shuttered lantern. Lovely and determined to leave, the idea of being married to him so distasteful she couldn't stand even a single night under his roof.

He didn't blame her after his outright lie and withheld truths. But he didn't want to send her away with poor memories of him. Mayhap if he did all he could to help her return home, she'd forgive him one day.

Malina sighed, a sound so discouraged it made him forget his own problems. The poor thing missed her family, her teaching. Mayhap she had pupils she was fond of. Mayhap the sire of her unborn bairn would be waiting for her. The thought scorched his heart and made his movements so tense Rand bobbed his head uneasily.

"Is he a good man?" he found himself asking past a throat tight with jealousy.

She looked up, startled. "Who?"

He shook his head at himself. 'Twas none of his concern, not when he was willing to toss aside the vows he'd made like scraps from the dinner table. But he still wished to ken what manner of man would get a woman with child and not marry and care for her.

"The one you're so eager to return to."

Her hand shifted from her box to her belly. "You mean, the man who got me pregnant?" A flicker of something that wasn't quite shame flitted through her eyes. "He has some good qualities," she said with furrowed brow.

Anger climbed his neck. She was eager to return, but the man waiting for her didn't inspire her confidence.

Rand protested his ruthless tightening of the girth with a grunt and a stomp of his hoof.

"Will he at least provide for you?" he asked, doing his best to keep his temper.

"No," she said. "He married another woman. But I don't need a man to provide for me." Her chin lifted with pride. "I have a good job and a comfortable apartment. I can take care of myself."

The wedding vows he'd spoken embedded in his gut like thorns. As he finished with Rand's bridle, his cut hand stung bitterly. The place where his blood and hers had mixed scorned him for being willing to let her go.

But he wasn't willing. 'Twas she who wanted to leave.

A sudden insight teased him. What if she didn't want to leave? What if she was just angry with him and acting impulsively?

He left Rand to kneel at her feet. She eyed him suspiciously. He hated that he'd given her cause to look at him that way.

"I will ask ye this but once. Do ye wish to forsake our bond and my offered protection? Do ye truly wish to return to your life of providing for yourself and working and raising your bairn alone? I would have ye stay here with me, and I would care for you your whole life. I would treat your bairn as my own. I have means, and I am a good man, though I ken I havena given ye cause to believe it.

"Stay with me, Malina. Let me prove to you the man I am. I wouldna expect your love, and I dinna expect you to share my bed. But I wish ye to stay and be my wife. I wish to be your husband. Will you release me from the vow I made to help ye return home?"

He made himself stop blathering and waited for her answer, drowning in the emerald pools of her eyes. Closing his hands around hers, around the box, he found some solace in the fact that she didn't pull away.

She appraised him with liquid eyes. Could that be tenderness he glimpsed? But it was gone too soon, replaced with suspicion. Och, he'd been so dishonest with her she likely would never be able to trust him. Mayhap it was for the best she was leaving. If she couldn't trust him, he'd nay be able to make her happy.

At last, she shook her head. "I suspect you're a good man, even though you lied to me. I see goodness in you, and honor. Any woman would be lucky to have you as her husband." His heart lifted with hope. "Any woman from your time," she added gently. "I don't belong here. I need to go back to my time. My being here is a mistake. This is all a huge mistake."

His heart crumbled as he released her hands and pulled the heavy velvet pouch from his sporran. "Then, take this. 'Tis my wedding gift to you. If I canna be with you to keep my marriage vows, I pray this will clear my name before the Lord."

She took the pouch and looked inside. Her eyes grew wide. "It's gold. I can't take this." She tried to push it back into his hands, but he refused it.

"You must. 'Tis the best I can do for you, Malina mine. I hope ye will remember me well when you use it. I hope this will provide for you and your bairn for many years." Not giving her a chance to reject his gift as she'd rejected him, he rose and blew out the lantern. He led Rand from the stables, and said, "Come, Malina. 'Tis time to send you home."

§

THE STABLE BECAME dark and quiet once more as Big Darcy and the ample-chested trollop he'd called his wife left with his beast of a horse. Anya crept from the shadows of the tack room to peek out the barn door. Silhouetted by the blue night, he held out his hand, and the woman reluctantly passed him what looked to be a box. After tucking it in the saddlebag, he helped the woman mount, then mounted behind her. They rode silently into the night.

She clapped her hands in delight. She'd just witnessed the heir of Ackergill agree to willingly dishonor his marriage vows by helping his wife run away. But even better, she'd just witnessed the man she'd ruined with rumors when he was little more than a lad get a taste of the rejection he'd dealt her time and again when she'd been blossoming into her womanhood.

Of all the young men in the clan, she'd chosen the tall and comely Darcy to give her maidenhead to. At first, he'd laughed at her, not in cruelty—for he had never had the stomach for cruelty—but as though he thought her advances in jest. But they had not been in jest. In fact, they had been so earnest and had so exposed her tender, young heart that his rejection had planted seeds of bitterness within her that had grown into thorns. By the time she'd learned the finer points of seduction and had finally lured him into kissing and fondling her in the stables, she had no maidenhead to give, and she realized she resented him for it. Vengeance had seemed a better reward than the long-awaited coupling.

When he'd shed his plaid, she'd seen her opportunity. The lad had been large. Not monstrously so, as she'd led him to believe, but larger than the others she'd seen, for cert. 'Twas almost a pity she hadn't permitted herself the pleasure of sitting astride such a magnificent manhood.

But kenning she'd so affected him that he'd never approached another lass in the years since made it worth the sacrifice.

Now Big Darcy was married, it seemed, and his wife didn't want him. Not only that, but she was asking him to help her run away. 'Twas a delicious discovery she couldn't wait to share up at the keep. Steafan would be furious. He may even disown his nephew. Too bad Big Darcy had a brother, or 'twould surely be Aodhan Steafan would set in line for the lairdship.

"There you are, lass," came a familiar voice out of the darkness. Aodhan. Her current lover and an important man among the Keith.

"You're late," she said, putting an extra sway in her hips as she approached him.

He swept her up in his strong arms and carried her to the dark tack room. "Business up at the keep," he murmured as he closed his mouth over hers. No apology for keeping her waiting.

But then she didn't expect one. Not from the war chieftain.

"Wouldna happen to have been a wedding, now, would it?" she asked as he set her on the workbench and helped himself to the pockets in her dress, searching for her vial of rose oil.

Aodhan tensed. His hand stopped in its search. "How did ye ken?"

"I saw Big Darcy with a strangewoman. I heard him call her his wife. Steafan must be pleased to have his heir finally wed." She toyed with the wiry hairs framed by the V of his shirt, pleased to ken Aodhan must have been so eager for her he'd undone the laces on his way to the stables.

"Aye," he admitted, but he said no more.

She didn't care for the caution in his eyes. He liked to tup her, but he wouldn't confide in her, the stubborn man.

"Who is she?" she asked, palming what he'd been searching for and pulling it from her pocket. 'Twas a vial of rose oil of her own making. She uncorked it and waved it under his nose, pleased with the way his eyes closed in bliss at the perfume's fragrance. Like a bull scenting the heat of a cow was Aodhan, mindless once his nose caught the promise of joining.

He took the vial from her and tipped it to coat two fingers before shoving up her skirts to rub it between her legs. In the next heartbeat he was there, loving her.

“You saw yourself,” he ground out. “A strangewoman. Dinna fash yourself over Darcy. I’m the only man ye need think about at the moment.”

“Yes,” she sighed, giving herself over to his forceful coupling. As always, his initial thrusts were uncomfortable, but the oil helped. Besides the customers who purchased her perfumes at market, a secret patronage sought after her scented oils designed to make coupling feel grand. But her personal supply did much more than that. Thanks to a dose of quinine mixed in, it kept her from catching a bairn. Of course, quinine was costly, so she only added it to her own supply and to the supply she sent to one unsuspecting couple.

But she couldn’t think of Steafan and Ginneleah now, not when Aodhan was hitting that secret place inside her over and over again. Not many men could find it, and Aodhan was the only lover she’d ever had who refused to release himself until he’d coaxed that spot into flooding her with ultimate pleasure.

Proving tonight was no exception, he reduced her to a crazed, mewling animal in mere minutes. When pleasure drowned her in a wild torrent, she bit back her screams, not wanting to wake the stable master. As she floated back to Earth, Aodhan’s growl of satisfaction rumbled through the dark tack room.

After they had both regained their breath, he lowered her to a bed of saddle blankets on the floor. “We wouldna have to keep quiet had we a marriage contract,” she said half in jest. Of all the lovers she’d taken, Aodhan was the first to make her consider marrying him instead of pursuing the goal that had driven her for the past four years. But Aodhan had never offered, and she would never beg.

Only for one man would she consent to beg. Only for her laird.

“Ah, Anya lass, keeping quiet is part o’ the fun.” He nipped her jaw, predictably avoiding her none-too-subtle hint. But she didn't mind much, not when he began lazily unlacing her dress and pressing hot, wet kisses to her breasts. Not when she kent he wasn't nearly finished bringing her pleasure tonight.

Besides, 'twas a laird's right to put away his wife if she failed to give him bairns. She may yet manage to wed Steafan. As long as that hope remained, she'd not seriously consider marrying another.

Chapter 7

MELANIE HADN'T RIDDEN a horse in years, not since childhood riding lessons back in Georgia. But lessons in an indoor riding arena on a gentle quarter horse had failed to prepare her for the terror of cantering through a night-darkened forest in a saddle as high as the roof of an SUV. She clung to Darcy's arm around her waist with one hand and to the horse's mane with the other, and tried not to contemplate how disastrous a fall from this height would be to her and her baby.

"Dinna fash, Malina," he said in her ear as the wind licked locks of hair out of her up-do. "Rand willna let you fall. Nor will I."

Her racing heart had the gall to calm at his assurance, and her body had the gall to settle into the cradle of his chest, arms and thighs. She wasn't enjoying the security of his embrace, she told herself. She was merely trusting her safety to an experienced horseman. Those weren't giddy butterflies dancing in her tummy each time his fists brushed her lap. It was just a side effect of trying not to hyperventilate.

The ride to Berringer's field took a fraction of the time their march to Ackergill earlier that evening had taken. Upon drawing his horse to a stop, Darcy dismounted and reached up for her.

"We're here already?" Her fingers curled into Rand's mane.

"Aye," he said. "Come along. The marker's just here."

She looked past him into the darkness to see muted moonlight making a blue edge on the leaning stone. A lump formed in her throat, which was silly since she was eager to return home.

She forced her fingers to release their grip on Rand's mane and trusted herself to Darcy's hands. He lowered her to the ground.

She didn't step away. She stood chest to stomach with him for a good minute, remembering their talk in the barn.

There was no way he could have faked the sincerity in his eyes when he'd asked her to stay and be his wife. Or the pain in them when she'd refused. If those vulnerable eyes of his hadn't convinced her of his honor, the precious gift sunk deep in a pocket of her gown was incontrovertible evidence. He had given her about five pounds of raw gold. In her time, it would be worth a small fortune, but in Darcy's time, it would be worth an immense fortune. In his mind, he was providing for her for her whole life, and providing for her well. The weight pressed her leg and her conscience. She didn't want to take this treasure from him. It might represent all his savings. But if she didn't take it, she'd be refusing him the means to fulfill his vows the only way he could. And she had no doubt that's what the gift was about. He might have married her for convenience, but he took the vows seriously.

She would never again question his honor.

She wouldn't have a chance to. She was leaving him. The permanence of the thought sat heavy in her stomach like the gold in her pocket.

Darcy's fingers felt snug around her waist. His linen and plaid-covered chest sheltered her from the night. Like in Steafan's office, she couldn't bring herself to look higher than his collar. The goodbye she owed him got lodged somewhere in the vicinity of that pesky lump still constricting her throat.

A sigh burst from Darcy's nose, and his warm breath stirred her hair. He abruptly released her and fumbled in the saddlebag until he pulled the box free. Placing it in her hands, he stepped back and petted his horse's neck, murmuring to the animal.

Seeking comfort? Communing with a friend who wouldn't leave him?

Guilt twisted her heart. "What are you going to do when I'm gone?" she asked. "Will Steafan try to bully you into marrying someone else?"

"He canna. He will likely pressure me to null the contract, but I willna do so. He will be forced to leave me be. Mayhap he'll name Edmund his heir."

She doubted Steafan would permit himself to be forced into anything he didn't want to do. She also feared what kind of "pressure" he might put on Darcy. But she shouldn't worry about him. She had enough problems of her own. Like impending time travel.

Would she get dizzy like when she'd left Charleston? Would she fall down and black out? Was time-travel safe for her baby? Would she remember Darcy, or would all this fade like a dream?

Regardless of the risks, she had to go home.

Swallowing past that persistent lump, she said, "Well, good luck. Thank you for taking care of me while I was here." *I will miss you,* her heart whispered. She turned her back on him and strode to the standing stone, cursing herself for not having the courage to give him a proper kiss for his trouble.

The box hard and cold in her hands, she stepped into the stone's black shadow and repeated her wish, turning the box and waiting for the telltale sounds that would precede her magical trip home.

Nothing happened.

Tears pressed at her eyes as she tried again, and she couldn't tell if they were tears of frustration, exhaustion, or relief. "Please," she begged the box, uncertain what, precisely she was asking it for.

Maybe that was the problem. The history around her was warm and alive, intoxicating in its vibrant proximity. What if her fascination with this place, and perhaps with a particular man, was keeping her from making a sincere wish?

No. She refused to consider that. She loved her parents, her friends, her job, being an American, enjoying twenty-first century privileges of freedom, equality, medicine, and convenience. Getting home was non-negotiable. It was most definitely a sincere wish. She tried again, voicing her wish while she imagined her mother's round face, surrounded by gracefully styled, shoulder-length, blond hair, her father's bearded, smiling face as he opened his arms to hug her.

Still nothing.

"No," she whispered, tears splashing onto the rosewood finish. "Please don't abandon me here. I'm afraid. I want to go home." The inlaid pattern on the box's lid twinkled with night-blackness as she shook it.

Her last few grains of hope slipped through a sieve and blew away on a brisk Highland wind.

§

DARCY COULDN'T TEAR his gaze from Malina as she bent over the meddling bit of wood and metal that would take her away from him forever. He wouldn't take for granted a single moment he had left with her.

His fingers tingled with the memory of her curving waist, still narrow as her unborn bairn made no more than a gentle swell beneath her gown. As he'd held her, the inner edges of her eyebrows had tipped up in regret, no doubt over the marriage he'd forced her into, but the regret was hers alone. His only regret was that he was not enough to entice her to stay.

A sob cut through the night. Then another. Malina bent forward to press her forehead to the ground.

Pain squeezed his heart. The next thing he kent, he was

kneeling beside her, gathering her to him and soothing her with words his mother had used when he'd been a wee lad and his favorite mutt went over the cliffs to chase a stick he'd thrown too far.

"Let the tears come, Malina. Let them come. They wash away what we canna bear."

Her shoulders shook with silent sorrow, and he wished he could bear the pain for her. He kissed her forehead before he realized what he was doing. The sweet scent of her heather crown filled him with longing until he ached to hold her closer. He resisted the urge, letting her go instead. She didn't need a clumsy oaf crowding her.

His body immediately missed the contact with hers. Swallowing thickly, he held out a hand. "Let me try it. Mayhap I can get the contrary thing to work."

She sniffed and handed him the box. The look in her moist eyes was nothing he could name. It wasn't quite hope, but nor was it despair.

Forcing his gaze to the box, he turned it over the way he'd seen her do. He rotated it, even shook it gently. It did nothing.

"Did it do aught that was special when you came here?" He was nervous to ken how her magic worked, but willing to dabble in it if it would help her.

Another sniff. "I had just read the inscription on the bottom and was turning it back over when it made some soft mechanical noises like a cuckoo clock about to engage. Then the lid just popped open. I didn't even get to look inside before I wound up here, lying on my back in the grass."

He studied her. Convinced she was telling him the truth, he flipped the box over to read the date as she'd described, then righted the thing. Still nothing. He inspected the tight seam. It lacked any sort of hinge or clasp. He tried to wedge the blunt nail of his thumb along the seam to search for a hidden catch, but his nail was too thick. Always, he was too large.

He took up one of her soft hands, inspecting her neatly trimmed nails that were much thinner than his. “Try running your fingernail along here.” He guided her hand to the seam and she did as he asked. “Do you feel a catch? Aught out of place or uneven?”

She shook her head. “It’s no use. It’s not going to work.” She raised her tear-streaked face and her lips pressed into a sad smile, the sight filling him with a hollow burn. “It looks like you might be stuck with me after all, Darcy Keith.”

His heart jumped. She would stay with him.

But not by choice. His poor Malina hadn’t chosen to marry him, either. Well, he supposed she had, but he’d pressured her just as Steafan pressured him. He couldn’t stand to see her choice taken away again.

His hands surrounded hers and the box for the second time that night. He rubbed his thumbs over the cool satin of her skin. “Mayhap for now,” he said. “But we shall keep trying. We’ll come back at all times of the day and night until it works.” In many of the stories he’d heard, women appeared by the stones on the eves of Samhain or Beltane. Beltane, the first of May, was only a few days away. Mayhap the magic would work then. “I willna rest until you are returned to your people.”

She shook her head and slipped her hands from his to leave him holding the box. “That’s sweet. But I’m not sure I should get my hopes up.” Using his shoulder for balance, she pushed to her feet. Her posture sagged. “I’m so tired,” she said. “I can’t think about it anymore tonight.”

“Will ye come back to Fraineach with me and rest for what’s left of the night?”

“Only if you promise I can sleep late tomorrow.” Had that been a wisp of humor he heard in her voice? What a resilient woman his Malina was. And not so mistrustful of him that she coulda bear to stay under the same roof with him tonight.

"You may sleep as long as ye need," he said roughly, his gut flopping wildly at the idea of her sleeping in his parents' long unused bed with him down the hall in the room he'd slept in since he was a bairn.

Och, he'd have to change the dusty linens before she could lie down. And she might require a light meal before bed—didn't pregnant women get hungry more often? Urgency to see to her needs pulled him to his feet. He swept her and her recalcitrant box up into Rand's saddle and cantered home, eager to make her feel welcome at Fraineach.

It was her home, after all. As long as her box forced her to stay.

§

ANYA LACED UP her dress, smoothed her glossy chestnut hair, and slipped from the stables after Aodhan had gone. But she didn't head for the cottage she shared with her ageing da. She turned onto the road up to the keep. She wished to tell Steafan about Big Darcy in time for her laird to send someone after his deceiving nephew and catch him in the act of disowning his wife.

'Twas shameful enough for a man to be so poor a husband that his wife wanted to leave him, but to go so far as to help one's wife run away, 'twas inexcusable. Surely Steafan would release the man as his heir, and she would have that much more leverage to convince him to put away his useless Ginneleah and take her to wife instead.

The sound of hoof beats distracted her from her musing. 'Twas late for anyone to be about the village ahorse. Tiptoeing between cottages, she looked in the direction of the sound and saw Big Darcy on his big horse coming up the lane to the stables. Alone.

She gasped and crouched behind a rain barrel as he went past. What happened to his wife? She'd thought he was helping her run away. She'd assumed such an activity would take several days at least. But here he was, back at Ackergill after no more than two hours away.

Wending through the tight alley to the back of the stables, she stepped up on a crate and peered through a barred window. Inside, Big Darcy lit a lantern but kept it shuttered so the dim orange glow gave him just enough light to store away his tack and brush down his sweaty beast.

She took a moment to appreciate the strong line of his shoulders as he worked. He still wore the crisp new plaid and fine shirt he must have gotten married in. His shoulder-length sandy hair was swept back from his face so his proud cheekbones and the clean-shaven angle of his jaw gleamed in the lantern light. She could see why Steafan had named him heir. He was an impressive man, if one went by looks alone. But his overripe sense of honor and his timid nature would make for a terrible laird. Besides, she lusted to give birth to Ackergill's future laird.

Steafan wouldn't need his nephew once she succeeded in seducing him.

She watched the man closely, looking for some sign of what might have become of his wife, but nothing stood out as unusual as he put his horse away, except mayhap the swiftness with which he worked. Only after his jogging footsteps faded into the night did she steal around to the front of the barn and make her way to the tack room for a more intimate investigation.

Mayhap she would find some evidence of treachery in his saddlebag.

Kenning the tack room as well in the dark as her own bedroom, she quickly found Big Darcy's saddle and flipped open the leather flap on the attached bag. Inside, she found not a weapon but an exquisite rosewood box with a broad border of silvery decoration that glinted in the meager light coming through the window. She had never seen the box's equal. 'Twould be worth quite a lot, a wee treasure like this. Might he have stolen it from his wife? What if he'd murdered her for it?

No. That made no sense. He didn't need to steal. His mill was profitable, and his home was grander than any other in Ackergill except for the keep. He'd even given his wife a pouch of gold, alerting Anya to just how well-off the big Keith was. Had she kent the extent of his wealth when she'd been a girl and that a skirmish would take Steafan's only child and leave Darcy as heir, she might have wooed him to wed her, rather than embarrass him publicly.

But the past was past. Ever since Steafan's first wife had died, Anya had been determined to share the laird's marriage bed. Something nefarious had occurred here tonight that she could twist to her advantage. She was sure of it. She just had to find proof.

Hoping the box hid something incriminating, she tried prying the thing open, but the lid wouldn't budge. She turned it this way and that, searching for a latch or some kind of trigger for the lid. No means to open the box revealed itself. Huffing with frustration, she lit a lantern to study the thing more closely. Writing on the bottom caught her eye. She read the date and frowned. What kind of wood-worker would date his creation twenty-five years anon?

As she stared at the date, she recalled something Big Darcy's wife had said that she'd thought odd. *"I need to go back to my time. My being here is a mistake."*

She had thought mayhap "back to my time" was a saying of the woman's people, but what if the woman was truly from the future? What if she was a witch and she and this box had come here by magic?

Oh, sweet saints, what if the woman had tried to hex Big

Darcy and he'd slain her to defend himself? If he'd killed the witch, the saints might withhold their curses on the Keith for accepting her as one of them, but if she yet lived, the woman posed a danger to Ackergill. She needed to take this box to Steafan immediately and alert him to the abomination he'd unwittingly welcomed into their midst.

A noise at the barn door made her heart leap into her throat. The box slipped from her hands. Only her deer-skin-sheathed toe kept the thing from making a racket as it hit the floor.

She bit back an oath as the corner bruised her foot.

Not wanting to be caught lurking in the stables lest her best place for fornication be lost to her, she blew out the lantern and dove under the workbench to hide among the saddle blankets. A moment later, Big Darcy strode into the tack room. His plodding steps came to a stop when his boot nudged the box on the floor. Stooping, he picked up the wicked contraption and dusted it off with his sleeve.

"What are ye doing on the floor, ye wee conniving devil?" he asked it.

She tensed at the familiar way he spoke to the object. 'Twas almost as if he expected it to understand him.

She held her breath, hoping she'd arranged the blankets well enough to hide herself.

She'd never been afraid of him before, but he frightened her now. He might have done murder tonight. He spoke to an object mayhap created by the devil himself. She itched to clean her hands of the vile touch of the box, but she forced herself to remain still.

"You arena happy enough to bring trouble to my doorstep?" he asked the thing. "Ye must leap around stables, too? I should chop you into bits and bury you in the forest where you canna tempt me with things I am nay meant to keep."

She gasped, then clapped her hand over her mouth. Is that

what he'd done to his wife?

Chopped her up and buried her in the forest? And what did he mean by accusing the box of tempting him? Did the thing speak to him as he spoke to it? Had it incited him to murder?

Big Darcy stiffened, and she held her breath. Saints, she hoped he wouldn't hear her pounding heart.

The man turned his great head in her direction. He scented the air like a hound from hell, his eyes searching the dark. She resisted the urge to whimper.

His gaze passed over her hiding place without stopping. He turned on his heel and left, tucking the box under his shoulder wrap and darting guilty looks from side to side.

Once he'd gone, she released her breath in a whoosh. But the relief didn't last. 'Twas plain to see Steafan's heir was involved in wickedness. 'Twas her duty to inform the laird.

Mayhap in his gratefulness, he would reward her with a visit to his bedchamber. She dashed up to the keep fast as her legs would carry her.

Chapter 8

ANYA AWAITED THE laird in the library, a richly appointed turret room, dark at this hour except for a lone candle lit by a sleepy maid. At the sound of Steafan's approaching footsteps, she fluffed her bosom and spread her hair over her shoulders. He strode through the door in naught but a nightshirt and a wine-colored robe, but carried himself like a man clad in his best finery.

She curtsied, which was not required but would stroke his sense of importance. "Laird Steafan, thank you for seeing me at such a late hour."

"Speak, woman. For what have ye made Hamish pull me from my bed?"

She stepped close enough to scent the smoky sweetness of whisky on his breath. "'Tis your nephew. Big Darcy. I couldna sleep, so I went for a walk and passed by the stables." She ignored the roll of Steafan's eyes, but stored it away for later consideration; if Aodhan was blabbing to the laird about their arrangement, she'd find a way to humble the proud war chieftain. "While I was out, I saw him ride away with the strangewoman ye married him to. He spoke of helping return her to her home in a most blatant betrayal of his marriage contract. I thought that was bad enough, but a short time later, he rode back to the stables. Alone. Without his wife!"

Steafan's gaze sharpened with interest, and she preened under his scrutiny. "After he left, I poked about in his saddlebag and found a wee, fancy box that must belong to the woman. 'Twas made of rosewood and had silvery markings, which is odd by itself, but there was somat even more strange about it. 'Twas dated 1542."

His eyes widened, then narrowed in skepticism.

She pressed on urgently. "Your nephew spoke to the thing as though it had a mind to understand, and he accused it of tempting him."

She took another step, bringing herself close enough to kiss him if she were to tilt up her chin. In a low tone, she said, "I dinna ken for cert what it all means, but I fear the woman may be a witch. Kenning your nephew, he has either slain the woman for being wicked or has let himself be pulled under her spell. Either way, I thought you should be aware."

His handsome, dark eyes pinned her as he considered her words.

She parted her lips, inviting affections.

The man took a long step back and scoffed, "Nonsense. You had Hamish rouse me from my bedchamber for this?"

His look of disdain cut her pride. Anger made her next words sharp. "'Tis nay nonsense. Recall where the men met the Gunn this afternoon. Berringer's field. There are standing stones there." She raised her eyebrows, willing him to see reason. "Ye've heard the stories. Women appearing from out of nowhere spouting stories of being from strange lands and distant times.

What if they arena just stories? What if Big Darcy's wife is one of those women, one of those witches who come to stir trouble for peaceable clanfolk? I heard her speech. She isna from Scotia or any place nearby, that is for cert. Did ye even ask her where she was from before ye opened your arms to her?"

His nostrils flared at her thinly veiled accusation. Mayhap she'd been too bold. She dropped her gaze in submission, lest he suspect she challenged his good sense. 'Twould not do to enrage the man, despite how magnificent he looked when riled.

"Do ye have this box to show to me?" His quiet voice made her raise her gaze to his.

"No," she admitted, pouting and lowering her eyelashes. "Big Darcy returned to the stables and I hid while he took the thing away with him. But he surely has it up at Fraineach. 'Twould be a simple matter of searching for it."

At his uncertain look, she closed the distance between them and clenched the lapels of his robe. He was close to believing. She just had to nudge him a little farther.

"Steafan." Her whisper promised intimacies if he would only accept. "You canna keep Big Darcy as your heir. Whatever has become of his wife, 'tis clear he meant to betray you. Ye married him so he would have bairns, but he didna even spend a single night with his bride. I dinna blame him if he suspected the woman a witch, but if so, why did he not bring her to you for your judgment? Why does he sneak about at midnight and converse with her strange box?"

She turned her hands so her palms pressed his firm chest. The warmth of him teased her through his robe and shirt. "If 'tis an heir you desire so badly, why not let me give you one of your own blood? Take me to wife, and I swear I will give you bairns."

Using just his fingertips, he removed her hands from his chest and dropped them as though she were vile to touch. His lip curled. "I already have a wife, if you'll recall. I didna accept your offer two years ago, and I havena changed my mind since. I willna have my heir be the get of Ackergill's whore."

She gasped as if Steafan had struck her. "You confuse me with my sister," she bit out, too offended to strive for the subservience the man seemed to prefer. "I may freely sample Ackergill's men, but only because they desire me. I canna understand why you pretend not to. I could be yours, and all the other men would be jealous, kenning they can never again have what their laird has claimed."

"They only tup you, woman, because you throw yourself at them. You arena as desirable as ye suppose. You are merely accessible." His words lit a fire of indignation in her. "Now, be gone with you and your gossip. Respectable women are in bed at this hour and not eavesdropping in stables and running to their lairds with wild tales."

He turned and strode from the library.

Rage burned every inch of her skin. She nearly unleashed a very unladylike tirade on the haughty man. But she bit her tongue. Her words wouldn't hurt Steafan. She had another way to punish the laird, a way she'd been employing ever since that rejection he so callously referred to.

She rushed home and set to preparing a fresh batch of quinine-laced rose oil. At times, she'd felt guilty for sending him and Ginneleah an annual gift of perfumed oil under the guise of a laird who lived leagues away. But if he was foolish enough to use the oil and believe it a helpful gift from across Scotia rather than a spurned-woman's revenge, then he deserved the monthly disappointment of his wife's flow.

As she arranged the vials she would need for preparing the oil, she smiled to herself. 'Twas a delicious sensation, having power over the most powerful of men.

§

STEAFAN WENT TO the kitchen to rinse his hands. He didn't like having touched that snake Aodhan insisted on tupping. Any man with sense should be able to see the glint of rebellion in Anya's eyes, the selfish set to her mouth. She was bonny and built for a man's pleasure to be sure, but only a fool would put his cock in such a trap. Once that woman had her hooks in a man, she wouldn't let go without a fight. He had no wish to be caught. He liked being the fisherman, not the fish.

And his Ginneleah was a fine fish, indeed. Aodhan had raised the lass well. His body sang with desire just thinking of his bonny young wife. He lusted to go to her, but the lass would be asleep at this hour, as he should be. As he would be, as soon as he shared Anya's unlikely story with Hamish.

Darcy was such a good lad he wouldn't have even bothered, save for the fact that Anya made some sense. Reluctant though he was to admit it, in his excitement at finding his nephew had claimed a woman, he had neglected to interview her properly. He doubted Anya's claim that Melanie was a witch, but he did find her strange accent and bold manner suspicious. Mayhap he should have learned more about her before granting her access to his nephew's home. 'Twas an oversight he would soon correct.

He found Hamish's room below the kitchen and spoke briefly with his chief guard before climbing the stairs to his bedchamber, passing Ginneleah's on the way. He paused in front of her door, his body tight with need and his mind craving the peace that came from sating himself in her sweet arms. He'd be within his right to wake her. And the obedient lass would be welcoming.

But he didn't wish to disturb her.

He wished to look on her, though. He didn't glimpse her in slumber often, but when he did, he fell in love with her all over again. Mayhap just a peek would ease his mind and body.

He pushed open the door as quietly as he could. The room was near black, the only light a scant line of gray coming through the narrow window. His eyes already accustomed to the dark, he stepped up beside the bed and gazed on his treasure.

What blasphemy Anya seethed! His Ginneleah might be barren, but his eyes refused to see her as aught but perfect. He would never put her away, especially no' for somat beyond her control.

Peaceful as an angel she was in her large bed, and more lovely by far. Her skin, naturally tan like her da's and even more golden for the afternoons she liked to spend in the garden, gleamed with youth even in the darkness. 'Twas a pity many women shielded their faces from the sun as the fashion was in France. Life came from the sun. Death from shadow. His Ginneleah was life itself. Bonny, sunny life. Her thick hair, burnished gold in color and silky in texture, fanned over her pillow in a temptation he couldn't resist.

He reached out and smoothed his hand over the soft strands.

"Steafan, is that you?"

Damnation. He hadn't meant to wake her.

"Hush, lass, back to sleep. I only meant to gaze on you. I'll go."

She breathed a deep sigh, and the linens rustled with her stretch. "Ye dinna have to."

"I ken it well. But I shall. And curse ye, lass, for sleeping so lightly. I would like the chance to watch ye rest on occasion. It puts my mind at ease." He kissed her forehead and turned to go.

"'Twill be a blessing, my light sleeping, when there are bairns down the hall needing me in the night." Her wistful tone tugged his heart and made him stop with his hand on the latch.

"Aye," he said, his voice soft, as he only permitted with her. "'Twill be a blessing, indeed."

"Come to me. Let us try again. It has been nearly a week."

Ginneleah didn't like coming together nearly as much as he did, though the sweet lass never complained. He kent himself to be a fine looking man, but he was elder to her da by five years, and he never fooled himself into believing she could ever look on him as aught more than a duty. He should let her rest, especially since 'twas plain to see they weren't meant to create life together.

"I shouldna," he said, but he was already hard. He was going to let her talk him into staying, and he hated himself for it.

"Of course you should," she said, holding out her hand to him.

"You need an heir, and I want to give you one. We shouldna let it go a week in between. Have you been busy? Sometimes when you have much work, you dinna come to me as often."

He returned to her bed and sat heavily on the edge. Predictably, his wife knelt at his back and wrapped her arms around his neck. Her scent of honeysuckle and herbs soothed him.

"Aye. I have been busy," he said, fingering her soft locks as they fell over his shoulder. "And so have you. Been in the garden today?" He inhaled deeply, letting the scents of innocence and sunshine caress his soul.

She murmured somat in the affirmative as her hands slipped over his collar and into his robe. Her fingers tugged at the laces of his nightshirt.

Utterly defeated, he stood and threw his night clothes aside then crawled on the bed, settling between his wife's cool thighs. He pulled the vial of rose oil from the drawer in the nightstand, frowning at how light it had become since they'd gotten it as a gift at the first anniversary of their wedding. He'd received a vial shortly after their nuptials, too, accompanied by a missive of congratulations from Laird Wilhelm Murray of Dornoch, a man he'd never met, but whose wealth and standing were regarded throughout Scotia.

'Twas a point of pride that such a great laird kent his name and cultivated his alliance by sending exotic gifts. In the missive, Murray had credited the rare and expensive rose oil for the siring of his six sons, and hoped it would do the same for him. He had hoped so too, but 'twas not why he used the oil with Ginneleah and 'twas not why he looked eagerly forward to the arrival of the next vial, should Murray be so generous again come their anniversary next month. Darcy wasn't the only man in Ackergill with a sizeable cock, and he didn't think his wife would find him comfortable without the oil.

He'd had no such ointment for use with Darla, God rest her

soul, and she had been far less accommodating than his sweet Ginnie. After Darla had given him his son, she'd claimed her duty as laird's wife was done and refused to welcome him to her bed. He had commanded her to capitulate a time or two when 'twas either that or lower himself to ease his strain with one of Anya's ilk, but he found he didn't like an unwilling woman beneath him.

He would never command Ginneleah to his bed. But then, he didn't think his wife would ever deny him and tempt him to. If he had to make do without the rose oil, he'd find somat else to make their joining tolerable for her. Surely there were ointments for sale in Inverness or Edinburgh.

But 'twas a problem for another day. At present, there was enough of the blessed nectar left for several couplings. He coated the tips of two fingers with the rose-scented slickness and rubbed her gently.

"You're a good lass," he said as he worked himself inside her, inch by slow, tight inch.

Her body tensed before he was halfway seated, and he kent she was struggling not to whimper.

He stopped his advance and merely stroked her hair and whispered to her. "Lovely as the sunflowers in the garden you are, my sweet lass. As warm and gentle as the summer breeze. Easy, sweet lady. Relax, and it willna bother you so much."

"It doesna bother me," she said in a strained voice that betrayed the lie. "Go on with it."

He afforded her a moment before proceeding, disliking this part despite the blinding pleasure of sinking into her oiled warmth. Thankfully, it always became more comfortable for her once he began moving. And tonight was no exception. She relaxed for him in stages, her body changing from a clenched fist to a perfect, welcoming sheath. Her face smoothed. She even favored him with a tender smile.

He made love to her slowly and gently, basking in the sounds of her quickened breaths as his heart sped and he neared the end; he always made it as quick for her as he could. As he finished, he held her tightly and praised her for her sweetness and willingness.

Leaving her to her privacy, he went back to his own bedchamber. He felt worlds better for his wife's soft embrace. He could think again, and this night had given him much to think on.

God help Darcy if the lad had truly helped his wife run away. God help Melanie if she was a witch. God help Anya if he found out she had roused him from his sleep for a hoax.

Morning would tell which of his charges was in need of divine assistance.

Chapter 9

MELANIE WOKE UP in a large, unfamiliar bedroom. The furnishings were simple and suited to a well-to-do merchant's home in sixteenth-century Europe. Fraineach. She groaned at the now irrefutable evidence that she was stranded in the past.

"And married to Darcy, let's not forget," she muttered as she kicked off layers of cozy quilts. She'd said it with as much sarcasm as she could muster, but the tone didn't match the soothing effect the words had on her. "Married to Darcy," she repeated, and her lips curled into a lopsided smile.

Damn the honorable Highland warrior for making her care about him. That very care might be keeping her here against her will. She had to figure out a way home. If the box refused to help her, maybe she could find the maker. Surely this MacLeod, whoever he was, would know how to manipulate whatever crazy magic the box contained. Although, whether the maker was established or not twenty-five years before he'd made the box was anyone's guess. Maybe she could talk Darcy into taking her to Inverness to investigate.

Encouraged by her new plan, she slid from the soft, clean bed. She still had on Darcy's mother's dress, which made sense since she didn't remember getting undressed last night. Or crawling into bed. Come to think of it, she didn't remember much of anything since collapsing by that standing stone and crying her eyes out all over Darcy's shirt. She must have fallen asleep during the ride back to Ackergill. Which meant Darcy had carried her up to bed without waking her.

And she'd thought him utterly lacking in chivalry. Marveling at how thoroughly she'd been proven wrong, she removed Fran's pins from her hair, ran her fingers through it, then set off in search of a place to relieve herself.

Fraineach's outer walls of stone and mortar and inner walls of painted wood slats marked it as a nicer than average home for the period. Had garderobes come into fashion by 1517 and if so, had Darcy's family been well off enough to have one? Searching along the upper hall, she peeked in the first doorway she came to. It opened into a spacious room cluttered with stored items and furniture draped with sheets. Amidst the clutter, she spotted a wire rack for sewing dresses, a stick topped with a carved horse's head, complete with leather reins, and a bassinette with chipped paint. Had Darcy's mother placed him in that bassinette when he'd been a cuddly little baby? Had the wooden horse served as Darcy's childhood steed as he chased Edmund around the windmills, pretending he was leading a skirmish?

A thick layer of dust on the floor suggested the room hadn't been visited in years. The dry and earthy smell of disuse reminded her of the museum. A heavy melancholy stole over her as she pulled the door shut on the forgotten treasures of daily life. A life every bit as vibrant as the one she was trying to get back to.

Farther down the hall she found a small bedroom with a narrow, neatly made bed and an open wardrobe with a length of forest-green wool trailing out onto the floor. Darcy's formal kilt.

Had she displaced him from the larger, nicer bedroom? Likely not. With its clean furniture and half-full oil lantern on the table, this room conveyed an air of regular use. He must sleep here every night. The master of Fraineach had never moved into the largest bedroom. A strange sympathy tugged at her until her bladder reminded her she'd been on a mission.

Continuing her search, she found what she was looking for, a small stone chamber with a raised privy shelf and a small window for light. No toilet paper. No toilet seat. But a welcome sight nonetheless.

With one bodily demand taken care of, she ventured downstairs in search of food to pacify her rumbling stomach. A faint fishy smell led her to a large kitchen with two stone ovens and a central workbench overhung with an assortment of cast-iron and copper cookware. At one end of the workbench rested a silver-rimmed china plate of radishes, crusty bread, a heaping pile of cold oatmeal, and a headless fish. She devoured everything except the fish, not sure how to get past the scales when the only utensil left for her use was a silver spoon engraved with a delicate floral pattern and the initials, *J.M.K.* at the base of the handle. Steafan had referred to Darcy's mother as Janine. Could the spoon have been one of his mother's most prized possessions?

Last night, he'd claimed he would be a good husband. She saw proof of his claim everywhere she looked.

She owed him a ginormous thank you. For his hospitality, for his genuine attempt to help her return home last night, and for his gentleness when she'd been simultaneously relieved and crushed as the box had refused to work.

Wondering where he might be, she shifted the curtains in the parlor to look out at a lush, green hillside sloping down from Fraineach to the village below. To her left, three squat windmills with fabric sails and exteriors of weathered wooden tile marched along the hill's crest.

The sails of two of the mills turned smartly in the wind rushing up and over the cliffs. The ocean, though invisible from the window, made itself known by a pleasant, briny scent in the air.

Movement at the base of a mill caught her eye. Darcy. Back in his plain brown kilt and battered leather ankle-boots, he passed from one mill to another, ducking his tall frame to go through the arched doorway. Had he managed to get any sleep before getting up to run his mills this morning, or had he spent the entire night taking care of her?

Guilt gnawed at her. When he'd headed out to battle the Gunn yesterday, he probably hadn't planned on getting stuck with a temporally challenged, knocked-up southern girl. He probably hadn't expected to spend the night getting married and gallivanting all over the Highlands as his new wife enlisted him to help her run away. She wasn't the only one who had been significantly put out by that blasted box. Darcy had sacrificed a lot for her yesterday. His time. His bachelorhood. His pride, perhaps, as his new wife broke down in heaving sobs at the prospect of having to stay with him.

Ugh. Poor Darcy. She owed him one heck of an apology. Add that to the thanks she owed him, and she might as well throw in a proper kiss, too. She winced at the memory of their fiasco of a wedding. That was not how she'd envisioned her first kiss as a married woman, and it probably wasn't what Darcy had hoped for either.

Determined to start fresh with him, she strode to the door and flung it open to a crisp spring morning and a short, glowering Highlander.

"Hamish," she blurted as her hand flew to her chest.

Steafan's enforcer narrowed his eyes. "Good morn', lass. 'Tis glad I am to see you." He didn't look glad. He looked dangerous. "Is Darcy about?"

Warning alarms went off in her head. She couldn't imagine what Steafan's enforcer was doing here, but he'd surely know by the turning of the sails that Darcy would be at the mills doing his work for the day.

Smiling brightly, she said, "Why, good morning. How lovely to see you. I trust your day is off to a shining start. I was just on my way to find my husband. Would you care to join me?"

Without waiting for his answer, she breezed around him and down off the porch.

A meaty hand landed on her shoulder and stopped her. "Where's the box, lass?"

Fear coiled in her stomach. How did he know about her box? Had Darcy said something to him or Steafan?

No. He wouldn't, not after he'd gone to such lengths to hide it from her so she wouldn't accidentally mention it to anyone.

She thought better of admitting she knew anything about the box. She also knew she needed Darcy. "He's at the mill, I'm sure," she said, ignoring Hamish's question. "I think I'll just say good morning and then I'll be happy to help you with whatever you need."

He didn't release her shoulder. He moved in close behind her and said in her ear, "What I need is that box." When she turned to face him, she met a sharp, beetle-black gaze. "You ken the one I mean. Rosewood. With silvery touches. And a date of 1542 on the bottom."

Her heart sank. Somehow, Steafan had found out about the box. Maybe Darcy *had* told him. She had tried to leave him last night, after all. What if he'd gone to Steafan in the night and confessed everything? What if this was how Highland husbands showed their appreciation for wives who tried to desert them?

No. She had meant it when she'd determined never to question his honor again. It couldn't have been Darcy. But if Steafan knew about the box, what else might he know about?

Did he know she'd tried to run away last night and that Darcy had tried to help her? Should she pretend not to know what Hamish was talking about, or should she own up to her involvement with the box?

"Where is it?" Hamish demanded.

"I don't know." That was the truth.

His eyes gleamed with satisfaction.

She'd inadvertently admitted to knowing about the box. Darn. "I mean, I don't know what you're talking about." It came out as more of a question than a statement. Double darn. She needed Darcy's cool head and careful speech. He'd know what to say to get the enforcer from hell to back off.

Hamish chuckled and it was not a happy sound. "Come wi' me, lass. We'll look for it together."

With little choice but to go where he dictated by the unyielding clamp of his hand on her arm, she followed him through the house as he poked around looking for the box. She willed Darcy to come to the house, but from what she knew of the Highland work ethic, she doubted he'd make it back to Fraineach before dinnertime.

Hamish looked in cupboards and chests and eventually dragged her into what looked to be an office with a small desk scattered with papers and quills. He pulled drawers out haphazardly. One drawer fell to the floor and the bottom splintered.

"Hey!" she protested. "Take it easy."

He did no such thing. Tugging on a large, lower drawer, he frowned when it wouldn't open. Removing his dirk, he released her and jimmied the lock, damaging the drawer's frame.

She ran for the door.

"Do ye ken what box I'm referring to now, lass?" His voice made her pause.

Looking back, she saw him lift the damning artifact from the drawer.

She said nothing, but her face likely proclaimed whatever guilt Hamish assumed was hers. She pushed through the door, shouting for Darcy. When she ran down the steps, a guard leaning on the porch railing out of view from the front door deftly caught her around the waist and swung her around.

"Watch yourself, Glen," Hamish said from the doorway.

"Bind her mouth so she canna hex you."

She kicked and fought the two men, but she had no chance against Hamish's cruel hands and the burly arms of the guard. They stuffed a rag in her mouth and kept it there with a kerchief knotted at the back of her head.

"Come," Hamish ordered the other guard. "Steafan will want to question the witch." After frowning at the date on the bottom of the box, he tucked it against his shirt in the wrap of his kilt. "And he'll want to see her wicked box as well."

He pulled her from the house and down the footpath, away from the windmills.

She looked back longingly at the three sturdy structures, willing Darcy or one of the other men whose voices and laughter occasionally caught the breeze just right for audibility to poke a head out and witness her—what was this, anyway, an arrest? Hamish had called her a witch. Did that mean she was on her way to a burning at the stake?

She had to get someone's attention. When a cart laden with wheat rattled by, heading for the mills, she gave up trying to keep her footing and let herself go limp. Hamish had to slow and take her weight. Giving the enforcer no help whatsoever, she turned imploring eyes to the driver of the cart. It was no use. The gray haired man looked resolutely ahead, ignoring the spectacle.

Hamish bruised her arms and tore her dress at the sleeve as he yanked her to her feet. One of her breasts spilled free of the dress's neckline. Oblivious to or uncaring of this humiliating exposure, he plowed ahead, propelling her toward the castle. Within ten minutes, she was back in Steafan's office.

The laird of Ackergill stood before her with an icy expression void of the warmth he'd shown when he'd embraced her last night.

Fear iced her skin and made her shake.

Hamish forced her to her knees. They cracked on the floor so hard she had to blink back tears. The guard pressed her shoulders to hold her down as Hamish handed Steafan the box. The laird inspected it for a long minute during which her heart drummed with terror. He gave special attention to the inscription on the bottom.

"Curious," he muttered to himself. "How does it open?"

She shook her head, trying to convey that she didn't know.

Steafan put the box on his desk and took two brisk strides to bring himself so close his kilt brushed her nose. Tears filled her eyes as he pulled his *sgian dubh* from its sheath.

So this was it. She was about to die at the hands of a paranoid Highland laird. Her parents would never know what happened to her. She would never meet her precious baby. Darcy would hate himself for failing to protect her. She didn't blame him for this, but she knew him well enough by now to figure he'd blame himself.

Steafan put the tip of the blade against her cheek. "Are you a witch or no?" he asked bluntly.

She tried to say no past the handkerchief. Tears freely flowed down her cheeks. Craning her neck to look up the laird's imposing body, she searched for a flicker of reason in his eyes, finding only cold calculation.

Without warning, the dirk moved. She cringed, waiting for the sting of a cut. But no sting came. Instead, the gag fell away. She spat out the soaked wad of fabric in her mouth, licked her lips and said, "I'm not. I swear to you I'm not a witch."

"Explain the box, then."

She paused, undecided as to whether to tell the truth or try to make something up, aware her life meant little to the man frowning down at her. "A forgery," she said.

"Lie," he said. "Hamish."

The enforcer stepped up and slapped her solidly across the cheek. The blow whipped her head around and left the side of her face numb.

Stunned by the quick violence, she stared into Hamish's black eyes.

"Explain the box," Steafan repeated, but she hardly heard him.

"Why did you hit me?" she asked, in a daze of shock. She had never been hit by a man before, had never been hit by anyone before. It rocked the foundation of her confidence. She felt shattered. She felt alone.

Some fundamental part of her cried out for Darcy. She desperately wanted to rebuild herself in the comforting circle of his arms. "I want my husband," she whispered.

"You'll nay be married much longer," Steafan said, nodding to Aodhan as he entered the room.

Aodhan's blue eyes found her kneeling on the floor and widened with concern before settling into guarded indifference.

"Her silence is as good as a confession," Steafan said. "I willna suffer a Keith to remain married to a witch. Bring the contract that it might burn along with her.

"A few more questions, lass, and I'll have Hamish see ye to the dungeon, where you can pray for your soul 'til nightfall."

§

DARCY PULLED THE door on the grain chute to send the coarse kernels hissing onto the grinding stage. Sweat dripped from his brow to sting his eyes as he worked with more haste than usual, eager to return to Fraineach and discuss with Malina how they might return her home. But the mill was no place for distracting thoughts. He'd already nearly caught his plaid in the winch when he'd hoisted the day's second bag of raw bere to the grinding floor. The last thing he needed was to injure himself and thus fail the woman relying on him. So focused was he on his task he hardly heard Edmund's call above the music of the cogs.

"Darcy! Tallock's backing his wagon in! Send down the hooks!"

He did as his brother asked, then climbed down the ladder to greet Tallock and help the Wick farmer unload his supply. He'd hardly set foot on the dirt floor when Fran came whipping in like a stiff wind, and threw herself into his arms.

"Melanie," she managed between panting breaths. As her chest rose and fell, he realized her bairn was pressed between them as well as a meal sack meant for Edmund. "Hamish. Dragging her to the keep."

His body went tight with readiness. He tensed to flee after his wife, but Edmund's hand fell on his shoulder.

"What's this about, lass?" he asked, guiding Fran from Darcy's arms to his own. "Slow down. Tell us what happened? Why are ye breathing like a mare run twenty leagues?"

"Coming up the path," Fran gasped, looking back and forth between them like a weathervane in an indecisive gale. "Saw Hamish and Glen. Pulling Melanie along. I hid behind the cart so Hamish wouldna see me, but I saw them through the tack. They have her gagged! She fell, and Hamish pulled her up none too gently and tore your mother's fine gown, and poor Melanie popped out of the top. And Hamish has a lump of somat under his plaid. Looks mayhap like a box of some sort."

His vision went red with fury. Hamish had mistreated his wife! His heartbeat pumped in his ears, deafening him to whatever Fran said after she took a mighty gulp of air. Leaving Fran to Edmund, he sprinted from the mill.

"Hail, Big Darcy," Tallock greeted as he spun the farmer around in his haste to get to the keep.

"Edmund will see to you, Tallock," he called, not slowing.

His gaze fixed on the keep. His stomach lurched with dread as he pushed his legs to run faster. His Malina was being treated like a criminal and not twelve hours after Steafan had married them and granted her the protection of the Keith. His uncle was feared for his swift changes in mood, but this was strange even for him. What had caused the paranoid bugger to turn on Malina in the span of a single night?

He remembered Fran saying Hamish had somat under his plaid, somat in the shape of a box. The memory collided with another. The faint trace of rosy scent he'd noticed in the tack room last night when he'd found Malina's box on the floor.

The box hadn't merely fallen from his saddlebag, as he'd assumed. Someone had found it and dropped it. Someone who tended to be in the stables at odd hours, who smelled like perfume, and who liked to stir up trouble.

Anya.

Snarling, he stormed through the keep's doors and made straight for Steafan's office, taking the stairs three at a time. Bursting through the closed door, he was met with a sight that turned the red rage of his vision to a fiery blaze. Glen had Malina on her knees, and Hamish stood ready to strike her. Tears streaked her face and one of her eyes was swollen shut. In her struggles, one of her breasts had spilled from the low neckline of her dress. One sleeve hung by mere threads.

In Steafan's hands was Malina's box.

"Release her!" he shouted, advancing on Glen.

"Easy, lad," said a voice behind him. Aodhan. "'Tis just talking the laird wants with your wife. Isna that so, Steafan?"

"Aye," Steafan said. "I have some questions for her. Questions she willna answer to my satisfaction, and Hamish has been good enough to persuade her. Hamish, again."

Hamish cuffed her across the cheek, his hand spanning from her reddened jaw to her swollen eye.

His wee bride cried out as the slap echoed through the room.

He tensed to lunge, but Aodhan caught his arm. "Calm

yourself," he whispered urgently. "Dinna make this worse. If Steafan makes me bind you, ye willna be able to help her."

He froze as Aodhan's words sunk in. Growling sounded from somewhere, and he realized it came from him.

"Easy," Aodhan rumbled, his fingers digging into his arm. "Answer the question, lass," he said to Malina. "Answer and Hamish willna strike ye again."

"Fail to answer truthfully," Steafan said, "and 'twill be fists next."

"I already answered," she said, and her voice was steady and strong despite her trembling. His poor Malina. He shouldna have left her at Fraineach alone. He should have hid the box better. Christ, he shouldna have been so absent-minded as to leave the box in the stables for anyone to spy. He'd let his desire to make her comfortable in their home distract him from keeping her safe.

"I told you the truth," she insisted. "I'm not a witch, and I don't do magic. I don't know how to open the box. It's not even mine. I'm just taking care of it for someone."

Steafan's eyes darted to Hamish, as if he were about to command more violence.

"'Tis not hers," Darcy found himself saying. "The box is mine, and the date is merely a forgery. A simple matter of changing a one to a four." His heart slammed against his breastbone at the lie, but it was for Malina. It was to spare her from his uncle's suspicions.

Steafan's gaze snapped to him. "You never could lie well, lad. Stop defending the wench. She is nothing to you. Had I kent she was a witch, I wouldna have wed you. Hamish, fists."

"No!" he shouted. "I lied, but Malina is telling the truth." When Steafan held up a finger to stay Hamish's ready fist, he pressed on. "I found the box where I found her on Berringer's field. By the marker. She isna a witch. I'll swear to it. Mayhap 'twas magic brought her here, but 'twas nay by her doing."

Steafan flicked a look at Hamish, and the brute relaxed his fist.

He ventured to press his advantage. "Dinna lay another hand on her. She is my wife. A Keith. You married us yourself last night, and I willna agree to a null. And she is with child, damn you. She doesna deserve this. If you must have Hamish using fists, have him use them on me. Malina is my responsibility. I will bear whatever punishment you feel she deserves."

"With child?" Steafan sneered. "A bastard child? What is that to me? And will you bear a burning on a pile of tinder for her? 'Tis what any witch deserves and well you ken it. The longer we abide her presence in our midst, the more her wicked spirits will seek to ruin us."

"I'm not a witch," Malina said faintly. "Oh, God. This can't be happening."

His uncle had that gleam in his eye that meant reason was leaving him. The first time the laird had gotten that look had been after Creag Kirk, just before he'd tortured to death with his own hands the traveler to whom he'd granted hospitality but had turned out to be an English spy.

Not a dwelling in Ackergill had escaped the grief of the two-day skirmish that spy had instigated, and the keep was no exception. Steafan lost his brother, Darcy's da, and his son, aged sixteen years, born him by his wife, Darla, who had died of grief soon after. Since then, Steafan had become overly protective of the clan. Any threat, real or merely perceived, was dealt with swiftly and decisively, to the extent where Darcy feared innocent men had suffered unfairly at the laird's hand. But so far, no woman had been slain. Beaten, aye. Humiliated in the stocks, aye. Imprisoned in the dungeons, aye. But now Steafan was threatening a woman who was neither a stranger nor a threat. A woman who carried a precious, vulnerable bairn.

A woman who had caused his heart to sprout the first tender

shoots of love.

He could answer that he was willing to burn in Malina's place, but he kent Steafan wouldn't be swayed from what he thought must be done. The gleam in his eye meant his mind was fixed and there would be no talking him out of it.

At his silence, Steafan told Hamish, "Put her in the dungeon. Prepare the pyre and alert the village. We will light the lawn of Ackergill Keep tonight with the spirit purging of a witch."

Darcy glanced over his shoulder at Aodhan. An understanding cut between them. Once Malina was under guard in the dungeon, he would be powerless to rescue her. 'Twould have to be now or never.

Aodhan afforded the smallest of nods.

He sprang forward and swept his wife up in his arms, tearing her from Glen's grasp. Cradling her to his chest, he ran.

Steafan's shouts and Hamish's surprised stammering sounded behind him on the stairs.

As he threw himself into the daylight, the last things he heard from within the keep were Aodhan's raised voice and then Steafan yelling, "I'll burn whomever I wish!"

Flying down the steps of the keep, he nearly collided with Edmund, who was leading a trotting Rand up the road.

"Best hurry," Edmund said as he took Malina from him so he could mount.

Once in the saddle, he drew Malina up to sit before him.

"There's food in the bags and a wee bit of coin," Edmund said. "I'll mind the mill for you, brother."

His chest tightened as Edmund slapped Rand's rump. Steafan's shouts meant he and the others had emerged from the keep.

"Thank you, Edmund," he called as his mount lurched into a full gallop. "Move Fran up to Fraineach. The house is yours."

He didn't look back to see Edmund's reaction. He would

never look back.

Chapter 10

"GOOD LAD," DARCY said with a pat of Rand's frothy neck. The gelding had raced southwest through Keith and Gunn land and well into the hills of the MacBane by the time the sun dipped too low to risk a gallop. He had stayed off the established paths, but kept a keen eye and ear out for signs of pursuit nevertheless. He didn't expect Steafan would be able to reach them tonight; even with two riders, Rand was faster than any other mount he'd heard of. But he wouldn't risk Malina to a MacBane out for a hunt, or a wolf stalking for prey.

All was quiet as he reined Rand into a dell beside a creek. He hadn't spoken to his wife during the harried ride, but had taken comfort from the way she leaned forward with him and clung to Rand's mane without complaint like she understood the necessity of their flight.

He spoke to her now in the quiet of gloaming. "Malina." He tugged her back against him and searched her face. She raised her gaze to his and his gut kicked with the sight of her puffy left eye. Her cheek was pink, the skin tight and swollen. He lowered his cheek to hers, overtaken by an impulse to comfort her. "I'm so sorry," he said as the heat from Hamish's abuse seared his whiskered skin. "Can ye forgive me, lass?"

She pulled back to look him full in the face. How it pained him to see just one green gem sparkling at him; the other nearly obscured by swelling. "Sorry? You're apologizing to me? Darcy, I'm the one who's sorry. I've—I've ruined your life, haven't I?"

She ducked her face and heaved an agonized sob. “I’m so sorry. So sorry for everything.”

He lifted her chin with a finger, hoping only to meet her gaze and tell her she had no cause to apologize, but before he got the words out, she pulled him down to her and pressed a lingering kiss to his lips.

His eyes flew wide in surprise, then drifted closed with bliss. Her lips were soft and cool as the most delicate rose petals. Her hand on his neck swept down his arm, her fingers leaving a tingling trail along his skin until they sought the valley of his palm. He closed his hand around hers, so cool and tiny. So fragile.

Mine to protect, his heart decreed.

He hadn’t kissed a lass in six years, not since Anya. He hardly remembered what to do.

Panic made him freeze. Until Malina parted her lips in an invitation his mouth heeded without consulting his stunned mind. He parted his lips too, and tilted his head to slant his open mouth to hers. Their tongues met in a rush of moist heat and he felt the stars fall to Earth to bathe him in their splendor.

He held her close, his one hand squeezing hers possessively but not too tightly and his other wrapped around her middle, touching the firm mound where her bairn grew. That was his to protect, too. All of her was his to guard, to provide for. Only, he had no home now. No income. No laird nor clan. He had only his sword, his dirk, his wits, and whatever Edmund—bless him and his foresight—had packed for them. Sobered by the dire situation into which he’d dragged his bride, he relaxed his hold on her and pulled his reluctant lips from their heaven.

Malina drew her plump lower lip between her teeth. “I owed you a proper kiss, husband of mine,” she said, her right cheek turning pink to match her left. A wee smile faded from her lips as soon as it had come. “And I owe you a very big thank you. Thank you, Darcy.”

"If that is how a lass shows her thanks, I shall endeavor to earn more of your gratitude in the future."

He held her gaze, feeling as proud as he could remember, then swung down from the saddle. He brought her down, too, and they stood for some time, his hands on her waist, hers on his chest. She chewed her lower lip again, and if he wasn't mistaken, he thought she might want to thank him in her special way again. But his cock, hard as steel and reaching for her under his kilt, couldn't take any more of her thanks. He forced himself to let her go and began removing Rand's tack.

"How can I help?" she asked, her voice small.

He ached to soothe her hurt. Mayhap he could comfort her by caring for her as well as he could in the wilderness. He wasn't terribly familiar with living away from Fraineach, but his da had taught him how to make a bow and arrows for hunting, and, thanks to Edmund, he had a full sack of jerky and dry parritch. She wouldn't go hungry between here and Inverness, where he'd be able to find work and lodging. He wouldn't be able to provide for her as well as he would with the income from his mill, but he was strong and able, and would work what jobs he could find to give her and her bairn all they desired.

Until he found a way to return her to her home as he had promised.

"Rest, Malina," he said. "Just rest, and let me tend to you."

§

MELANIE DIDN'T WANT to rest. She wanted to help, needed to help, because whenever she stood still, the pain from the wounds to her face made her relive the senseless horror of being hit over and over again. Refusing to give the memories purchase, she searched for a distraction while Darcy wiped down his horse.

Remembering Edmund saying he'd packed some food, she

peeked in the saddlebags, thinking she could prepare something for dinner. When she found mostly jerky, figs, and dry oats, which either required no preparation or more preparation than she knew how to provide, she frowned and looked for some other way to be helpful. She tried filling Darcy's water skin after she'd emptied it, but he intercepted her and went to the creek to take care of it himself. She started to gather sticks for a fire, but he informed her they shouldn't make one until they were farther south.

She felt worse than useless.

She was no fool; she knew he couldn't go back to Ackergill after snatching her from Steafan's clutches. In fact, Steafan would probably send men to look for them so he could watch them both burn for daring to defy him. Darcy had been in line for the lairdship. He had run a profitable business. He'd had an impressive and comfortable home that held for him memories of his deceased parents. And because of her, he'd lost it all.

She was a freaking albatross.

She had nothing to offer to even remotely make up for what she'd cost him. Well, she briefly entertained the thought that she had one thing to offer, one thing that wouldn't be much of a sacrifice considering how incredibly attracted she was to him, and not just because he had the most lickable male body she'd ever seen, but also because he was genuinely kind and honorable and sincere and now literally her hero.

But he didn't even seem to want that. She'd practically thrown herself at him, but he'd taken just the one kiss—and wow, what a kiss! Then he'd pulled back from her physically and emotionally. He'd hardly spoken to her since, except to command her to sit and rest and continue being useless.

Maybe she wasn't exactly his type. A big, strapping warrior, Darcy probably preferred his women tall, leggy, and gorgeous, not short, pregnant, and in constant need of saving.

Whatever the reason for his reluctance, she refused to embarrass herself any more by offering what wasn't wanted. She had enough to recover from without adding the insult of his rejection on top of it all. *Keep your hands off the gorgeous Highlander,* she coached herself while he sat beside her on the ground and handed her figs and strips of jerky.

"We can make parritch, once it's safe to have fires, but for now, this will have to do," he said.

"This is fine." She took a sip from his water skin to wash down the savory saltiness of the jerky.

"In the morn, I'll find us some greenery. And there will be villages we'll come across. Edmund packed us coin enough to buy a proper meal now and then along the way." He scrubbed his hand over the back of his neck.

"And I still have the gold in my pocket," she offered.

His eyebrows lowered, and offense made the line of his jaw sharpen. "That is yours, Malina, for when you return to your kin. I will provide for you while you are with me. Mayhap not as well as I might back at Ackergill, but you shall nay go hungry."

Her throat constricted with emotion. He still planned on helping her return home. She'd liked it better when he was begging her to stay. Now, it seemed like he couldn't wait to get rid of her. And no wonder. She was nothing but a burden.

"Thank you," she said, feeling about as small and annoying as a gnat. She sniffed back the urge to wallow in self-pity and said, "I like the jerky. And Fran's meal plus the breakfast you left me this morning probably met my caloric requirements for the whole week. Thank you for that, by the way." Her cheeks grew warm. "It seems I'm always needing to thank you."

Her mind wandered once again to the possibility of thanking him in more intimate ways.

As if he'd read her mind, he looked at her softly, his gaze dropping to her mouth. He promptly cleared his throat and looked away. A faint blush crept up his neck, tugging a smile from her.

He might pretend not to want her, but the truth was in his gaze, fixed on an utterly uninteresting twig. Seizing on the proof of his attraction, her brain spun out of control with thoughts of pulling him down on top of her there on the forest floor and discovering the bounty hidden beneath that plain kilt of his.

Just thinking about it made her body tighten with need. And it wasn't a need based purely on lust. She genuinely liked him. Heck, she more than liked him. A day ago she'd been furious at being coerced into marriage to a near stranger. Tonight being married to Darcy felt like a safe harbor from a hostile, alien sea.

But his harbor was starting to feel like a dry dock. And it irked her more than it should.

She blamed pregnancy hormones for her preoccupation with sex after the day she'd had. And just like that, her mind was back on the brutality of Hamish's hand slamming into her face, each curled finger bruising like a lead ball bearing.

It had been awful. It could have been so much worse.

Clutching her belly, she said, "You mentioned there would be villages on the way. On the way where? Where are we going?" She needed conversation or she'd start to cry and there was no telling when she'd stop.

"To Inverness," he answered. "I can find work there. And 'twill no' be difficult to hide from Steafan in such a well-travelled place. Besides, your box was made there." He frowned. "Or it will be made there." He shook his head, the scenario apparently hurting his brain. "So mayhap we can learn how to return you, even though we dinna have the box any longer."

"Will we have to meet the laird there before being allowed to stay?" She accepted the water skin he passed her. His fingers brushed hers as their gazes held.

"Nay. They arena all paranoid canker-blossoms," he answered with a wink. They laughed together, and if it went on a little too long, she suspected it was because they both needed some joy tonight.

"I don't know what that means," she said as their laughter faded. "But it seems to fit Steafan." Sighing, she turned her face up to the night sky. The cloud cover had rolled back to reveal a stunning array of stars. The air had a crisp bite to it. The scent of trees and loam soothed her. It was beautiful here, but that was probably no consolation to her homeless husband. "Oh, Darcy, I'm so sorry."

"Whist. Ye did nothing wrong."

She shook her head. "My simply being here is wrong. It's all wrong." Fighting a choking sense of despondency, she stared into the dark forest.

After a minute of silence, he said, "Tell me about your home. It must be a fine place for you to want to go back so badly."

A tear leaked from her good eye at the memories his words conjured. Talking about home would undo all the mental buttresses she'd been relying on to keep it together. "I can't," she whispered.

His arm went around her shoulders and she couldn't resist settling against his side. She'd take the comfort of his touch, even if it didn't mean what her body wanted it to mean.

"Tell me about your home," she said. "Please. Tell me about your parents." She needed a distraction or she'd be tempted to pine for what might be lost to her forever.

He was silent for several seconds. Then he said, "My mother was your size, which comes as no surprise to ye since you're wearing her gown—I wish I could mend it for ye, but I have no sewing things. Though, she didna look like you, ye ken. She had eyes as blue as yours are green and hair as dark as yours is fair. I can still remember how it curled when the rains came. She was a fine mother to me and Edmund. My da was a tall man, but no' so tall as me. He had red hair, but a shyer shade than his brother, who ye've met." He said the last part darkly, and she realized he meant Steafan.

"My da ran the mill like his uncle before him, who built the place after seeing such mills down in Aberdeen. 'Tis the mill that makes Ackergill fair profitable for such a wee village," he added with no small share of pride.

His brogue brightened as he spoke about his mill, and she sensed he'd rather talk about his work than his parents. She understood that.

"I love windmills," she said. "But I don't really understand how they work. Will you tell me about what you do every day?"

He launched into an energetic description of everything from the hand-sewn sails to the timber cap that could be rotated into the wind to the gears, and the process of grinding wheat and barley into flour and grains as fine or coarse as desired. He'd removed his arm from her shoulders to gesticulate while he spoke. Though she missed his touch, she delighted in his enthusiasm and was pleased she'd seemed to successfully distract him from their predicament for a time.

After a while, he began to wind down. He yawned several times and she remembered he likely hadn't slept much the night before.

"We should rest," she said, her stomach fluttering at the thought of lying down in his arms.

"You rest," he said. "I will stand watch."

"I don't think so. If anyone stands watch tonight, it will be me."

He raised an eyebrow in reply, but didn't say anything as another yawn overtook him. He pushed to his feet and stalked into the trees. She thought to try to hide another yawn. But when he came back several minutes later with an armload of ferns and pine branches and spread them over the ground where they'd been sitting, she realized he was making a little bed. She set to gathering soft-looking foliage as well.

It felt good to work. It would feel even better to see Darcy get some much-needed sleep while she watched over him, serving him for a change.

"Lie your head down, Malina," he said, spreading his horse's blanket over the bed.

She snorted. The man whom she'd judged lacking in chivalry was suddenly taking his duty as husband and protector to an unhealthy extreme. "And when will you sleep?" she asked sweetly. "When we're riding in full daylight tomorrow, perfectly visible to anyone who happens to look our way? What am I to do if you tumble off your horse and bash your head on a rock? Who will protect me then, hmm?"

He frowned as if he hadn't thought through the implications of his staying awake two nights in a row. His lips pursed in that thoughtful and completely guileless expression she'd come to adore on him.

"Are we really in any danger?" she asked, looking around the clearing and feeling nothing but secure within the shelter of the thick growth. "We could both rest." Her breath quickened at the possibility of lying down tightly wrapped in his arms, her face pressed to his bare chest, at the thought of kissing him again, of giving him more than just kisses. She bit her lip, gathered her courage, and completely disregarded her promise to not embarrass herself anymore. "We could lie down together."

His eyes widened. His throat rippled with a swallow. Then he shook his head. "No."

His rejection stung, but she shoved the useless hurt away. Darcy needed rest. "How about you sleep for a few hours while I sit watch and then I'll wake you and you can watch while I sleep?"

He cocked his head while he considered it. Uncertainly, he said, "'Twould be dishonorable for a man to rest while his wife guards him. ’Tis a husband’s duty to protect his treasure.”

Her heart flip-flopped. Was he speaking hypothetically, or did he consider her his treasure?

“It seems to me a good wife ought to take care of her husband,” she said. “If we were back at Fraineach, I’d be expected to make your meals for you, wouldn’t I? I’d be expected to keep the house.” *To share your bed,* she wanted to say. She felt her face flushing, but hoped the darkness hid it. “Why don’t you lie down, and let me take care of you for a change? Please?”

He looked like he might argue, but grimacing over another yawn, he capitulated. “Dinna let me sleep long.”

“Okay.” *Who’s to say what a long time is?*

When his hands went to his belt, her pulse sped. He froze and stared at her like a deer caught in the headlights.

“Don’t mind me,” she said. “Make yourself comfortable.”

His lips quirked and he laid down fully dressed, which for him meant wearing his kilt and boots. Except for when they’d gotten married, she hadn’t seen him in a shirt. That was far from a complaint, though she wondered how he’d stay warm if the temperature dipped much more.

As soon as he lay down, his breathing deepened and she knew he was asleep. She was tired, but not overly so. Staying up tonight shouldn’t prove much of a problem. She could doze in front of Darcy tomorrow and trust her husband to not let her fall out of the saddle.

Her *husband.*

The word felt right. Terrifying but right.

She was married. As in no longer single. As in Mrs. Keith. As in bonded ’til death to a man who had sacrificed everything for her. To a man who would never abandon her.

A man who wouldn’t stand in her way as she abandoned him.

She frowned as she settled back against a boulder to watch and listen for danger, unsure what bothered her more, that she was leaving Darcy or that he didn't care enough to try and stop her, that he, in fact, planned to help her.

Would they still be married after she left? What if he found someone else he might like to marry, but his honor kept him from doing so? Would she ever feel right about dating, knowing she had a husband in the past?

Oh, God, when she made it back home, Darcy would be long dead.

Her lungs locked, refusing to breathe through the pain accompanying that thought.

No. She couldn't let herself dwell on that. It wasn't her fault she was here—okay, maybe if she hadn't made that wish—but if she didn't do everything possible to return home, her parents' grief would be her fault. Her friends' grief. And she couldn't risk having her baby in a time with such rudimentary medical practices. If anything happened to her baby, that would be her fault too.

How could she live with herself if she didn't focus all her energy on getting home?

Forcing her thoughts away from Darcy, she tried plotting her return to the twenty-first century, but couldn't come up with anything to add to the current plan of traveling to Inverness and looking for MacLeod. She sighed with frustration. As the night wore on and weariness undermined her best efforts not to think about Darcy, she found herself plotting something much more exciting than time travel: the seduction of her reluctant husband.

Chapter 11

DAWN BROKE FOGGY and chill. It would have been a perfect morning for snuggling up with a cup of tea and a romance novel, but excitement kept Melanie from regretting too badly that she didn't have either on hand. At first light, she hopped up, eager to implement her new plan.

Over the course of the long night of remaining alert for non-existent threats, she had realized a few key things. One, she cared for Darcy. Two, he cared for her. Three, they were married. Four, she wanted—no, needed—sex with him. Her hormones had been screaming for sex for months and there was absolutely no reason she could fathom as to why she shouldn't get her needs fulfilled by her husband and meet his needs in turn. Five—and she'd grappled with this one for more than half the night—getting home wasn't a given. She'd keep trying, but this was magic she was dealing with. If she managed to find a way home, and that was an awfully big *if*, she'd simply have to cross the bridge of what that meant for her and Darcy when she got to it.

But right now, in this moment, with the sun peeking through the mist and her gorgeous husband stretched out in an ungraceful but completely adorable display of deepest slumber, her heart knew a deep peace that, once she had the courage to acknowledge it, eased the bulk of her fears. Feeling lighter than she had since arriving in the sixteenth century, lighter, in fact than she'd felt long before that, she strolled through the trees to the creek and undressed for a freezing cold bath.

After slipping back into her dress, careful not to make the tear at the shoulder any worse, she leaned forward to fluff her breasts. Nodding with satisfaction at the pale mounds, larger since she'd entered her second trimester, she turned her attention to her hair, fluffing that too, and arranging her layered fringes around her face. If she was lucky, her hair would distract from the swelling around her left eye, which she could open only with the help of her finger and thumb. It would be a challenge to seduce her husband with one eye puffy as a donut hole and probably sporting an array of interesting colors, but a challenge was precisely what she needed today.

As happy as she would ever be with her appearance, she headed back to the clearing. Not halfway there, she heard Darcy's panicked voice.

"Malina! Where are you, lass? Malina!"

She dashed through the bracken and trees, mentally kicking herself for worrying him.

"I'm here! I'm coming!"

The sounds of the forest yielding to a large and possibly crazed Highlander preceded Darcy's crashing into sight. Twigs jutted from his hair. His shoulder wrap had slipped partway down his arm. His chest heaved, and his eyes were wild. Yup. Crazed was an accurate assessment.

"Christ, lass, I thought—" He scrubbed a hand over his face, wiping away the wildness.

"Thought what?" She closed the distance between them. Seeing him so worked up over her stroked something possessive and feminine within her. "That I had run off in the night?"

His eyes darted away. He pretended to inspect the forest. "Ye didna wake me," he said, bringing his gaze back to hers, accusatory and more than a little angry.

"I wasn't tired," she lied. "Plus you looked so delicious lying there all stretched out and handsome." She inched closer to him and laid her hands on his chest, swirling one finger in the soft hair there. He would receive no mercy today. "I couldn't bring myself to ruin the view." She tugged her lower lip seductively between her teeth and released it, remembering the way he'd stared at her mouth the last time she'd done it.

"Christ," he breathed. Without another word, he stepped around her to go to the creek.

She smiled and headed back to the clearing to say a cheerful good morning to Darcy's horse.

§

WHAT IN BLOODY hell had gotten into his Malina? And was it possible she looked more beautiful than he'd ever seen her? How could that be, since she hadn't slept and had been beaten by Hamish yesterday? He'd hardly noticed her swollen eye for the perfect pout of her rosebud mouth, the silvery-blonde halo of her wind-tossed hair and—Christ—the lush pillows of her breasts that he longed to fill his hands with.

It was going to kill him, being so near to her when she looked so bonny and insisted on saying things to make him feel like more of a man than any lass had yet made him feel. If only he weren't such a large man, if only he could be the husband she deserved, mayhap she would stay with him.

He stomped through the creek, splashing himself clean on his way to the other side, where he'd spotted yellow dandelion heads peeking out from amidst the creek grass. He gathered up their green leaves to supplement the figs in his saddlebag.

When he got back to the clearing, he found Malina stroking Rand's nose and murmuring to him in her sweet voice. His horse had his eyes half closed, enjoying the bliss of her attention.

When she tugged gently on one of his relaxed ears, the bugger pressed his head into her hands to give her better access. If Rand wasn't already gelded, Darcy might have done the job himself then and there.

Seeing him, his wife pranced in his direction with a breathtaking smile on her lips. His eyes locked onto the mesmerizing bounce of her breasts. His mother's dress was mayhap just a touch too tight for her up above and her creamy, bountiful flesh pressed dangerously against the neckline as though only a wish kept her bosom from spilling out. With a twist of his stomach, he recalled the way Hamish's rough treatment had made her reveal one of those precious mounds to anyone who cared to look.

For the first time in his life, he had the treasonous thought that his uncle wasn't a respectable laird. Permitting his paranoia to master him until he treated an innocent woman so harshly was the final insult. There was somat wrong with Steafan, somat that had mayhap broken when he'd lost Willie and then Darla. He didn't ken if such a flaw could be fixed, but he hoped it could, for the sake of those he'd left behind in Ackergill.

Aodhan had surprised him, though. He seemed to have a fondness for Malina and yet he bore Darcy no ill will for claiming her. The normally stoic war chieftain had shown himself to have a caring heart. He best not let Steafan see it, or the mad bugger might just try and rip it out.

"What's for breakfast?" Malina asked, interrupting his thoughts.

He was more than happy to concede thoughts of Ackergill Keep to her. They shared a pleasant if simple meal and were soon continuing south. He kept Rand to a walk to give the gelding rest after his hours of galloping yesterday. To his mixed pleasure and dismay, Malina began smoothing her fingers over his hands as he held the reins.

"I like your hands," she said. "They can wield a sword as large as a fence post and operate the large gears of a mill, but for all their strength, they have a surprising capacity for gentleness. I enjoyed watching you wash those dandelion leaves. Such a delicate task for such large, capable hands."

He could hardly breathe for the emotion swelling in his chest at her praise combined with the thrill of her soft caress.

"And your hands have the ability to comfort. I was so distraught the other night. You know, when I realized the box wouldn't send me back. But you held me and took some of that pain away. And these quick, brave hands saved me from something too horrible to contemplate yesterday." Her voice hitched along with his heart. "These hands make me feel safe."

He wouldn't have been surprised if his chest burst with the joy she was thrusting into it.

"My hands werena quick enough to take your box from Steafan. I am sorry."

"It's all right. I don't think the box was going to work, anyway. Maybe it only works once for a person. Or maybe it has its own agenda. Let Steafan keep it. A temperamental artifact for a temperamental laird. Maybe it'll curse him for us."

They chuckled and relaxed into each other. Malina's hands settled over his and he let his wrists rest on her thighs. Her hips rocked with Rand's walking stride. Her body molded comfortably to his. He was hard as a flagpole against her backside, but she didn't fash about it.

She didn't seem to mind at all.

As they rode through a grassy valley that took them far wide of the medium-sized village where most of the MacBane resided, he searched for some compliment to pay her as she'd complimented his hands. His mind tripped over so many he couldn't settle on a single one.

Before he could give voice to any of them, Malina said, "You asked me about my home. I'll tell you a bit about it, if you're still curious. I'll warn you, though. It's very different from your

Highlands." She paused, as if waiting for his permission.

"Aye," he said. "I'd like to hear about it." He loved her unhurried voice. He could listen to her talk all day, every day. For the rest of his days.

He listened as she spoke about her country, America, and the king, whom she called a "president," and about mechanical inventions she called "cars" that took the place of horses and carts and about how easy it was for her to buy all the food she needed from a single storehouse that she called simply "the store" using coin she earned at her "job." It seemed she was much more than a teacher, but rather a keeper of historical artifacts. She told him of her family, and he was stunned to learn it was not uncommon for young women to live away from their parents and remain unmarried for many years.

While she spoke of all these strange ways and wondrous inventions, he slipped the reins into one hand and took one of her delicate hands into his other. He ran his thumb over her knuckles, loving the feel of her smooth skin and delighting in the way her fingers gripped him back, as though she craved his touch as much as he craved hers.

"Where is your America?" he asked, content with the cool sunshine on his shoulders and her pure, unique scent, a faint sweetness like sugared custard, filling his lungs.

"It's across the Atlantic Ocean," she said. "It's very far away, and, um, in this time, it's only just been discovered by the Europeans. Though in my time there are millions of people who live there, having come from Europe, Asia, Africa, all over the globe."

"How did so many people settle in your land in twenty-five years?" he asked. "They must come to your shores in droves in the years to come."

Malina was silent for a time. She clutched his hand with a new tension. "Not twenty-five years," she said at last. "Closer to five hundred. The box was very old when it came to me at the museum."

Her quiet admission stopped the breath in his throat. "Five hundred," he repeated. "The year you come from would be two-thousand seventeen?"

"Close enough," she said miserably. "What's a few years when you're talking that big a difference? So, are you totally freaked now?" She loosened her grip on his hand as if she expected him to pull away.

He didn't. He held her tight. "I dinna ken what freaked is, but I dinna wish to release your hand. Whether twenty-five years, five hundred, or a thousand separate my place from yours, I am glad to have you with me now."

Malina turned to look at him, and unshed tears trembled in her eyes. "That's very sweet. I'm—I'm glad to be here with you, too."

Her smile wavered. She didn't look glad. She looked heartbroken, his poor Malina. And no wonder. Her America held wonders his people hadn't dreamt about. And in her time, her parents were alive and well. Though she didn't live with them, she spoke to them often using one of her curious mechanical items that could carry voices over long distances. They would be worried about her, and she missed them terribly. If his parents were still alive and he'd been separated from them by magic, he'd not rest until he found them again.

He'd not rest until she was home. He'd vowed it before, but 'twas more than a vow now.

'Twas his purpose. He'd not fail her in this. He'd never fail her again.

As if the Devil had heard him and thought to make him prove himself, the breeze carried hoof beats to his ears. He let go of her hand to take the reins properly. He hoped his horse was rested, because it seemed the time for walking was over. He urged Rand into a trot and took him up a low hill where he could look back at the valley and see who rode behind him.

Keeping them mostly hidden behind a scrubby outcropping, he spotted five horsemen a few furlongs away. Even over the distance, he recognized Hamish's squat form atop his black horse. And Gil's spiky red hair. Gil was the one who had taught his da and the other Keith elders how to track.

"Damn."

"Is it Steafan?" Malina asked.

"Aye. 'Tis as I feared. He's named us fugitives." He cursed again, both fearful of what it meant that Steafan had sent such a large party and his best tracker after them, and annoyed that his pleasant ride with his wife had been interrupted. "Hold on, Malina mine. 'Tis time to fly."

A nudge of his heel and a spoken command sent Rand into a gallop. He didn't fash about being seen; with Gil riding along, the party would ken he was there.

They must rely on Rand now, and if he had to rely on a horse, he was glad for it to be Rand. But he was just one horse and he carried two riders. He wouldn't be able to outpace Steafan's party perpetually, and even if he could, 'twas more than capture he feared. They would likely spread word round every village they passed that he lacked good standing with the Keith.

'Twould be just a matter of time before the whole of Scotia kent to look for a tall man and his wee wife and send word to Ackergill when they were spotted. 'Twould be no life for his Malina, running from place to place, always looking behind them for signs of Hamish or Aodhan or Gil or Steafan himself.

He searched his wits for a way to escape his uncle and not just for today, but for all time.

Only one possibility came to mind, and it might not even work. He also wasn't fond of the idea. But for Malina, he'd try it.

"I've changed my mind," he called to her over the wind.

"Inverness will have to wait. We ride for Dornoch."

§

"YOU'VE GOT TO be kidding me!" Melanie exclaimed, looking up at the enormous castle jutting up through the trees. Despite the darkness that had fallen in the last hour, the impressive sandstone building with its glowing windows and steep, stacked-stone foundation looked startlingly familiar. It had been thoroughly documented in People magazine when she'd been a senior in high school, and she'd come across a more recent article featuring the historic site in her research for the exhibit.

"Is that Skibo Castle?"

"Ye ken it?" Darcy asked as he guided Rand through the town and toward the towering structure.

"It's where Madonna and Guy Ritchie got married back in 2000. And in 1898, it was purchased by Andrew Carnegie and completely rebuilt after centuries of lying in ruin. Must have been one heck of an accurate reconstruction, because it looks just like the pictures."

"I wouldna mention any of that to The Murray, especially the part about his home falling to ruin."

She huffed a mirthless laugh. "Don't worry. I don't have a death wish."

"Except when you have to listen to Edmund and Fran tupping."

She really laughed then, a full-throated release of the tension that had built over the course of the day. As it turned out, leaning over the neck of a galloping horse for hours on end with a party of rabid Highlanders hot on their trail was a tad stressful; though to be fair, she hadn't seen any sign of their pursuers since that glimpse of them back at the valley.

"Why Dornoch?" she asked as Rand rounded a stone wall to

bring them up to a large barn. "Will we be safe from Steafan's henchmen here?"

"Aye, for a day or two at least. Rand will have bought us some time with his speed and I took us the long way, through the clay hills. They willna expect us to have turned east after entering the hills, and horses dinna leave tracks on the rock." Darcy had slowed Rand to a brisk walk through the red, rocky terrain. "We may have lost them altogether. Though if Steafan is determined enough, he'll find us eventually."

Leaving her with that less than comforting thought, he dismounted and led Rand to the barn entrance, where a lanky boy rushed out to meet them. Darcy dropped a few coins into his hand and instructed, "Be sure to walk him for a spell. He's had a hard run. Then give him all the oats he wants." He helped her down, then landed several firm pats on the horse's soaked shoulder. "Good lad, Rand. Good lad."

He turned his concerned gaze on her. "Are ye all right?"

Her legs felt rubbery, and her face and knees were still sore from the unpleasantness in Steafan's office, but otherwise she was doing remarkably well, considering they'd been running for their lives for the greater part of two days. "Fine," she answered. Thanks to Rand. Giving the horse a rub between his flaring nostrils, she said, "Thanks, big guy. I know that couldn't have been easy."

The horse gave a weary bob of his head and then the stable boy led him to a paddock to cool him down.

"What now?" she asked Darcy.

"We go up to Skibo," he said, his face grim. "And see if the rumors are true."

Chapter 12

FROM THE IMPECCABLE Roman cut of his white-gray hair to the polished silver-and-jeweled hilt at his hip and his luxurious sporran Melanie recognized as traditional rabbit-hair, Laird Wilhelm Murray looked the epitome of a Scottish warrior king. He wore a burgundy great kilt wrapped over a leather shirt that would double as light armor. The rich wool shifted majestically with his every step as he descended a curved stairway. On his arm was Lady Constance Murray, who looked just as regal in her maroon, flat-fronted French-Renaissance gown and with her salt-and-pepper hair swept up and encircled within a silvery tiara. A roomy hood of Murray plaid loosely covered her head and flared behind her like a cloak.

Caught up in the grandeur, Melanie curtsied on her wobbly legs.

Laird Murray's silvery-blue eyes fastened on her. His lips twitched. "No need for that, lass. A laird isna royalty, though some like to pretend they are." He came to a stop in front of Darcy, his hands clasped at his belt. He was easily over six feet tall.

Lady Murray hung back and studied her with shrewd hazel eyes.

"My chief guard tells me you are a Keith and that you wish an audience with me," the laird said.

"Aye," Darcy said. "I apologize for the intrusion. We come begging refuge from Laird Steafan of Ackergill."

Laird Murray emitted a very Scottish sounding harrumph that held more consonants than she had imagined possible to squish together in a single syllable. “Mayhap you’d better sup with us and tell me what this is about. I dinna suppose you’ve eaten.”

“We gratefully accept any hospitality you see fit to extend to us,” Darcy replied.

A plump, aging maid escorted them to a beautifully furnished bedroom with a high, curtained, four-poster bed and a pair of ewers for their washing.

Darcy tossed down his saddlebag and propped his sword against the wall. He looked around the room with his hands on his hips. “I didna expect such a warm welcome,” he said with lowered eyebrows and those pursed lips of his that meant he was thinking hard. The expression endeared him to her, and she realized that during their harried flight, she’d completely forgotten about her resolve to seduce her husband. As long as they were truly safe tonight, she looked forward to carrying on with her plan.

“Does Laird Murray have a reputation for being inhospitable?” she asked, going to one of the ewers and running a damp cloth over her face and chest. She squeezed a little water out so it left dewy drops that ran into her cleavage.

Darcy’s gaze followed the rivulets. He swallowed audibly and turned away. “He has a reputation for being as ruthless in the protection of his clan as Steafan is paranoid.” He put his hand on the door handle. “I’ll step out while ye wash.”

She didn’t give him the chance. She came up behind him with the freshly wrung cloth and ran it down one of his dusty arms. “I’d prefer for you to stay.”

When he didn’t work the latch, she kept washing his muscular arm, smoothing her fingers over the tawny satin of his water-chilled skin. Needing to dip the cloth again, she tugged him to the dressing table and sat him down, then continued to remove dust from the sculpted mound of his shoulder and the sinewy column of his neck.

As she worked her way down his other arm, she noticed his ears had turned red and he'd clenched his fists on his thighs. His shoulders bunched as if he might bolt any second.

Not quite the reaction she had been hoping for.

The mystery of Darcy Keith deepened. He was attracted to her, wanted her as his wife, but he didn't want a physical relationship with her. That much she knew already. But this shyness seemed incongruous with his warrior build and his chiseled good looks. It was almost as if he wasn't accustomed to a woman's attention.

She was tempted to stop tormenting him, not liking to see him uncomfortable, but couldn't bring herself to end this quiet moment after the ride they'd had. She also couldn't deny herself the thrill of this large, beautiful man submitting to her care. But Darcy's comfort was important to her, so to distract him from whatever had him so tense and embarrassed, she asked him questions about the Murrays. Did they have a history with the Keiths? Was Wilhelm a fair laird? What did it mean to ask another laird for refuge?

Darcy's coloring returned to normal as he answered, and she learned that he knew very little about Wilhelm, aside from rumors of fiery rampages that had left entire villages and even churches leveled when other clans had dared to cross him.

"Though I wouldna mention those rumors to him," he tacked on at the end.

"Don't mention his home falling to ruin. Don't mention his rampages," she said. "Is there anything I can say to Laird Murray?"

He pursed his lips while he thought about it. "Mayhap you'd better—"

"Leave the talkin' to me," she finished for him in her

laughable impression of a Scottish brogue.

Their eyes met in the mirror over the dressing table. "Aye," he said with an unguarded half smile. His gaze traveled from her face to the tear in her dress. The sleeve was nearly separated from the bodice, making the neckline sagged precariously. She needed to move carefully or flash everyone Janet Jackson style. "Mayhap I can ask for some thread and mend your dress for you before dinner."

Of all the things for him to be concerned about at the moment, it touched her for him to worry about her dress. "That's sweet, but do we have time for that? It feels like dinner time to me and the little one." She rubbed her hollow-feeling belly.

He shrugged while he watched her hand in the mirror. "I dinna ken. Mayhap they'll send someone for us when we're wanted. Shall I fetch ye some figs from the saddle bag?"

She shook her head. She'd clean her dinner plate for sure, but she wasn't ready to fall on it like a ravenous beast. Not yet anyway. If she had to wait another hour for dinner, she refused to be held responsible for her actions. But at the moment, she was more concerned with studying her husband. Here he was in a powerful laird's home, and he seemed unconcerned about impressing or infuriating Wilhelm Murray. Confidence or naivety?

Confidence, she decided. She'd seen Darcy with his uncle, and knew he was not naive when it came to dealing with men of power. From all he'd told her this evening, he'd given this meeting with Laird Murray a lot of thought during their ride. Even so, she couldn't help but worry about what it might cost him to assure their safety from Steafan. Laird Murray did not strike her as one to give something for nothing.

Regardless of what their future held, she had Darcy with her now, and he was relaxing in stages. Moving to stand between his spread knees, she began washing his face with gentle strokes of the cloth over his smooth, tan brow.

His eyes drifted closed, and she took the opportunity to drink in his stunning masculinity.

Cinnamon-colored beard stubbled his strong jaw since he hadn't shaved in more than a day. His nose was straight and broad and slightly reddened by the sun. Between his proud cheekbones and slashing eyebrows, a shade darker than his dark-blond hair, he looked every bit as intimidating as she'd first found him at Berringer's field. Except now, she wasn't afraid. Now, he was hers.

Tentative wonder filled her chest.

She set down the cloth and, starting at the tips, began combing her fingers through the wind-blown tangles falling around his face. The prolific number of split ends didn't detract from the beauty of his majestic mane. In fact, they leant his soft locks a roughness that reminded her of the way his warrior exterior disguised the core of vulnerability he hid from the world. What she wouldn't give to see his hair washed and combed properly, to have those strands skate over the bare skin of her stomach, her breasts. She sighed. She was a goner for Darcy.

Well, if you're in serious lust with a man, it might as well be your husband.

By the time she finished untangling his hair, there wasn't a trace of tension left in his shoulders. His hands were no longer in fists but splayed open on his thighs. He still had his eyes closed. His lips parted with a release of breath and she needed to feel those lips on hers again.

She brought her lips to his in a slow and tentative kiss, careful not to stretch his comfort zone too far. When his hands came around her waist and he drew her down onto his knee to take control of the kiss, she knew she'd won a small victory.

Her husband might be averse to having sex with her, but he did not seem to mind kissing her. And what a kisser he was! His tongue gently pushed into her mouth and stroked hers, around and around, over and under. He explored her as thoughtfully and masterfully as he did anything he set his mind to, and she was glad she had his solid thigh under her because her legs might have given out from sheer sensual delight.

A knock at the door was the only warning they received before the maid bustled in with an armload of clothing. Darcy ended the kiss and went on tense alert again.

She bit back a curse.

"The laird said to give ye these for dinner as your own clothes are a bit travel worn," the maid said. She dumped the things on the bed and left as abruptly as she'd come.

Darcy cleared his throat. "We shouldna tarry," he said, standing and setting her on her feet. Without a look back, he went to the bed to study the clothes, a dress in a rich chocolaty-brown brocade with ivory ribbon trim for her, and a folded bundle of burgundy plaid and a large linen shirt for him. He frowned at the kilt.

"He wants you to wear his tartan," she said, forgetting her frustration over their interrupted kiss. She put a supportive hand on his arm as he weighed the wool in his hand.

"That's significant, isn't it?"

"Aye," he said, without looking at her. "It means he expects me to give him my fealty tonight."

"Please don't." He had given up next to everything for her. She couldn't stand to have him give up his clan by allying himself with another.

"It would be a grave insult for me not to don this."

"I think it's a grave insult for Wilhelm to put you in this position." She folded her arms and scowled at the crisp tartan, completely ignoring the lovely dress she'd been offered.

"No. I've asked for his help," Darcy said. "This is what he wants in return."

"He wants you? He wants you to forsake your home, your family? For what? Will he protect us from Steafan's bounty hunters? If so, for how long? Are we supposed to live here in Dornoch forever? I don't understand. If you put that on, does it mean you can never go back to your mill? To Edmund and Fran?"

"We can ne'er go back, as it is."

"No." She shook her head. "I refuse to believe that. There must be a way." She yanked the plaid from his hand and tossed it on the bed. "It's your home. And Steafan is being completely irrational. Won't he come around? Eventually?" She winced, suspecting she already knew the answer.

Darcy's droll look confirmed her suspicion. Steafan was not the kind of man to "come around" merely because a little time had passed.

"You can't just give up on Ackergill. It seems impossible now, but maybe after a while we can write to Steafan and explain things. Or maybe there can be a trial or something. Isn't there a judicial system for clan disputes? A third party who can examine our case and make Steafan take us back?"

"The laird is the only judge a clan needs."

"But he's being unfair." Her grandmother's voice echoed in her head, *"Life isna fair, child. If ye go about expecting fairness from all and sundry, ye shall be a disappointed soul, indeed."*

"Aye, but he doesna see it that way. And offering my sword and strength for the Murray can ensure that Steafan willna get his hands on you. He wouldna cross the Murray."

"Those are facts, Darcy. What does your heart say?" She moved close to him, her face in line with the organ in question. She placed her hand over his breastbone and gazed up at him.

"How do you feel about this?"

His lips pursed. "'Tis no' important how I feel. 'Tis my duty to protect you. And the Murray are a large clan. 'Twould be a fine place to live, Dornoch. And not far from Inverness. I can still find your MacLeod for you."

"Never mind about the box. And never mind about me. This is about you. Dornoch might be a nice place to live, but it's not Ackergill. Don't do this if your heart tells you not to. We can find another way to stay safe."

His gaze pierced hers. "We would have to keep running. 'Tis no life for a woman, especially a woman with child."

She didn't particularly want to keep running either, but she didn't want Darcy to lose even more for her sake. An idea struck her. "Maybe we can meet Wilhelm half-way."

§

MALINA LOOKED LIKE a dream of cream and silk in the dress the Murray had sent for her.

Darcy's chest puffed with pride as he escorted her to the laird's private dining room, even as his stomach churned with unease at how Wilhelm would take his appearance. He had put on the new shirt but had left the burgundy plaid folded on the bed, wearing instead his plain brown one.

Instead of offering his fealty this night, he and his bride had talked about what else he might offer. He had to admit, she had a fine mind on her. If they were lucky, Wilhelm would be too intrigued to take offense.

As they approached the dark-wood door, guarded by a barrel-chested, freckled man with forearms the size of clubs, the savory scents of *collops* and roasted grouse, the briny bite of salted herring, and the sweetly flavored air that spoke of apple *frushie* for dessert had his mouth watering despite his nerves. If he angered the Murray and went to the gallows for it, at least he'd go with a happy stomach.

The guard flicked his eyes up to Darcy's in a look that passed quickly from surprise at his height to cautious respect. He inclined his head and pushed open the door to the dining room while Darcy schooled his features into the relaxed smile he always wore when hoping to put Steafan at ease. He didn't ken if Wilhelm was as prone to tempers as his uncle, but it wouldn't hurt to start things off with a disarming countenance.

The table was set with porcelain trenchers, silver utensils, simply adorned wooden mazers, goblets of pewter, and lace-trimmed linens of the kind that would have pleased his mother. Wilhelm broke off his whispered conversation with his wife and rose from the head of the six-seater table. The laird's expression was unreadable as he took in Darcy's dress, but a slight smile curved the lips of the laird's wife. Her eyes were unsurprised. Mayhap even a little pleased.

He had good reason to observe the reactions of both his host and hostess, for it was not Wilhelm's reputation for ruthlessness alone that had drawn him to Dornoch. Rather, it was the rumors of the cause of that ruthlessness, the Lady Constance Murray, whom Wilhelm was said to have rescued from a burning pyre down in Edinburgh thirty years ago, before he'd become laird.

He hoped that mayhap he and Wilhelm shared a commonality that might sway the laird's sympathy in his favor. They both cared for women who had been accused of witchcraft. And they'd both risked much to protect those women.

"Was there a problem with the fit of the plaid?" Wilhelm asked.

"I dinna ken," he replied. "I didna try it, but I have other things to offer you in exchange for your hospitality."

"Such as?" Wilhelm asked coolly.

Lady Constance rolled her eyes and nudged her husband's hip with her elbow. The laird gave her his attention, and a single look from her had him glancing sheepishly back at Darcy.

"Where are my manners," he bit out. "Sit. Eat. And tell me what brings you to Dornoch."

The laird sat down and Darcy breathed a sigh of relief as he and Malina took their seats across from a wryly smiling Constance.

While they dined, he told Wilhelm about Hamish taking Malina away not twelve hours after Steafan had married them. Avoiding the detail of the box, he said simply that his paranoid uncle had found improper cause to accuse Malina of being a witch, and that he'd hastily given the order to have her burned.

"I wouldna stand by and let him take from me what he had just given. She is mine to protect, and protect her I will, even if it means ne'er returning to Ackergill." He caught Malina's approving eye. "Though, as Steafan's heir, it is my hope that Ackergill willna be lost to me forever." He didn't expect to still be heir to the lairdship after fleeing the way he had, but it couldn't hurt to mention his standing among the Keith to Wilhelm.

Back in the bedchamber, the sight of Murray plaid in his hand had made the hackles on his neck rise. He would join the Murray for the sake of Malina's safety, but his very heart would break to turn his back on Ackergill forever. And his wife had kent it. She had convinced him not to disregard a possible return, and at her prodding, he'd permitted himself to imagine coming home to Fraineach with Steafan's blessing.

There was but one way he thought it possible. If Malina was not with him.

He had vowed to return her to her home, and he meant to see it through. And with her safe in her own time, he would mayhap be permitted back, though he feared Fraineach wouldn't feel like much of a home without her. Yet it was the only home he had, and Malina was right, he couldn't leave it without first trying everything in his power to return.

"If ye grant us your protection," he continued, "I will promise you a fifth-share of my take at the mill once I return. And I will come to your hand and fight with the Murray whenever ye send for me, so long as I am able."

Wilhelm leaned back in his chair and sipped his wine. "You plan a homecoming? You assume whatever offense your wife has done to your laird, he will eventually forgive her?"

Constance spoke for the first time. "No. He plans to return without her. Don't you?" Her English was not accented with the brogue of Scotia, nor the softer, cultured strains of England. In fact, it wasn't so very dissimilar from Malina's. "You plan to send her back through time."

Chapter 13

MELANIE'S PULSE PICKED up at Constance's words. And her accent. She was from modern-day America. She knew about traveling through time.

But more importantly, Darcy didn't deny what she'd just said. He planned to return to Ackergill alone. As in, without her!

"Darcy?" she asked, her delicious meal forgotten. She didn't care that he'd advised her not to speak in front of Wilhelm. Keeping her accent a secret didn't matter anymore. Not when it was so similar to Constance's.

He turned to her with resigned eyes. "I gave ye my word. I intend to keep it. We may have lost your box, but I willna stop until I find the maker. If he could make one magic box, he can make another."

A surge of hope at the thought of returning home warred with a pain in her chest at the thought of leaving Darcy. When she'd talked him out of putting on the Murray tartan, she'd thought they could find a way to get back to Ackergill together. It shocked her to realize she hadn't thought of Charleston once during their strategizing session. How was that even possible?

Maybe she had been too distracted by seeing Darcy's full torso for the first time, as he'd slid down the wide swath of wool that usually covered most of his golden, muscled chest to put on the shirt. Or maybe it had been the look in his eyes, all at once heated and shy, when she'd dropped her ripped dress to the floor, leaving herself in nothing but the thin shift Fran had given her before finding her way into the intimidating tent of the Renaissance-style gown. They'd talked while they dressed, but their eyes had roved over each other as though talking were the only thing keeping them from more kissing.

Lust. It was only lust, she told herself. Of course she still wanted to go home. Of course she still wanted Darcy to help her.

Too bad the thought had the flavor of a lie.

She gave him a thin smile. She ought to thank him for his devotion to her cause, but her tight throat couldn't form words.

Constance spoke, saving her. "So it was a magic box for you?"

"Aye," Darcy answered for her, not bothering to deny her association with magic.

Apparently, he knew Constance and Wilhelm weren't strangers to this kind of thing. "But Steafan has the box now."

"Which doesn't matter," Melanie piped in. "The box wouldn't work for me again. We tried, but it didn't work." Her voice got small toward the end as Constance's gaze met hers.

Those eyes were a mite too shrewd for her liking, as if they might see all the way through to what she didn't want to face. She looked at her plate and pushed some fish around with her spoon.

Wilhelm spoke. "So your laird married you but then he found out about the box and decided your Malina was a witch and wouldna make a good Keith after all. And you stole her before he could carry out her sentence."

Darcy nodded.

Wilhelm scoffed a humorless laugh. "And ye think he'll take you back after you've helped your witch of a wife use her magic to travel through time?"

Darcy grimaced. "I dinna plan to tell my uncle I helped her use magic. I will simply go home once she is safe, tell Steafan my wife left me, and beg his forgiveness."

Wilhelm arched an eyebrow in what might have been

amusement.

Constance said, "I wonder what Malina thinks of all this. Or is it Melanie? Where are you from, dear?"

"Charleston," she answered. "And yes. It's Melanie. Melanie Burns."

"Melanie Keith," Darcy corrected, taking her hand. "You may always keep my name. 'Tis my gift to you. If ye want it."

She bit the inside of her lip to keep her rising emotion at bay. Melanie Keith. She liked hearing that way too much, and she liked the sentiment behind it even more.

How could she be having verklempt thoughts about last names when she was sitting at a dinner table with a woman who had traveled through time like she had? A woman who might know how she could get home.

A woman who hadn't returned home, herself, and was looking at her with twinkling eyes.

"Come, Melanie," Constance said, rising. "Let's leave our husbands to hammer out their contract."

She looked between Constance and Darcy, torn.

"Go," Darcy said. "I'll find ye later."

She squeezed his shoulder in parting and left with Constance, who led her to an upper room lined with gilt mirrors and boasting a large marble tub that looked remarkably modern with its bronze faucet and heavy, lever-style handles.

"I missed hot baths the most," she said with a flip of one of the handles. Water poured from the spout, and to Melanie's astonished eyes, it began to steam. Constance draped her cloak over an overstuffed brocade chair and flipped the other handle up halfway. She gave Melanie a wink. "Wilhelm insists this room remain secret, especially from the staff who keep a raging fire going under a tank below stairs from dark to midnight every night. We've endlessly debated whether Scotland is ready for heated indoor plumbing. I vote yes. He thinks it could unravel the fabric of time or some nonsense and I might never come into existence as a consequence. Thinks I might evaporate into thin air if I let the wrong thing slip. He's so dramatic. Well, what are you waiting for? Take off your dress."

The woman tried to hide it, but the faint lines around her mouth suggested the Lady Murray took a great deal of pleasure in sharing her little haven with her guest.

She shucked her dress and shift, the hot water beckoning her past any issues she might have had about stripping in front of a stranger. "How?" she asked, dipping her fingers into the water. The temperature was perfect. She sank in with a sigh and let the tub fill up around her.

"I was a mechanical engineer. Before. 1981 is when I came through the stones. And Wilhelm is no slouch in the brains department. That, and he's very wealthy and determined to give me anything I want."

As remarkable as the hot water was, something else in what Constance had said caught her ear. "Through the stones?"

"Standing stones." Her hostess seated herself on the edge of the tub. "You know, like Stonehenge? The circle that brought me through is near Inverness. When I was vacationing with my mother and sister, it was called Druid's Temple. It has no name today that I know of." She waved away the enormity of time travel via ancient stone formation and raised her eyebrows at Melanie's belly. "Your first?"

She nodded, her hands rubbing her baby bump beneath the steamy paradise. Despite the gentle flutters deep inside that usually made her ridiculously happy when she was still enough to feel them, a deep melancholy overcame her. She had a woman from close to her own time, who'd gone through a similar experience to her own, making herself graciously available, yet her thoughts kept turning back to the way her heart had ached when Constance had said, *"You plan to send her back through time,"* and only incriminating silence had followed.

"You've got it bad, darlin'."

She looked up with a start and realized her hostess had been talking and she'd been spacing. "I'm sorry. What were you saying?"

Constance gave her a knowing smile. "I was saying I was terrified about giving birth here, but it wasn't so bad. I managed it quite a few times. But I have a feeling giving birth isn't the top totem on your pole right now."

She felt herself blush and let her head rest back on the tub as she focused on the woman before her instead of the man across the castle. "How many is 'quite a few?' Boys? Girls?"

"Later. Let's talk about that top totem. You thought you wanted to go back, but now you're not so sure."

The truth of the other woman's words kicked her in the gut. She wanted to deny it. Wanted to say, "That's absurd. Of course I want to go back." But she couldn't. She could only soak there and look guilty.

A soft laugh parted Constance's lips. "Boy, have I been there, darlin'."

"Did you look for a way back?"

"No," she said softly. "At first it was all I could think about, but I didn't have the opportunity. Within an hour of coming through the stones, I was imprisoned under suspicion of being an English spy." They shared a sympathetic smile. "There was no trial. No opportunity for escape. The word *witch* was thrown around. Before I knew it, I was naked and tied to a stake with a pile of wood on fire at my feet."

But for Darcy's snatching her from Steafan's clutches, Melanie would have died like this remarkable woman almost had.

As she continued her story, Constance's hazel eyes went back to that day. "Wilhelm had been riding through the clan-lands educating the lairds about alternatives to unnecessarily cruel punishments—my husband has always been a thinker out of place in time." She beamed with pride and added with a conspiratorial wink, "It's one of the reasons we get along so well." She rose and rifled through a cupboard while Melanie tried to reconcile the man with the compassionate agenda with the ruthless laird Darcy had told her about.

"Well, as you can imagine," Constance went on, "his ideas weren't too popular. But being the oldest son of the laird of Dornoch, he was humored, though no one took him seriously. Until he rode through that crowd, sliced the head off my executioner, and pulled me from the flames like a warrior possessed by righteous justice."

There it was, the missing piece. Wilhelm was ruthless in his compassion. The thought made her smile. She imagined Darcy would ride through flames, beheading executioners, to rescue her as well.

Constance turned from the cupboard with her arms full of pressed soaps, glass bottles, sponges, and loofas. "Dunk your head and I'll wash your hair," she said, uncorking a bottle.

Melanie obeyed, her eyes drifting closed with pleasure as her hostess lathered her locks with the gentle fingers of a woman who had raised several children, the strong fingers of a modern woman who had made a life for herself five hundred years in the past. The sweet fragrance of honeysuckle drew her deeper into bliss.

"So, he saved you," she said, her voice slurred with relaxation. "That's so romantic. What happened then?"

Constance was quiet, so Melanie cracked an eye open. Her hostess smiled down at her, the mischief in the look hinting at sensual memories. "Well," she said, "I found my rescuer *verra* handsome. And, as you can imagine, I was *verra* grateful."

They sighed in unison, and she wondered if her hostess had ever been a reader of romance novels.

Pouring a pitcher of warm water over her head, Constance

said, "Wilhelm's father married us the next week, and I never did get around to looking for a way back to the corporate grind."

Melanie availed herself of the soaps and loofas while her hostess told her about her six sons, the oldest three now married and with children of their own.

She let herself imagine Constance thirty years ago. The woman had a stately beauty about her now; she must have been absolutely ravishing back then. And Wilhelm, who still looked as though he could more than hold his own in a battle, must have been quite the warrior back in the day. What color had his hair been then? With his silvery-blue eyes, probably blond.

"And you never looked back?" she asked at last.

"Never." She put away the bath things, and Melanie stood and toweled herself dry.

"That's not to say it wasn't difficult at times. I grieved for the people I loved whom I knew I would never see again. I hated myself sometimes for not at least trying to find my way back to them." She regarded her with serious eyes. "But whenever I thought about what it would do to Wilhelm if I left—" She shook her regal head as if the thought was too terrible to voice.

Her face softened. "And then we had our first son. Seeing Wilhelm as a father changed me. Made me realize that nothing mattered but us. Our family. Those who would have missed me would have forgiven me for taking this happiness for myself. I stopped beating myself up about it and just…lived."

Constance's story sat like a stone in her gut. It both anchored her and made her feel ill.

"Didn't you ever worry about how your life would likely be shorter here, without modern medicine? Didn't you think about all the conveniences you would miss?" Even to her own ears, those concerns sounded trivial in contrast to the love Constance had found.

The older woman cocked an eyebrow in response, showing

she felt the same way.

"Let's keep the hot water just between us girls." Her hostess showed her back to the bedroom then left her to contemplate all they'd talked about.

Darcy wasn't back yet, so she sat before the dressing table and combed her damp hair.

She didn't know if she could stop looking for a way home. She had feelings for Darcy, sure, and her leaving would hurt them both, but in the end, her leaving would actually help him. He'd be able to go back to Ackergill if she wasn't with him. The whole agreement he was working out with Wilhelm assumed he would eventually be allowed back. In time, he would be glad to have her gone so he could have his life back, and she would be glad to get back to Charleston and the museum and to the people she loved and who would be so worried about her.

But the way back home, if there was one, waited for her in Inverness. For now, she was in romantic Skibo Castle in picturesque Dornoch. And she had a husband to bend to her seductive will. Darcy had vowed to help her return home. Rising from the dressing table, she vowed she wouldn't go without having given him as much affection and pleasure as he deserved.

With her hair all combed out and drying in chunky waves, she stretched out on the bed in her shift, lying on her side to face the door with her legs bent to alluring effect and one arm framing her breasts.

"Come and get me, you sexy Highlander."

§

AFTER DISCUSSING A contract with Wilhelm for over an hour, Darcy made his way back to the room he and Malina had been given. They'd finally agreed the Murray would provide them protection in Dornoch for up to two years, and in exchange, Darcy would serve the Murray with his sword for those two years and for the following five years, answering as many as four calls per year so long as the skirmish was not against the Keith or an ally of the Keith. When he eventually returned to Ackergill, he would send Wilhelm a quarter share of his take at the mill until the end of the seven-year contract. It was a larger percentage than Darcy was comfortable with. After Steafan's take of thirty percent he would be left with just over forty percent for running the mill and to live off of, but he'd agreed to the sum thinking that it didn't cost much for a man to live alone.

Mayhap it was optimistic to believe Steafan would abide his return, but he had value to his clan as a warrior, and being near kin to the laird may serve him well. So long as Malina wasn't with him, he stood a chance, however small, though he wouldn't be surprised to spend some time in Steafan's stocks or to suffer a scourging for his rebellion.

'Twas only fair. He had defied his laird. But he didn't fash overmuch about it. A little pain would be nothing compared to the ache of losing Malina. Any wounds his uncle saw fit to carve into his flesh would heal.

Malina's absence would be a never-healing agony.

He walked the grand halls of Skibo and pictured his wife's bonny face and her sweet mouth. Would she mayhap kiss him again before he took his place on the floor tonight? Her kisses, her touch, the soft look in her emerald eyes that made him unashamed to stand to his full height, those would be the things he would live for until he had to say goodbye. He would spend however long they had together flooding his mind with memories he could cling to on the cold nights that awaited him after she returned home.

He came to the door and opened it quietly, not wanting to wake her if she was already asleep. But the faint glow of a shuttered lantern met him, along with an enticing honeysuckle scent. He stepped inside and his lungs forgot how to breathe.

Malina was lying on the bed in her shift lazily stroking a finger over the velvety bedcovers. Her hair surrounded her shoulders like silky ropes of silver and gold. And, sweet saints, her breasts plumped against her low neckline like cream about to overflow a pitcher.

While he stood stunned in the open doorway, one of her delicate hands curled in her shift and tugged up her hem to reveal the pale, smooth lines of her shins. The gentle curves of her knees.

Christ, higher.

"Shut the door, Darcy, and come to bed."

He shut the door all right, sealing himself outside the bedchamber, eradicating the vision that had made his cock spring instantly to attention. 'Twas more than kissing his wee temptress of a wife had in mind. She would kill him with the wanting of her.

He turned on his heel and fled at the fastest pace that could yet be called a walk. Where he might go, he had no idea. It didn't matter. So long as he got himself away from the temptation that was his beautiful Malina.

"Darcy! Where are you going?"

She was coming after him. His muscles coiled to run from her. But the Keith didn't run. They faced what terrified them with bravery and honor.

He stopped and turned, facing the most terrifying and wonderful thing he'd ever laid eyes on.

Her silvery eyebrows slanted with concern. "Darcy?"

"Malina—" He didn't ken what to say to her, so he said nothing.

She closed the distance between them and took his hand. He was too startled by the contact to yank it back.

"Come on, husband of mine." Her smile did a poor job of masking her hurt. "I'd rather behave myself and have you stay with me tonight than try to seduce you and chase you away. Tell me about the contract with Wilhelm," she said, leading him back to the room.

§

SHEE-YIKES, COULD THAT have gone any worse?

Doing her best not to take Darcy's rejection personally, Melanie pulled a blanket around herself and curled into as unsexy a ball as she could manage against the bed's many pillows. She listened as he paced the room and told her of his contract with Wilhelm. It pleased her that the meeting had gone so well and that he seemed to look forward to his eventual return to Ackergill.

"What did you talk about with Lady Constance?" he asked, hands on his hips, back to the brocade curtains pulled across the window. He offered her a smile that seemed to acknowledge the awkwardness of what had happened earlier.

Hoping her embarrassment wasn't too obvious, she briefly told him about how Constance had come through standing stones from close to her time and about her and Wilhelm's fast and fiery courtship. She skipped over the part where Constance had said that once she'd chosen Wilhelm she'd never looked back.

Darcy took the Murray kilt and spread it on the hard floor, then blew out the lantern. In the dark, his boots thunked to the floorboards, one after the other, then the clinking of a belt buckle cut into the silence. The sound of rustling fabric told her he was unfurling his kilt and wrapping himself in it. She'd never been jealous of a piece of fabric before, but she would've given up a whole shelf of romance novels for the chance to be wrapped around Darcy in his kilt's place.

"Tomorrow, Wilhelm will show me around Dornoch," he said as he lowered himself to the floor. His voice came from close to where she lay in the bed, so she knew he was sitting up.

She could reach out and brush her fingers through his hair, but she kept her hands to herself, remembering her promise to behave. "He'll show me where I might best serve him while we are here. I imagine ye can spend more time with Lady Constance. We should get our rest." After a pause, he said, "Thank you, Malina. I am content with the arrangement we have with the Murray. And I wouldna have thought of such a thing on my own. You have a fine mind on ye, lass." He sighed and lay down.

As her eyes adjusted to the dark, she peered over the edge of the bed at her husband. When he rolled to one side and then the other and finally settled for lying on his back, she arched an eyebrow. "Comfortable?"

He made that Scottish harrumph sound.

"Come on up here," she said, patting the bed. "I promise to keep my hands to myself."

He made no response.

Fine. Be that way.

She scooted out of bed and unabashedly stretched out alongside her tall Highlander. The burgundy kilt did nothing to disguise the hardness of the floor, and her hip protested when she turned on her side to face him.

"What are ye doing, lass?" His voice was so soft and close in the darkness, it made her shiver.

She forgot all about the hard floor. "I always imagined that once I got married, I'd finally know what it was like to spend the night in a man's arms. Will you hold me, so I can feel what that's like? I won't ask for more than that. Just hold me."

He rolled to face her and touched her cheek. "Ah, lass," he sighed. "How can I deny you when you ask so sweetly? If 'tis holding ye want, holding you shall get. But the floor is no place for you and your bairn. Up in the bed with you."

"It's no place for a married man, either," she said, smiling at her small victory.

He sighed again, a sound heavy with sentiment she could only guess at. She climbed under the blankets and held them up for him, but he was taking his sweet time.

"Are you coming?"

"Aye, lass. Just donning my plaid."

She bit back a huff of frustration. She determined to enjoy what little affection he would give her and didn't want to push her luck by asking for more. Her hormones would have to learn patience; this was going to be a painfully slow seduction.

When Darcy slipped into bed, bare-chested, but wrapped in layers of wool from the waist down, she cuddled into his open arms. All her frustration drained away as he gathered her in and the heat of his chest turned her into a melty puddle of contentment. She nestled her nose into the tuft of hair between his mounded pectorals and inhaled his scent of saddle leather and faint, masculine musk. Beneath her closed eyelids, her eyes rolled back in her head with bliss.

Kyle had held her on sufferance when she'd demanded it of him after their all too brief trysts at her apartment, but he never held her for long, and he never gave in to her increasingly adamant invitations to spend the night. But being in Kyle's arms had never felt like this.

This felt…it was hard to put into words. But it reminded her of a fond memory. About six months after moving to Charleston to take the job at the museum, she had walked into her apartment with an armload of groceries and been struck with a sudden and profound sense of homecoming. She'd stood in her kitchen in her coat and scarf and shed a few tears because in that moment, she'd known that her parents' house in Georgia would never feel like home again.

She would always feel comfortable there. She would always be welcome. But she'd never again long to stay there day after day, night after night. She'd grown up. She'd moved on.

The first hot tears of a similar realization snuck out and onto Darcy's chest before she could stop them. He felt like home.

She'd known him less than three days and yet being in his arms overwhelmed her with the kind of peace she'd known that evening in her apartment. This was where she belonged. And if that was true, then if she managed to find a way back to Charleston, it might never feel the same to her.

Confusion tied her up inside. She wanted to return to Charleston. She wanted to stay with Darcy. Her heart ached with an impossible dichotomy of desires.

Constance had stayed. She'd never looked back. But Wilhelm had wanted her.

Darcy might have feelings for Melanie—he might even be attracted to her—but his life would most definitely be simpler if she went back to her time. He hoped to return to Ackergill, something he couldn't do if she stayed with him.

No matter what she truly wanted, she would have to keep looking for a way home. And when she found it, she would have to leave Darcy. And her heart would break.

Chapter 14

SINCE HE'D MET her, Malina had felt like a wee, delicate flower to Darcy. Oafish as he was, he'd been afraid of hurting her merely by being near her. But holding her like this, in a big, soft bed in the peaceful dark, she didn't feel so wee. The vast difference in their heights didn't seem to matter so much when they lay down together, and the darkness hid the fragile lines of her delicate face and frame.

She felt solid and sure in his arms. She felt like she belonged there. Like a cog rotated into a companion wheel, Malina fit him perfectly. She moved him.

The skin of her bare shoulders cooled the sensitive underside of his forearm. Her belly, rounded and firm with the bairn inside, pressed the hard muscles of his stomach, and he lamented the thin fabric of her shift between them. Her breath ruffled the hairs on his chest, and he became jealous of those hairs for being so near to that lovely rosebud mouth. Bath fragrances from her time with the Lady Murray made their bed smell like a bower lined with blooming honeysuckle.

He craved her kisses like the crops craved spring rains. Would she give him those lips freely if he tilted her face up and took them? He thought she would. Judging by the way he'd found her tonight—his arousal throbbed beneath his doubled-up plaid at the memory—he thought his Malina would give him everything if he asked for it. And he'd take it if he could. But he couldn't, not without hurting her and embarrassing himself. So he didn't ask for her kiss or anything else.

Instead, he merely held her, and when the feel of her, so cool and soft and trusting in his arms, had his body strung so tight he didn't think he could bear it, he forced his thoughts to the mystery of her wanting him. His da had taught him that proper women didn't much care for meeting their husbands' bodily needs except mayhap on rare occasion, but that a good wife offered her body willingly nevertheless just as her husband faithfully provided her food, shelter, protection, and leadership. His da had said only wanton women craved a man's attentions. "Wed a woman like that," his da would say, "and ye'll be a cuckold in no time."

Anya had been a wanton woman, which was why he'd avoided her for so long. If Malina desired him, did that make her wanton? He didn't wish to think of her as such. With her sweetness and bravery and her selfless spirit, she was nothing like Anya. And yet she had gotten with child without a husband. Mayhap she had been wanton and she was trying earnestly not to be any longer. Or mayhap she wasn't wanton at all but merely wished to meet the bodily needs she assumed he had, as a good wife should.

He should explain to her that she didn't need to fash about that particular duty. But something in the way she clung to him told him she desired him beyond a wife's duty.

His Malina was a mystery, a lovely and welcome mystery.

He couldn't resist smoothing his palm over her silky hair. Stroking her like that, over and over again filled him with peace. Concerns about his mill and Steafan and all that Wilhelm might expect from him floated away on a cloud of contentment.

Until he felt warm wetness on his skin where her face nestled.

"Are ye weeping?"

"No," she said, but her voice caught on a sob.

"There," he said, "now we have both told a lie to the other. We are even."

Whatever had her distraught, her heart wasn't so heavy that she couldn't give a small chuckle. "Maybe I'm crying just a little," she said. "It's fine, though. Don't worry. Get some sleep."

"I canna. My da told me a good husband doesna lay his head down for the night if his household isna in order and his wife isna content."

"He sounds like a very responsible man. Like father, like son."

No one had given him as much to feel proud over as this woman. "I do my best to be like him. Now tell me what's fashin' you. Is it Steafan? Your eye? Are ye in pain?"

Her head rocked on his arm. "No. It's nothing. Really. Pregnancy can make a girl a little emotional. That's all."

"Ye miss your home," he guessed again, ignoring her excuses. "Are ye worrit over finding your box maker?"

She was quiet for a moment. "I suppose you could say that."

"Dinna fash. I will do all I can to see you home safe."

"I know," she said, but she didn't sound happy.

After long minutes of quiet in which he thought she'd gone to sleep, Malina said, "Is it because I'm pregnant? Or too short?"

She was asking about earlier. His heart clenched. "Nay, lass," he said with a sigh. He tilted her chin up then, not for the kiss he longed to take from her, but to find the moist sparkle of her gaze in the darkness. "There isna a thing wrong with you. You are lovely as a lily in the morning mist. Any man would be proud to have you as his wife."

"Are you any man?"

"Aye, lass. I'm as proud of you as I can be. Never doubt that."

"I suppose I can live with that," she said with a wee smile. "If you won't make love to me, then I'll take your pride."

His heart stuttered and his cock jerked at her bold words. He hoped his plaid kept the bugger from bothering her.

"I can live with it," she pressed on, "but it would be easier for me if I knew the reason. Is it because I'm planning to leave you?" She said the last words so quietly he had to strain to hear her.

Guilt lashed at him; she was desperate to understand why he didn't want to bed her.

He cupped her face, his hand covering her delicate cheek and jaw. His thumb stroked the swollen skin around her eye. It was tight and hot with healing. Malina was wounded because he'd failed to hide her box well enough. Her injury was his undoing. It tugged at his heart and made him willing to do anything to make it up to her.

"Malina." Her name was a balm on his tongue. It flowed out of him as naturally as breath from his lungs. But he lost the ability to speak aught more when his eyes roved over her plump lips. They looked like velvet in the night.

Unable to resist any longer, he dipped his head and kissed her. She tightened her arms around him with soft strength as their mouths joined. Her lush curves molded even closer to him.

When she parted her lips, he delved inside, lost to sensation, oblivious to reason.

She was sweeter than sugared custard with cream, and more decadent than dessert wine.

Without him meaning them to, his hips pressed forward, seeking a connection that wasn't meant to be. But she didn't ken that. She pushed back, and the suggestion in her movement stirred heat low in his gut. Need racked him. An urge to make promises to her with his body had him delving deeper into their kiss. He would drown in the warm waters of her affection and die a happy man.

His wife pulled back, breathless. "Is this really what you want?"

Her whisper brought his sense back. His lungs devoured the air in gasps as he fought not to reclaim that sweet mouth. He needed more of her. But he made himself back away.

"Och, lass, 'tis not what I want that matters." He sat up and slipped out of bed, his body aching with loss.

"I'm sorry. I shouldn't have kissed you," she said in a rush. "Please, don't go back to the floor. I'll behave. I really will."

The desperation in her voice made his stomach burn. So did the realization that came to him as the feel of her left his body and his mind cleared. "We canna share a bed. I'll hold you all ye want by day. But I will ne'er be able to lie down with you and find sleep. Rest, now. I'll just go for some air. When I return, I shall sleep on the floor, and you will obey me and stay in your bed. Understand?"

"Please don't go. I didn't mean to scare you away."

He bit back a bitter laugh at her words. "'Tis nay fear I feel when I'm with you, lass. Sleep, now."

He left her in the dark bedroom and wondered if there was mayhap an icy loch about he might dunk himself in.

§

THE DOOR CLICKED closed and Melanie fell back on the bed. "Stupid, stupid, stupid." Darcy had kissed her, and she'd lost her head completely. She should have pulled back from him much sooner. She shouldn't have asked those stupid, needy questions.

"Why, Darcy, oh, why won't you do me?" she mocked. "Could I have sounded any more desperate?"

The sad fact was when he touched her, her brain went on vacation and her hormones ran the show. Maybe it was some primal female need to be securely mated that came on with pregnancy. Whatever the cause, she needed to rein it in or she'd just keep pushing him away.

"Think, Melanie. Think." It didn't take a rocket scientist to know he'd wanted to throw off his kilt and bury himself inside her. He'd been hard as marble, and even if she hadn't felt his arousal through his layers of wool, the way his hips had rolled forward in unconscious search of coupling would have been enough of a give-away.

He wanted her. But he didn't want her.

It wasn't that she didn't look good to him. It wasn't that she was pregnant. It wasn't that she was planning to leave. What else was there?

He had commanded her to sleep, but how could she possibly find rest when she had such an impossible puzzle to work out? How could she relax when she missed his warmth in the bed?

How would she survive when she left him and it wasn't just his physical warmth she missed, but the soul-deep warmth of knowing he would always be there for her?

If only she could find a way to break through his barriers and make love to him so she could take the steamy memory with her when she returned to her life. Surely that would sustain her when her heart iced over without him.

She tossed and turned, wanting to obey because she sensed that earning his trust was paramount to getting under his kilt. But with her body burning and her mind churning, she couldn't even keep her eyes closed, let alone sleep.

"Sleep, my patootie," she muttered, kicking off the blankets. Darcy wasn't the only one who needed some air.

Wrapping the Murray plaid around her shift like a blanket, she slipped out of their room and padded down the halls of Skibo Castle. The lush, late-medieval decor tried to lure her into stopping and studying each sconce, mirror, and tapestry, but if she was going to clear her head enough to get to sleep sometime tonight, she needed the crisp air of the Scottish countryside.

Stepping into the night, she inhaled the clean, chilly air. Dornoch didn't smell like the ocean, like Ackergill, but like grass and loam and horses. Stars blazed above in a stunning canopy of light. Though no lanterns or torches lit the outside of the castle and the moon was a mere crescent, the stars gave enough light that she could hold out her hands and make out the white tips of her short nails.

It was beautiful here. By daylight, Dornoch bustled with the busyness of a good-sized town, and after dark, all was harmonious with the stillness that came after a day of honest labor.

A place like this could grow on a girl. But it wasn't Ackergill with its quaint village, loping fields, and towering cliffs overlooking the ocean. She'd been at Ackergill less than a full day, but she'd fallen just a little bit in love with it. No wonder Darcy wanted to return so badly. She would too, if she'd grown up there.

She set off on a stroll, not sure where she was going. Predictably, her feet took her to the door of the barn; besides the castle it was the only other place she'd been in Dornoch.

She pushed through the tall door, breathing in the sweet scent of hay and clean horses, thinking she'd give Rand a rub on his nose and ask if he had any insights about his master.

"You are a disobedient wee thing. If you were staying with me, 'twould be my duty to discipline you."

She smiled to hear Darcy's voice rumble softly through the dark, belatedly realizing what he'd said. Her smile turned wry. "I'd like to see you try, big guy. I might be small, but I'm quick."

"I'm quicker."

She couldn't see him, but she'd heard the lift of a smile in his voice. She itched to flirt with him and ask how he'd discipline her. With spankings? By tying her down and torturing her with his brain-melting kisses? But she remembered her earlier promise to behave, and the rush of embarrassment resulting from her failure to do so.

"Maybe I should have stayed in bed, like you'd said, but I couldn't sleep. I needed some air, too." She scanned the dark for her husband, not seeing anything but the doors of stalls. If he wanted her company, he'd probably show himself. Disappointment made her sigh. "Well, I suppose I've gotten my air. I'll go back." She turned to go.

"What is it ye hope to gain from sharing my bed?" His voice stopped her. "You already have a bairn." The creak of a stall door followed his question. Footsteps whispered on the packed-dirt floor. With her eyes adjusted to the dark, she saw him as a towering shadow emerging into the broad aisle of the barn. He must have been checking on Rand.

She frowned at his question. He made it sound like she had some ulterior motive besides being attracted to him. "I'm not sure what you mean," she hedged.

"You want to couple with me. Why?"

She rolled her eyes; she'd understood that much of the question. It was the part where he seemed to have a problem with "sharing a bed" with her she didn't get.

Tamping down her offense was getting old. If he was going to be bold, she would be, too.

"You're easy on the eyes," she clipped. "I'm attracted to you, and we're married, so why not, right? Am I missing something here? Shouldn't I be the one asking you why you don't want to 'couple'? Oh, wait, I did. And you wouldn't give me a straight answer."

He moved closer, stopping a foot away, which meant his voice now came from high above her. "Are you a wanton woman?"

The question had been dark. Dangerous. And it kicked her offense into full-on anger.

"I'm knocked up and I want sex with my husband. If that makes a girl wanton, then I suppose I am. What of it?" She lifted her chin in challenge.

"I'll ask again. What is it ye hope to gain? The truth,

Melanie."

Her heart sank to hear him call her by her given name, and this sudden edge of hostility confused her. It felt like he was accusing her of something, but what? She was also insanely aroused. Not only had her eyes adjusted to the dark well enough to see his serious and seriously handsome face, but his looming presence filled her with an irrational sense of security. Add to that his scent of leather and man, and her lips trembled for another kiss.

She didn't want to lash out any more. Anger released itself to the night like steam from a mug of cocoa. "Pleasure," she whispered, her breasts reaching for him with her quickening breath. "That's the truth. I want to feel your body under my hands. I want to feel you inside me as you make me your wife in more than just name. And I want pleasure for you, too. Especially for you. You've given up almost everything for me. Giving you pleasure is the only way I can think of to thank you."

He blinked with surprise. "I dinna expect your thanks. 'Tis not why I stole ye away from Steafan."

She rolled her eyes, but this time with affection instead of annoyance. "Duh, I know that. You're so darned honorable you'd never do anything for something as paltry as my thanks. It's not just about thanks. I love you, you stubborn Highlander."

She cupped her hand over her mouth. The ornery thing had just blurted that which she had yet to fully admit to herself. Considering how much it hurt to have Darcy reject her physical advances, she was in no mood to bear his inevitable rejection of her heart. Mortified, she turned to run away.

But his arms went around her. He hadn't lied when he'd claimed to be quicker.

"Do ye mean that, lass?" he asked, bending over her back, holding her.

"No," she lied, trying to pry his arms away. "I'm out of my mind. Don't listen to a thing I say. Let me go."

"No. I willna. And I think a confession spoken in ire is more trustworthy than one spoken in calm." He turned her around and lifted her face to his. "I love you, too, lass." He kissed her.

The world spun into a kaleidoscope of brilliant sensation. Everything around her went off balance, but Darcy was solid and real beneath her clutching hands. He was her everything.

She didn't worry about where home was or whether she'd ever find it again. Darcy loved her. She loved him. Right now, that was enough.

She parted her lips as she had in bed, inviting him deeper, needing him inside her any way she could get him.

He gasped and broke the kiss, holding her possessively tight, but with a rigidity suggesting he couldn't decide whether to accept her invitation or not. It didn't escape her attention that he held her against his hip rather than straight on. He didn't want her to feel the evidence of his desire. She wasn't the only one wanting more than she was getting from her spouse.

Whatever held him back from loving her with his body, her newly acknowledged love for him made her sympathize. Instead of rising up on her toes and coaxing him down into another kiss, she said, "It's okay. I won't ask for more than you can give. I won't even press you for an explanation. Not tonight, anyway—if you come back to bed with me and hold me."

"You think ye can set terms with me?"

"A girl can try."

"I dinna ken what to do with you." His tone was somewhere between playful and exasperated. "You are a contrary and demanding thing, but you make me smile, and so I canna hold it against you, try as I might." He sighed. The sound was significant, as if he'd released something that had been pent up along with the breath.

"Ye may not press for an explanation, but I shall give you one. I canna lie with a woman. I am too large. I didna expect it to be a problem as you are already with child and I kent when I married you we'd have but a short time together. I didna expect you to want me in that way. But though I canna give you what ye seek, I shall give ye everything else a husband ought to and more. I vow this to you, Malina. You shall want for nothing while you are with me."

She stared at him in the dark. Her jaw went slack with shock. So that's why he kept rejecting her advances. He thought he was too large.

Did he mean his height, or his uh-hem?

"What do you mean, you're too large?" she asked carefully. "Do you mean you're too tall?"

"'Tis not for my height they call me Big Darcy," he said, and she heard the shame in his voice.

Her shock collided with a girlish impulse to giggle not just at the topic at hand, but at the ridiculous notion that a man might be too big for a woman. She had felt him—behind her in the saddle, lying in bed mere minutes ago. His erection was impressive to be sure, but too large?

Was there such a thing as too large? If so, she'd never heard of it.

Judging by his grave tone, he truly believed his boy parts were too big, not just for her, it seemed, but for any woman. Suddenly, she didn't feel like giggling any more. In fact, a profound sadness weighted her down as she considered how he might have come to such a conclusion.

What if he had tried to be with a woman and hurt her? Judging by what she had overheard between Edmund and Fran, that scenario would make sense. If Edmund's total lack of foreplay had been representative of lovemaking Highland-style, she could understand how an awkward first experience might lead Darcy to the conclusion there was something physically wrong with him.

She wanted to pepper him with questions. She wanted to

demand to see him, all of him, so she could judge for herself whether he was "too large." But she sensed he had just laid his heart open to her and if she immediately questioned him, it might undermine his willingness to be open in the future.

Slow. She needed to take this slow.

"Thank you," she said. "Thank you so much for telling me. It doesn't change how I feel about you. I didn't mean to say it earlier, but I do love you. Even if we won't fit together. If intercourse is out of the question, I can live with that." She highly doubted intercourse would be out of the question, but this moment was about his need for acceptance.

Her eyes grew warm at the way tension eased from his shoulders and his gaze softened with relief. His hands transformed from heavy weights on her shoulders to lithe butterflies as his fingers traced up her neck. She wrapped her arms around his waist and hugged him tight, molding herself along his front. He didn't stop her, and she felt him hard, pushing at her stomach.

Neither of them spoke for several minutes. At last, he cleared his throat and said, "Does intercourse mean what I think it means?"

She smiled against his breastbone. "It means joining together, coupling."

"'Tis sorry I am I canna give you that, lass."

"I don't mind. There are plenty of other ways you can give me what I've been craving."

He went tense in her arms. "What are ye speaking about?"

She ignored the question. "And there are ways I can bring you pleasure, too. We don't have to have intercourse to consummate our marriage and to enjoy each other in bed." She tilted her face up to find him looking at her with wide eyes, as if he'd never contemplated intimacy as anything more than intercourse.

His breath rasped in the darkness. "I'd think you were trying to make a fool of me, but ye're no' the sort to take joy in making another person feel foolish."

"I'll never try to make you feel foolish. Never."

"I willna pretend to ken of what ye speak, but ye've caught my attention to be sure."

"Would you like to come back to bed and trade pleasures?"

"Och, lass. You're serious." When she only nodded in response, he said, "What did ye have in mind?"

"I'd like to use my hands on you and feel your hands on me." Just imagining his large hands teasing her sensitive nub made moisture gather between her legs. Thinking about wrapping her hands around him, seeing the look on his face as he lost himself in pleasure—her breath quickened and her body swelled with desire. "I'd like that very much. And using just our hands, there's no danger of you hurting me."

"And this would make you happy?"

"Very happy."

"Christ. You may be a wanton woman, but you are my wanton woman. Show me where to put my hands, and I'll be happy to bring you what pleasure I can."

Chapter 15

MALINA SAGGED IN his arms there in the aisle of the stables.

"Are ye all right?" he asked as he scooped her up. Concern for her eclipsed the stirrings of desire her bold words had caused.

"Uh-huh. Just horny."

He didn't ken the meaning of the word. "Is there aught I can do to help?"

"Yes. Take me to bed. Now."

He carried her from the stables and made haste for their room. Mayhap 'twas the bairn inside her, making her weak. Or she might be exhausted. The poor thing had nay gotten proper rest the night before.

When he took her into their bedroom and laid her down, she pulled his face to hers and captured his mouth in a kiss that set his soul on fire. She nibbled at him with her lips and teeth.

Her hands kneaded his back. The soft noises coming from her made him hard as steel beneath his kilt.

"Are ye feeling well, lass?" he asked, the words garbled because she wouldn't stop kissing him.

"*Mmpf-hm*," she said without taking her lips from his. "Light. We need a little light."

He didn't ask why; between relief that she wasn't ill and renewed arousal, he wasn't thinking clearly enough to ask questions. He just obeyed, lighting the lantern and returning to his ravenous wife.

When he bent over the bed, she tugged at his belt and said,

"Off."

He froze with uncertainty.

"Now," she demanded.

"I dinna need to be naked to use my hands."

Malina growled, a throaty, frustrated sound that belonged in Africa's jungles, not in a bedchamber in a Scottish keep. "Fine. Have it your way."

There was nothing graceful about her normally delicate hands as she clawed up her shift, revealing the ivory length of her legs and higher. "Touch me here," she commanded. When she pressed his hand to the warm place between her legs, he gasped with shock and lost his footing so he fell on the bed.

He pulled his hand back instinctively. He'd believed for so long he couldn't tup a woman and had convinced himself 'twould be wise to never touch one and stir temptation. Now his wife was asking for the most intimate of touches. Once he touched her there, he would lose his head as surely as he'd already lost his heart. Every touch on the secret places of her body, every caress of her most precious treasure, would sear Malina on his soul.

'Twould be hell to let her go after this.

But that fear wasn't enough to make him put an end to what was happening. Not that his wee tigress of a wife would have permitted such a thing. Taking advantage of him being off-balance, she pounced, pushing him onto his back and straddling his legs far more swiftly than he'd imagined a woman with child should be able to move. In one brisk gesture, she pulled her shift over her head. It fluttered to the floor like a swan alighting on a loch.

"I'll let you keep your kilt. This time. But you're going to have to tolerate at least one of us being naked."

He barely made sense of her words for the shock of seeing a woman completely bare and sitting astride him as bold as a cock in a henhouse. Malina was glorious. Her body was a beautiful miracle.

Her rounded belly held the gift of life, her creamy breasts the gift of nourishment. His mouth watered at the sight of those abundant mounds, but not for the taste of mother's milk.

'Twas the taste of her skin and the feel of her rosy nipples pebbling on his tongue he craved. At the juncture of her thighs, soft curls protected her fertile soil, soil another man had planted his seed in.

Rage surged.

He gripped her satiny thighs. He needed to make her his. However he could. He wasn't too proud to let her show him the way.

"Show me. Tell me what to do."

"First, I think a demonstration is in order." Not waiting for him to respond, she skimmed her hands up his legs to explore the very thing he'd spent his adult years being ashamed of.

When she found him beneath his plaid, he sucked in a breath, waiting for her reaction.

Dreading her reaction.

"Oh, Darcy," she sighed.

He closed his eyes as mortification climbed his neck in a hot pulse. She would send him back to the floor for being too large. She might laugh at him as Anya had done. She might take back her love, which meant more to him than aught else ever had or ever would.

But when her hands began doing incredible things to him, he realized she wasn't overly upset with his size. Mayhap his warning had prepared her.

He opened his eyes to find her gazing softly at him, her teeth releasing her plump lower lip. "You're perfect. Just perfect."

Her words sent a wash of peace over him as her touch pulled fire through his loins. If it were possible to feel too much in one's heart, to feel too wonderful in one's own skin, he felt that way now.

"Christ," he breathed, his hands gripping her hips, drawing her forward so his plaid lifted up and she stroked him against her pale belly. Unbidden, his hips thrust forward. He pushed himself deeper into her hands, needing things from her he couldn't name.

"That's it, baby. Let me take you home. Let go. Let go for me."

Neck straining with pleasure, he closed his eyes and gave himself over to his bride. In less than a minute, his stones drew tight to his body as carnal delight built in his belly.

He couldn't stop the growl that burst from his throat as liquid fire surged up and out of him. He spilled over her hands. His heart pounded like a wild thing. His body was more alive than it had ever been, but he didn't think he could move so much as a finger.

She stroked him lightly as he came down from a cloud of debilitating pleasure. Her lips curved up at the edges in a smile that meant she'd enjoyed touching him. It hadn't been a chore for her. And she didn't seem to care that his seed covered her belly and hands.

"Malina mine," he whispered. He could say no more for fear his shaky voice would reveal too much of himself to her. Her affection and acceptance had cut him to the quick. He was raw. He was in love, deeply and frighteningly so.

"When you're recovered, I expect you to return the favor," she said with an impish smile.

Certain there was nothing he could do for her to match the joy she'd just given him, he said, "I will do my best, lass."

§

MELANIE HAD NEVER felt more confident in her body than when she'd begun showing her pregnancy. Always a curvy girl, she now felt at home with those curves instead of at odds with them.

Her body was doing what it was made for. Carrying a baby made her feel feminine and beautiful. Powerful. She felt even more so as she sashayed from the bed to the ewer, knowing Darcy's eyes followed her every move.

She wrung out a cloth and cleaned herself, then returned to him, letting her hips sway, feeling her breasts jiggle with her steps, proud of her rounded belly. When she unfastened his belt, he merely watched her, a wonderfully sated look in his eyes.

She'd put that look there. She'd shown him the acceptance he'd been lacking, and he trusted her now, perhaps more than he'd ever trusted before. Her heart soared with satisfaction.

Her body burned with desire.

"I'm going to undress you, now," she said, giving him a chance to protest if he had any lingering discomfort.

Not only did he offer no protest, but he flaunted his trust by lacing his fingers behind his head, showing off his strong triceps. "Go on with it, lass. 'Tis no use hiding from you now." His voice purred from his chest, soft and relaxed.

She grinned as she peeled back layers of muted brown wool. Her breath caught when she spread his kilt and he lay completely naked before her. He was all long, strong limbs and hard-working muscle. The sun had burnished his shoulders and arms a rich, satiny gold. His torso and stomach were a lighter tan, his natural color, and dusted with dark blond and cinnamon-colored hairs that beckoned her fingers to play. A line of darker hairs led from his belly button to the rich tuft of sandy brown between his legs. Curving to the side from the center of that tuft, long and broad, even in his semi-softness, was the most mouthwatering male member she had ever seen, and that included the ones she'd imagined in her fantasies.

"You are beautiful," she said as she wiped him clean with loving, gentle swipes of the cloth.

"I am pleased ye arena too disappointed."

"Disappointed? I'm not disappointed at all. I'm pleased. I have a big, strong, handsome, capable husband. I find you completely stunning. Completely desirable."

Skepticism tightened the corners of his eyes. "I ken you doona jest, but I canna believe you are truly pleased with my form. How can ye be?"

She finished cleaning him, smiling at the way he thickened and lengthened in her hands. Tossing the cloth on the floor, she climbed over him and nipped his ear. "Would you like me to prove it?"

His hands rubbed up her back, making her moan with the tingling sensation of his rough fingers over her skin. "How can you prove such a thing? How can you show me what's in your mind when ye look on me?"

She reached around to guide one of his hands from her back to her bottom and pressed the tips of his fingers to the moist heat between her legs.

He inhaled sharply. "Ye're slick as river-weed growing on the rocks in the creek." To her delight, he didn't pull his fingers away, but skated them over her in tentative exploration.

"A woman gets wet when she is full of desire. It's the body's natural preparation for intercourse." She kissed him slow and deep while his fingers made her tremble with need. "It means I want you," she breathed between kisses.

"How do ye want me, lass? Tell me what to do."

She rolled off him, lying back on the bed.

He turned onto his side, taking the liberty of rubbing a hand up her stomach to cup one breast.

"You can start by kissing me. Here." She circled a finger around her nipple.

Obeying instantly, he pressed a close-mouthed kiss to her as if he were bestowing a reverent peck on her cheek.

"No. Kiss me like you kiss my mouth. Devour me. Play with

me."

His eyes went dark with desire. Holding her gaze, he closed his mouth over her nipple and swirled his tongue. Heat darted from her breast directly to her womb, making her gasp with shock.

They said pregnancy made a woman's nipples more sensitive. Whether it was that or the fact she'd been beside herself with need for Darcy, his mouth on her there felt better than anything she'd ever experienced.

When he pulled at her with gentle sucking, she dug her heels into the bed and her back bowed. A strangled moan tore from her throat. Good grief, she was close to climaxing just from a little nipple action.

Focus, Mel. You can't come yet. Make it last.

At her response, Darcy groaned, and his eyes rolled back in his head. He required no more instruction than her sounds of pleasure, proceeding to tease and torture her sensitive peaks until she was writhing beneath him and crazed with longing.

She had to tug on his hair to get him to stop. "Please. I need you to touch me. Now." She throbbed for more than just his hands, but she retained the presence of mind to take things slow.

She had always been a master at delayed gratification, and making love with Darcy was a reward she wanted to build up to, not just for her own sake. She wanted to initiate him to sex in a way he'd never forget. She wanted to savor him and teach him how to be a thoughtful, talented lover, to watch the wonder in his face as she guided him in exploring her with his eyes and his hands.

When she'd brought him to climax with her hands, the look on his face had been rapturous. That moment had been Christmas morning, birthday, and summer vacation all rolled into one for him. She couldn't wait to see his reaction when she gifted him with the knowledge that they could, in fact, come together in the way he'd never thought possible.

But that would come later. Tonight was for lithe fingers and stroking hands.

"How shall I touch you?"

Gliding a finger over the smooth head of his fully engorged shaft, she said, "You are very sensitive here, yes?"

"Aye, lass," he growled. "Your touch feels divine there."

"I have a place between my legs that is just as sensitive, but it's very small. Would you like to see it?"

His breath caught. He nodded, eyes wide. Just as she'd suspected, her Highlander had had no idea a woman could be stimulated externally. She'd thought Highland men suffered from a chronic lack of romance, but now she knew it was merely an epidemic of ignorance.

No surprise. She hadn't discovered her clitoris until her sophomore year in college, and then she'd only found it after her roommate had joked about double-clicking her own mouse and Melanie had asked her what she'd meant. She'd learned more about sex in a fifteen-minute conversation with Hillary than she had from her mother and her high school's pathetic excuse for a sex-ed program combined. And when she'd explored her own body in her bunk that night, she'd been astounded that a potent little pleasure button had been hiding right under her nose all those years. It had been the Rosetta Stone of personal discoveries.

And now, she could share that discovery with her husband.

She spread her legs. Just the feel of the air cooling her moist, plump tissues made her gasp with pleasure. Threading her fingers into her curls, she gave a little tug to reveal her swollen clitoris.

She directed Darcy to scoot down the bed so he could inspect her closely, and showed him with her fingers where she was most sensitive. Her own touch felt incredible, but when he took over without being asked, her head fell back on the pillow and she cried out.

"Yes. Right there. Oh God, don't stop."

She closed her eyes and reached behind her head to grip the pillow. Her hips shifted up and down, mimicking the motion of mating. She ached to be filled, but knew it would be sweeter if she let this climax come and then showed him how to give her another later.

"Can you keep doing that and kiss me at the same time?"

He responded by moving up her body and capturing her mouth with hot, open-mouthed kisses. His fingers didn't waver.

"Harder," she moaned into his mouth as something beautiful built deep inside her. "Faster."

Darcy took direction well. A handful of seconds later, a ragged cry erupted from her throat as waves of frantic bliss crashed over her. He swallowed her scream, moaning himself as she shuddered beside him.

Panting, she pushed his hand away from her over-sensitized nub. "So good. That was so good."

"Christ, lass," he said, his face solemn. "I never kent a woman could *feel* like that. You are a miracle to me."

He kissed her, and she melted into him. When he pulled back to gaze lovingly at her, she grasped his straining erection and said, "It looks like you're ready for round two."

§

MALINA SLEPT SOLIDLY beside him, gloriously naked and cool as a lily in his arms. He couldn't sleep, so enchanted was he with her. A few days ago he'd not even kent her, and now she was the most essential part of his soul. She'd accepted him where others had ridiculed. She'd shown him worlds of delight he'd believed could never exist for him.

Tonight, her hands had brought him more pleasure than he'd ever managed to bring himself in those weaker moments a man succumbs to, and her mouth—good Christ, her mouth was a portal to heaven. And he liked pleasing her with his hands and his mouth just as much as he liked receiving from her. There was once that they came together with their bodies reversed, their lips and tongues exploring and sucking each other, their hands gripping each other's hips and buttocks; he grew hard again just remembering it.

She was his wife. His lover. His everything.

And when she left him, he would become a shell of a man.

But he had vowed to help her. He wouldn't fail her, even if it meant his demise. He'd help her discover the magicks she needed to navigate time, and then he'd give himself to the Murray. He'd tear up the bloody contract, don Wilhelm's tartan and forget he'd ever had a home and a family who loved him in Ackergill.

He might as well remain in Dornoch. There was no home without Malina.

His heart aching, he stroked a hand over her silky hair and watched her sleep. She was beauty itself. She was goodness. She was purity and carnal decadence all wrapped together. He counted himself blessed to have been given charge over such a creature, for however short a time.

Restless, he slid from the bed and poured some wine. He paced their darkened bedchamber and drank and realized he needed to get her home as soon as he possibly could because if he dallied, he'd risk becoming weak and breaking his vow. His hands trembled with the urge to shake her awake and tell her that he would never permit her to leave him. His loins throbbed with need for her, and not just for the nearly unbearable pleasure she'd shown him tonight, but for the closeness he felt with her.

Before he could change his mind, he threw on his plaid and took a candle to Wilhelm's study, where they'd negotiated their contract. The room was unlocked, so he went in, helped himself to paper and a quill and pulled up a chair to a table by the window.

As he worked, the faint light of sunrise seeped into the room to color the paper lavender.

"I canna believe that with a wife as fair as yours you'd rather be composing letters at first light than lying in bed beside her." Wilhelm stood in the doorway, smirking.

The laird strode in, fully dressed in his armor shirt and burgundy plaid, the metalwork on his belt polished to perfection, every hair on his head strictly in its place.

"I could say the same for you," Darcy said with a good-natured smirk.

Wilhelm chuckled. "Ah, lad, leisurely mornings of tupping are for younger men without such responsibilities as I have. I am laird of Dornoch. What's your excuse?"

"I must go to Inverness," He paused in his writing to give Wilhelm his full attention. "But I canna take Malina. With Steafan's men about, 'tis too dangerous for her, and I can ride faster alone. Will ye watch over her while I make my errand? When I return, I shall be your man for as long as ye need me and in whatever capacity ye decree."

"I thought ye wished to return to Ackergill. I thought ye'd be sending me a quarter share of your mill's take."

"I do wish to return. But I dinna think I ever shall. Things have changed, and it all hinges on Inverness."

Wilhelm raised an interested eyebrow, so he elaborated. "If I fail to find a way to return Malina to her time, I will have to keep searching. I canna do that from Ackergill and keep it secret from Steafan. But nor can I return if I have success in Inverness. Ackergill wouldna be the same for me. No' without her." He shook his head, shocked at his own forthrightness with a man he'd only recently met.

Clearing his throat, he turned the conversation to business. "Either way, I shall nay be going back to Ackergill. I shall be your man as ye wanted. There will be no need for our contract. Instead of having a quarter of my worth, ye shall have all of me. I shall swear my fealty and wear the Murray plaid."

Without Malina and without purpose, he feared he'd waste away. But if he indentured himself to Wilhelm, he would at least feel obligated to carry on.

He quickly finished and signed the letter he'd written to Malina. He handed it to Wilhelm. "Will ye see that my wife gets this when she rises? I intend to leave immediately."

Wilhelm took the letter and appraised him with shrewd eyes. "You think ye can find her box maker?"

"I hope so."

Wilhelm grunted. "Well, come on, then, lad. Let's break your fast before ye leave."

§

"WHAT DO YOU mean, he's gone?" Melanie's shriek echoed off the windows of the sunny breakfast room.

Wilhelm held out a folded piece of paper like a shield against her panic. "He left ye this. Dinna fear, lass. 'Tis only an errand. He doesna plan to be gone more than a half-week at most."

"Half a week? I want to talk to him now!" She snatched the paper from Wilhelm and opened it, scowling at Darcy's slanting signature. The last time she'd seen it was when he'd signed their marriage contract in Steafan's office.

Her eyes raced over her husband's words, her vision blurring as she read that he'd gone to Inverness without her to look for *your Mr. MacLeod*. He still wanted to send her home. Even after all they'd shared last night. And he hadn't even had the decency to say goodbye.

She thought they'd forged an incredible bond last night. She'd fallen so deeply in love with him that she'd firmly decided she wouldn't try to get home to Charleston. While Darcy diligently brought her to peak after peak of pleasure, her heart had rejoiced and wept at the same time—rejoiced for the treasure she'd found in Darcy and wept for the loss of all she loved back home. She'd grieved for her parents even as she'd clung to her husband and kissed him and made love to him every way short of intercourse.

For better or for worse, she was going to stay with him and be his wife and—gulp—have her baby in 1517.

She'd planned to tell him tonight and to reveal that he could, in fact, make love to a woman, that he wasn't some freak of nature that needed to be ashamed of his large body. But he'd taken off before she'd had the chance. He'd snuck out while she slept, intending to send her away forever.

Her heart broke. She turned her back on Wilhelm, not wanting a witness to her tears.

"Fetch the Lady Constance," he said quietly to a maid. "There, there, lass," he said with an awkward pat of her shoulder. "He is a man of his word. Ye'll be kenning that, I'm sure. He doesna see he has a choice but to help ye find your own time again, not when he vowed he would do such."

"I know," she said past a tight throat. "He's a stubborn idiot." Turning to meet Wilhelm's sympathetic eyes, she sniffed. "I don't suppose you'd let me go after him."

He smiled, but showed his teeth in warning. "Nay, lass. Ye'll no' be leaving. I have charge over you, and I intend to keep you safe while your husband is away."

She huffed, embracing her outrage rather than think about how alone she suddenly felt.

"Well, what am I going to do with myself while he's gone? Sit around and file my nails and be barefoot and pregnant?"

"Oh, no," Constance said, breezing into the breakfast room.

Wilhelm wasted no time extricating himself from the critical, emotional-female situation, ducking out of the room.

Constance helped herself to the breakfast buffet. "I need help in my garden. And we need to find you a decent wardrobe. And there's a ton you need to learn if you're going to be hanging around in this century."

"But I won't be," she protested, fighting the urge to start crying again—damn her hormones. "Not if Darcy has his way." When did the idea of getting home to Charleston and the twenty-first century become a bad thing?

Constance threw a conspiratorial smile over her shoulder as she poured some tea and prepared a plate of bread, raisins, and cheese. "When a man acts rashly, say for example, galloping off at the crack of dawn on some cockamamie errand without so much as a goodbye, it doesn't necessarily mean he knows what he's doing. In fact," she added, falling into an overstuffed chair and popping a raisin in her mouth, "it often means he's running from something."

"Yeah, from me," she huffed. She felt too upset to eat, but her little one had other plans.

She couldn't stop herself from grabbing half a loaf of bread from the sideboard and tearing off a hefty bite. It was so good. Starchy and grainy and utterly healthy-tasting. She helped herself to the brie, spreading a generous glob over the bread before devouring more.

While she ate with Constance, she couldn't help thinking about last night. Poor Darcy had never been with a woman before, and suddenly she was pawing him, throwing herself at him, demanding his compliance as she had her wicked way with him.

He'd shown absolutely no sign of distress—if he had, she would have backed off. But passion could mask deeper feelings. Maybe deep down, he'd been battling regrets, and when morning came and the passion had worn off, those regrets had shone as starkly as the sun.

He'd told her he hadn't intended to remain married for long. He hadn't intended to become intimate with her. Maybe now that he'd let her seduce him, he was more determined than ever to get her back to her time, before she could sink her claws into him any deeper. To Darcy, she must seem like a needy succubus of a woman, desperate for male attention—a wanton, he'd called her. Remembering the bite in the word as he'd spat it at her in the barn, she winced.

He probably thought she was trying to seduce him into taking care of her and her baby, that she was using him.

No wonder he was in a hurry to ditch her. Her eyes burned with fresh tears.

Constance rolled her eyes as she set down her plate. "Honestly, dear, if you can't tell that man is completely head over heels for you, you need your eyes checked. He's not running from you. More likely, he's afraid of what you make him feel. As a general rule, men don't like to be out of control. That's especially true for our rugged Highlanders. They are men of action."

Constance sipped her tea. "Hunt it, terrify it, dominate it, kill it. And if it can't be hunted, terrified, dominated, or killed, than it's best to leave it alone."

"Wilhelm didn't leave you alone," she said, more than a little jealous of the woman for being happily married while her husband was miles away searching for a way to get rid of her.

"No, he most certainly didn't. But he did try to terrify me. And when that didn't work, he tried his hand at dominating me." The defiant gleam in her eye spoke to the effectiveness of those attempts. "It wasn't until the poor man realized he could dominate me through tenderness and that when a woman loves a man, she is innately terrified of losing him, that he finally began to trust what we had."

"You're saying Darcy's just trying to make sense of what he feels for me, and he's doing it by immersing himself in action. But what if he actually finds a way to return me to my time?"

"He might find your box maker. He might even learn the

secret to returning you to your time. The question is, what will he do with the information?" Constance leaned forward, turning the full power of her shrewd gaze on her. "Perhaps a better question is, if he arrives at a decision you don't like, will you roll over and accept it, or will you fight for what you really want?"

Chapter 16

DARCY GLARED AT the stenciled sign for MacLeod's Fine Furniture. He'd half hoped to nay find any hint of Malina's box maker. She would have been distraught, but he would have comforted her with kisses and the touches that brought her so much pleasure. He'd hold her through her grieving and stroke her hair and tell her how sorry he was. But inside, he'd be joyful at the prospect of keeping her with him as they searched for another way to return her to her home.

But the first bloody man he'd asked once he'd arrived in Inverness had kent of MacLeod and directed him to the cobbled close in which he currently stood. Beyond the wide archway he'd ridden Rand under minutes ago, the street stunk of refuse and garbage as the streets in larger towns tended to, but once in the sunny courtyard, away from the rattling pony carts and crippled beggars, he smelled only the clean straw and animal scent of the stable where he'd stored Rand for the day, and fresh-cut timber.

While he glowered at the stone and mortar furniture shop, a patron pushed out the front door, tucking his purse in his sporran. The man started when he noticed Darcy's height, but he quickly recovered and gave a cordial nod before continuing on his way.

He wouldn't be doing himself any favors by blocking the entrance to MacLeod's shop all day. Blowing out a resigned breath, he pulled open the door and went inside.

The centerpiece of the shop was a grand dining table the likes of which Steafan had up at Ackergill Keep. It had ten matching chairs, each with intricately worked arms and legs. Darcy didn't much care for finery, but even he could tell the set was well made and expensive. A dozen or so patrons ran their hands over the table and chairs as well as the other wares lining the walls, a chest of drawers, two armchairs with matching footstools, smaller chests and tables, and slabs of stained wood that might serve as mantles for fireplaces in well-to-do homes. At the back of the shop was a shelf covered with smaller items, candlesticks, carved children's trinkets, shaving kits, and—he gulped—boxes.

A white-haired man, far along in age but agile and strong of build, gestured as he spoke with a smartly dressed man and woman eyeing a chest of drawers.

Darcy moved close to listen, pretending to study a circular table with spindly legs.

"Och, 'tis a fine piece," the white-haired man was saying. "Worked it last winter. Notice the inlaid foils of cherry wood about the edge. 'Tis a technique you'll nay find used elsewhere in Scotia."

After bending their heads together for a conference, the man and woman agreed to the high price, and the white-haired man led them to a counter where they made arrangements for payment and delivery of the item. At a sharp call from the white-haired man, another white-haired man hurried to the counter from a door tucked away behind the shelf at the rear of the shop. He moved with such haste that Darcy missed the man's face and saw only his back. It was a strong and straight back, too fit to match the hair atop the man's head. He couldn't look away, struck by the contrast between the man's auld hair and youthful movements.

The new man bobbed his head earnestly at the various commands issued by the first. "Yes, Mr. MacLeod," he said in the squeaky voice of a lad not quite settled into manhood. He turned and rushed back to the hidden door, and Darcy saw his face. He had to stifle a startled intake of breath at the sight of pink eyes and skin whiter than a cloud.

'Twas no second auld man, but a young man with the coloring of a pail of milk.

The young man kept his eyes downcast as he rushed back to the hidden door. Except for his face and neck, he kept the rest of his skin covered. He even wore trews in place of a plaid so no skin on his legs showed. With gloved hands, the lad pushed through the door and disappeared into what must be MacLeod's workroom. He must be MacLeod's apprentice.

Returning his attention to MacLeod, Darcy watched the finely dressed couple exit to the courtyard. Before he could step in and meet the furniture maker, a plump woman in a peacock-blue dress too fine for day wear in his opinion tugged on the man's elbow. "A moment of your time, sir," she said, dragging him away with a string of questions about an upholstered armchair near the front of the shop.

He sighed. It might take some time to meet the man. Mayhap he should return at the close of business. In the meantime, he perused the items on the shelf, eyeing the boxes in particular.

They didn't look unlike Malina's box, but none were quite the same as hers, either. Some were rosewood, some maple, some cherry. Most had inlaid bits of different colored wood or carvings in lovely patterns, but none had patterns done in metal of any kind.

He itched to peek at their bottoms to inspect the dates, but he couldn't quite bring himself to touch them, afraid of what magicks they might possess.

But that was daft, wasn't it? Surely MacLeod kent better than to keep nefarious objects that could send people hurtling through time just lying about his shop for anyone to touch.

Reaching out, he stroked a finger over a box about the size of Malina's. When it didn't bite him or do aught else suspicious, he lifted it from the shelf to inspect it.

It was lighter than Malina's box. A sturdy brass latch kept it shut. He worked it with a nudge of his finger and peered inside. The thing was lined with velvet. He closed it and turned it over. The date read 1517. The dark brown ink beneath the stain looked familiar, but the script that read *MacLeod* and listed Inverness as the place of manufacture was larger and more slanted, written in a different hand.

He put the box back and looked at the others, finding the writing and the date the same on them all, with the exception of a few 1516's and one 1514. They were just ordinary boxes designed for keeping ladies' jewelry or precious trinkets.

"Is it a gift ye're looking for, for your wife, mayhap?"

He turned to find MacLeod at his side and realized with a flop of his stomach he had no idea what to say to the man. He couldn't very well blurt out the question foremost in his mind: Do ye make magic boxes? At least, it wouldn't be wise to do so where the other patrons might hear him.

"I was hoping to have a word with ye," he settled on. "Mayhap after ye close for the day. At the pub down the way?"

MacLeod narrowed his eyes. "I dinna imbibe in spirits," he said in a clipped tone. He passed his gaze over Darcy's dull brown plaid, bare arms, and scuffed boots. Compared to the other patrons, he was woefully underdressed, but he hadn't felt such until MacLeod looked at him that way. "If you are nay here to browse my wares or purchase somat, I'll be asking you to leave. I am too busy for idle chit chat."

The man turned to stalk away. To stop him, Darcy blurted, "Have ye ever put magic into one of your wares?"

MacLeod stopped mid-stride. His shoulders went tight. He slowly turned. His voice low so no one else could hear, he said, "I'll nay have men speaking of heresy in my shop. Be gone with you and your devil-talk, and let me see you no more."

The man hurried away to serve another patron, casting Darcy

sharp looks until he made his obedient way out into the courtyard. As he closed the door behind him, he wiped a hand over the back of his neck and cursed himself. If he couldn't get MacLeod to talk with him, how would he find a way to help Malina?

"Sir?" A quiet voice pulled his head around. Pink eyes peered around the corner of the stone building. "A moment, sir?" the young man said.

Darcy followed him into a shadowed alley that stank of stagnant water. What could the lad possibly want with him? The alley opened into a smaller courtyard where stacks of fresh-cut beams, sawdust, and wood stain scented the air.

The workroom behind MacLeod's shop opened to the outdoors with a door as big as the side of a barn propped in a horizontal position with poles. Three men in the workroom sawed and hammered and bantered and ignored him as he followed the white-haired lad into a narrow, leaning outbuilding.

Dust motes floated above a bowed workbench in the meager light from a single window. Mismatched scraps of materials filled the cramped space.

The lad crouched at the workbench and pulled out a crate covered with a ratty cloth. He hugged it to his chest as he stood up.

Darcy got an unhurried look at the lad as his gaze darted everywhere but Darcy's face. He wasn't tall, but he had good, strong shoulders and a broad chest that would serve him well as apprentice to a wood-worker. But he appeared painfully shy.

Darcy waited for him to speak, afraid that if he spoke first, he might cause the lad to faint.

"P-pardon me, sir," the lad said at last, "but I overheard ye asking Mr. MacLeod about magic, and—" His gaze cut to the door, which Darcy had left cracked open. At hearing the word *magic*, Darcy yanked the door shut, kenning a stray ear could spell danger for them both.

“Well, I suppose I was wondering what ye might have meant by it,” the lad went on. Those strange eyes turned up to him, and they were full of hope. “Have ye seen magic, sir? Do ye ken how it works? How to…control it?”

“No. I havena seen it. But I ken someone who has. ’Twas magic in a box, a box not unlike the ones your Mr. MacLeod sells at the back of his shop.” Taking a chance, he added, “In fact, ’twas a box with the very name of your mentor on the bottom.”

The lad’s eyes went wide. He hugged the crate so tight that the wood creaked. He shook his head, white hair flopping. “Surely not, sir. I dinna mean to argue, but Mr. MacLeod has no tolerance for aught deemed improper by the church.”

“I saw the inscription with my own eyes. MacLeod. Inverness. ’Twas a box with no clasp and with patterns on the lid in white metal.” He kept the date to himself, not willing to give away too much before he understood the lad’s purpose.

The lad’s expression didn’t change. If he’d ever seen such a box, he gave no indication of it.

Darcy tried not to be too disappointed and reminded himself the box wouldn’t be made for another twenty-five years.

“You’re certain it was magic?” the lad asked. “What—” He looked down and scuffed his toe in the dirt. “If you dinna mind me asking, sir, what did the box…do?” He whispered the last word.

“It brought a fair lass through time. From far in the future.” He watched closely for a sign of recognition.

If the lad could have grown any paler, he might have done so then. “The future,” he whispered as if it were the answer to a question that had long plagued him. He stared at Darcy in an apparent state of shock before spinning to put his crate on the workbench.

Making a racket, he pulled the cloth off and unpacked an armload of tools, horseshoes, and haphazard bits of metal. He paused with his gloved hands clutching a second cloth, one much cleaner and finer than the one that had been on top. The crate was like a cake with layers.

No one would look twice at the junk making up the top layer, which served as a disguise for the second layer.

He leaned over the lad's shoulder, anxious to see what the second cloth hid.

The lad pulled it away to reveal a mass of objects the likes of which Darcy had never seen before. There was a shiny object the size of a man's palm with wee decorations—no, not decorations, but raised bumps declaring the letters of the alphabet, numbers, and other symbols.

A similarly shaped flat object looked like a rectangular stone, so black and glossy he could see his reflection in it like an expensive mirror. There was a large sheet of parchment somehow made stiff. Across the top, it read, *Rise and Shine Bed & Breakfast, Inverness, in business since 1928.* Below that were lists of foods, some he kent well, like blood pudding, kippers, eggs, and smoked eel, but many of the foods sounded foreign to him. Pancakes? Waffles? Hash browns? A heavy, porcelain cup with a handle had bold black letters across it saying, *SCOTS DO IT WITH A BURR.* Do what? And why would someone paint such large letters across a perfectly good cup? Several spoons jutted from the pile and several spoon-like objects that had tines like a pitchfork, rather than a broad surface for scooping. Amidst the strange trinkets, he recognized a circular face that reminded him of the big pendulum clock in Steafan's office, but this clock was set into a strip of leather as if it were meant to be worn on a man's wrist.

His fingers twitched, wanting to explore the contents of the crate, but his neck prickled with warning.

"Some of them would glow when ye touched them just right," the lad said. "But the glowing always stopped after a few days.

Except this one," he said, lifting out the wee clock. He touched it with his gloved finger and thumb on each side of the face, and the thing gave off an unearthly green light.

Darcy jumped back. "Christ," he breathed. 'Twas surely magic making that light. 'Twas likely magic that crafted such curious objects…or brought them here from a future time. Magic the likes of which might help Malina.

He bent closer, his initial fear forgotten as hope for his wife rose to the fore. The lad beamed at his interest as he released his hold on the clock and the light went out. "I've had this one for nigh on six months, and it still does that when I touch it so. And I havena had to wind it once, yet it still keeps the time." His look of pleasure at revealing his secret to a stranger made Darcy worrit for him. Did he not realize what ill fate might befall him if he showed his collection to the wrong person, or if anyone stumbled across it?

"Put it away. Put it all away. In fact, you should bury it. What are ye thinking, keeping such things where anyone might find them?"

The lad's eyes dimmed. His shoulders fell forward as he pulled the cloth over the strange items and began piling the tools back in. Working with his back to him, he muttered, "'Tis only me that uses the shed, and I keep it locked."

He'd kept Malina's box locked away, but that hadn't stopped Steafan from finding it.

Though he hardly kent the lad, he couldn't help the urgency that sharpened his tone when he countered, "Any fool kens locks can be broken. Are ye mad to trust this pitiful shed to keep safe that which might condemn you?" A twitch of the lad's shoulders, like a dog expecting a beating, made his scolding fizzle out. Gentler, he said, "You may trust my authority on this. Ye dinna want anyone to find these objects."

The lad crouched down and scraped the crate back into its

hiding place. "I ken as much," he said with more than a trace of wounded offense. Still low to the dirt floor, he turned his fair head just enough to show his profile. Though old enough to shave, he still carried a child's roundness in his cheeks. He would be about sixteen, an age at which a lad thought he was a man and hoped to be treated as such by other men. "Ye willna tell Mr. MacLeod, will you?"

Sympathy doused him. He didn't understand what manner of burden bent the lad's sturdy back with shame, but he'd borne his own burdens long enough to ken only understanding and acceptance would make that back straight and proud. "What's your name?"

Eyes that looked pale lavender in the dim light turned up to meet his gaze. "Timothy, sir. Though most call me Milky." He grimaced with the nickname.

"I shall call you Timothy. And you may call me Darcy. And you may be assured I willna be speaking to your Mr. MacLeod about that crate or aught else. The man doesna seem to care for my company."

Timothy's face relaxed. "Darcy. A French name, no?"

"My mother fancied French fashion," he said, offering somat of himself to befriend the lad. "Arcy is a province there, or so I've heard."

"Mr. MacLeod doesna care for fashion of any sort. But he studies woodworking methods from all over. Dinna think ill of him, please, sir—Darcy. He is firm in the teachings of the church, but that makes him charitable as well. If it werena for him and his wife taking me from the orphanage in Edinburgh, I'd surely be begging on the mile with the lame lads." A frown furrowed Timothy's white-fringed brow. "But if he kent the odd things that happen around me, he would send me away for being wicked."

"Happen around you?" He tried not to sound overly eager. He also tried not to dwell on the inevitable loneliness and heartache that awaited him once he found what he was after. “You refer to these objects? How did ye come by them?”

“’Tis my blood that does it.” Timothy’s eyes searched his face.

Darcy worked to keep his features free from condemnation or disbelief.

He must have succeeded, because the lad went on. “Ever since I was a wee ane in the orphanage, when I’d scrape my leg on a stray nail or get a bloody nose from one of the bigger lads, odd things would appear at my feet. At first ’twas toys and trinkets that amused me, but as I counted the years, the objects grew more complex and less obvious as to their function. And though I dinna like to say such things, I suspect the objects may be made by the fair folk, for I ken of no substance nor craftsman, at least nay in Scotia, that can create such things.”

“I dinna ken about fair folk, but I ken where such things may have come from.” At least, he’d heard descriptions of similar objects, wondrous objects made of materials called “plastic” and “batteries,” objects that could fit in a man’s hand and bring the world to him, and send him out to the world in return. He hardly understood why a man would need the world in his hand or why he would want to send part of himself away into the air, but Malina seemed to miss such “conveniences.”

The fine hairs on the back of his neck rose with the suspicion that some of these objects, mayhap all of them, had come from Malina’s time. But he had more questions than answers, such as if Timothy’s blood could bring these objects here, could it also send them back? Were aught from Malina’s America or were some from Scotia as the stiff parchment and the cup indicated?

Could Timothy access a specific time and place with his magic? He suspected not, since it seemed the lad was looking to him for help.

Timothy raised his eyebrows in desperate curiosity, but

before Darcy could say more, a lady's high-pitched scream grated through the cracks in the shed.

He threw open the door and charged toward the main courtyard, Timothy close behind.

What met them when they plunged from the alley was a sight so outlandish, he didn't ken whether to jump into the fray to assist the screaming woman or to laugh. 'Twas the same overdressed patron he had seen in MacLeod's shop, only when she'd been inquiring about the armchair, she'd not had a shrieking monkey in red trews jumping upon her head.

The woman's hat lay trampled on the cobbles like a wounded game bird, and great chunks of her graying hair had come loose from her pins. As she flung her arms about her head in an attempt to rid herself of her meddlesome cargo, she called to mind a twirling mop. Her violet-faced husband bounced from foot to foot, clutching his coin purse as though he might use it as a weapon, should he summon the courage to come to his wife's aid.

A tinkers' cart painted a garish shade of pink burst through the archway into courtyard, followed by a crowd of gawkers apparently drawn by the woman's screams. Within seconds, the close was packed to overflowing until it seemed the white carthorses with feather plumes on their bridles were the only two souls in Inverness not gawking at the debacle.

A bow-legged dwarf jumped from the rider's bench and began leaping around the woman in his attempts to call the monkey down. The driver, a slender man in a lacy shirt and high-waisted breeches, drew the horses to a halt and glided from the bench. His embroidered boots with their stacked heels that added to his already substantial height landed lithely on the ground.

Unconcerned with the spectacle, the man sent his onyx gaze searching the crowd as though for a particular acquaintance.

Deciding someone other than the shortest man in the vicinity should help the poor woman, Darcy elbowed through the crowd. He shot an arm out to scoop the gleeful creature off the woman's head. Unfortunately, the woman's husband must have assumed he meant her harm, because the change purse, which was lamentably heavy despite his wife's effort to empty it in MacLeod's, slammed into his eye, causing him to stumble back.

Stars burst in his vision, and not the pleasant kind Malina had made him see the night before. They cleared in time for him to see the man come at him with an odd sort of cane that looked to be wearing a frilly gown. The man attempted to beat him with it, but his new friend intervened.

Timothy grabbed the end of the cane while the man had it reared back and said, "Here now, sir. The big man's only trying to help your lady."

The patron wheeled about, and his eyes grew round with a crazed sort of fear when he looked on Timothy. "Accursed tinks, all of you! A giant, a dwarf, a Rom, and a pale man! Devils you are! You'll be leaving my wife alone!" He ripped the cane from the lad's gloved hands, and the fabric of the cane's gown spread between fingers of wood until the thing became round like a wagon wheel with the stalk of the cane acting like a spoke.

Darcy hardly had time to contemplate what manner of weapon the odd thing was before the man swung it at Timothy's face. The pointed tip sliced across the lad's cheek, leaving behind a path of torn flesh that welled with blood.

No sooner had stark red appeared in the snow of Timothy's cheek than a great rumbling cut the air. The ground quaked, and between one breath and the next, a boulder of shiny black steel and glass appeared in the street.

Chapter 17

THE RUMBLING WAS like nothing Darcy had heard before. It sounded like a boar about to charge—if the beast didn't need to take a breath. On and on it went, steady and deep as night but with a subtle brightness to it that called to mind the far-away clang of a smith's hammer. The sound spoke to his gut, and he grinned, realizing what the large object was.

'Twas an "automobile," or a "car" for short. Malina had talked at length about them, especially when the soreness in her bottom and legs from riding Rand all day had become enough to turn her sweet spirit a mite contrary.

Of all the wonders his wife had told him of, cars were the one thing he thought he'd have a use for. He'd even imagined himself in the driver's seat of one, racing down one of the evenly laid roads she'd told him of, with the wind whipping his hair, not stopping or even slowing for a hundred leagues and only then so he could fill the thing's belly with "gas." As fast as Rand was, Malina claimed a car could go even faster, and ever since she'd said so, he'd longed to see the proof of it for himself.

But this was no fantasy. This was nay Malina's land 500 years hence. 'Twas an Inverness that wouldn't ken what to make of such a thing. He wouldn't ken what to make of it either, had he not been prepared by Timothy's crate.

The lad's blood had done this. And judging by the stricken horror on the lad's face as he stared at the car, he had neither intended it nor had aught control over it.

He considered all this in the space of a single heartbeat, and that was all the time he had for the luxury of thought, because the car hadn't just appeared and had done with it. The bloody thing was moving.

Though its pace was slow and its black wheels soundless on the cobblestones beneath the growl of the "engine," it rolled steadily forward. Toward MacLeod's shop. And its door was flung wide to reveal an interior of dark leather, shiny gears, and the ominous lack of a driver.

The crowd went utterly still in a moment of collective shock. Then it erupted in screams that swallowed the noise of the car. Above the racket, the monkey shrieked and hopped from the head of the woman to the shoulder of the slender man. That onyx gaze twinkled with amusement as it fell upon Timothy.

Men, women, and children scattered as though the Devil itself had appeared in their midst, but the people weren't his top priority. That distinction was reserved for MacLeod as he emerged from his shop to put himself directly in the path of the car.

When Timothy caught sight of his master, dread drew his face taut. He clapped a gloved hand over his cheek and took off running from the close. He blended with the scattering crowd, and Darcy lost sight of him.

"Timothy!" he called, worrit for the lad, but more worrit for MacLeod, whose hand suddenly clutched the shirt over his chest when he caught sight of the car. The man collapsed where he stood.

Darcy was torn. Attempt to drag the auld man from the path of the car, or stop the car itself? Before he could decide, the slender man glided to MacLeod, lifted him in his arms in a startling display of strength, and dashed out of the way.

That left him to deal with the car. Without a moment to lose lest MacLeod's livelihood go the way of his auld heart, he leapt through the open door, arranged himself in the tight quarters of the driver's seat, and thrust both feet against the pedals he kent would be on the floor.

He recalled one would make the car go and the other would make it stop, but there wasn't time to test them each.

The engine's rumbling increased to an alarming roar, but the car lurched to a stop mere inches from the open shutters of MacLeod's shop.

He didn't relax, though. He dared not move his feet until he'd found a way to stop the engine. Combing his memory for the details Malina had shared about how cars were driven, he scanned the confusing dials and controls. His wife had told him all about how one must "shift gears" with a stick and use the gas and brake pedals, but he couldn't remember her telling him how to stop and start a car.

"What are you waiting for, *mon ami*? Drive us out of here!"

He whipped his head around to see the slender man climbing into the seat beside him and slamming the door shut. Neither MacLeod nor the monkey was with him.

Deep in concentration over his dilemma with the car, he hadn't noticed when exactly the screams of the crowd had turned to angry shouts, but in the mirror before him that reflected the courtyard, he saw the people of Inverness topple the tinkers' cart and set fire to it. The horses reared as the tack broke around them from the blows of axes. More townsfolk were striding toward the car, shaking their fists and raising sundry weapons. Sharp thuds echoed through the car. The crowd was throwing rocks.

"Now would be a good time to depart," the slender man urged.

"I dinna ken how!" He had to shout over the furious growling of the engine and the even more furious chorus of "Burn them in their devil's cart!"

The car began to rock as the crowd shook it. Torches came

into view.

"Moving us backwards would be a good start!"

He didn't spare his gaze for the roll of eyes the obvious statement warranted. Instead, he located the gear stick Malina had mentioned. It jutted up by his knee and had at its base a nonsensical series of letters and numbers that didn't spell any word he'd ever heard of. One letter stood out to him, and he worked the stick in line with it. He hoped it stood for what he thought it did: *Retreat.*

Taking an even chance, he lifted his left foot just a fraction. The wheels screamed against the cobblestones. Black smoke choked the crowd. The car shot backward, knocking people out of its way.

He didn't relish causing injury, but his life was being threatened, and he didn't appreciate that. If it was a choice between him or his enemy, no matter how misinformed his enemy might be, he'd choose himself every time. 'Twas the Keith way. 'Twas a warrior's way.

Besides, it was all he could do to keep the car from crashing into the flaming tinkers' cart. Yanking the wheel to one side and then the other, he steered the car around the cart and the bulk of the mob and turned it to face the archway into the close. He stomped on the left pedal at the same time he shoved the stick into the position marked with the numeral "1," all the while keeping the right pedal pressed full down.

More screeching and smoking came from the wheels, and the car lurched forward onto the street. He turned the steering wheel to aim the car out of town, but the thing hardly went fast enough to outrun the mob.

A rock hit the rear window, and a lad wielding a spade came up alongside them, arms and legs pumping. He jabbed the spade at the window, and Darcy held his breath until he was certain the glass would hold.

"Come on, ye growling beasty," he urged amidst the thuds of more rocks and more blows from the spade. He'd thought a car would go much faster than this. Then he remembered that amidst the nonsensical letters, there was also a numeral *2*. He moved the stick there, and the car went marginally faster while its mad growling grew a mite quieter, but the feel of the machine was discordant, as though it were fighting him.

Wishing for a *3* or, better yet, a *4*, he did the only he thing he could think of to hasten their flight. He moved the stick to the next position, marked with a *D*. The car's growling dropped to a gentle hum, and it glided forward with a blessed burst of speed. His veins thrummed with excitement as the mob grew smaller and smaller in the mirror.

He would have sped them all the way out of Inverness if he hadn't spotted Timothy running for all his worth down the main road.

He stomped his foot down on the left pedal, bringing the car to a screeching halt and bringing his nose to within an inch of the glass in front of him.

His passenger threw up both arms to brace himself, and even that maneuver he managed to make graceful. The man threw his door open. "Come aboard, *mon ami*! Quickly!"

Obeying despite his scairt eyes, Timothy climbed into the rear seat.

The car sounded agreeable, so he didn't fash about the stick. He thought mayhap the *D* meant *drive*. Focusing his attention on operating the pedals smoothly, he let off the left and gently pressed the right. The car went quietly and powerfully forward. He grinned broadly. "I think I ken the way of it now. Hold on."

And off they went.

§

'TWAS ALMOST A shame no one chased them out of Inverness. Darcy would have liked to test the car against a horse. At least he would have liked a test on the even roads in town. When the smooth, tended roads changed to a wheel-rutted cart path at the town's outskirts, he revised his thinking on the matter. A horse would have the clear advantage on the terrain they currently bounced over with a spine-jarring racket.

Keeping their speed low lest the car rattle to pieces, he followed the slender man's instructions and steered onto a path through a field. He wondered vaguely how he was going to get back to the stables to retrieve Rand, especially since that man had called him a giant and accused him of association with the now unwelcome tinkers.

He didn't mind the association. It might actually protect him from Steafan's men, as any news of an unusually tall man in Inverness would be followed with talk of the tinker caravan he kept company with. He'd be dismissed as a travelling anomaly and not the fugitive nephew of a northern laird. But it took no more than a glance in the mirror at Timothy's slack face to ken that the lad saw no such benefit to his association with the tinkers. He must be fashing over losing his home and position with MacLeod.

"I dinna think your master saw what happened," he told the lad. "And even if he did, he wouldna ken to blame such a thing on you." He didn't say as much, but he figured MacLeod would save all his blame for the man beside him. Tinkers were typically welcomed as travelling performers and merchants, but this particular tinker had a way about him that made a person think of magic. Mayhap 'twas the mischievous twinkle in his eyes or his flamboyant dress better suited to a French courtier than a poor traveler. Whatever the reason, he was sure Timothy would be welcomed back. So long as MacLeod survived to do the welcoming.

"What happened to the auld man?" he asked the slender man.

"A doctor took him from me," he replied in an exaggerated French accent.

Timothy's face appeared between the two front seats. "Why did he need a doctor?"

"Ye didna see?"

"See what? What happened?"

"His heart seemed not quite up to the level of excitement in the street," he said delicately, sharing a sideways glance with the tinker. Odd though it was, despite their brief acquaintance and kenning the man wasn't half as French as he pretended, Darcy trusted him, liked him even.

"What are ye saying?" Timothy squeaked. "Is he dead?"

"He was very much alive when last I saw him, *mon ami*. I am certain all will be well."

Darcy doubted that, but he appreciated the slender man's optimism. He hoped it would put the lad more at ease.

"This is Timothy," he said, rounding a copse of scraggy Hawthorns overrun by brush. Having a feel for the car by now, he moved the stick to the *1* and inched through a puddle of unknown depth across the path. "I'm Darcy Keith of Ackergill and only a visitor to Inverness," he said as he shifted back to *D*.

Despite Steafan's men scouring the country for him, he didn't think twice about telling his name to the slender man. *Trustworthy* wasn't exactly the word that came to mind, but *loyal* seemed to suit him. He couldn't explain how he kent such a thing beyond crediting his warrior's instincts, but ken it he did: the moment the slender man had slipped into the car, he'd declared himself an ally. If Darcy was going to find a way to return Malina to her home, he had a neck-prickling feeling 'twould take both this man's help and that of the scairt lad behind him.

"Bastien Gravois, at your service, Monsieur Keith." He pronounced his name in the French way, *Bas-tay-on Grahv-wah*, as he made a grand gesture with his hand. “And what is your surname, Master Timothy?” he asked, turning in his seat.

“I have none, sir. But Mr. MacLeod permits me the use of his when necessary.”

Gravois pushed out his lower lip in polite surprise, then motioned ahead toward a creek that separated the field from a rise of rocky hills. “Our camp is just over that bridge.”

He looked in the direction the man pointed, but saw no signs of a camp. In fact, from this vantage, the bridge looked precariously narrow and poorly maintained. When he drew the car up close, it looked even worse. He wouldn’t have trusted the crumbling stone and wood structure to support a pony and dogcart, never mind a piece of machinery that likely weighed four times as much. “How did ye get your cart over this?” he asked, coming to a stop at the foot of the bridge.

“It is stronger than it looks,” Gravois said.

Darcy gave him a doubtful look, which earned him a purring chuckle.

“Have no fear, *mon ami*. Things are not always what they seem.”

He suspected the statement applied to the man beside him as much as to the bridge.

“Might there be a bit of the magician in you, Gravois?” He hoped so, lest his trip to Inverness be for naught.

The man’s reply was a smile caught between mischief and mystery. “Go on,” he said. “There is no time to lose. Once we are across, we will be safe from pursuit.”

Darcy shrugged and eased the car forward, figuring it wasn’t his, so if it fell into the creek, it would cost him naught but a wet pair of boots. The moment the wheels touched the bridge, his vision blurred and then cleared to reveal a startlingly different sight.

The bridge transformed from a near ruin to a solid affair in good repair. Across the bridge, the grass became greener and stretched farther before the rocky hills jutted up, creating a lush sanctuary for four colorfully painted tinkers carts arranged in a half-circle. Strung between several trees that hadn't existed a moment ago were ropes tethering eight fine horses, two of them of the draft variety.

Several people milled about the camp. Some were arranging wood for a fire. Others were skinning a small boar. Others groomed the horses and shined the tack. Still others lounged against rocks with their bare feet cooling in the creek. Not a single one of them had been spared from some physical malady or unfortunate distinction. There was a hunchback, a man whose face and hands were covered in thick hair, a dark-skinned woman with thousands of exotic plaits hanging past her shoulders, a true giant that must have been nearly eight feet tall, an old woman with a curved back and gnarled hands, a tattooed man with disks in his ears, a woman from the east with slanted eyes and rings about her neck, a female dwarf with pale hair and wooden shoes, a lad with a tail protruding from his trews, and, as Darcy stopped the car beside a bright yellow cart, he was stunned to see the dwarf from Inverness trot across the bridge atop Rand. Atop the dwarf's head rode the wee monkey, proud as a prince to his coronation.

A bit of magic, indeed. Never mind the hidden camp, the dwarf must ken how to fly to be able to mount Rand.

He looked at the smug Gravois. "Ye might be just the man I came to Inverness to see."

§

"ALLOW ME TO test my understanding," Gravois said in his fake French accent as he dabbed away a spot of grease from the corner of his mouth with an embroidered handkerchief. "A magic box brought you a wife and you tried to get it to take her away again. Are you mad? I would be counting my blessings, not throwing them away at the first opportunity." He accentuated his words by tossing his trencher to the ground.

Night had fallen. The fire for cooking the boar stew had long since been banked, but a scatter of torches behind them made a dark slash of Darcy's shadow across the grass on which he sat. Gravois, clearly the leader of the tinker caravan, reclined on an ornate pillow propped against a crate of cooking supplies, and sipped brandy from a tin cup. Darcy had slung his brandy back in a single swallow after listening to the various tales of how Gravois's fellow travelers had come to keep company with him. As it turned out, being chased from villages by angry mobs wasn't uncommon for a man who kept company with misfits, especially misfits who tended to possess magical abilities.

He suspected Gravois sought to add Timothy to his troupe, but he doubted the lad was interested. Though Timothy had partaken of the boar stew made by the hunchback and the eastern woman, he still darted his eyes about like a rabbit in a circle of foxes. Sympathetic though he was toward the lad, 'twas time to focus on keeping his word to his wife.

"'Tis sorry I am I gave my vow so hastily, but the deed is done, and I canna take it back."

He clapped the lad on the shoulder. "Between what Timothy can do with his blood and the magic I've witnessed here this day, surely a man of your talents and decency can devise a way for my wife to return to her time."

The slender man gave him a mildly chiding look in acknowledgement of the flattery, then swirled his cup as he studied Timothy. "I am afraid there is nothing I can do, *mon ami*," he said while his gaze remained locked on the lad. "At least not at present." He finished his spirits and leaned forward, elbows on his knees, hands free to elegantly gesture. "Your bloodmagic is like a child without proper rearing," he said to Timothy. "Without any rearing at all, in fact. That clumsy display in the close proves it." He clucked his tongue in disapproval. "Magic requires discipline as it matures, if it is ever to be useful. I can teach you that discipline, but it will take time, perhaps years, to counteract the damage done by your neglect of your gift." He faced Darcy. "I do not suppose you would be willing to wait years for such help as you request."

He felt the blood drain from his face. He would lose his very heart and soul when he sent Malina away as it was. What would it do to him to send her back after he'd had years to cherish her? It must be soon if at all—But the point became moot when Timothy suddenly sprang to his feet and shrieked, "I willna do it, I tell you! You're all wode! 'Tis a curse, magic. I dinna want it!" He took heaving panicked breaths as his fists curled at his sides. "I must return to Mr. MacLeod. He'll be fashing over my absence, and he doesna need that on top of heart pains. That, or he'll be furious with me. Either way, I need to see him." He turned and strode toward the creek.

Darcy couldn't let him go like that, thinking his only interest in him was for his *bloodmagic*, as Gravois had called it. Tossing a look at the slender man that said they weren't through talking, he jumped up and stalked after the lad. "Wait, Timothy. I'll give ye a ride back."

The lad spun to face him, fear and indignation warring on his face. "I willna get in that thing again." He pointed at the car, which sat cold and dark as the boulder it resembled by the bridge. "Ye're as wode as the tinks. Leave me be."

"I meant on my horse, Rand," he said gently. "Come. Let's get ye back to check on your master."

He made it back to the tinkers' camp 'round midnight. Gravois met him as he crossed the bridge and helped him tend to Rand and Shirebrand, the gray gelding Gravois had let Timothy take back to Inverness and whom Darcy had led back on a tether. Shirebrand was primarily a carthorse, but like Gravois and his fellow tinkers, the horse had varied skills. He was trained as a saddle horse as well as a performing horse. The lad with the tail did handstands and flips on his back for coin, Gravois had told him.

'Twas the tinker way to accept coin for their enterprising entertainments. The old woman told fortunes. The eastern woman sold potions. The giant, the hunchback, and the Negro lass stood in curtained booths where the curious could pay Gravois to peek in at them. The tattooed man performed feats of strength. The dwarf didn't perform, but he was the one to cast an illusion over the camp. Gifted with bending another's perception of reality, he was, and Gravois honored his refusal to be gawked at so long as he made himself useful in other ways. The dwarf woman also didn't perform, but kept Gravois's accounts and managed the troupe.

"Madame Hilda wishes to tell your fortune," Gravois said to him as they finished wiping down the horses. "Go find her in the purple cart. Then you may bed down with the men, if you wish, in the yellow. I have some business I must attend to, but we can talk more in the morning."

The man patted his shoulder. "Though I am afraid there really is nothing I can do for you, *mon ami*. My advice is to go home and enjoy your wife. It is not breaking your word if it simply cannot be done."

He wouldn't accept that. Mayhap Gravois couldn't help him and mayhap Timothy wouldn't, but he would keep seeking a way. 'Twas not just that he'd given his word. 'Twas that Malina missed her modern world. After the excitement of driving the car, he understood a little better the magnitude of convenience she was accustomed to. Her world was truly wondrous. No wonder she wanted to return so desperately. He wouldn't rest until he'd sent her back to where she longed to be.

Subdued, he said, "I have already seen my fortune, and it is lovely and transient as a rainbow. But I thank you for your time. I'll compensate Ferdinand for my meal." He nodded toward where the dwarf sat on a moonlit log smoking a pipe with the hunchback.

"You insult me, *mon ami*. You saved my life today. The very least I can do is see you fed before your journey home. I hope you will break your fast with us in the morning as well, as I would like to hear all you know about this miraculous device." He motioned toward the car. "Now, do not insult the *madame* by refusing her. She does not offer free fortunes to just anyone. The sooner she reads you, the sooner the *madame* can get her rest."

Only because Gravois pricked his guilt did he seek out the auld woman in her purple cart. That, and he was mayhap a mite curious to meet her, since neither she nor the eastern woman had supped with the others. He would meet the woman, listen to her daft fortune and then snare a few hours of sleep before returning to Malina.

A day and a night was far too long to be without her. Though he supposed he'd have to spend more days and nights apart from her as he sought another way to keep his word.

He didn't allow himself to dwell on the razor sharp twinge of dread that accompanied the prospect of spending a lifetime of days and nights alone after he sent her away.

Golden lamplight glowed from the cart's cracked-open rear door. He rapped twice.

"Enter, Highlander." The woman's voice rolled with the accent of the Rom—the gypsies—and rasped with age.

He ducked through the door and was immediately startled by the dimensions of the cart, which appeared grossly larger on the inside than he'd have guessed looking at the outside. In fact, his head didn't even brush the ceiling, though he'd have sworn the height of the cart a full hand under his own height. He should have had to bend nigh in half to fit. Figuring the cart to be one of Ferdinand's illusions, he resisted the urge to step outside to reassess the exterior, and looked around the generous space.

Netted shelves littered with supplies and wares lined both impossibly long side walls, and a hanging rack of women's clothing occupied the rear wall. Despite all the space for storage, plenty of room remained for the two cots toward the rear of the cart and the low table atop a woven rug toward the front.

The auld woman, Hilda, sat on a three-legged stool at one end of the table, embroidering a colorful scarf with crystal beads. He wondered how she did it, because being so close to her for the first time, he noticed her brown irises were milky with more than the effects of age. She was either blind or close to it.

The Eastern woman—Gravois had told him her name, but he didn't recall it—sat cross-legged and stiff-backed on a cushion at the other end of the table. She rolled herbs into squares of paper and nodded in polite greeting. The movement was slight due to the rings elongating her neck.

He nodded in return, but inwardly cringed at the disfigurement.

"Sit, Highlander," Hilda said, indicating another cushion on the floor. "I must study your aura to tell your fortune."

He obeyed, though it irked him to sit lower than the woman. "I thank you for your consideration, Madame Hilda," he said warily, "but why did ye wish to tell my fortune?" He didn't trust anyone who offered somat for nothing, especially somat of a magical nature.

Without answering, she closed her eyes and when she opened them again, the milky color of her irises and the black of her pupils had clouded to the pure white-gray of an overcast sky.

He scrambled for the door. Surely the woman was possessed of some vile spirit to alter her appearance so grotesquely.

"I did not take you for a coward," the woman said, stopping him on the threshold.

His heart racing, he turned back to face her. The doorframe creaked under his grip as he struggled to meet her white gaze. "Answer my question or I'll be leaving your camp tonight to take my chances with the dark road. I dinna like magic." Ferdinand's illusions he could tolerate, and Timothy's inadvertent bloodmagic he could sympathize with, but he could not completely unearth the notion ingrained in him since childhood that magic was inherently evil.

"Yet it blessed you with a wife," Hilda said. "And you seek it out for her sake with intent to use it yourself if need be." Gravois must have told her of their talk after dinner. Either that or the harridan's ears were far more hale than her eyes to have overheard them from this cart.

"I only seek to undo the unnatural thing that's been done." His heart squeezed with denial. "She belongs in her own time. Now answer the bloody question or I'll take my leave of you." He didn't like to use foul language with women, but Hilda tried his patience by reminding him he had magic to thank for granting him a taste of heaven and he would have magic to curse for taking his heaven away again.

She shrugged one shoulder. "There is a blight on your aura that intrigues Monsieur Gravois."

So Gravois had put her up to it. That gave him pause. Mayhap his mysterious new friend sought to help him in this way. He kent in his vitals Gravios wouldn't intend him harm. The certainty gave him the strength to take up his seat on the floor again, though he scooted back to put inches between his knees and Hilda's skirts.

"What do ye mean by 'blight'?" he asked suspiciously. "And 'aura,' for that matter?" 'Twas the second time she'd used the word.

The Eastern woman answered in heavily accented English. "Aura the energy of life. Each have it. Many in camp can see, but only Madame can *see*—see deep inside. See danger."

"Energy of life" meant naught to him. But he understood danger. "I am a warrior for my clan," he said. "Danger isna unusual for me."

"If Monsieur see danger so he ask Madame to see, you let Madame see or very bad happen. Let Madame see." Her voice was gentle, her face full of concern.

He harrumphed. "Well, let's have done with it then."

"Be very still," the Eastern woman said. "Take time to *see*."

He harrumphed again.

"Quiet," the auld woman barked.

He ground his teeth in indignation, but he sat still and resisted the urge to grumble.

Hilda leaned forward, her brow layered in wrinkles that deepened in her concentration. Her white-gray eyes bored into him, making his skin crawl.

At long last, she spoke, but not to him. "Chi-Yuen." It was a sharp command, given as she stretched a hand toward the Eastern woman, who rose from her cushion to take it.

Standing behind Hilda's shoulder, Chi-Yuen closed her eyes and inhaled sharply. Her painted lips pursed. She shook her head. The auld woman huffed. Chi-Yuen tilted her head as though listening, then reluctantly nodded.

His gaze darted between the two women. Were they somehow communicating with each other? If he'd been at the limit of his patience before, being ignored while two women held a magical conversation tipped him well past.

He shot up off the cushion to glower at the pair. "If you're through, I'll take my leave." He turned to go, surprised when neither woman tried to stop him.

Drawing cool night air into his lungs, he shook off the

neck-prickling feel of magic and strode to the yellow cart. He doubted he'd be able to sleep after such an unsettling handful of minutes, but he wouldn't ride Rand back to Dornoch this eve. Even if he wouldn't rest well, his mount deserved to spend the remainder of the night in peace.

To his dismay, the yellow cart dared to boast an even larger interior than the purple, though the outer dimensions were the same. It served as sleeping quarters for all the men in the troupe. No less than ten cots filled the space, each with a trunk at its foot, and like the purple cart, a table occupied the entrance and netted shelving lined the walls. He turned around and marched right down the stairs to lie on the ground near the horses.

He woke at dawn, bleary-eyed and even more tired than when he'd lain down. Sitting up to stretch his stiff neck, he found a refreshed and energetic-looking Gravois holding out a cup of tea. "I trust you slept well, *mon ami.* "

He snatched the cup with a harrumph. "What were those two women about? Did your auld fortune teller get what she was after?"

Gravois's smile faltered. "I shall tell you what I can over eggs. Come. Eat."

He followed the man to the fire, where Ferdinand spooned cooked eggs from a pan onto a trencher for him. Eyeing the curious dwarf, he shoveled in the offered nourishment while Gravois blathered some nonsense about the Rom being forbidden to reveal certain fortunes.

"It means naught to me," Darcy said. "I didna seek the fortune, so I dinna mind leaving without hearing it." He rose to saddle Rand.

Gravois followed, wringing his hands. "But it is of grave importance, *mon ami.*"

"Tell me or no. I dinna care which. But speak quickly if you mean to tell it. I must return to Dornoch and my bonny wife." He winked at his new friend, feeling more cheerful after breaking his fast and kenning he was but a day's easy ride from holding Malina in his arms again.

As he slipped the bit into Rand's mouth, Gravois made a sound of frustration he somehow managed to make elegant. "Madame Hilda saw your death, Monsieur Keith."

He froze, hands about to give the girth a final tug. He faced Gravois, not kenning how to respond to such a statement. Would he die heroically? Would he die an honorable member of the Keith clan, or a forgotten fugitive? How many years would he live with the agony of separation from Malina?

"The Rom are strictly forbidden from speaking *le mort ne prophetiser*—death prophesies. At the risk of losing her sight and perhaps even her life, the *madame* would not tell me exactly what she saw. But Chi-Yuen saw. She will not speak of the fortune either, but after the *madame* went to sleep, she made you this potion." Gravois extracted a vial of whitish liquid from an inner pocket in his jacket and held it out to him. "Keep it with you at all times, for Chi Yuen believes it may save you from whatever it is the *madame* saw."

The liquid reminded him of the color of Hilda's eyes when they'd clouded over. He shuddered and shook his head. "Nay. I want naught to do with potions. I will only use what magic I must to help my wife, and that I do at the peril of my soul." He rolled his eyes heavenward. "If the Lord hasna already crossed my name off his list, he certainly will do so by the time I've found a way for her to return home."

Gravois clucked his tongue. "Do you honestly believe magic is evil? After all you've witnessed? Knowing it brought you your wife. Knowing our gentle, pale friend carries it in his veins, and that it favors many in this camp? Do we strike you as evil, *mon ami*?"

He didn't feel like having a philosophical discussion. "I only ken I was raised to revile aught that runs contrary to the natural way of things, as does the church. Though I've had reluctant dealings with magic and will deal with it further for my wife's sake, I dinna do so lightly, and I dinna expect to escape punishment."

"Am I in need of punishment? Is Madame Hilda? Master Timothy? Is it so difficult to believe magic might exist under the approving eye of the Almighty?"

He huffed in annoyance. Rand, sensing his mood, stomped an impatient hoof. "Gravois," he warned. "I dinna have the patience for this debate. My clansmen hunt me, my wife is leagues away under the protection of a man I hardly ken, and I've had my fill of shocks in the last day."

He swung up into the saddle and gave the tinker a curt nod.

"Wait," Gravois said urgently. "I forgot, I have a gift for your beloved wife. A moment, *mon ami*, and I will fetch it," he said over his shoulder as he jogged toward the green cart.

He waited, though both he and Rand lusted to run.

Gravois returned a few minutes later with a package the size of a flintbox. 'Twas wrapped in canvas and tied with twine. "*S'il vous plait*, tell your wife that I wish her well, and that this gift is to be opened only—how do you say?—when the sheet hits the fan. It is very important you use those exact words, *mon ami*."

He raised a brow at the odd phrase, but took the package.

"It was my immense pleasure to make your acquaintance." Gravois stepped back from Rand and made a grand, graceful gesture.

Darcy couldn't help his smile. He nodded toward where the car sat. "Unless you'd like to face another angry mob, I'd be ridding myself of that thing." Guiding his eagerly prancing mount toward the bridge, he called back, "Take care of yourself, Gravois."

After he crossed, he looked back to see nothing but a

dilapidated ruin of a bridge and a barren rise of rocky hills.

Chapter 18

MELANIE KNELT BESIDE Constance in Skibo's terraced garden. Beneath them, the village of Dornoch bustled with activity. The sounds of rolling carts, haggling merchants, and laughing children drifted up to the castle on the gentlest of breezes. Mild sunshine warmed her shoulders, and freshly turned loam cooled her knees through her apron-covered kirtle. The mingled scents of a hundred varieties of flowers and herbs christened the morning perfect.

She should be cheerful, darn it, but each stab of her trowel into the soil punctuated one of the many questions that had been sawing through her mind since yesterday morning. Had Darcy made it safely to Inverness? When would he be back? Was he thinking about her? Did he regret what they'd done the night before he left? How would she react if he returned claiming to know how to send her back to Charleston? Would she go so he could return to Ackergill, or would she expose her heart to him in the most irrevocable way and tell him she wanted to stay? He had told her he loved her, but what if he loved his home more?

"Honestly, dear. It's like talking to a sheep."

Constance's voice brought her back from the brink of insanity at the same moment the tip of her trowel struck impacted earth. She'd dug far too deep for the young sprouts they were planting. She looked up to find her hostess's gaze sympathetic, despite the annoyance in her tone.

She cocked her gloved hands on her hips and grumbled, "Did

you hear a single thing I said about agrimony?"

In the past two days, her hostess had tried everything to distract her from her sour mood.

But no amount of being fitted for pretty dresses, going on scenic walks, gardening, or learning about the medicinal properties of various herbs, barks, and ointments could make her forget the raging pain of Darcy's rejection.

Apparently, her heartache was having an adverse effect on her concentration. She chewed her lip and shook her head. "Is it the Scottish term for a terrible marriage?"

Constance chuckled. "No, but failing to use it for fresh breath might cause even the most devoted of spouses to run for the hills. It's an astringent, dear, and can also be used in tea to help cure the common cold and diarrhea." She frowned at the small grave Melanie had dug. "But if you plant it that deep, Skibo will suffer a plague of halitosis come winter."

"Sorry." She began filling in the hole, packing the cool loam tight with her trowel.

"It's all right." Constance patted her shoulder. "I know what it's like to have your husband away. It never gets easier. But at least you know he hasn't run off to a skirmish. He's just gone thirty miles or so to Inverness to talk to a box maker."

Melanie rocked back on her heels and used the back of her wrist to drag a lock of hair off her forehead. "But what if he runs into Steafan's men on the way? What if he attracts the wrong kind of attention with his questions and winds up accused of witchcraft? What if he's being burned at the stake as we speak and I never see him again?" Her chest tightened painfully at the thought.

"Yes, poor helpless Darcy," Constance said. "Do you really think he'll be unscrupulous with his words or that he can't hold his own against Steafan's men if it comes to that?"

"You're right." Her chest relaxed. Darcy was nothing if not

scrupulous and capable. "I'm worrying about things that don't even make sense."

"It's what we do," her hostess said with a shrug. "We're wives. But if we're smart, we keep friends around us who don't let us moon around when our hormones try to turn us into worthless, dithering lumps." She winked, and Melanie realized with a rush of warm surprise that Constance was her friend.

She had a husband and a friend in sixteenth-century Scotland. And in just a few short months she'd have a baby, too. She hadn't even been here a week yet and she was already starting to build a life. The idea of staying was growing less frightening by the hour.

"Speaking of hormones," her new friend said. "Have you given any thought to whether you'll plan your future pregnancies or just let things happen?"

Her heart swelled at the thought of carrying Darcy's child. After a moment's fantasy, she cocked an eyebrow at Constance. "Don't women in this time just kind of let it happen? I mean, there's no pill, and coitus-interruptus isn't exactly reliable."

"Well, Mother Nature is certainly a persistent bitch," Constance said with a wry smile. "But there are a few things that can take her down a peg or two. Bradley was born when I was forty-five, but before him, I managed to use seeds of Queen Anne's Lace and home-made suppositories as birth control for several years. Of course, they call it Wild Carrot since Queen Anne won't sit the throne for nearly two hundred years. But it works just the same."

Melanie had met twelve-year-old Bradley and his seventeen-year-old brother, Marcus, at meal times. Constance and Wilhelm's three oldest were married and lived in estates spread over Wilhelm's territory, and the nineteen-year-old was at University in Edinburgh.

"I stopped bothering when I started 'The Change.'" She dramatically deepened her voice. "But soon realized that just because you're getting older and you miss two periods doesn't mean your ovaries have given up the ghost." She smiled wistfully as she stood and stretched her back. "Bradley's was a hard delivery. An even harder recovery. But I don't regret it. I don't regret him. He's wonderful. They're all wonderful. But you do have to consider that there are no hospitals. No blood transfusions. No monitors to show when the baby is in distress. No perfectly controlled little incubators for preemies."

She sighed, and the sound was heavy with sadness. "I lost three over the years, two of them during delivery. One two weeks after. Two of them were girls, including the one that lived for those precious two weeks. Maryanne. She was a month early. Easiest delivery I'd ever had. Hardest loss." Constance's haunted eyes looked out over Skibo's grounds.

"I'm so sorry," Melanie said inadequately.

Constance's lips lifted in a small smile. "Still no regrets, though. If someone had given me the ability to go back and change my mind about staying, I wouldn't have done it. Come on." She extended a hand to help Melanie up. "We'll finish planting tomorrow. Let's go to the storeroom. I'll show you how to prepare seeds of Queen Anne's Lace and make the suppositories so you can use them when you feel the need. You can also simply add quinine to scented oil. It works as a spermicide. But Wilhelm and I never liked using oils. Didn't need them," she added with a wink, and just like that, the mischievous joy of a sexually satisfied woman shoved away the shadows in her eyes.

Would thinking of Darcy bring her back from dark moods in thirty years? Yes. She was sure of it. And that certainty cemented her decision to stay.

She was his. He was hers. She wanted him for all time. If that meant he could never return to his home, then she'd make sure he felt at home wherever they went. Darcy was her home. She'd be his, too.

Regardless of what he would discover in Inverness, there was no way she'd let him send her back. Her decision was cast in the iron of her love. If only her stubborn Highlander were here so she could tell him.

§

DARCY ROCKED IN the saddle as he cantered Rand north toward Dornoch. He hadn't found what he'd been looking for in Inverness, but then, it was a quarter century before the date on Malina's box. He vaguely wondered whether a visit to Timothy at MacLeods in twenty-five years would find the lad matured not just in physical form but in his ability to control his bloodmagic as well. But in the next thought, he kent that even if Timothy could create the box in 1547, he'd sooner die than let her go after loving her for so long. He'd have to find another way.

And soon.

Feeling like a failure for the time being, he considered taking the ten leagues between Inverness and Dornoch slower to put off disappointing his wife, but with Gil, Hamish and the others about looking for him, he thought it unwise to dally. Besides, Rand liked to run. If the gelding had his way, he'd be galloping full out, but Darcy didn't want to spend him too soon. If he ran into Steafan's men, he'd be needing Rand fresh.

Once they crossed onto Murray land, he thrilled at kenning Malina was so near. He forgot his hesitancy. Even if she was disappointed with him, 'twould still be heaven to hold and kiss her.

Sensing his master's eagerness to reach Skibo, Rand pulled at the reins. They were close enough now, with only a league or two to go, that he gave the gelding his head and let him run as fast as he lusted. With his ears pricked forward and his stride long and joyful, Rand raced through the forest skirting the southern border of Wilhelm's land.

As they ran, horse and master cutting a defiant streak through the air, he thought about his last night with Malina and a grin settled on his face. Would she be too disappointed to grant him another such night? Was he a cad for wanting another? And then another after that and another yet again until he lost count?

She was his wife, after all. If ever 'twas acceptable for a man to act on his desires, 'twas with his wife. But it felt wrong when he kent he was nay meant to keep her.

One moment thoughts of losing Malina had his gut in knots. The next, he was flying through the air as Rand tumbled beneath him.

He sailed over Rand's head to land hard in the road. Rocks bit his shoulders and knees as he rolled. The ear-splitting scream of a horse in pain had him springing to his feet the moment he came to a stop.

Rand was trying to get his feet under him, but somat was wrong. Darcy's chest contracted with dread.

Ignoring his scrapes and bruises, he ran to his horse. Blood flowed from both the gelding's front legs. The white of shattered bone glistened through the red.

"No. No!" He fell to his knees and clutched Rand's thrashing head. The horse ceased struggling and collapsed on his side. His nostrils flared and his eyes flashed their whites. "Rand, lad, what happened?" Grief tightened his throat around the words.

Rand was as good as dead with two broken legs. He would have to use his sword on his faithful friend.

"What happened?" he repeated helplessly.

The road had been flat, a little rocky in places, but not enough to prove dangerous to a galloping horse. Tearing his eyes from Rand, he glanced back along the road, looking for what might have caused his horse to fall.

Nearly invisible, a rope was strung tight across the road, tied to trees on either side.

"Christ," he breathed, his muscles tensing. "A trap."

No sooner had the words left his lips than he heard the scuff of a boot in the dirt behind him. He lunged for his sword, still strapped to Rand's saddle. He drew it and spun around in time to meet Hamish's thrust. The bastard had been aiming for his throat.

"Dinna kill him, Hamish." Gil's voice.

Keeping an eye on Hamish, he found the red-haired man standing with his hand on his hilt at the side of the road where one end of the rope was tied. Though Gil made no move to attack, Darcy angled himself to keep both men in view.

"Why spare him?" Hamish sneered, setting himself up for another strike. "Steafan said to bring him back alive or nay. 'Tis only the witch he demands alive, and that only so he can watch her burn."

When Hamish struck again, his arm shook with the block. 'Twas not Hamish's strength, which was no match for his when it came to swordplay, but bitter betrayal that seized his muscles. Not only did it seem his uncle was intent on pursuing Malina for a witch's spirit purging, but he'd given the order to treat him as the worst kind of traitor.

If any hope of returning to Ackergill had remained, Hamish's words snuffed it out. A part of his heart sheared off like a cliff crumbling into the abyss.

Gil said to Hamish, "The laird gave that order in haste." To Darcy, he said, "Dinna fight, lad. Come along with us, now. Steafan's temper will have cooled by the time we get back."

"Will his temper have cooled toward my wife, too?" He kent the answer already.

"Ye ken she must burn," Gil said, and Darcy despised his calm. "'Tis the best thing for her everlastin' soul."

"Malina is no witch," he said, refusing to give ground to

Hamish, who tried to crowd him toward the edge of the road. "And I willna be returning to Ackergill." He cut a sharp look at Gil. "Alive or nay. Leave me and my wife be and tell Steafan I have aligned myself with the Murray, or you shall fall under my sword here on this road. The choice is yours."

He prayed he didn't have to make good on the threat, but he was no fool. Gil was capable of great cunning, and Hamish of great cruelty. And he saw no sign of the other three riders he'd glimpsed in that valley. The missing Keith might have been searching for Malina that very moment. His gut coiled with fear. He was assailed by an unbearable urge to lay his eyes on her and assure himself she was safe.

"No," Hamish said. "The choice is yours. Come along with us or I shall make use of your wife while ye watch. I'll show her what a man can do when he isna scairt of his cock. I'll have the bitch praising me for sating her when her husband couldna as she goes to the fire."

Fury tightened his movements. He blocked Hamish's sword, then threw him back with a roar. "You willna touch my wife! Not ever!"

It took every honorable fiber in his body for him nay to thrust his sword through his clansmen, especially when he remembered his wife's cries as Hamish had struck her.

"Then ye better come along, lad," Gil said, quick as a rabbit. "Because we have her already. The others collected her from the Murray for a wee sum of silver. Dinna give Hamish cause to touch her. Lay down your sword."

He stopped listening after Gil said the Keith had Malina. His mind snapped with rage. He imagined her wrestled onto the back of a horse, bound and gagged and on her way to Ackergill.

What evil would Steafan's guards do to her before he could find her? What evil would Steafan do to her if he failed to reach her in time?

He didn't even have Rand to chase them down.

He roared with frustrated fury. He couldn't afford to dally in the road any longer. Malina needed him.

Her bonny face fixed itself on his heart. He struck out with his sword and took Hamish with a ruthless jab to the belly. The man's eyes flew wide with shock.

He spun around to find Gil gaping with equal surprise. But despite his shock, the man didn't back down. He positioned himself for defense and Darcy didn't disappoint him.

They battled. He took Gil's blade to his shoulder and thigh, but his strength and size didn't fail him, nor did the training he'd gotten from Aodhan, the only man he'd ever met who he thought could best him with a sword.

When Gil finally fell, blood gushing from his side, the tracker wheezed, "You would betray your clansmen for a witch? Ye'll burn in hell for this." He coughed and died.

Horror tried to pull him to his knees as he panted over the bodies of his clansmen, but he couldn't let himself regret what he'd done. Not when Malina could be suffering.

But there was one task he must see to before rushing to her rescue.

Poor Rand lay in the road, broken and bloody, trembling with pain. He didn't permit himself to hesitate. His dear friend had suffered too long already. He knelt as he drew his dirk and dragged the blade firm and true under Rand's bridle.

"You're a good lad," he told the gelding, rubbing his ears as his life spilled onto his lap and the dusty road. "You are the best horse a man could boast. God grant ye endless pastures to roam in heaven."

When Rand's eyes stilled, he rose a harder man than he'd been a quarter hour before. Icy determination in his veins, he sliced the blasted rope across the road, threw himself on Gil's dappled gelding, and raced for Dornoch.

Chapter 19

THE RICH SCENTS of lavender, thyme, mint, and countless other plants and flowers bombarded Melanie as she followed Constance into the storeroom. It reminded her of stepping into the Yankee Candle shop in the Charleston mall. Oddly, the modern-day memory lacked the bite of fervent longing she'd braced herself for.

Following Constance's example, she harvested seeds from a basketful of delicate, lacy, dried flowers. That done, she learned how to mix honey and the expensive but highly effective spermicide, quinine, which Constance ordered from an apothecary in Edinburgh.

The thought of using these things to keep from getting pregnant seemed as strange as making her own sausage and sewing clothes for her children, both things that Constance insisted she would teach her. A week ago those tasks would have seemed terrifying, maybe even impossible. But with her competent friend showing her the way, she believed she could not only survive in the sixteenth century, but thrive in it.

An unexpected fondness for Ackergill made her chest tight as she thought about thriving at Darcy's side. Steafan was a paranoid bastard, and she'd just as soon see Hamish ride his black horse and his even blacker heart off a cliff, but she found herself missing Fran. Edmund, too, and their baby. And Fraineach. She'd spent no more than a few waking minutes in the manor home, but longed to see its sunny rooms again and to breathe deep of its crisp ocean-side scent. In fact, she missed Faineach more than her apartment back in Charleston.

In her dreams the night before, she'd seen herself rocking her baby in the dusty room that had become Darcy's storage place for the things a single man had no need for. In her dream, the bassinette had been freshly painted and lined with fluffy blankets. The skeletal wire rack had had a dress on it that she would mend while her baby napped. The spinning wheel with a sheet over it would be oiled, and, thanks to Fran, she would know just what to do with it when the wool was ready to be made into skeins.

Fraineach wasn't just Darcy's home. It was hers.

"I wish there was some way to get Steafan to take us back," she mused out loud as Constance tied a ribbon around the jar they'd just filled with the honey mixture.

"Here," Constance said, handing her the jar. "It'll keep forever, but you'll need to stir it very well each time you use it. Just use what drips off the stick to coat the wool before inserting it. Consider it a welcome home to Ackergill gift." At her dubious look, her hostess lifted her chin. "We are two intelligent, determined women, and the Keith laird is just one paranoid man, a man who's reputed to be afraid to leave his keep at that. Surely we'll think of some way to reinstate Darcy. He is the man's heir, after all."

"Obviously, you haven't met him. He's not going to budge. His mind is made up that I'm a no-good witch and his nephew has been corrupted by me. Nothing's going to change that."

"Pish posh," Constance said, waving away her concerns. "Nothing is impossible. Just look at my private bathroom. Now, let's start by considering what matters to the laird of the Keith, shall we? What does he value above all else?"

She scoffed. "That's easy. Power. He's the kind of man who likes to see everyone around him cower. He likes to think he's more important than he is."

"Well, we certainly don't want to give him any more power. Is there anything he wants that might be within your power to give him?" Constance took her arm and led her from the storeroom.

"Nothing comes to mind." She doubted Steafan could be bought off with the gold Darcy had given her; he seemed the type to gain a lot more enjoyment from a grudge than from wealth. "Personally, I don't want to give that jerk anything except maybe a lit stick of dynamite. Why do you ask? And where are we going?"

"To Wilhelm's study. We've received some correspondence from Ackergill Keep in recent years, and Wilhelm keeps everything, especially correspondence. And I ask because no man, however stubborn, makes up his mind so firmly that the right woman can't change it."

"Well, we'd better write to Ginneleah then. According to Darcy, Steafan's ga-ga over his wife."

"Now you're on to something, my dear Malina." Constance used Darcy's name for her in affectionate jest.

She liked the easy friendship she'd found with this woman, even if she thought Constance a tad crazy for taking the comment about Ginneleah seriously. Melanie hadn't even met the girl; Darcy had told her she was only 17, and she'd married Steafan two years ago, at the tender age of 15. She shuddered. The poor thing.

In Wilhelm's study Constance poked through a cherry wood cabinet until she came away with two sheets of paper. "Here they are," she said, showing them to Melanie. "It was the strangest thing. Wilhelm received these a year apart. The most recent came in June last year."

Constance was quiet while she read the short letters. They were essentially thank you notes for a perfumed oil Wilhelm had sent the couple as a wedding gift and then as an anniversary gift the next year. "Why strange?" The letters seemed quite thoughtful to her. If there was anything strange about them, it was seeing Steafan so cordial and gracious in writing, proving he wasn't a perpetual ass.

"They're strange because Wilhelm has never sent a single thing to Ackergill keep, gift or otherwise. To be honest, I don't think he'd even heard of the Keith laird by name until we received the first letter."

"Maybe Steafan mistook a gift from someone else as being from Wilhelm," she said, frowning at the letters.

"The second one seems to refute that." Constance pointed at a line she hadn't understood the meaning of. *Ginneleah and I hope and pray the saints will bless us through your kind gift as he has blessed you so greatly.* "I think this is a reference to our six sons. I think he assumed the oil is a conception aid and that Wilhelm and I credit something of the sort with our good fortune in bearing so many healthy children."

"But you didn't use anything like that. You told me so this afternoon."

Constance nodded significantly.

"Why would Steafan assume it then?"

"Since you arrived, I've been wondering the same thing. Thinking we credit a perfumed oil with the birth of our sons is an oddly specific assumption unless the gift arrived with a note. Surely there had to have been a note if he was certain enough to write a letter of thanks to Wilhelm. Twice." She narrowed her eyes and tapped her chin with a slender finger. "What if someone sent him the oil in Wilhelm's name?"

"Why would anyone do that?"

"To get him to trust the oil is innocuous or even helpful to conception." Constance gave her raised eyebrows, waiting for her to make a connection.

It took several seconds, but logic snapped into place. She

gasped. "You think someone sent Steafan a gift of perfumed oil and purposefully led him to believe it might help him and Ginneleah conceive?" As her brain spun with sickening possibilities, Constance cocked her head in affirmation. "But they haven't conceived, not in the two years they've been married. And Darcy told me Steafan hasn't been himself since losing his only child to a terrible skirmish a few years ago. He wants another son, a true heir, more than just about anything."

"And when a man wants something that badly…" Constance trailed off, gesturing for Melanie to finish the thought.

"It broadcasts his weakness, makes him a potential target for foul play. What if that oil has quinine in it? What if it's doing the opposite of what he thinks?"

Constance smiled, but it wasn't a happy expression.

"But to work, they'd have to use it every time, wouldn't they? Is that realistic? What if they don't use it at all and we're making something out of nothing?"

"Does Steafan strike you as a man who would send a sincere thank you note for something he tosses in a drawer and never uses?" Constance didn't give her a chance to respond. "Plus, some couples are far from creative in the bedroom. I'd imagine if they used the oil once and liked it, they'd continue using it merely out of habit. I'm by no means certain, but I have a strong suspicion that someone's taking a great deal of pleasure in Ginneleah's apparent failure to give her husband what he most desires."

The thought made her skin crawl. She pretty much hated Steafan, but she wouldn't have wished that kind of deception on him, especially when having more children might mellow the man. "Okay. Say you're right. If we suspect something like that, we have to do something to help. But what? It's not like we know who it is. Steafan's probably got a list of enemies a mile long. It could be anyone sending him this oil every year."

Constance nodded. “I imagine we’ll receive another letter in a month’s time, just like the others. Unless our culprit has given up her grudge.”

“Her?”

“Oh, please. Don’t tell me you think a man could be this devious. If we’re right about the oil, it could only be a woman’s work.”

“Hell hath no fury,” Melanie recited, to Constance’s approving nod.

“Steafan thinks you’re a witch, my dear. I wonder if he’d change his mind about the wiles of a magical woman if you were to ‘say a spell of fertility’ over his wife and offer her an oil of your own making, one free from anything harmful.”

She gaped at her friend. “First, that’s awful. That would be perpetuating a lie. I don’t want him to think I’m a witch at all. And if you think he’d let his beloved Ginneleah within ten miles of me, you’re nuts.”

“Not nuts,” Constance corrected. “Optimistic, maybe. As devious as Steafan’s secret admirer, definitely. I’m sure we can come up with something that makes a hero out of you—without perpetuating a lie,” she added with a roll of her eyes as Melanie made to argue. “If nothing else, we can simply tell Ginneleah our suspicions. If we determine she’s using the oil consistently and suggest she stop using it, she might just conceive. Think how grateful Steafan would be. Maybe even grateful enough to invite you and Darcy back.”

“Doubtful,” she said, but regardless of Steafan’s gratitude or lack thereof, she was on board with alerting Ginneleah to the potential harm of the mysterious oil. She’d certainly want to know, if it were her. “So, how do you propose to tell her? It’s not like she’s got an email address or a cellphone. A letter?”

Constance shook her head. “It’s not like the U.S. mail, where the recipient is the first person to open it. If I wrote to Ginneleah,

Steafan would see the letter first. And if he didn't deem it suitable, she might not see it at all. No. Such sensitive news must be given in person and only to Ginneleah. Besides, can you imagine how furious Steafan would be if he found out he's been tricked in the most personal way imaginable? What if he takes out his anger on his wife?"

Melanie cringed at the thought. "He'll blow a gasket, all right." She didn't want to be responsible for the damage he'd be likely to cause in his fury.

"We don't even know if it's true," Constance said. "We'll get Ginneleah alone and talk to her about it. See if we're even in the ballpark with our suspicions."

"How do you plan to do that?"

"I'm going to have Wilhelm write to Ackergill Keep and invite the laird and his wife to Dornoch. What better way to give the happy couple their next installment of perfumed oil, than to do it in person?"

She scoffed. "Steafan hardly leaves the keep, let alone the village. According to Darcy, he hasn't even led his men in a skirmish since losing his son. There's no way he'll come to Dornoch."

"That's the beauty of it. The laird himself may not come, but if he's truly as thankful for the oil as his notes suggest, he'll certainly want another year's supply. He'll likely send his wife as his representative rather than decline the invitation outright and risk offending Wilhelm."

Constance lit up with the brilliance of her plan. She clapped her hands once and strode from the study. "Oh, there's so much to do. We need to prepare the finest guest suite and order caviar from Edinburgh."

Melanie chased after her with panic fluttering behind her breastbone. "You can't be serious. What are we going to do, bring her here and start drilling her for details of her sex life? 'Hi, nice to meet you, Ginneleah,'" she mocked. "'So, how often do you lube up for your husband? Every time?'"

"Please," Constance chided. "You're going to be much more subtle than that."

"Me? This whole thing is your idea!"

"But *you* need to worm your way into Ginneleah's confidence if you and Darcy are going to have a snowball's chance at earning an invitation back to Ackergill. Remember, dear, Ginneleah is Steafan's biggest weakness. That makes her your best shot."

It seemed awfully manipulative to plan on making a friend as a means to an end, but Constance did have a point. It wasn't like she would be disingenuous in her offer of friendship, and she did want to get to the bottom of this perfumed oil mystery. If she managed to secure a spot in Steafan's good graces, she'd consider it a bonus. She was willing to try for Darcy's sake.

Constance sailed to the kitchen and instructed Skibo's head cook to order some special things from Edinburgh. "Now, let's find my husband and tell him he's got a letter to write tonight."

They found Wilhelm in the practice yard, throwing knives at a target painted in the shape of a man. It reminded her of a modern-day shooting range, minus the firearms and ear protection.

"Wilhelm, a moment, love," Constance called.

Her husband turned to them with a warm expression that made Melanie blush just from catching the run-off of that much affection.

Before Wilhelm had taken two steps, a servant dashed into the yard. Between panting breaths, he managed, "The Keith. Riding up the road. Covered in blood and screaming like a wild banshee. And he's riding a different horse than the one he left on. Come quick!"

Her stomach dropped to her feet as Darcy's frantic shouts met her ears.

"Wilhelm! Ye bloody better have my wife! Malina! Where are ye, lass? Malina!"

She grasped Constance's hand, and together they ran after Wilhelm toward the road.

§

DARCY URGED GIL'S horse up to Skibo, his gaze scouring the keep for any sign of Malina.

Just a glimpse of her, he petitioned the saints. *Please.*

Just a glimpse of her silvery hair and bonny face would ease the terrible knot in his chest. Just a glimpse and he'd be able to breathe again.

Never before had he felt such agony as the fear of having his wife hurt or worse.

Damn him for leaving her in the care of a near stranger. Damn him for neglecting his duty to her. He'd failed to protect her from Hamish's cruel hands, and now trusting in Wilhelm may have precipitated her capture.

If Wilhelm had sold her to the Keith, he'd bloody well ride with Darcy to retrieve her, or he would see him pay for his broken promise in blood.

"Wilhelm!" he called again. "Show yourself!"

Wilhelm and a pair of his guards rounded the keep at a run.

He reigned in Gil's horse. "Where is she? Where is my wife?"

"Right behind me. What happened, man? Are ye wounded?"

Malina came running around the keep with Constance. Relief surged through him to see her blessedly unharmed, though her face was drawn with concern. She was worrit for him.

He flew from the saddle and dashed to her. His ripped thigh protested, but he didn't falter in his steps. Pain was nothing compared to the need to hold his sweet wife in his arms.

Sweeping her up, he pinned her to his chest. Their hearts

reached for each other with every beat. She clung to him as fiercely as he clung to her, and some of the horror of the last hour lifted from him.

"Christ, lass, I thought…I thought—" He buried his face in her hair.

She smelled of herbs and flowers, and underneath was her own scent of sugared custard.

She wore a lovely kirtle of sapphire blue and an apron smudged with dirt as if she'd been doing chores in the garden.

Her hair flowed like silk through his fingers as he ran his hand over her head and face, assuring himself she was hale, all except for the purple marks around her left eye from Hamish's hand. Passing over her cheeks, his fingers came away wet with her tears.

"Dinna weep, Malina mine. All is well."

"You're hurt," she cried. "Let me see. There's so much blood."

"What happened?" Wilhelm demanded.

"How much of the blood is yours?" Constance asked.

He ignored all but Malina. "I'm all right, lass. I'm all right. Just a few scrapes." He permitted himself a relieved breath as her face smoothed somewhat, but he refused to let her go. He couldn't even bring himself to lower her feet to the ground. With Malina in his arms, he was whole. She wasn't only his to love and protect; she was part of him.

Realization struck him with blinding force. "I canna let ye go back," he said. "I willna. You are mine, and I willna send you away to your time." The tightness in his chest unfurled.

Malina's eyes widened with shock. Her rose-petal lips parted to say somat, but he silenced her with a kiss. He couldn't help himself. Let her hate him for a time. He would find a way to earn her love and forgiveness. He'd earn them every day for the rest of his life.

Christ, it felt wonderful to have the decision made. He showed her how wonderful it felt with his lips, feasting on her, loving her, pushing his tongue inside of her as he longed to do more privately with her skirts up around her hips

He expected her to shove him away, to pummel his shoulders with her wee fists and demand he keep his word to help return her to her time. But she did none of those things. Instead, she tightened her arms about his neck and kissed him back with all the urgency and passion coursing through his own veins. Her tongue plunged with his, and her lips stole his breath. Her taste exploded in his mouth as they fought to meld together as one.

Whatever his Malina thought of his declaration, 'twas nay hatred she felt for him.

He kissed her harder, deeper. The joy of their reunion made him deaf and blind to all else.

Pressing her legs around his waist, he turned toward the keep. He would die if he didn't prove his love to her in every physical way he could.

Wilhelm's voice broke through his haze of desire. The laird's hand clapped his unwounded shoulder. "There'll be time for that later, lad. But first, your wounds need seeing to, and I need you to tell me what's happened." To Constance, he said, "Take Malina and make arrangements to sew him up."

Constance reached a hand toward Malina, but his wife refused to leave him. His chest swelled with pride that she would cling to him against their host's wishes, even after he'd decreed he would be breaking his word. He didn't wish to release her either, didn't think he'd survive another minute without her after their two-day separation, which had felt like two years.

"Come along, Melanie," Constance said in a firm but compassionate voice. "It seems our lessons today must include doctoring a bleeding husband."

Malina searched his face.

"Go, lass. I'll come find you shortly." As much as he wanted to carry her to their room and forget the last hour in the haven of her arms, Wilhelm was right. There were bodies in the road needed tending to. A horse and two men, men whom he had killed, it seemed, for no better reason than they'd lied to him about having his wife. Regret plowed him over.

Malina released her fists from his plaid and slipped from his arms, glaring at Wilhelm as if warning him not to keep him for long. Then she tugged him down for a parting kiss. He let her lips soothe the raging guilt that would be sure to eat him alive the moment she stepped away.

He'd acted rashly and the price would be a never-healing wound on his conscience. He'd killed when killing hadn't been necessary. May the Lord deal mercifully with him.

Malina's lips left his, and he felt bereft. Though Constance led her into the keep, she kept her gaze locked on his until the door shut behind her.

"Where's your horse?" Wilhelm asked. "And whose blood are ye covered in?"

Chapter 20

"No," Wilhelm said in a tone only a fool would argue with.

"I must," Darcy insisted. "They are my clansmen."

Wilhelm didn't pause in saddling his chestnut stallion. "They played ye false and made ye fear for your wife. Not to mention ruining your fine horse. I would have done the same as you, and I wouldna be flogging myself for it. Go find your wife. My men and I will see to the road."

He meant the bodies. Wilhelm was being delicate about it, but Darcy didn't want delicate. He wanted Wilhelm to rage at him, to condemn him as a murderer. He wanted to be punished for what he'd done. If no one would punish him, then he had to at least see to Hamish and Gil as the kin they were.

"'Tis my responsibility. I willna find solace unless I lay them to rest myself." Mayhap not even then.

Wilhelm slipped the bridle over his horse's ears then turned to him. Though the man stood several inches shorter, the laird of Dornoch had a way of looking at him so he felt small.

"'Tis not your solace I'm concerned with. You're bleeding all over the place. You need to be sewn up, and I dinna wish to answer to your wife if ye put it off and fall over dead while ye see to men who would have killed you for protecting what's yours."

Wilhelm's hard expression softened. He lowered his voice. "If you hadna slain them, man, I would have. I'd have tracked them down and done it myself, and I'd not have been as quick about it as you were. They trespassed on my land, threatened what was mine to protect, and besmirched my name. 'Tis only because they were kin to you that I dinna burn their bodies where they lie. We'll bring them back and you can witness their rights come morn'. Now go to your wife and let her tend to you. I willna hear another word about it."

Without giving him a chance to respond, Wilhelm led his horse from the stable and mounted up. Five of his men accompanied him, two of them in a cart equipped with blankets and shovels.

As the dust of their departure rose up along the road, the weight of too many losses crushed him. Rand. Gil and Hamish. Ackergill. Edmund, Fran, and wee Jaimie Darcy. No miracle could give him back his home now that he'd taken the lives of two of his clansmen.

Steafan would see him as an enemy forever and more, and with just cause.

How much heartache could a soul sustain before crumbling?

He'd lost everything that had mattered to him most except Malina, including a large part of his honor, and yet he hadn't crumbled. It was because of her. Somehow, in the short time she'd been his, the woman had infused his heart with enough love and strength to sustain him through this most dire of trials.

Turning his feet toward the keep, he determined to make a home for her in Dornoch, a home worthy of the treasure she was. Starting now.

§

AS MELANIE PACED the bedroom, her emotions teetered like a stone on a precipice. A single jostle in any direction and she'd tumble over into tears. Relief at Darcy's return to Dornoch tipped her one way, while the shock of seeing him sticky with blood tipped her another way. Elation at his pronouncement that she was his and he would not be letting her go tipped her yet again, only to have the wounded horror in his eyes tip her in the opposite direction.

Not knowing what he'd been through was killing her. Had he run into Steafan's men?

Had he fought them? How bad were his injuries? Had Rand been injured or worse?

"A few scrapes, my ass," she muttered, wringing her shaking hands.

Constance shoved a bulb of garlic at her. "They're Highlanders, dear. They'll get themselves stabbed, dragged through a briar patch, thrown over a cliff, and punched in the face all before breakfast and call it 'a fair interesting morn'.' Now, peel those and put the cloves in the hot water." The older woman nodded toward the steaming kettle a maid had deposited on the hearth. "Garlic water cleans wounds better than plain water and keeps infection away."

She latched onto the competence Constance radiated. While calming her with brisk assurances that all would be well, the older woman deftly deployed a small army of castle servants on various missions relating to "doctoring a bone-headed Highland husband." She'd set the kitchen staff to boiling buckets of water and the maids to preparing a hot bath for Darcy in front of the unlit fireplace. A footman hurried in with an armload of medical supplies from a room behind the kitchen that Constance said was the late-medieval equivalent of a field hospital.

The Lady of Dornoch herself laid out clean bandages and spread blankets on the bed to protect the linens. Melanie focused on the garlic, and as she plunked clove after clove in the kettle, her hands shook less and less.

Slowly, the scent of garlic thickened the air. Two nights ago, this room had been a lantern-lit haven of intimacy for her and her husband. Now it was overly bright with late-afternoon sunlight and unseasonably warm with too many bustling bodies and vessels of steaming water. The biting odors of garlic and witch-hazel obliterated any romantic vibes that had lingered in the long-lost scents of honeysuckle soap, saddle leather, and sex.

Sweat trickled down her back and caused fringes of hair to stick around her face as she finished peeling the garlic and wiped her now steady hands on a damp rag. Constance, also looking pink in the cheeks, told a maid to open the window. Then she addressed the room at large. "Thank you all for your help. Now, everyone out. There's no room in here for the poor Keith. Shoo, out."

As the room cleared and a spring breeze stirred the drapes, Melanie breathed easier. But her stomach was still in knots. Only laying her eyes on an ambulatory Darcy could fully ease her anxiety.

At last, the sound of approaching footsteps in the hall trained her attention on the door.

Her heart hammered. Her arms ached to hold her husband and never let him go.

Darcy ducked into the room. Blood and dirt streaked him from head to toe. His right arm was caked with blood from the wound in his shoulder, and she suspected he had a wound in his left leg, too, judging by the criss-crossing streams of blood matting the hair on his shin. But it wasn't his physical state that tore a cry of sympathy from her and sent her hurtling into his waiting arms; it was the haunted weariness in his eyes. Something had broken inside him.

Something had chased away what little of boyhood had remained.

"Oh, Darcy," she breathed into his neck as he bent around her. "What happened?"

"'Twas Gil and Hamish," he said, his voice tight with pain. "They set a trap for me, and it took Rand." His chest heaved with a repressed sob. "I fought them. I was worrit about you, and I fought hard. They are dead. I've killed my clansmen." In the shudder that wracked his body, she felt his grief and guilt.

"I'm so sorry, baby." She'd take his pain into herself if she could. "So sorry." She stroked his hair, giving him what comfort she could.

Constance cleared her throat. "You did what you had to do." Her voice was firm and compassionate, a combination Melanie was learning to appreciate.

Darcy nodded against her cheek. He held her locked in his arms as if she were all that stood between him and breath-stealing sorrow.

"Which are the worst wounds?" Constance asked. "Let's get this done with and then I'll have an early dinner sent up for you both."

Hidden behind the fall of her hair, Darcy wiped his eyes on her shoulder and straightened.

"My leg and shoulder need sewing up. The rest are just lumps and scratches."

For the next half hour, Melanie did her best to ignore her frayed emotions and concentrate on Constance's crash course in stitching sword gashes. The lady of Dornoch sewed up the deep wound in Darcy's thigh, and then Melanie did the seeping cut in his shoulder, wincing more than him with every poke of the needle.

Wiping her hands, Constance led her to the door and nodded at the linen bandages draped over the chair in front of the dressing table. "Rinse the wounds with whisky when he gets out of the bath. Then use the poultice and bandages to bind them. I'll have your dinner left outside your door." With a wink, she added, "I know food isn't your highest priority, hon, especially once you get him out of that plaid, but he's going to be starving. Make sure he eats well and drinks plenty of milk and tea. Go easy on the wine or he'll get a terrible dehydration headache after all that blood loss."

"Thank you." She gripped the older woman's hand, knowing she wouldn't have made it through the past hour without her cool-headed friend.

"It's nothing, dear. I'll see you when I see you." With another wink, Constance left.

Clicking the door softly closed, she turned to find Darcy sprawled on the bed with one arm over his face. A tuft of soft brown hair shaded his under-arm. His tangled locks lay limp across the blankets protecting the bedding from his grime. His long limbs rested on the bed with the fleshy bulk of relaxed muscle.

He was the most beautiful thing she'd ever laid eyes on.

She went to the foot of the bed and wiggled one dusty boot from a long foot.

"I love you, lass," he said quietly. She looked up to see him watching her from under his arm. "More than I thought a man could love."

Her stone tumbled off its precipice. Tears heated her eyes and moistened her cheeks as she pulled off the other boot and let it fall to the floor. Happiness infused her, making her body warm and heavy with longing. "I love you too."

"Enough to forsake your home?" He sat up and swung his legs over the edge of the mattress, waiting for her response. His face wore a much more jaded version of the vulnerability she had grown used to.

She went to him and undid his belt, shaking her head. "I'll never forsake my home."

When he closed his eyes to shield her from his disappointment, she let the undone belt fall to the blankets and framed his face with her hands. "My home is where you are. I will stay with you. Forever."

He opened his eyes and searched her gaze with shocked wonder.

"I would have told you as much if you'd bothered to ask before leaving for Inverness." She softened the rebuke with a smile. "But I understand why you went, I think. You were trying to keep your word to me."

He nodded. His throat rippled with a swallow. Then he crushed her to his chest. His breath seared her neck as his kisses landed hot and urgent on her skin.

Joy washed over her. For the first time in her life, she felt complete. She hadn't known she had been incomplete, but the sensation of her body molding to Darcy's and her soul aligning with his filled her up in a way she'd never imagined possible.

"Malina," he murmured, finding her mouth and taking her breath away with a desperate kiss. "My Malina."

"My Darcy," she said past a silly grin as she submitted to his ravishing mouth and roaming hands.

"I *am* yours," he whispered between kisses. "I give myself to you, lass, now and for all time. Your happiness shall ever be my greatest goal, your pleasure my greatest desire."

That was the sweetest thing anyone had ever said to her. She could only kiss him back and hold on for dear life as he flipped her beneath him. His touch lulled her into a lust-hazed dream place where nothing mattered but need and love.

"My heart is sore with what I've done today," he murmured as he kissed his way down to the neckline of her dress. He was already undoing the buttons marching down the bodice. "Your cries of pleasure can be my only solace."

Yes, yes, her body said, but her brain retained a shred of reason. "Bath first," she managed, tugging at his kilt and exposing the sweaty, warm skin beneath.

He growled. "You would make me wait to taste you?" Moving faster than a wounded man should be able, he whipped her skirts up and buried his face between her thighs.

"Oh!" she cried as he began kissing her most intimate place with the same desperate passion he'd given her mouth. And then she had no more breath for speech.

Heat and desire swelled as she arched under the voracious tenderness of oral sex performed out of passionate love. As if his motivations weren't apparent enough, he moaned in decadent proof that this was his heaven as well as hers. The vibrations penetrated her womb and sent her spiraling into ecstasy. Her vision went white hot like lightning. She clenched her fingers in his hair. She was flying. She was home.

While she tried to blink the world back into focus, her husband crawled over her like a lion with a fresh kill. "I will bathe now under one condition."

She nodded, limp with satisfaction and drunk with love. If she could have roused her voice, she'd have asked what his condition was, but it didn't really matter. After that enthusiastic performance, Darcy could have whatever Darcy wanted. She hoped her pathetic nod conveyed all of that.

Judging by the twinkle in his eyes, it did.

"My condition is that ye let me do that again, as often as I want. For the rest of our lives."

A laugh bubbled up and out of her. "And here I thought you were a brilliant negotiator. You could have asked for me to return the favor. You could have asked for anything and I would have given it." Her stomach leaped with anticipation as she realized he still didn't know they could have intercourse. "I'll tell you what. Because I'm feeling generous, I'll agree to your condition and I'll even give you a bonus."

"I dinna ken what 'bonus' means."

After a moment's thought, she said, "It's a boon. An extra special gift."

"What boon can a man ask for when he already has all he

wants?"

Her heart squeezed. "I'll show you after your bath."

§

DARCY LEANED HIS head back on the rim of the copper hipbath. With each stroke of Malina's hands over his skin, the guilt that would overwhelm him lost ground to peace. How could he regret defending this precious treasure? She had never actually been in danger, but he hadn't kent that. In fact, Gil and Hamish had convinced him of the opposite.

Thinking his wife had been captured and on her way back to Steafan had broken him the way nothing else could. And then returning to Dornoch to find her safe and hearing her say she'd never leave him had rebuilt him stronger than he'd been before.

"My home is where you are," she had said. *"I will stay with you. Forever."*

Ackergill was lost to him, but he wasn't without a home. Malina was his, as he was hers.

His heart swelled with contentment as her gentle fingers spread warm lather over his collarbones and shoulders, then dipped into the water to clean his chest. She seemed to take great delight in toying with the wee hairs that coursed down to his nether region. And when she washed him down there, he had to bite his lip to keep from begging her for more than her fleeting, teasing touches.

The vixen kent what she did to him. Her sparkling emerald eyes confirmed it, as did the blush in her cheeks and the sly smile curving her mouth.

She had him completely entranced, completely at her mercy. He'd do aught she asked to keep her fawning over him as she was, moving slowly around the tub in naught but her shift, pressing her breasts to his neck and shoulder as she washed him.

Malina didn't speak. Nor did she make him feel as though he ought to. She didn't ask him to recount the horrors of his day. She didn't ask about Inverness. Mayhap she never would.

He'd tell her, of course, about Gravois's odd tinker camp and about Timothy and how if 'twas his magic that brought her here, 'twas nowhere near sufficient at present to send her back.

He'd thought the news would destroy her. But now he looked forward to sharing his unusual experience with her the way a man talks to a trusted friend. But not until he'd loved her senseless. Not until he'd begun proving how much he needed her and what a good husband he would be.

Malina's hands kneaded his neck and shoulders with surprising strength. The mound where her bairn grew cushioned his wet head. He tilted his chin to gaze up at her. So lovely she was, watching him with smiling eyes, her hair loose about her face, her breasts rising and falling with the tide of contented breaths. He wanted to see those breasts bare again. He wanted to see them tremble with sensual excitement as he loved her with his mouth again. He wanted her silky hair wrapped around his hands as she loved him with her mouth.

"The water's growing cool," he said. "Help me out, *mo gradhach.*" She truly was his beloved. His most precious treasure. That which he would kill for. That which he would die for.

He stepped out of the tub, and water sheeted down his legs to pool on the hearth. Malina wrapped him in linens and dried him, her bare feet leaving small, wet prints on the stone. Done drying him, she stepped into his arms, and he held her tight to him. Her warmth chased away the evening chill wafting through the open window. She didn't protest when he lifted her and carried her to the bed.

"I want you," she said. "So badly. But you must be hungry. You should have something to eat first."

"Aye. I'm famished," he said, pulling her shift over her head.

He laid her down and pressed their naked bodies together. His lips claimed hers in a kiss that would leave no doubt in her mind that she was the only nourishment he needed.

"You've lost a lot of blood," she said.

He kissed her harder, smiling when she arched against him and gave up speaking in favor of those wee moans that pricked him deep in his belly.

His fingers found her dewy petals, and the evidence of her desire for him. The need to be inside her consumed him. It could never be what he most desired. But he'd be more than content to bring her pleasure with his hands and his mouth. 'Twas all he could think about. 'Twas his entire purpose.

He plunged his tongue into her mouth as he slipped a finger inside his wife's tight heat.

Christ, feeling her like this, wet tongue to wet tongue, softness between her legs to his hard digit.

Heaven.

His heart burst with love. A sense of belonging flooded him as she clung to his shoulders and pushed her hips forward, asking for more. He gave her more. He stroked her, slow and sure.

He kissed her, deep and hard.

She broke away, panting. "Sit up against the headboard."

He didn't argue. The one glorious night they'd shared in this bed, he'd learned obeying his wife when her voice was breathy and demanding like that led to grand things for them both.

What miracles of pleasure would she show him tonight? Would they come together all the ways they had that night? His cock jerked with hope, but he tried only to think of her, of how he could serve her and prove to her she would never regret staying with him.

She crawled off the bed, eliciting a growl of impatience from him. Only the delight of watching her move about their room completely bare kept him from demanding she return to him so he could finish what he'd started with his finger. When she lit a lantern and came to the bed with bandages and poultice, he realized she was putting off her own desire to care for him.

"I need naught but your cries of pleasure," he said, gripping her arm and trying to tug her up onto the bed. "Ye can fix me later."

"Maybe I want to be rough with you. You've whet my appetite. I want to be wild. I don't want to have to worry about your stitches. So hush. Let me do this, and then you'll get your boon."

He'd forgotten about his boon. Judging by the glow of desire in her eyes, 'twould be a boon for her, too. Good. Her pleasure was his sole focus tonight.

He reluctantly acquiesced, relishing the visual bounty of her pale, lush form as she tended his wounds. She hid no part of herself from him. Pride filled him to ken this caring, lovely creature was his and she trusted him fully with her body and her heart. The saints had truly smiled on him when they'd permitted magic to touch Malina and bring her to him.

Past the nose-tingling scent of the poultice, he scented her desire, that barely there, sweet musk that would drown him with lust when he once again buried his face between her thighs.

With his gaze caressing her breasts, he inhaled deeply, imagining her taste and her soft cries. His eyes closed with the decadent fantasy.

Her touch lifted from him after she fastened the bandage on his thigh.

He reached for her. His hand found only air. The sound of the door latch made him open his eyes. Every muscle in his body tensed as he prepared to defend his woman. But 'twas only Malina bringing in a tray with cold meats and cheeses and a loaf of bread.

"I dinna need food," he said. His stomach promptly betrayed

him as she set the tray on the bed and the savory scents of their dinner made their way to his nose.

"Maybe I do," she said, politely ignoring the grumbling sounds of his gastronomy.

Kneeling beside him, she spread a slice of bread with brie and folded a thinly cut bit of peppered mutton on top. Her teeth sank into the small feast. He had never witnessed anything so sensual as his naked wife closing her eyes in bliss while she indulged her palate.

"Christ," he breathed. "Give me some of that." He guided her hand to his mouth and ripped off his own bite. The bursting flavors of seasoned mutton and tangy cheese had him moaning around his mouthful.

Laughing together like children around a stolen pie, they fed each other and sipped lukewarm tea and milk. When he voiced his desire for wine, his wife refused him.

"Only one glass tonight, and only after I've had my wicked way with you."

Her lips on his cheek helped him be content with the tea and milk. And when she moved her lips to his neck and then his chest, he forgot all about food and drink. He forgot he'd intended to focus his attentions on her. Within moments of finishing their supper, she had him hard and straining for more than the gentle hand play she teased him with.

But he refused to ask for more. He would serve her tonight. He would serve her every night, for she was his.

Malina sat herself astride his thighs so his arousal was trapped between their bodies.

Smoothing his hands down the cool, satiny skin of her back, he cupped her bottom with one hand and traced the other around to stroke her sensitive nub. She was drenched with desire for him. He felt proud. Her want of him satisfied him like nothing else ever would.

"Yes, Darcy," she whispered as she moved with him, reveling in his touch. One of her hands splayed into his damp hair. The other rubbed him intimately against her rounded belly. Her mouth nibbled at his chest. He was on fire for her and she for him.

Christ, to have a wife on his lap and a growing bairn between them was more erotic than anything he'd ever dreamt of. He closed his eyes in rapture and gave himself over to the feel of her, to the feel of the three of them together. His family.

"Look at me," she said.

He lifted his lids lazily. Malina rose up on her knees. Her grip shifted and she sank down over his crown in a rush of liquid pleasure. She held him in her gaze as she drew her lower lip between her teeth. She hissed in a breath, and it wasn't an expression of pain.

He was inside of her.

Panic tensed his muscles.

But Malina didn't look distressed. Her lips parted around a soft sigh as she took even more of him. Inch by slow inch, he filled her, and when her bottom met his thighs, sealing them fully together, her eyes gleamed with wicked delight.

He breathed a curse and stared at his bride, stunned.

He was afraid to trust the incredible pleasure racing in his blood. He was afraid to move and cause her pain. He was frozen in wonder.

But Malina wasn't frozen. She began to move, caressing him in the most intimate way, making them one.

Ecstasy took the place of concern and thrust him to heights of joy he'd never dared to imagine. His wee bride was taking him, all of him, and liking it.

"How?" he asked, fighting the urge to release himself within her. 'Twas too soon. He kent as much, even though he'd never been inside a woman before.

She wound both her arms under his and clutched his shoulders as she continued her sensual undulations. "You're large," she breathed, pleasure written on her bonny, blushing face. "But you won't hurt me as long as I'm ready for you. You're not abnormal, baby. You're perfect." Her eyelids fluttered closed as a little cry parted her lips. "Oh, God, you feel so good. You're perfect, and you're—oh!" Her movements quickened. Her fingers dug into the skin of one shoulder and the bandages on the other. 'Twas a good thing she'd bound his wounds, after all. "You're mine!" she cried as she found her peak.

He couldn't help himself. Lightning struck his spine. He shouted as he followed his wife into purest bliss.

Never before had he felt anything so all-consuming. He could have sworn he rose above his body for a moment, above the Earth, and glimpsed stars and angels and mayhap the Lord, himself.

"I love you, Darcy," Malina whispered against his chest. "I'm sorry that was so fast. We'll get better at it the more we practice."

"Christ almighty," was all he could make himself say.

Chapter 21

MELANIE WOKE TO the familiar pressure of Darcy touching her belly.

Using the width of his fingers as a ruler, he stacked hand over hand until two fingers came to rest at the place where her baby bulge met her sternum. It had become part of their Sunday morning routine in the month they'd lived at Skibo.

"Ye've added three fingers since we came to Dornoch," he said. "Your bairn is growing fair well, I'd say." His soft gaze caressed her face as he leaned over her.

She reached up to smooth his sleep-mussed hair behind his ear. The soft skin at his temple heated her fingers, and she was tempted to trail them all over his body in initiation of the more blush-inducing part of their Sunday morning routine.

"You chose the wrong occupation," she told him, pushing herself up to kiss his nose.

"You should have been a midwife."

"Och, 'tis only *your* legs I care to look between." He moved onto all fours, placing himself over her like a dog with a prized bone. He worked his way down her body with kisses until he was there, doing much more than looking.

A long while later, she ran a washrag over him as he reclined on the bed pillows, utterly relaxed, utterly hers. "I love Sundays," she said, stretching the post-coital tinglies from her limbs as she climbed from the bed to dress for the day. In fact, she loved almost everything about her life with Darcy. If she could change one thing, it would be his homesickness. He never complained, but she'd caught him up on the roof more than once gazing to the north and sipping scotch. If it weren't for his obvious but unspoken longing, everything would be perfect.

"Aye. 'Tis a day of worship," he agreed sagely. "A day to dwell on the Lord and all he has done for those who honor him."

She caught the twinkle in his eye as she pulled on her shift and dress—Darcy never acknowledged the divine except when he was loving her and cursing under his breath.

"I was thinking about the morning sex," she said, earning a grin from her Highlander.

"There is that."

She wadded up the washrag and tossed it at his face, but his quick reflexes had him catching it and tossing it back as he lunged from the bed to spin her around. The playful embrace turned sensual as he hardened against her belly and they lost themselves in kisses.

"I suddenly find myself not minding so much if we miss breakfast this morn'," he said, his fingers undoing the clasps she had just fastened on her dress.

It was another hour before they ventured down to the breakfast room.

She wasn't surprised to hear voices inside as they approached, even though it was almost noon. The briskly turning cogs of the castle's goings on always slowed to a near stand-still on Sunday mornings. It was the one day of the week Darcy didn't rise before her and stay gone until dinner time, building a watermill with Wilhelm at a site up-river from Dornoch. It was also the one day of the week Constance was likely to be late to breakfast, often looking rather tumbled and acting even more cheerful than usual.

But this morning, Constance's voice floated from the breakfast room with the put-on British accent she slipped into when dealing with esteemed guests, whom she'd once told

Melanie wouldn't know what to make of her casual American speech.

Having grown used to her hostess's frequent entertaining, she released Darcy's hand and smoothed her dress as they entered the sunny, glass-enclosed room. She expected an introduction to another merchant from Inverness or a notable tenant from Murray lands.

Instead, she met a pair of ice-blue eyes that flew wide when they spied her and Darcy.

Darcy's hand clamped on her shoulder, and he shifted in front of her. "Aodhan," he said.

Aodhan shot from his overstuffed chair and opened his mouth to say something, but Constance clapped her hands once and chirped, "Good morning, you two. I trust you slept well." She surreptitiously put herself between the two battle-hardened bodies that had just gone on high alert. To Aodhan and her other guest, whom Melanie had barely glimpsed before the solid wall of her husband blocked the room from her sight, Constance said, "You both know Darcy, of course, but have you had a chance to meet his wife, yet? This is Melanie Keith." Constance gripped her hand and attempted to pull her out from behind Darcy.

There was a brief tug of war in which she felt like the rope, but Darcy eventually relented when Constance huffed, "Honestly, it's just a friendly breakfast. Sit. Have some tea and sausage." To Melanie, she said, "Meet Ginneleah Keith, my dear." She led her to the young woman rising hesitantly from the chair beside Aodhan's. "Darcy's aunt by marriage and Lady of Ackergill."

She gaped at the young woman. She was pretty. Very pretty, with flawless, sun-kissed skin, long golden waves pinned back on the sides, and a dress the color of robin's eggs bound around her tiny waist with a yellow ribbon. She transferred her gaping expression to Constance.

She'd been so content at Skibo that she'd forgotten all about her hostess's plan to bring Ginneleah to Dornoch for an intervention regarding the mysterious rose oil.

She couldn't believe Constance had done it. She'd actually gotten Ginneleah here without Steafan.

"You're catching flies, dear," Constance said.

She snapped her mouth shut. Facing the young woman, she recovered and managed an unsteady smile. "Pleased to meet you." When Ginneleah only stared at her with caution in her eyes, she bit back the urge to blurt out, "I'm not a witch." Instead, she took a step back and tried to look as non-threatening as possible.

Darcy was at her side an instant later, Aodhan with him. The men still looked tense, but neither of them were brandishing dirks or snarling threats. In fact, Aodhan's expression warmed when he looked from Darcy to her.

"You look well, lass. 'Tis sorry I am that ye left Ackergill under such unfortunate circumstances." He drew Ginneleah forward with an arm around her shoulders. "I never did think you were a witch, and I might even manage to convince Steafan of it one day. I will say I am surprised to see you both," he said with a look at Darcy. "I doubt Steafan would have permitted Ginnie to come if he'd kent ye'd be here."

"That's why I didn't mention it in my invitation," Constance said. "Now, everyone eat before the tea goes cold."

§

AS THE SERVANTS cleared the breakfast dishes, Constance suggested the ladies take advantage of the warm May sun and walk Skibo's gardens. Melanie's stomach fluttered with nervous butterflies. Did Constance expect her to jump right in with personal questions? She was still recovering from the shock of the first half of their plan having worked. She wasn't prepared to force a friendship down this poor girl's throat if she didn't want it, and Ginneleah definitely seemed shy, if not downright wary.

"Where Ginneleah goes, I go," Aodhan said, cutting into her thoughts. He rose from his overstuffed chair to lay a hand on his daughter's shoulder. "The laird made me vow to nay let the lass out of my sight."

Great. How would she and Constance get Ginneleah alone to talk to her about the rose oil when the girl's father was sticking to her like wool on a sheep?

As usual, Constance was not without a plan. She herded them all from the breakfast room saying, "Then it's settled. Aodhan will escort the ladies to the gardens and oversee their talk of babies and gowns and Darcy will find Wilhelm in the practice yard." Tugging on Darcy's elbow, she added, "I believe the laird mentioned Ian the Bowmaker would be demonstrating his newest creations this afternoon. Perhaps he'll arrange a competition for the men. I'm sure Aodhan will enjoy hearing about it at supper."

Aodhan's shoulders stiffened.

"Are ye sure ye dinna wish to come, Aodhan?" Darcy had apparently caught onto the fact that Constance wanted Ginneleah away from her father. "How long has it been since ye've tried a new bow? It's been years for me. I wonder if I can still pick a pear off a fencepost."

Aodhan grumbled a very Scottish sounding harrumph before pulling Ginneleah aside.

Father and daughter exchanged a few hushed words. Ginneleah rolled her eyes. She might be the lady of Ackergill, but at the moment, she was every bit a teenager seeking independence from an overbearing parent.

Finally Aodhan cleared his throat and said, "I shall accompany Darcy to the practice field, then seek Ginneleah in the gardens in one hour."

Constance said, "What a pity. We understand, though, and I shall personally vouch for the safety of Laird Steafan's lady." She took Ginneleah's arm and gave Melanie a private wink before whisking the girl away.

She followed, but not before Darcy kissed her goodbye and whispered, "Tonight, you will be telling me what you and Constance are about, lass. I dinna trust 'tis bairns or gowns ye'll be discussing."

"Later," she breathed near his ear and sent him off with the Keith war chieftain to play with weapons.

"It seems you're surrounded by protective men," Constance said to Ginneleah as they emerged into the kitchen garden.

The fresh scents of rosemary, parsley, and dill eased her nerves. So did Constance's confident manner. At least one of them seemed to know what to do.

"Aye, but they mean well," Ginneleah said diplomatically. She had a soft alto voice that probably had a soothing effect on Steafan. What kind of effect might Steafan have on Ginneleah?

The girl didn't look depressed. Maybe because she was away from him for a time.

"Then you must consider yourself blessed," Constance said. "As I do, dear. I have a protective husband as well. And from what I've observed, so does Melanie."

Ginneleah glanced at her and some of her wariness thawed. She stopped short of smiling, however. "'Tis glad I am that Big Darcy is wed. And sorry I am that my husband thought so poorly of you as to force his nephew to run away to keep you safe."

The sentiment appeared genuine, though Ginneleah obviously harbored some reservations where she was concerned. She thanked the girl and smiled warmly, hoping to put her at ease. It seemed to work, because soon, they were talking freely about how Darcy's mill was running and how Edmund and Fran were faring up at Fraineach.

When they'd wandered deep into Skibo's manicured paths of blooming bushes and trees and were surrounded by nothing but fragrant nature and warm sunshine, Constance settled herself on a stone bench and said, "Ginneleah, I've wanted to meet you for some time, dear. Ever since Wilhelm received a note of gracious thanks from Steafan for a gift of rose oil."

Ginneleah's tan cheeks took on a hint of pink. "We're verra thankful for the gift."

"Lovely, dear. But I have a confession to make. Neither Wilhelm nor I sent that oil to you, and I fear whoever did has misused our name and may mean you harm."

Constance was no mincer of words. Melanie cringed in sympathy as Ginneleah blinked in surprise and then paled.

"Harm? What do ye mean?" Her blue eyes darted around, as if looking for protection from the father she'd so confidently dismissed a little while ago.

Constance pulled a small velvet pouch from a pocket in her dress and carefully unwrapped two glass vials protected within. One had a clear stopper, the other a blue one. The contents of both vials looked indistinguishable from ordinary olive oil, pale gold in color and mildly viscous.

"I ordered these from Inverness when I sent for you," she said. "One is a lubricant meant to assist marital relations. The other is used to prevent a woman getting with child. They both smell of roses or whatever perfume the maker chooses, and they both can make joining more pleasant, but—" Constance tipped the vial with the blue stopper to moisten the tip of one finger.

She placed her finger to her tongue and made a face. "The one with quinine in it has a bitter taste while the other tastes only of perfume and oil."

She held the vials out to Melanie and said, "Take a taste. It's perfectly safe taken orally, and can, in fact, be given in quite high doses, even to pregnant women, to treat malaria."

She raised her eyebrows, impressed as always with Constance's knowledge. She inspected the vials under

Ginneleah's worried gaze and dabbed a drop of each oil on her tongue to compare them. The one with the clear stopper dried her tongue and sent sharp notes of rose scent straight to her nose. The one with the blue stopper did the same, but when she closed her mouth to moisten her tongue and swallow, a bitter taste made her wrinkle her nose.

The anxiety in Ginneleah's eyes vanished as she watched. Her eyebrows lifted with curiosity, then furrowed. "Do ye mean someone might have sent the oil as a gift meaning it as a curse?" When Melanie handed her the vials, she didn't hesitate to sniff and taste them for herself.

"I'm afraid so," Constance said. "Although you won't know for sure unless you taste a drop of the oil you have at Ackergill. That's why I invited you to Dornoch. Not to give you more oil, unless you'd like the one in your right hand." She nodded at the vial with the clear stopper. "But to warn you. I wouldn't use the oil you have at home again, or trust any more that comes in Wilhelm's name."

Ginneleah made a face and shivered at the taste of the quinine oil. She searched Constance's face with wide eyes. "But who would do such a thing?" she said in a voice so vulnerable it melted her heart. Tears pooled behind the girl's lashes as she looked down at the two vials. "Steafan wants an heir so badly, and I want to give him one. To think of all the time we've wasted." Ginneleah loved Steafan. It was clear from the sorrow in her voice and the disappointment etched on her young face.

Melanie touched Ginneleah's knee. "Someone must have a grudge against your husband," she said gently. "But we've found them out. As long as you don't use that oil any more, you'll get the better of them, whoever they are."

"All this time, I thought…I thought..."

"That you couldn't conceive," Constance offered, her voice more tender than Melanie had ever heard it. "It's possible. But I'd test that oil if I were you before you go thinking anything is wrong with you."

Ginneleah sniffed. "What shall I do without the oil?" she said so quietly she might have been talking to herself. She turned imploring eyes to Constance. "I fear using anything now," she said, thrusting the vials into Constance's hands. "But—" She looked down again, her cheeks pink.

"I'll go see how lunch is coming along," Constance said, wrapping the vials and tucking them away. "If I see your father, I'll point him this way." She gave Melanie an encouraging nod.

As Constance disappeared down the path toward the castle, she had the urge to take the despondent Ginneleah into her arms to comfort her. But they'd only just met. Instead, she said, "Here we are, me pregnant without meaning to get that way and you having tried so hard and been disappointed time and again." She gave a mirthless chuckle. "My grandmother used to tell me you can never count on life to be fair. I guess she was right."

Ginneleah attempted a smile. "Mayhap things will change for me and Steafan now. Oh, but I shallna enjoy telling him of this discovery. He will be furious. Anger comes so easily to him."

She didn't know what to say. Was Steafan abusive to her? As soon as she had the thought, she dismissed it. Ginneleah didn't give the impression she was mistreated in any way.

But from her quiet plea from a few moments ago, Melanie doubted Steafan was as talented a lover as Darcy had proven to be. She decided to get right to the point, hoping to say everything she needed to before Aodhan found them.

"Do you find it necessary to use oil?" She winced at the bald question, but she wasn't sure how else to start.

The girl's cheeks pinked up again. "Aye. As you must with Big Darcy." She met her eyes with no small difficulty. "I may be young, but I've heard the rumors. If what the lasses say about your husband is true, ye have it harder than I do by far."

She smiled gently. "Never trust a rumor. Especially one started by a spurned woman."

Ginneleah gave her a curious look, so she shared with her the tale Darcy had told her one quiet night. Holding her in his arms, he'd told her about Anya, the woman who'd laughed at him in that most vulnerable moment of first showing himself to a potential lover, the woman who'd outright lied to make him think he was too large.

The bitch. She hoped she never met the woman, because she'd never been so tempted to slap anyone before.

"Oh, that's awful." Ginneleah's face was free from her earlier wariness. "Would ye believe *that* one tried pushing herself on poor Steafan while he courted me? I dinna like the woman, and nor does Steafan. In fact, she's the reason my husband took such umbrage to you. She's the one who told him of your wee box. To hear Steafan tell it, she found it in the stables and described it perfectly. She was the one to call you a witch, and once the word was uttered, Steafan…well, he is verra protective of the clan. Mayhap too protective. But he's a good man. In his heart, he wants to do what's right."

Clearly, the girl—no, the young woman, for Ginneleah had wisdom in her eyes that spoke of girlhood being past—was devoted to her husband. That was good. If she was afraid of him or disgusted by him, no amount of sex-ed would help them.

She stored away the information about Anya for later consideration. At the moment, Ginneleah desperately needed some encouragement in matters of intimacy.

"You love him, don't you?" Surprisingly, she was glad Steafan had such a sweet, positive influence in his life. Without Ginneleah, he might be even crankier.

"He is my husband," she said modestly. "'Tis my duty."

Love wasn't always part of marriage. Not in her time, but especially not in this time. She didn't bother Ginneleah with the observation.

"You wear your duty well," she said, nudging her arm and smiling a little wickedly. "I can tell you care for him, and I'm glad. I might not be in a hurry to ever see him again myself, but I can appreciate that he's an attractive man, and if he's good to you, and you care for him, then I wish you both every happiness."

"My thanks. I wish the same for you and Big Darcy."

"Please, just call him Darcy. He's not as big as all that. In fact, I don't really think it's possible for a man to be so big as to make joining with his wife impossible."

Ginneleah snorted, then blushed and covered her mouth with her hand. "How unladylike of me." She smiled shyly, but then her eyes darkened with sadness.

"It hurts, doesn't it?"

Ginneleah looked away.

"Intimacy between men and women can be wonderful," she said carefully, "but it takes practice and some skill and knowledge to make it so."

Ginneleah turned curious eyes her way.

They spent the next half hour talking about female anatomy, foreplay, and pleasures that could be had without intercourse. Eventually, the poor young woman stopped blushing. She even laughed some, and her mirth rivaled the joyous calls of the birds in the garden. It was easy to see why Steafan was rumored to be quite smitten with her.

By the time Aodhan clomped into the little clearing, Ginneleah was holding her hand and thanking her. "I shall speak gently to Steafan of the things you have told me today. I dinna think he is ready to accept you back to Ackergill, but mayhap if I can give him a bairn, I will inform him 'twas you and Darcy who found out about the oil."

"It was Constance who thought of it. Not me."

"Mayhap. But the Lady of Dornoch isna in want of my

husband's good graces."

Ginneleah sealed herself in her heart with a conspiratorial smile before rising to greet her father.

Melanie dared to hope they might meet again one day, both of them with babies on their hips.

Chapter 22

A FEMININE SHRIEK of delight made Steafan look up from his ledger. Golden and fresh as a sunflower, Ginneleah dashed around his desk, all shimmering hair and shining eyes the color of pale skies. A garden of innocence she was, and her exuberance lifted his spirits. The keep hadn't been the same without her presence warming its halls.

"Ginnie," he whispered into her hair as he swept her up in a tight embrace. She flung her arms around his neck and kissed his face, just in front of his ear. He grit his teeth to keep from taking her mouth in a deep kiss. Nearly two weeks she'd been away with her da, gone to Dornoch at the Murray's invitation. 'Twas the only separation from her he'd kent since they'd wed. He wanted her badly, but he would hear about her travels first.

"Are ye well?" he asked. "Is your da seeing to the horses?"

She nodded in a circular way, ending with a shrug. "Da is seeing to…things. I am well, and happy to be home, but I have much news." Dark thoughts clouded her eyes. "I'd like to wait for da. We agreed to tell ye together. I should go up and change. I'm dusty from the road."

"Go on," he said, letting her feet to the floor. His arms released her reluctantly. "I'll send up a bath. We shall have a private dinner tonight. Just the three of us."

Ginneleah pranced from his sight, whatever sadness he'd glimpsed in her eyes no match for her youthful stride.

Two hours later, he met his bonny wife in the private dining room. She and Aodhan were already seated, but they both rose when he came in. Ginneleah curtsied in the formal way, which she didn't have to do, and Aodhan inclined his head in greeting, his eyes guarded as usual.

Pleasantries were exchanged. Dinner was served. Then Aodhan began with, "Hamish and Gil are dead."

He stared over his full trencher. Of all the news his second might bring from Dornoch, that had been the least expected and the most unwelcome. He'd assumed Hamish's and Gil's absence when the rest of the search party had returned meant they'd caught the scent of his wayward nephew and his witch of a wife and were travelling far to capture them. He'd thought his loyal servant and the Keith's best tracker merely thorough and obedient. Now he kent better.

Fury climbed his neck and heated his face. Two of his best men, gone. "How?"

Aodhan's gaze was unflinching. "Darcy killed them."

Ginneleah gaped at her da, a look of betrayal in her eyes he didn't understand. But he was too shocked and angry to consider his wife's feelings.

Rage pushed him to his feet. He gripped the table, the wood creaking in his hands.

"'Twas no' enough for him to flee with a condemned witch and turn his back on his responsibility? He had to take from me two of my best men? His own kinsmen?" His nephew would pay for his sins.

"They ambushed the lad on the road outside Dornoch," Aodhan said. "Killed his horse. Ye ken how your nephew loved that horse. 'Twas a gift from your brother. They tried to take him as ye wished, and he fought. He fought well, and mayhap didna ken his own strength. Mayhap he was a wee bit crazed thinking his wife was in danger from them."

"Dinna make excuses for him. He is a murderer. And his wife

deserves what danger she meets."

"We dinna ken what happened on that road," Aodhan said evenly. "Mayhap Darcy meant to kill them. Mayhap he didna. It happened well before Ginnie and I arrived. I will say the lad confessed it to me as soon as we came to Dornoch, and when he showed me their graves, he wept bitterly in my arms for the loss of his kinsmen. My heart tells me many of those tears were for Ackergill and Fraineach. He is a Keith, Steafan, your brother's eldest, and you have set yourself against him."

Indignation puffed his chest. "He set himself against me." He thumped his fist on his breastbone. "He chose a witch over his clan, over his responsibility. He was my heir. He could have been master of Ackergill Keep one day, yet he tossed it all away. And now he is a murderer."

Disappointment and grief pricked his temper as the weight of Hamish's and Gil's deaths settled on him. And Aodhan was defending their murderer, a young man with such promise who had been ruined by association with a witch. Since Darcy had met the wicked woman, he'd been a different man, a far less obedient and far more reckless one. What a fool he'd been to marry them!

He'd been thinking only of Darcy having bairns to carry on his brother's blood, nay of what kind of woman the stranger might be.

He slammed a fist down on the table, making the platters dance and Ginneleah jump. The poor lass stared at her trencher, her face drawn with fear.

He forced himself to calm. "Dinna fear me, lass," he said as he resumed his seat and took her hand. "My anger isna for you." Never for her. She was the ray of sun to the pall of his duty, the refreshing spring in the parching desert of leadership.

Aodhan cleared his throat. "Whatever your nephew is or isna, there is more news from Dornoch. Ginnie?"

"Wait," he said. "Were Hamish and Gil seen to in the proper

way?"

"Aye. The Murray and Darcy saw to them before I arrived. They are laid in the churchyard in Dornoch with markers to say they were Keith."

He bowed his head and remembered his men. He hadn't considered his nephew might fight rather than be taken. Always a peaceable lad, he'd been, until the witch. He shook his head.

His stomach burned with regret. He should have sent Edmund to reason with Darcy. He should have foreseen the woman's influence on him.

The weight of Aodhan's and Ginneleah's gazes made him look up at last. "So my nephew hides with the Murray," he said. Anger coursed through him. If he had suspected Darcy and the witch might be at Dornoch, he never would have let his wife go, not even with Aodhan as her escort. "Why would he flee there rather than to Inverness or further south?"

"I think he went to the Murray because of the rumors of the laird's wife."

Aodhan's words parted the curtain of his memory. Long ago, when he was just coming into manhood, the young and impetuous heir to the Murray was rumored to have razed an entire village to save the woman he later took to wife from a burning at the stake. If the rumors were true, the Lady Murray was a condemned witch. How could he have forgotten? Och, he'd let his pride at being noticed by the much-feared laird blind him to possible danger. If aught had happened to Ginneleah, he'd never have forgiven himself.

He gripped his wife's shoulder and searched her face for aught sign of illness or, saints forbid, corruption. "My nephew sought the help of yet another witch and my Ginneleah was exposed to a double portion of evil? Why did ye no' bring her straight home when ye realized ye were surrounded by witches?" he growled at Aodhan.

"The rumors arena true," Ginneleah interrupted. Her face was as innocent as ever, her guileless gaze a balm for his fear. Bless the saints, she hadn't been changed.

When he didn't discourage her boldness, she added, "Lady Constance is a fine, upstanding woman. She was a most kind hostess and saw me and da well cared for."

Had any other lass of seventeen spoken with such confidence of something she should be far too innocent to ken aught about, he would have dismissed her words. But he couldn't discount the earnest plea in her countenance. Ginneleah may be young, but he had never kent her to judge another's character poorly. 'Twas one of the qualities he admired so well in her. She had wisdom others her age would lack even the wits to covet.

He exhaled and released some of his rage. Kissing her head to show his approval of her speech, he drew her soothing fragrance of gardens and sunshine into his lungs.

Remaining with an arm on Ginneleah's chair, he eyed his second. "And what think ye of the woman?"

"Ye dinna believe my assessment of Darcy's wife. Why should ye believe it of the Murray's?"

He showed his teeth. "I asked what ye think. What I choose to believe after isna your concern."

Aodhan's eyes twinkled with disarming humor. Steafan could never quite cow the man, not even when they'd been lads and he five years Aodhan's senior. 'Twas one of the reasons he respected him so well.

"Neither of them are witches," his second said. "Darcy didna go to Dornoch for a witch's help but for the help of another man who loved a woman wrongly accused."

"The box," he said by way of defending his actions. The wicked bit of wood and metal sealed Melanie's guilt. He took a confident sip of wine, daring Aodhan with a glare over the brim to counter that proof.

"'Tis a strange item, indeed," Aodhan agreed, no doubt recalling Steafan's attempts to burn it, chop it with an axe, even grind it beneath the massive stones in Darcy's mill, all to no avail. 'Twas impossible to even scratch the accursed thing. In a fit of fury, he had hurled it over the cliffs where if it dared to spite him and not be dashed to pieces on the rocks, at least he wouldn't have to witness it. "But ye have no proof your nephew's wife has aught to do with its magic. She claims to be a victim of the thing, to have no understanding of its workings. And I believe her."

Ginneleah's hand on his arm made him look at her. Her brows were slanted in a silent plea.

"I suppose you agree with your da," he said with resignation. "Go on. Speak your mind, lass."

"Melanie is no witch," she said without hesitation. "At least, well, I dinna ken any witches, thank the saints, but I ken goodness when I see it and both Melanie and Constance are good and true. I believe Darcy brought his wife to Dornoch because he thought Laird Murray would offer them refuge. To his mind, his wife was unfairly accused, though I ken you only thought to protect Ackergill when you arrested her. He hoped the Murray would sympathize, and he was right. As for Gil and Hamish, he only fought them because of his love for his wife. Ye'd do the same for me and ye'd be just as ruthless. But because you are such a good man, I ken ye'd mourn the unfairness of having to slay your kinsmen, just as your nephew does."

She pinched her lips shut and looked at the table, mayhap embarrassed she'd said so much. 'Twas, in fact, the most he'd heard her speak in one go and certainly the most disagreeable he'd ever found her. He almost smiled at her daring, but the last of her words reminded him just how bleak the facts were.

He released a sigh. His heart was heavy. He'd lost Gil and Hamish. Darcy, too. And his only remaining nephew and current heir, Edmund, refused to look him in the eye. Was all this loss worth pursuing an evil that seemed to be gone from their midst?

Quietly, he said, "I canna risk Ackergill by permitting my nephew's return. Nor can I forgive his slaying of our kinsmen. If he or his wife set foot on Keith land, they will face just punishment for their sins. But I will nay hunt them."

Ginneleah faced him, her eyes at once bright with hope and weary with sadness.

He cleared his throat. "'Twould be foolish to set myself against the Murray and risk more of my men for a pair of loathsome sinners. Let them be Dornoch's problem."

Her lips smiled, but her eyes remained sad. He wished he could wipe the sadness away, but he couldn't give the tender-hearted lass aught more than his promise to leave his nephew and his wife to the inevitable consequences of their wickedness.

Aodhan said, "'Tis a fair pronouncement." He sipped from his goblet and glanced at Ginneleah. "There is more news from Dornoch." His tone implied Steafan was apt to like this news about as much as the last.

He harrumphed. "It'll wait until morn. I have need of my wife." Looking into her eyes, he said, "I am no' accustomed to being without you for so long, and I have missed ye greatly."

She paled and ducked her head to stare at her hands.

Panic gripped his heart. Ginneleah had never shown reluctance before. Had the Lady of Dornoch or Darcy's wife turned her against him? A spark of anger made his pulse tick in his throat. He should never have let her out of his sight.

A tear rolled down Ginneleah's cheek, and his anger yielded to sympathy.

"What's happened, lass?" He tilted up her chin to capture her gaze. Fear drew her features taut, but there was tenderness there as well. She didn't shy from his touch. Relief made his breath catch. "Go on, Ginnie. I see a storm of words wanting to get out.

Dinna be afraid of me."

She glanced at her da, who nodded his encouragement, then she took a shaky breath.

"Laird Murray never sent you any rose oil," she said. "He showed me his seal, and 'tis different from the one on the vials we received."

He tensed. There were too many surprises in this conversation. His body strained in his chair. He wanted to pace and yell and throw somat that would make a mighty crash to startle the servants, but he refused to upset his wife any more than she already was.

"What are ye saying?" he asked as civilly as he could. "Where did it come from then?"

He looked from Ginneleah to Aodhan, whose face was grave.

"Now that is somat we can discuss in the morn," his second said. "Let it be sufficient for tonight that you shouldna trust what ointments ye've been sent in the past." His gaze darted to Ginneleah and his lips pressed hard and white. "They might be dangerous," he gritted out.

His fists clenched. Looking at Ginneleah, he saw more tears leak from her eyes.

"Dangerous in what way?" he asked, lifting his wife's chin to capture her attention. Torn between commanding Aodhan to speak plainly and comforting his wife, he chose to comfort Ginneleah. He made his tone soft and stroked her cheek with his thumb.

"It's laced with quinine," she whispered, her chin quivering in his grasp. "Someone did not want us to conceive." She tried to say more, but shook her head, overwhelmed with grief.

He took her into his arms and smoothed her hair with a hand he forced not to shake. He tried to meet Aodhan's eyes over her head, but his second looked away, no doubt furious with him for failing to protect Ginneleah. He had every right.

Steafan should never have trusted such an intimate gift from a man he didn't ken.

Ever since Willie's death, he'd been so careful to protect Ackergill. He'd hardly left the keep for fear of meeting with an untimely death and leaving his lands without a laird. He'd been stern with visitors, hardly suffering them to set foot on Keith territory. But he hadn't been diligent enough.

He seethed with self-loathing.

Aodhan shoved away from the table. "I'll take my leave and see you in the morn'. Ginnie, goodnight, lass."

She nodded but made no move to leave his embrace. The lass sought his comfort even though the responsibility for two years' perpetual disappointments lay with him. She was a far better mate to him than he'd been to her. He would never forgive himself.

After Aodhan slipped out, she sniffed and dabbed at her eyes with her napkin. "I'd like to tell ye more about the oil," she said. "But not here. Can we retire for the night?"

"Of course, my sunflower." He owed her compensation for his grievous failings. She would ask for naught the rest of their days together that he would deny her.

§

HER ARMS FULL of supplies from her ride to Wick, Anya used her hip to nudge open the door to her room. Her da's raspy nagging faded behind the rough planks as she kicked it shut behind her. When he finally shuffled out for his nightly visit to the pub, she muttered, "Good riddance."

Dropping her basket on the workbench that took up one whole wall of her room, she looked about for the vial she'd filled for Steafan. Thanks to her trip, she had the quinine that still needed to be added and enough to make herself a new supply, besides. Her belly heated at the memory of the last time she had used the oil.

She hoped Aodhan would return soon from his errand. Two weeks was far too long to go without a tup.

Lifting the vial meant for her laird, she added the quinine, doubling the dose, just to be sure Aodhan's brat would never have the privilege of carrying the laird's child. A quick stir and she corked the vial and reached for the wax to seal it. Where she should have felt the smooth stick of wax in its cubby, her hand only found the flintbox she kept beside it.

"Where are ye, ye bugger?" She searched her various cubbies by lantern light, but didn't see the wax, nor the counterfeit seal she'd bought to trick Steafan into believing the vial was from the Murray.

A commotion in the main room of the cottage made her think her da had returned for his purse, but she realized it wasn't her da when her door burst open and Aodhan's muscular shoulders filled the space it had occupied. His eyes cut to her, sharp as broken ice.

Her heart leapt. He craved a tup even more than she did, by the looks of him. Forgetting her wax and seal, she rushed to him, expecting him to sweep her up in his arms.

"What are ye doing here?" she asked, wondering why he wasn't wrapping himself around her and kissing her face. He usually sent a message to her when he wanted to meet. He never came to the cottage she shared with her da, nor did she ever seek him out at the keep. "Ye must be in poor shape, indeed, to come directly to me. Let me care for ye, Aodhan, but we shouldna remain here. My da may return."

Aodhan shoved her away so hard she stumbled into her workbench, bruising her hip. She gasped with shock. A forceful lover Aodhan was, indeed, but he had never been violent before.

Fear spiked in her chest as she watched the man prowl forward, a dangerous animal about to strike.

"Aodhan, what's come over you?"

"Give me one reason I shouldna bind you and toss ye in the

dungeons to await Steafan's judgment." His voice was a growl of scarcely contained fury.

Her heart fell into her stomach. "What are ye babbling about?" She kent the answer already. Confirming her worst nightmare, Aodhan pulled from his sporran the wax and seal she'd been looking for a moment ago. He slammed them down on her workbench, crowding her, frightening her.

"I searched your room upon my return, hoping I wouldna find these." The anger drained out of him as he studied her face. "What made ye do it? What turned you against your own laird?"

Her mind reeled for only an instant before self-preservation forced her to sort out the facts. She was found out. But by Aodhan, who had some affection for her. All was not lost.

She fell to her knees, clutching at his plaid. "I let jealousy tempt me, Aodhan. Please show me mercy. I'll never send another vial. I'm sorry. I'll do whatever ye ask to spare me and nay tell Steafan." She trembled with very real fear as she realized the anger filling Aodhan's eyes again was beyond that of a loyal second. 'Twas the fury of a da and mayhap that of a betrayed lover.

How had he found out?

Had her da spied on her possessions while she'd been gone? The ungrateful cur! After all the care she'd given him, all the meals she made him, all the perfumes she painstakingly made and sold to support him when she could have moved to Thurson and made four times as much in the bawdyhouse her sister lived and worked in.

"Up with ye." Aodhan left her no more time for wondering, and pulled her up roughly by her arm. His face an inch from hers, he spat, "You will be gone from Ackergill by dawn or you will face Steafan for your two years of treachery."

He would let her flee. Mayhap she could even finagle an escort out of his deal. No gentleman would send a woman off on her own, and Aodhan was the most courteous gentleman she'd ever lain with. Surely he'd send her off with a guard whom she might bribe into playing spy for her so she could determine whether 'twas her da or some other who needed paying back for this betrayal.

She twisted her face as if she were in pain. "Ye ask me to leave my home? For how long? Where shall I go? Who will go with me and protect me?"

Aodhan released her. "'Tis no concern of mine where ye go or how ye fare," he said with a voice as frigid as his glare. "But ken ye this. If I ever lay eyes on you again, I will bring ye straight to the laird for him to do with as he wills." He released her, and the sharpest edge of his icy expression thawed. "I tell him at dawn. You best be gone by then."

He turned and left, taking with him the wax and seal. He didn't even pause to look over his shoulder when she feigned a faint and let herself collapse to the floor.

Cold disbelief washed over her as she pulled herself up by her workbench. Aodhan was abandoning her to the wilderness, to possible thieves and rapists. How dare he! He'd been her lover for more than a year; surely she warranted more consideration from him.

Aodhan would pay as would whoever had revealed her plot with the rose oil.

Her face hot with indignation, she began shoving her most precious possessions into a basket for the ride to Thurson. Her sister would help her. Seona loved plotting revenge, mayhap even more than she did.

§

STEAFAN ESCORTED HIS wife to her bedchamber. He couldn't bring himself to meet her eyes.

She would be justified in banishing him from her bed for a time. 'Twas the least he deserved.

Pausing before her door, he cleared his throat and said, "I'll leave ye, lass. Rest well. We shall break our fast together if ye wish."

Her hand tightened on his arm. "Dinna go." Pink infused her sun-kissed cheeks. "We have much time to make up for."

His heart squeezed painfully. Two bloody years his folly had cost his lovely wife the one thing she seemed to want more than aught else, a bairn, an heir to his seat.

She must have seen his disgust with himself on his face. Her lithe fingers traced his beard. "Dinna blame yourself. Stay with me. Let us comfort each other."

His young woman's resilience amazed him. He stood in awe of her apparent willingness despite his failure. "But without the oil—" He looked away, unable to finish. He didn't wish to hurt her as he'd hurt Darla. He wouldn't.

She pushed the door open and led him inside. "About that." Her full lips quirked in a smile he wasn't accustomed to seeing on her face. 'Twas a woman's smile, a seductress's smile.

"I believe I have a solution. So long as ye dinna mind spending more time in my bed than usual."

"Och, lass," he said, closing the door. "I could spend days in your bed and wish to spend days more."

"It shouldna take days, my love. Mayhap an hour or two, though." She stood on her toes to kiss his mouth.

He stiffened at her forwardness, then melted into her scent of sun-warmed gardens.

Mayhap 'twas the guilt making him softer than usual toward her. Mayhap 'twas the irresistible purity of his sweet wife. Whatever the reason, he didn't mind yielding to her bold advance.

"I am at your disposal, *mo gradhaich,*" he said when she broke the kiss. Heat filled his loins as she skimmed her hands up his shirtfront and toyed with the laces at his collar. That seductress's smile looked more and more appealing on her bonny face. "Do with me as ye will. For as long as ye will."

Chapter 23

One year later

DARCY WOKE WITH the tickle of an ant crawling along his wrist. Blinking the sleep from his eyes, he watched the wee, black creature navigate the forest of hairs on his arm as it made its way to the crease of his elbow. A soft snore made him turn his head toward Malina.

They'd lain down in the long grass in the shade of a great ewe tree overlooking Skibo, but the sun had shifted during their nap to shine full on them. He ought to wake his wife and move her back to the shade lest her fair skin turn too pink. But his limbs were heavy with relaxation, and he didn't wish to do aught more than gaze on her bare form for a while.

Malina lay on her stomach atop the burgundy Murray plaid he'd worn since the day she had forsaken her own time for his sake. Her smooth back curved like an ivory valley toward the succulent hills of her bottom. Her hair glistened around her shoulders like mica spun into fine strands. Her bonny face rested on her arm, pink lips parted, the tips of her white teeth showing.

And beneath that delightful exterior was a woman who was his perfect match in every way.

How he loved her!

He'd loved her when he'd wed her. And now, after being wed for more than a year, seeing her through the birth of their cherub of a daughter, and making a home for the three of them in

Dornoch, he loved her more than he'd ever imagined possible. Would he love her even more in another year? Ten years from now? When their children were grown, like Wilhelm and Constance's?

Aye. He kent he would. How could he not? She was his wife, his mate.

Her eyes eased open. Their gazes caught. She smiled. "Hi," she said and then she yawned.

"You are beautiful when ye sleep," he said.

"Only when I sleep?"

"Aye. The rest of the time, ye are merely radiant."

She wiggled closer for a kiss. He brought her into his arms and indulged in her sugared scent and her taste of wine and berries. He grumbled when she broke the kiss and said, "We should get back. Janine will be hungry."

"Constance will see to her. I am not nearly finished with ye, lass." He rolled to bring her astride him. Her yelp of surprise aroused him, as did the swell of her lush breasts before his face.

The generous orbs were still firm and full with milk for their daughter. "And if ye need some relief," he said, shaping those glorious treasures in his hands, "I am more than happy to ease your suffering." When she lowered herself to his mouth with desire-darkened eyes, he took her milk greedily, moaning with her at the decadent intimacy.

No pleasure could match making love with his wife under the summer sun. The only thing that could make an afternoon such as this better would be if they were back in Ackergill, under one of the cherry trees by the mills. A year hadn't eased his yearning for his former home.

He longed to walk the cliff edge with wee Janine in his arms and show her the sea and the islands that could be glimpsed on a clear day. He wished he could simply forget those desires. He wished he could be as content with Dornoch as Malina seemed.

But he never did forget. And each day when he donned the Murray's burgundy plaid, he felt a twinge of discord deep in his vitals.

"I love you," Malina said as she rode him gently "So much, Darcy." Her passionate words and the perfect vision she made warmed his heart and eased his useless longing.

"I love you too, lass. For all time."

The horizon had turned pink by the time they put their clothes back on and strolled back to Skibo. The keep rose up from Dornoch with its impressive towers and spires, a fortress built to be as pleasing to the eye as it was impregnable. So unlike the utilitarian keep glowering over Ackergill, the pinnacle of security that had fixed itself in his heart as the purest symbol of clan.

"You seem melancholy," Malina said as she linked her fingers with his and playfully swung their arms.

"Mayhap I'm a mite homesick," he admitted. "But lovesick enough to nay fash over it."

She rested her head on his arm. He wound it around her waist and drew her close for the rest of the walk. Upon entering the keep, a maid hurried from the kitchen and headed to the great hall with freshly laundered linens. "Lady Murray was looking for ye," she said when she spied them. "She'll be in the solar."

"Oh, I hope Janine hasn't been a handful," Malina said, her tone anxious. Her stride quickened, and she tugged him toward the room that was Constance's favorite for playing with Janine and her grandchildren when her elder sons visited with their wives.

Constance was on her hands and knees on the vibrantly colored oriental carpet, crawling alongside their nine-month-old daughter amidst a scatter of wooden toys.

The bairn squealed upon seeing her mother and opened and closed her chubby hands until Malina swept her up. The bonny lass had lips as lovely and pouty as her mother's, and flopping silvery-fair hair. Her eyes were the only thing she seemed to have gotten from the man his wife referred to as "the sperm donor." They were soft brown, and he could almost imagine the color had come from him instead of someone else.

Constance was not alone with Janine.

"Aodhan," he greeted as Malina cooed to their daughter.

"Darcy," the war chieftain said with a nod of respect. "'Tis good to see you, lad. Melanie, ye look well. I've met your bairn already. A fine wee lass she is, and lovely as her namesake."

He warmed at the acknowledgement of his mother as well as at the friendly words from a Keith he admired so well. But caution held that warmth in check. "What brings you to Dornoch? Are Edmund and my uncle well?"

Constance mentioned some chore that needed seeing to in the kitchen and asked Malina for her help. The women left, Malina with Janine on her hip and a concerned slant to her brows.

Aodhan watched them go, then cleared his throat. "Aye, your brother and uncle fare well. Verra well, in fact. They both have new bairns."

His heart leapt to hear Edmund and Fran had a new wee ane. Then it occurred to him that Aodhan had said *both*. He turned stunned eyes to the blushing war chieftain.

"Ye heard me right, lad. I am a grandsire. And you have a cousin at last."

§

"YOU'RE CERTAIN THEY'RE to come this way?" Anya peered through a scrawny bush to the narrow road below. Winding along the lichen-covered, ocean-side cliffs by Brora, this road was not only the shorter of the two a traveler might choose to go from Dornoch to Ackergill, but wide enough for a cart the whole way, and thus the more likely choice for the caravan she was hoping to intercept.

"Aye, An," Glen grumbled. "Cease your fashin'. I didna risk my neck to spy for you these months to let ye down now. They'll be leavin' this morn' and passin' by this way soon. But 'tis early yet." He pulled her back from the lookout and flipped her beneath him before wiggling his hips between her skirted legs. "There's time for another tup," he said with a grin.

'Twas with a great effort she kept from rolling her eyes. For months, she'd been meeting the cocky guard in secret and trading her body for news from the keep. Glen wasn't her first choice in allies, but her selfish sister had left her no choice. Some time before she'd fled to Thurson, Seona had abandoned her post at the bawdyhouse. It was rumored she'd run off with a patron without leaving word as to where she'd gone, or when she might return. Since Glen was the only man from Ackergill who regularly visited the bawdyhouse, he was the only one left whom she could rely on for information.

At least the randy bastard had proven useful. 'Twas because of him she kent Steafan's wife had borne him a son and Steafan had invited Big Darcy and his wife back to Ackergill.

She had seethed with rage upon hearing the news. Her laird could forgive a witch for tampering with evil and his nephew for rebellion and murder, but he couldn't forgive a fair lass such as she for giving him her heart and desiring to serve him as wife. Nay, he hadn't even been given a chance to forgive her, since Aodhan had never revealed her part with the rose oil. And, much to her indignation, Steafan had never asked where she'd gone, at least according to Glen. For all she kent, the man was deceiving her to keep her dependent on him.

He noisily licked her ear as he shoved up her skirts, and she had all she could do to not grind her teeth. Granted, Glen was better at tupping than most of the men she saw at the bawdyhouse, where she'd taken on Seona's duties in her stead, but he was a callous, wily bastard who she trusted as far as she could toss a caber, and he always had been. Glen had been the one to deflower her after Darcy had refused her, and he'd done it in a most unforgettable—and unforgivable—way. For her fifteen-year old self, the afternoon had been pure magic, until the lads Glen had arranged to hide in his parents' loft boomed a chorus of cheers at Glen's finish.

She had paid him back, of course, by slipping a triple dose of bowel-loosener into his flask the day of his first skirmish as a warrior for Ackergill, but pay-back, no matter how satisfactory, did not equal forgiveness. Now, her life lay in ruin, and Glen was her only hope to begin setting it to rights.

'Twas all the fault of Big Darcy's wife. She was the one to warn Ginneleah of the quinine. She was the one who would pay most dearly for ruining Anya's dreams. Even though Seona had abandoned her without a word, leaving her to plot revenge all alone, she was sure her plan was sound. The thought of that trollop suffering was enough to coax her body into taking a bit of pleasure from Glen as he sated himself on her, again.

After he finished, she busied herself applying the disguise he had helped her acquire.

"You look like my grandam," he said with a chuckle when she turned to show him the results.

He lay atop his plaid on his back with his hands clasped behind his head, flaunting his brawny arms and barrel chest. He wasn't a bad looking man if a lass didn't mind acres of thick hair everywhere but on his face, which was as smooth as a bairn's behind. She preferred a man to boast his vitality with a hearty beard and no' to shave his most masculine feature clean off, and she'd told Glen so often enough that she suspected he shaved twice in a day merely to annoy her.

"Are ye so complimentary wi' all the lasses?" she asked, noticing how the mask distorted her speech. 'Twas made of beeswax and stuck to her cheeks and forehead with tallow. If she moved her face too much, she risked popping it loose.

"Only with you, An. Only with you." He winked, counting his charm worth far more than it was in truth.

"Well, lookin' auld is the goal, so I thank ye." She sketched a mocking bow.

Glen sat up on his plaid and pulled his shirt on over his head. He tugged her to stand between his spread knees. She let him because she wasn't quite through with his help just yet.

"But ye dinna sound auld," he said as he scrutinized her. "And the mask willna fool aught but a blind man upon close inspection. I say it again, ye risk too much for your vengeance."

"Nonsense." She'd planned this encounter perfectly. Besides, Glen had no right to fash over her. At his raised eyebrow, she said, "I'll pull my plaid up as a hood to shadow my face, and I'll alter my voice. Not even Aodhan shall suspect I am aught other than an auld villager selling spring apples."

Glen shook his head, clearly lacking even the barest hint of faith in her. "Och, I fear you are more confident than is wise," he muttered as he crouched to fold his plaid.

As if Glen had any experience with wisdom.

Once fully dressed, he strapped on the small armory of weapons he liked to carry. While he did so, he looked her up and down as though considering her in a new way. He stroked his barely shadowed chin in thought and then nodded as though he'd decided somat.

"I shall make you an offer. If ye forget this foolishness and leave wi' me now, I shall take you to Torroble, where my cousin has settled with his wife's people. There I shall suffer to take ye to wife. Ye'll be a faithful wife, mind, and ye'll stop wi' the oils that keep ye from catchin' a bairn. If I find ye makin' a cuckold o' me, I'll truss you up and bring ye back to Aodhan myself. But so long as you do right by me, I shall do right by you, and you can forget about that flea-infested bawdyhouse."

She scoffed. Glen might as well have shoved table scraps at her like a master to his mangy pup. "Och, ye make a lass blush with your honeyed speech, Glen. How can I possibly refuse such a gallant proposal?"

"Ye best no'," he said, his voice dangerously quiet. He crowded her in a move that might intimidate a woman who didn't ken all the places he was ticklish. "Because I willna make the offer again, and 'tis a better one than a whore in her twenty-fifth year is likely to get again."

She let her hand fly. It connected sharply with Glen's cheek.

His eyes blazed with a moment's anger and then he shrugged one shoulder. "So be it. I shall help ye no further. You are a destructive woman who doesna even recognize how deserving of pity she is." He began saddling his horse.

"You canna leave now! You agreed to escort me back to Thurson!"

"An auld woman such as you shouldna attract trouble on the road," he goaded with a smirk as he mounted.

"Ye bloody bastard!" she called after him as he rode off. "You coward!"

"Come with me, An," he called back. "Last chance."

"Go to hell, you…you deserter! You ungrateful cur!"

"'Tis not me who is bound for hell's fires."

Shaking with indignation, she stuffed her few supplies into the saddlebag and wrapped her lady's plaid about her shoulders in the way that made a large hood for covering her head. "I dinna need him," she hissed as she saddled her borrowed mare with jerky movements that agitated the beast.

After several moments' indulgence in her rage, she willed her hands to uncurl. The horse she could afford to agitate, but not her unawares passenger. Carefully, very carefully, she lifted the crate that held the key to her vengeance and tied it behind her saddle.

Inside the crate was a bag of rare spring apples she'd spent a full week's pay to acquire and at the bottom of the bag was the thing she'd purchased from a turbaned man in Inverness: a viper of one of the most poisonous varieties on God's green Earth, deep in a digestive sleep and due to wake by nightfall.

§

DARCY LOVED THE briny scent of the ocean. 'Twas with great joy he turned the cart onto the seaside road that would bring them through the village of Brora. In fact, 'twas with great joy he did everything since Aodhan had delivered the news that Steafan had invited him and Malina home and promised they would face no consequences for their "unfortunate misunderstanding."

The war chieftain rode ahead on his gray warhorse, and Malina sat beside him on the driver's bench with wee Janine bouncing happily on her lap. The few possessions they'd acquired in their year at Dornoch filled the cart he had bought for the journey. 'Twas mostly gowns for Malina, dresses for Janine, and supplies they'd collected as the Lady Constance imparted the ways of a wife in this time.

Already, she could spin yarn, sew clothes for Janine, and cook delicious meals from the most basic of ingredients compared to the offerings of a "grocery store." He fondly remembered the laughter they'd shared over her early attempts at each of those tasks.

"I am fair proud of ye, lass," he said, nudging her elbow with his.

"For what?" She turned her bonny face to him, her eyes wide with curiosity and bright with happiness. He'd feared she would regret leaving Dornoch, but she'd bounded into his arms with a delighted squeal when he'd told her of Steafan's change of heart. And for the days they'd been packing and saying their goodbyes, she'd chattered without ceasing about her plans for Fraineach.

"For being who you are," he said. "For being mine." He wanted to pay her a dozen compliments, but noticed Aodhan drawing his mount to a halt to speak with a bent auld woman standing in the road. He slowed the cart horse and stopped just behind Aodhan.

"...but mayhap my companions would like some," he was saying.

The auld woman turned in their direction, all but the tip of her hooked nose hidden beneath her hood. "Apples," she mumbled in a voice dusty with age and disuse. "Spring apples, ripe and ready for baking. Treat for your lady, sir? Just a half groat for a bag."

He suspiciously eyed the bag she held out with a filthy, trembling hand. It being only the first of June, he worrit the spring apples would be too green to be of worth. But if they were truly ripe, he'd happily buy the treat for his wife. "Let me see the fruit," he said, leaning over the arm of the bench.

"Ooh, I could make a pie to share with Fran and Edmund," Malina murmured as she tried to peer around him.

The auld woman loosed the tie on the bag, her dirty fingers shaking to make her clumsy at the task. Finally, she pulled the bag open and he bent close to look inside. Though a touch of green remained, the apples were mostly red and yellow. He fingered out a half groat from his sporran, and didn't bother to haggle with the poor woman, who likely needed the coin far more than he.

"Thank ye, sir," she said as she took the coin.

He curled his fingers in the rough fabric of the bag.

Malina put Janine on his lap and reached for it while Janine let loose a gurgling laugh and clapped her hands.

The auld woman tried to pull the bag back, but he didn't relax his grip. "Ye canna change your mind now that I've paid ye," he quipped, giving the woman a smile, but she didn't tilt her face up to see it.

Seemingly reluctantly, she released the bag and the significant weight of it surprised him.

Mayhap he'd gotten a bargain for such a weight of rare spring apples. He let Malina snatch it from him and peer inside. Her exclamations over the fruit made him preen.

"Look, baby girl," she cooed to Janine. "Apples for Mommy! I can make you some nummy apple sauce and a pie for daddy!"

When he went to thank the auld woman, he found her already hurrying away without looking back. He shrugged and nodded to Aodhan, who urged his horse onward. He slapped the reins, thinking vaguely that the woman smelled strange. For her tattered cloak and threadbare plaid, she ought to have smelled of dirt and decay, but what had pricked his nose instead had been the feminine fragrance of roses.

Chapter 24

NEVER IN HER former life would Melanie have imagined a burlap bag of apples in early June would make her nearly weep with joy. Gone were the days of simply driving to the store and picking up a perfectly ripened pint of strawberries or a juicy honeydew melon or a slightly green bunch of bananas regardless of the season. She still missed that kind of convenience, but what she'd traded it for was well worth it.

That night in her office back at the museum, she'd made a tongue-in-cheek wish for a sexy Highlander to sweep her off her feet. She'd gotten her wish and then some. She'd gotten a treasured friend, a passionate lover, and best of all, a wonderful father to her child—their child.

She had her heart's desire. Everything was perfect.

Except she hadn't gotten to say goodbye to her parents. If she could have changed just one thing and left everything else the same, it would have been that. She wished she could tell them she was happy, that she missed them and loved them so much her heart ached when thoughts of them snuck up on her. She wanted to tell her mom how much she loved being a mom herself, tell her that having a baby without an epidural had been the worst kind of torture but the moment Janine had been placed in her arms, she'd forgotten the pain. She wanted to tell her dad that she'd married a good man, a man just as responsible and loving as he.

Breathing the moist, salty air deep into her lungs, she leaned on Darcy's arm and stroked Janine's baby-fine hair as she took her afternoon nap in her arms. White-gray cliffs rose to their left, and to their right, the ocean stretched pewter and choppy into the mist. Brora lay about an hour's easy pace behind them. While she gazed out over the North Sea, Darcy tried to sneak an apple from the bag at her feet.

"Oh, no you don't," she said with a swat. "I've got big plans for those apples."

He pulled his hand back as if stung. "Mayhap, but I'm the one who bought them for you," he answered with a smirk. "I only seek my fair share." Hooking a long foot around the bag, he inched it toward his side of the foot well.

She hooked her foot around his ankle, impeding his attempted thievery. They grinned at each other as they played their high-stakes game of footsie.

Suddenly, he jerked his leg away. "Christ! Get away with you!" He grabbed her shoulder and pushed her away from him until she clenched the rail to keep from tumbling out of the cart with Janine.

"Jeez, Darcy. If you want one that bad—"

His face turned red as a beet before her eyes. With jerky movements and labored breaths, he grabbed the sack of apples and threw it out of the cart.

The fruit pattered onto the road and rolled in every direction. The burlap thrashed, seemingly of its own accord. Then a huge brown snake slithered out and disappeared into the roadside bracken.

Darcy tried to call for Aodhan, but his hands went to his throat, the reins forgotten. Froth formed at the corners of his mouth.

A wave of horror doused her as a scream built behind her sternum. "Aodhan! Snake! Help! I think Darcy's been bitten!"

She set Janine behind her in the cart and caught him as he swayed. Struggling with the weight of his limp torso, she laid him along the bench and yanked the horse to a stop.

"Calf," he choked out, spittle flying.

She followed his panicked gaze and ripped the loosely tied boot from his foot. It took all the strength in her fingers, since his foot had already swelled until the skin was tight and painful looking. Blood trickled from a pair of puncture wounds several inches above his ankle.

"Oh, God, Darcy!" Her heart pounded. She clutched uselessly at his kilt, and looked desperately at his face only to find his handsome features disappearing behind the puffy evidence of poison coursing through his veins. His wild eyes darted to Aodhan as he jumped up into the cart.

He tried to speak, but she couldn't make sense of his wheezing. It sounded like he was saying, "Roses" over and over again. It made no sense to her, but a stream of curses erupted from Aodhan, who sliced his dirk across Darcy's ankle and squeezed out enough thin, bright red blood to fill a cup.

"It's too late," she murmured, half to herself. The venom was in him, and it was potent enough to be deadly within minutes. She was going to lose him.

No! Her soul rebelled at the thought. She couldn't lose him. Her love wouldn't permit it.

Janine's frightened cries faded into the mental background, as did Aodhan's urgent commands for Darcy to stay awake. The entirety of her concentration narrowed to a single memory. It was the morning after Darcy's return from Inverness. He'd told her about the albino, Timothy, and the gypsy with the fake French accent, Gravois. Darcy had given her a small box wrapped in fabric and tied with twine and told her it was a gift from the gypsy.

When he'd relayed to her Gravois's words, *"He said it is only to be opened when the sheet hits the fan, whatever that nonsense might mean,"* she'd stared at him, dumbfounded. *"Do ye ken what he might have meant?"* he'd asked, frowning at her expression.

Yes, she'd had an idea, but she had only shrugged noncommittally, granting Gravois the same kind of instant trust her husband had described having upon meeting the man. If her instinct was right, Gravois had used his accent to hide the meaning of his colorfully worded and very modern message from Darcy. And if he'd taken the trouble to do that, she'd take the trouble to treat his gift with respect. And caution.

She'd initially tucked the box away in a drawer to keep it safe, but while packing for their return to Ackergill, she'd felt compelled to keep it on her person at all times. Her neck prickling with certainty, she pulled it from a pocket in the folds of her skirts.

"Aodhan, your dirk." She held out her hand. He gave it to her without question, and she sliced through the twine.

"What are ye doing?" he asked.

"Saving his life. I hope." If the "sheet" had ever hit the fan in her life, it was now. She hoped she was doing the right thing and that Gravois was worthy of the trust she was placing in him.

Inside the box was a pear-shaped vial of milky-white liquid. Without daring to think, she wrenched the cork out with her teeth and climbed over Darcy. "Open his mouth," she commanded Aodhan. She refused to contemplate the fact that the red of Darcy's face had given way to a grayish pallor, that his eyes were swollen closed and his chest was hardly moving.

Aodhan obeyed, and she dumped the contents of the vial into Darcy's mouth. "Sit him up to help him swallow. Darcy, baby, you have to swallow this. Please. Oh, please," she added in a whisper. Her composure hung by a thread.

He didn't look conscious, but by some miracle his throat worked. When Aodhan laid him back down and she wiped the froth from his mouth, only the barest trickle of the milky liquid leaked out.

"What was that?" Aodhan asked.

Tears flowing, she said, "I don't know, but I hope it was magical." An unassuming box had brought her through time to find the man of her dreams. She hoped with every fiber of her being that a mysterious gift from a gypsy could cure a snake bite.

She met Aodhan's eyes, searching for an ally in her hope. He only shook his head and averted his gaze to Janine, who had quieted and now held out her chubby arms to him. He picked her up and put her on his hip while Melanie sagged on the bench seat and cradled Darcy's head on her lap. His damp hair clung to her fingers, face slick with cold sweat. His chest shuddered once, then froze in place, refusing to rise and fall with another labored breath.

"No." Her blood turned to ice. The universe came to a screeching halt. Every moment of her life, past, present, and future blew away on a fickle wind, leaving her all alone in this one pinprick point in time. "Come on, Darcy. Breathe for me." She bowed over him, squeezed her eyes shut, and prayed.

"He's gone, lass." Aodhan's voice trembled with grief. His hand fell like a lead weight on her shoulder.

Fiery denial shot through her, but before it could sear her soul, Darcy's chest stuttered under her hand. Though he looked no different, she could swear his sternum rose and fell ever so slightly.

"Aodhan, I think it's working."

"Lass," he warned.

"No, look." She stared at his chest and sure enough, his breathing, though labored, was even.

"Och, you're right." Their gazes locked. "Can ye drive the cart?"

She nodded and took up the reins, seeing on Aodhan's face the same tenuous hope holding the pieces of her heart together.

"If this is magic, I dinna trust it on its own. Let's get him to a physician back in Brora. I'll carry your bairn." He hopped down from the cart and, cooing to Janine, mounted his horse.

She agreed with his assessment. Darcy wasn't improving nearly as quickly as he'd succumbed to the poison. He could breathe, and under her fingers, his wrist gave a thready pulse, but there was no guarantee he'd survive this. Whatever was in that vial might have only bought them a little time.

Aodhan wheeled his horse around, then grabbed the bridle of the cart horse and helped Melanie turn the cart.

She slapped the reins. As tears dried on her cheeks, they raced back to Brora.

§

ANYA WASN'T SATISFIED.

As she guided her nag over the rocky hills and away from Brora, she tried to find peace in the fact that her vengeance was at long last complete. But peace eluded her. She told herself 'twas because she hadn't witnessed the results of her plot, that she didn't even ken whether it had been Darcy or his accursed wife who had been bitten or if the snake had yet awoken and struck at all. But she couldn't quite believe her satisfaction waited for confirmation of her success.

Rather, she had an unwelcome feeling her conscience was to blame.

She had bent the truth to her advantage and used her beauty to manipulate men all her life, but she hadn't ever done true harm to another. Until now. A corner of her innermost self trembled to ken she'd most likely caused someone's death today. Mayhap 'twould be the death of the strangewoman, but mayhap 'twould be her clansman or even a wee ane whose only crime was being born to a witch.

She wished that doubting part of her had shown itself before she'd stepped into the road to pose as an auld villager selling fruit. Then she remembered all she had lost. Her home. Her chance at living up at the keep and being the object of Steafan's desire, of bearing his children and having the honor of the entire clan. 'Twas only dishonor she had now, that and a pitiful income and the occasional pleasure of a talented lover at the bawdyhouse. And Seona, if she ever returned.

If she'd done wrong today, 'twas really her sister's fault; Seona should have been there for her and helped her come up with a better plan. Aye. She was not to blame for aught ill that had occurred today.

Her conscience appeased, she squared her shoulders and focused all her attention on navigating the treacherous rocks. There was no trail here, nor any way to be followed since there was no soft ground to leave tracks upon. But one wrong step by her mount and they could both tumble into a ravine.

Glen was a hog's fart for leaving her to find her way to the inner road by herself. But she'd kent better than to agree to marry him and then try to back out of it. Glen wasn't one to let another deny him what was his, and if she'd agreed to be his, he'd hold her to it. 'Twas for the best she'd refused him. Even if she broke her bloody neck out here on the rocks. She'd rather be dead than chained to a conniving, controlling, bald-faced husband.

She urged her mount down a steep incline and the clumsy nag stumbled. Loose rocks clattered under hoof as the horse struggled to remain upright.

She clung to the saddle, but couldn't hold on as the nag went down. Braced for the bite of the hard terrain, she put out her hands to protect her face. She hit with a mighty force and rolled downhill, arms around her head.

Then the ground went out from beneath her.

Time stood still as she threw out her arms to catch herself, but there was no stopping her sudden descent. Rocks like knives sliced her skin as she slid down, down, and down some more into a cleft of unforgiving limestone. Her fingers raked at the walls, nails tearing. When she hit the bottom, the crack of shattering bone filled her world with horror.

Pain scraped through her entire body. She screamed. And screamed. And screamed. She didn't give up her screaming even when her throat felt like fire. Panic was a noose around her neck, tightening by the hour, suffocating her.

Night fell. Her screams had become coarse whispers.

Ten lifetimes as Glen's wife would have been better than this agony. She'd been a fool to spurn his offer.

"I'm so sorry," she found herself muttering like a prayer. "I've done wrong, I've done wrong. Help me. I'll do anything."

Deity must have taken pity on her, because a familiar voice cut through her pain.

"Will you really, Anya? Will ye do anything?"

"Aodhan! Help me!" His deep voice far above her soothed the worst of her fear. He'd cared for her once. He would help her.

"Anything?"

"Aye! Aye, anything. I'll become your servant! I'll face Steafan! Anything!" She contorted as much as her twisted body would allow, trying to glimpse his face, but she saw nothing but darkness.

"Here's what I want," he said calmly, as though he were placing an order with the butcher. "I want you to confess to all ye've done."

"Aodhan, I'm dying! I've broken my legs. Please! Get me up and I'll confess to anything."

"Now, Anya. I want to hear you confess. Then I shall decide whether or not you are deserving of help."

A sob ripped from her chest. She could barely think for the pain that had become her world. "I did it," she uttered through clenched teeth. "I put the viper in the sack. I wanted to make that woman pay for ruining me."

"What else do ye have to say?"

"Are ye a bloody vicar?" Rage mixed with agony to make her vision wash crimson. "Shall I confess all my sins? Get me up, you self-righteous fool!"

"Do ye even care what happened with the viper?" His voice went cold as ice.

That stopped her anger. "Of course," she said after a pause. "What happened?"

"Darcy will live. But it was a near thing. And 'tis too soon to tell if he may keep his leg."

Faint emotion pricked her heart. Mayhap 'twas relief, but it paled in comparison to her will to survive. Aodhan clearly expected her to be sorry. If that was what he wanted, that was what she'd give him. "I am glad he lives," she said. "I regret what I've done. Please, help me. I'm begging you."

He ignored her plea. "Did you ken there was a bairn in that cart? Darcy's a da, now."

She scoffed. Aye, she'd kent he'd married a disgraced woman who'd let herself get with child out of wedlock. But even she had to admit, the child was the fairest bastard she'd ever glimpsed. Almost angelic enough with that crown of shining hair to have made her regret her plot. Almost.

"Why do ye tell me such things? Can ye no' tell the state I'm in? Please! I'll do anything ye ask. Anything!"

"Ah, but you canna do what I lust so desperately for you to do." His voice dipped with sadness. "I wished only for you to care for another above yourself. But you are too far gone to wickedness." He was quiet for so long, she thought he'd gone away.

"Aodhan! Dinna leave me! Please!"

"I'm here, lass. I'm here." Though she couldn't see him, she had the distinct impression he was shaking his head in disappointment.

"I do care! I didna wish harm to the child. I prayed the child would be spared," she lied.

"Too late, my dear. Too late. I have seen to the depths of your selfish heart." He sighed heavily, the sound slicing through the crevasse like a barren wind. When he spoke again, his voice was firm with decision. "I'll be leaving you, now. You'll die a slow, painful death, but 'twill be better than if I bring you back to Steafan. Consider it a mercy." The last word rung with dreadful finality.

"No! No, ye canna leave me! Aodhan!" Rocks shifting under his shoes spoke more baldly than any words. He was leaving.

She screamed and cried and begged, praying he'd only gone off for a time to frighten her.

When dawn came, and Aodhan never reappeared, she lost hope. She slumped against the wall of the crevasse, stared up at the sliver of mocking blue sky, and wished for death.

But it wasn't death that came for her.

"Good morning, *ma cherie*. It seems you are in need of rescuing."

She squinted at a dark figure haloed by sunlight.

"Bastien Gravois at your service."

Chapter 25

"PUT THAT DOWN, you ornery old fool." Melanie swatted at Darcy with a dishtowel, uncaring that her southern roots were showing.

"Och, I'm neither auld nor foolish, and I dinna ken what ornery means," he answered with a grin as he danced away with the pie that had been cooling on the windowsill. Curse the man's long reach!

"That's a lie. If I've told you what ornery means once, I've told you a dozen times. The fact that you claim not to remember just proves how apt a description it is." She reclaimed the pie, made with the cherries from Fraineach's orchard, and ordered her husband back to bed.

Two months had passed since they'd returned to Ackergill after their two-week stay in Brora. Darcy was still recuperating from the snakebite. He'd been in a coma for five days—the worst five days of her life—and had awoken ill and with no appetite. In the weeks that followed, he'd lost about 30 pounds by her estimate—two stone by his—which he was just now starting to put back on. He'd also lost all the toenails on his right foot, which had turned more shades of purple than she had known existed, but had never darkened to the black that meant tissue death.

He'd gotten his energy back just a few days ago, along with his appetite—for food and other things that she couldn't afford to think about unless she wanted to be blushing when her guests arrived—and it had been impossible to get him to rest ever since.

"I've been in bed for weeks," he argued. "Much as I love to do as ye ask where our bed is concerned, I willna go back to it while the sun is up unless you come with me." He waggled his brows.

She harrumphed Scottish-style, a habit she'd picked up from Darcy. "Well then, make yourself useful and go check on Janine."

Babysitting duty would be easier on his mending body than working on the broken sail at the mill with Edmund, where she had no doubt he would go if she didn't keep him distracted.

She could have wrung her brother-in-law's neck when he marched in first thing this morning and suggested Darcy help him with it. She'd only managed to keep her husband from the manual labor by improvising a strip-tease that led to another sort of strenuous activity, but at least one that didn't have him dangling fifty feet off the ground while he was weak as a kitten…well, judging by his performance this morning he was much more like a tiger than a kitten. And now she was blushing despite her best efforts.

Just in time for the knock at the front door.

"That'll be Fran, aye?" Darcy asked as he finger-walked Janine into the kitchen.

She turned to hide her blush, but not before catching his longing look at the freshly sliced pie on the butcher's block. Honestly, he was more work at the moment than her almost-one-year old.

"Aye," she said, "or Ginnie. Though it's early yet." It was her turn to host the Sunday afternoon tea the three of them had begun as soon as she'd arrived home. Ginneleah had hosted the first up at the keep, where Steafan had made an appearance and come as close to apologizing as he likely ever would. "Welcome home, lass," he'd said. "'Tis fair sweet to have ye back."

He'd kissed her cheek and then left the ladies to their tea.

She ran a loving hand over Janine's soft hair, kissed Darcy on the check, and went to answer the door, calling sweetly over her shoulder, "If I come back and find one piece of that pie missing, there'll be hell to pay, mister."

Behind her, she heard him conspiring with their daughter. "One piece, your mama says. Then two must be okay."

She grinned at his modern slang and the high-pitched giggle that meant he and Janine were availing themselves of her morning's labor.

She opened the door not to an early Fran or Ginneleah, but to a broad-shouldered man with a wide-brimmed hat that shadowed his face. When he looked up, she smiled with surprise.

Blue-tinted glasses hid the true color of eyes she knew must be pink based on the egg-shell white skin stretched across the fresh cheeks and chiseled jaw of a young man around eighteen.

"Good afternoon. I am Timothy MacLeod, come from Inverness to call on Darcy Keith."

§

DARCY STRODE TO the parlor, his spirits high despite the pain in his right foot. The muscles around the site of the snakebite still cramped with every step, but he never complained, so glad was he to still have a foot to pain him.

"You look like death warmed over," the lad, or rather the young man, said. Timothy had added half a hand to his height and lost the roundness of youth from his face. "Is that blood, man?" He motioned toward his own mouth while gaping at Darcy.

"Cherry pie." He tongued the tart filling from the corner of his mouth. "I'd offer you a slice, but I fear the penance I'll have to pay as is." He clasped Timothy's forearm. "Good to see you. What brings you to Ackergill?"

"Monsieur Gravois was worrit about you," Timothy said. "Somat about a fortune Madame Hilda read. By the looks of you, I'd say he was right to fash. What happened?"

"Bit by a fair poisonous snake," he said by way of justifying his pallor and thin frame, both of which would soon change now that he had the strength to return to work at his mill—though he didn't relish telling his wife of his plans for the morrow. "What of you? I thought you didna approve of the Rom, and now here you are running errands for him." He didn't bother hiding his pleasure at the fact. He liked Gravois even more since Malina had told him of the man's gift. There was no doubt in his mind that if he had never visited the gypsy camp, he would have died on the road near Brora. He also suspected Gravois could help Timothy and had hoped the lad might give the man the chance.

"We made our peace," Timothy said with a grimace. "Had to. There was another, uh, incident at the shop, and if Monsieur Gravois hadna been keeping an eye on me, I might have been found out."

"Another incident? That sounds like a story, and I'd like to escape the house before my wife's guests arrive and try to dote on me. I've got whisky up at the mill. Come. I'll pour while you talk."

§

OVER A DINNER of mutton, boiled radishes, and buttery rolls, all of which Fran had taught her to make, Melanie hooted with unladylike laughter while Darcy recounted Timothy's tale of cutting himself on a bill of sale and making a fire hydrant appear on the toe of a customer at MacLeod's shop.

"Oh, my," she sighed. "What did you do?"

Timothy had initially appeared uncomfortable with talk of magic at the dinner table, but he had eventually relaxed and even laughed along, though his manner remained reserved. "Well, to be honest, I was too stunned at my own stupidity to do aught—I kent better than to take off my gloves, but the paper was sticking, you see." As he spoke, he displayed his hands, covered with sturdy leather gloves that he hadn't even removed for dinner. "But Monsieur Gravois was there lickety-split, as if he forekent somat was about to happen. A nose for magic that tinker's got." He tapped his nose for emphasis. "He played it off as a jest and took a bow. Then he swept out of the shop with the—what did ye call it? A hydrant?—on a wee wagon and his screeching monkey on his shoulder. Those in the shop didna ken whether to applaud or run him out of town, so they just went back to their business as if nothing had happened."

They all laughed some more, and she got a sense of the young man's earnest nature. It wasn't hard to see why Darcy had taken to him so readily.

"So that's when you reacquainted yourself with Gravois?" she asked.

"Aye. 'Twas last winter. He's taught me a great deal since, even though we only meet when his troupe travels near Inverness. In fact..." He cleared his throat, and his eyes darted from her to Darcy. "I brought your wife somat Gravois thought she would like. 'Tis a piece we worked on together."

She exchanged a look with her husband. Judging by his furrowed brow, he didn't know what Timothy was talking about.

"Another gift from Gravois?" he asked, his tone darkly serious. "Does this mean one of us is in danger?"

Timothy shook his head. "No, no. Nothing like that, least not that I'm aware. It's just, well, Monsieur Gravois supposed my bloodmagic was like a child with no discipline, and he thought giving it some direction would help it to no' be so wild. He was right." Timothy's smile transformed his face. He'd smiled shyly before, but this smile was a soul-brightening one. He seemed lighter, as if a weight had lifted from his shoulders. "I dinna ken for sure if it will work as we planned, but I think it will. We did several tests first, you see." He looked back and forth between them expectantly, but she had no idea what he was talking about.

"Tests of what?" Darcy asked.

"To determine if I could put magic into somat and get it to do what I wish. I can. I have."

He shook his head as if his thoughts were getting ahead of his words. "I'll bring ye the piece and then explain." With that, he pushed away from the table and went outside.

Five minutes later, he tramped through the door bent under the weight of something heavy fixed to his back with thick leather straps. Darcy helped him lower it to the floor, and for once, she didn't scold him for the exertion. She was too shocked, because there on the rug in her parlor sat her grandmother's rosewood hope chest.

She heard voices, but they didn't penetrate. She went to her knees in front of the chest and ran her fingers over the stained and polished wood. There were the intricately carved roses at the corners, and there the inlaid, curving strips of mother of pearl—some of them would chip over the centuries—and there the black stain lending contrast to the tooled details.

Memory washed over her, bringing her to her grandmother's lilac-scented bedroom. She had been eight years old, and her grandmother was showing her the hope chest for the first time.

"'Tis a very special antique, my dearie. One of a kind, for cert. It's gone to each eldest female in the family. When I'm gone, 'twill be your mother's, and when she goes, 'twill belong to you. 'Tis how it's been since the auld days."

"Malina! Are you ill?" Darcy hauled her off the floor and into his arms. He ran his hands over her face and head, as if looking for a fever. "Speak to me." He shook her gently, but her tongue wouldn't work.

"You recognize it," Timothy said, his voice filled with wonder. "Monsieur Gravois said ye might."

She nodded, her eyes fixed on the chest.

"Say somat," Darcy urged, putting his face before hers and

capturing her gaze. The concern in his dark brown eyes broke the spell of her stupor.

"It's my grandmother's hope chest." Her slow smile stretched her cheeks. A little laugh bubbled out of her. "How?" she asked Timothy. "Why? I mean, you don't even know me. This is such a beautiful, valuable piece. Is it really the chest I know from my time?"

"What magic did ye put in it?" Darcy asked, cutting to the chase.

Timothy beamed, obviously pleased by her reaction. But when he answered Darcy's question, he sobered. "None yet. But with your permission, I hope to charm it tonight before I leave."

"Why would I want ye to do that?"

"It wouldn't be for you," Timothy said. "But for your wife." Turning to her, he said, "When I accepted Monsieur Gravois's offer to mentor me, I made a choice. I chose to cease running from what I have inside of me. But Monsieur reminded me that once the choice was made, I'd committed to a path that would lead to you being pulled from your time into ours. I dinna pretend to understand what magic brought ye here, and nor does Monsieur. But I ken now that the magic was mine.

"Between now and the date on your box, I'll have learned enough to make somat that changed the course of your life. I canna imagine I'll ever have unworthy intentions where my bloodmagic is concerned or that I would let loose a piece with such power, but I shall take responsibility for your unexpected departure from your time.

"The chest has a secret compartment." Timothy lifted the lid and fixed it in the open position. The entire panel lining the inside of the lid was braced open, revealing a recess about an inch deep.

She had dug through her grandmother's treasures a hundred times and had never suspected there might be a secret compartment in the lid. She stared in awe as Timothy continued.

"I would like to charm the chest so the compartment opens on the date of your choosing. That ye recognize it is a relief. It means that any message or mementos ye wish to leave inside have a good chance of finding the ones ye left behind. You may add whatever will fit, but once the compartment is closed, it will remain closed until the day you choose. 'Tis a small thing, but all I can do at present to ease what suffering ye've had because of me."

Tears spilled down her cheeks. She might have a way of saying goodbye to her parents.

Timothy toed the rug and looked at the floor at her feet. "We've tested the magic, and it should work. I just need to prick my finger and smear the blood on the release mechanism while I speak the date."

Her knees felt weak. She would have sunk to the floor if Darcy's strong arms hadn't already been around her. She steadied herself by breathing in his scent of saddle leather and man.

Her heart was bursting at the seams with joy and love. She didn't regret coming to the past one bit. If she could go back to Charleston, she wouldn't. She'd do everything the same to end up here in Darcy's arms, his wife, the mother of his baby girl—Darcy was the only father Janine would ever have. And she hoped she'd have more children with him.

She'd be able to write to her mother and father and tell them she was happy. She'd tell them about Janine, about the wonderful man she'd met, all the things she'd wished she could have shared with them over the past year. They might not believe her, but she'd do her best to make them. She'd pour her love for them into a series of letters, and they'd be able to read them again and again whenever they thought of her.

The chest was the missing piece of her happiness. That missing piece had shrunk over time until it occupied only a small corner of her heart, but no matter how small the pain became, the puzzle of her life was always going to feel incomplete. Now the puzzle was whole, and the picture was more beautiful than she could have imagined.

She sagged against her husband as she said in a hoarse voice, "Thank you. Thank you so much, Timothy. This is—" She shook her head. "Thank you."

Epilogue

One year later

MELANIE PUSHED THROUGH the door of the north-most mill, an almost two-year-old Janine on her hip. "They named the baby Rosalisa!" she called, placing Janine down so she could toddle to her daddy. Up at the keep, Ginneleah was recuperating from birthing a precious baby girl the night before.

Darcy cooed a jubilant greeting as he hoisted their little girl in arms that were as brawny and tanned as ever. He'd fully recovered from his snake bite, packing on every last inch of muscle he'd lost and then some by operating his mills and building a waterwheel with Edmund based on the design of the one he'd made with Wilhelm Murray.

"A bonny name," he said with a twinkle in his eye, coming to her and planting a kiss on her lips. "And have I told ye how lovely ye look pregnant?"

"Only every day for the last eight months," she answered, resting a hand on her enormous belly. Hooking her other hand around his neck, she pulled him down for a slower kiss.

He only broke it off when Janine started squirming and saying, "Up-down! Up-down!"

"Put me down, please, Daddy," she corrected as he set their daughter on the floor.

Since Timothy had given her the hope chest, she had been writing weekly letters to her parents. Darcy had proven quite the artist, sketching amazingly detailed pencil-drawings of Ackergill and Fraineach, her and Janine. He'd even done a portrait of himself at her urging.

Writing the letters had been a catharsis, but one little thing had still worried her. How would the chest find its way into her grandmother's hands? Even though the piece was a family heirloom, she refused to consider that her grandmother might be a distant descendant of hers. It was just too weird. She couldn't possibly be related to…herself, no matter how much time had passed.

But now she didn't have to worry any more.

Rosalisa was not a common name. Except in her family. It was her middle name. And her grandmother's name. And Ginneleah hadn't known that.

Darcy folded his arms around her and nuzzled her neck. "So, I take it you'll be passing the chest to my wee cousin one day, Malina Rosalisa Keith. Does it put your mind at ease?"

"Aye." She rubbed her hands up and down his back, pushing her fingers under the shoulder-wrap of his kilt to caress his warm skin. "Do you know what would put my mind even more at ease?"

"What's that, *mo gradhach*?"

"If you came back to the house with me for a long lunch break."

"Och, but I'm so busy today," he teased.

"Suit yourself," she said, pulling out of his embrace and heading for the door. "Come along, Janine. Your daddy needs to get back to work."

Darcy rushed her and lifted her into his arms as if she didn't weigh a ton and a half. He easily scooped Janine up as well and carried them both up to Fraineach, their home.

A note from the author

Thanks so much for reading *Wishing for a Highlander.* I hope you enjoyed it. This novel is the first in my Highland Wishes series. Next is *The Wolf and the Highlander,* due out May 2014.

Reviews make my day. Whether positive or negative, reviews help an author immensely. Please consider leaving an honest review at Goodreads and/or your favorite retailer.

About Jessi Gage

USA Today Bestselling Author Jessi Gage is addicted to happy-ever-after endings. She counts herself blessed because she gets to live her own HEA with her husband and children in the Seattle area.

Jessi has the attention span of a gnat…unless there is a romance novel in her hands. In that case, you might need a bullhorn to get her to notice you. She writes what she loves to read: stories about love.

Do use the contact page on jessigage.com and drop her a line. There is no better motivation to finish her latest writing project than a note from a happy reader! While you're visiting her website, sign up for Jessi's newsletter so you never miss a new release.

Find Jessi at the following online haunts:

Website http://jessigage.com/
Blog http://jessigage.wordpress.com/
Facebook https://www.facebook.com/jessigageromance
Twitter https://twitter.com/jessigage

Made in the USA
Middletown, DE
21 June 2019